BETTY

THE ULTIMAT

Betty Neels's
by millions of readers around the world, and this very special ***12 volume collection*** offers a unique chance to recapture the pleasure of some of her most popular stories.

Each month we're bringing you a new volume containing two timeless classics—irresistible love stories that belong together, whether they share the same colourful setting, romantic theme, or follow the same characters in their continuing lives...

As a special treat, each volume also includes an introductory letter by a different author. Some of the most popular names in romance fiction are delighted to pay tribute to Betty Neels; we hope you enjoy reading their personal thoughts and memories.

We're proud and privileged to bring you this very special collection, and hope you enjoy reading—and keeping—these twelve wonderful volumes over the coming months.

Volume One

—With an introduction from

Penny Jordan

Two heart-warming stories brought together for the first time:

NOT ONCE BUT TWICE
A GIRL NAMED ROSE

*We'd like to take this opportunity to pay tribute to **Betty Neels**, who sadly passed away last year. Betty was one of our best-loved authors. As well as being a wonderfully warm and thoroughly charming individual, Betty led a fascinating life even before becoming a writer, and her publishing record was impressive.*

Betty spent her childhood and youth in Devonshire before training as a nurse and midwife. She was an army nursing sister during the war, married a Dutchman and subsequently lived in Holland for fourteen years. On retirement from nursing Betty started to write, inspired by a lady in a library bemoaning the lack of romantic novels.

Over her thirty-year writing career Betty wrote more than 134 novels and was published in more than one hundred international markets. She continued to write into her ninetieth year, remaining as passionate about her characters and stories then as she was with her very first book.

Betty will be greatly missed, both by her friends at Harlequin Mills & Boon® and by her legions of loyal readers around the world. Betty was a prolific writer and has left a lasting legacy through her heartwarming novels. She will always be remembered as a truly delightful person who brought great happiness to many.

THE ULTIMATE COLLECTION

Volume One

NOT ONCE BUT TWICE

&

A GIRL NAMED ROSE

Two full-length novels

All the characters in this book have no existence outside the imagination of the author, and have no relation whatsoever to anyone bearing the same name or names. They are not even distantly inspired by any individual known or unknown to the author, and all the incidents are pure invention.

Harlequin Mills & Boon Limited,
Eton House, 18-24 Paradise Road, Richmond, Surrey TW9 1SR

ISBN 0 263 83643 6

Set in Times Roman 11¼ on 12¾ pt.
141-0702-109821

Printed and bound in Spain
by Litografia Rosés, S.A., Barcelona

Dear Reader

I started to read Betty Neels's books at about the same time as I started to write for Mills & Boon® myself, and her books were always a favourite read of mine.

She had a unique talent and a way of writing that was instantly recognisable and totally 'her'. There is a timeless quality to her characters and her stories, a real sense of security and the expectation of a wonderfully happy ending. I have always associated her books with a sense of comfort and well-being. I consider her to be one of my ten favourite romance writers, and I used to pounce on her books with delight whenever one came out. She was, I think, ahead of her time in the way that her heroines did not need to conform to thin model-like stereotypes to make us love them and want their happiness. She created terrific role models for any woman feeling insecure about her own body image.

I actually once had the pleasure of meeting Betty when we were both appearing in the same video tribute to our Japanese fans. She was in her eighties then, and arrived from her home by car, full of smiles and excitement. Watching her with the young people around us, I learned a very valuable lesson. Within ten minutes of her arrival Betty, in the warmest way possible, engaged the make-up artist in conversation, asking genuinely interested and informed questions about her work, and I could see the respect in the girl's expression as she talked to her.

That personality and warmth live on in her books for all of us to read, enjoy and learn!

Penny Jordan

THE ULTIMATE COLLECTION

Don't miss **Volume 2**, on sale next month!

Two charming stories that will bring you the magic of *summer proposals...*

BETTY NEELS

Volume 2

THE MOST MARVELLOUS SUMMER

and

A SUMMER IDYLL

NOT ONCE BUT TWICE

by

Betty Neels

CHAPTER ONE

IT HAD BEEN raining heavily from a leaden sky, so that the late September afternoon was already settling into an early dusk. People were hurrying home from work, their faces for the most part ill-tempered, for the morning had been fine and umbrellas had seemed unnecessary. The bus queues were long, impatient to get home; surging to and fro to avoid the fine sprays of dirty water thrown up by the traffic. The girl who joined the queue outside St Athud's Hospital sighed gently; if she hadn't been so late off duty, she would have missed the evening rush hour and been home by now; as it was the shops were already shut and she would have to change her plans for the evening meal. She frowned a little, debating the advantages of sausages over macaroni cheese. Sausages were quick of course...a sharp prod in her back reminded her that the queue was moving, but there were so many people ahead of her she had little chance of getting on the bus. Indeed, she was at the steps when the conductor came rattling down the stairs, bellowing 'Full up!' and rang the bell. At the same time he saw her and swung her on board just as the bus pulled out.

'Cor, Sister, almost left yer be'ind,' he declared cheerfully. 'Yer should 'ave shouted...'

She smiled at him and shook her head. 'That was nice of you, Mr Collins. How's the chest?'

He handed out a few tickets before he answered her and she listened gravely, her fine grey eyes on his cheerful face. They were quite beautiful eyes, heavily fringed with curling dark lashes, redeeming an ordinary face from plainness, for her mouth, though sweetly curved, was too wide and her nose tip-tilted, and her light brown hair was drawn back too severely from her face, although the damp air had allowed one or two curling tendrils to escape. But the conductor could see no fault in her.

When he had been stricken with asthma, unable to breathe and scared to death, it had been she who had been ready with the ephedrine when the wheezing started, and if it grew worse, the aminophyline injections, and she who had calmed him down, assured him that he wasn't going to die, restored his cheerful Cockney humour. He thought of her as an angel and good looks didn't come into it.

He went on down the bus presently, leaving her standing crushed against the door with an over-large woman flattening her on the other side, a circumstance so common to her that she hardly noticed. She was a serene young woman with plenty of common sense and while not quite content with her lot, prepared to accept it—indeed, she had reminded herself on several occasions, she hadn't much choice. She was twenty-seven, and while not exactly unkissed, certainly unwed and as far as she could see, likely to remain so.

Her journey was a short one. She got off at a busy junction and turned into a road of mid-Victorian houses, their uniformity broken here and there by a shop and occasionally by a small block of modern flats. It was a depressing road, still respectable and reasonably quiet, but she had never quite got used to it. At the end of the second terrace of houses there was a crossroads and she turned into the left-hand road, to stop a few doors down before a house which was rather better maintained than its neighbours and whose door bore a brass plate with 'Doctor G. H. Forbes' engraved upon it. It was still ajar, for although evening surgery was over the receptionist would be tidying up and getting things ready for the morning. The bleak little lobby opened on to a narrow hall carpeted in a useful brown and brightly lighted, showing a door on either side, shut, and one at the end, half open. She shut the door behind her and her brother's voice called: 'Christina, I'm in the study.'

She went to the half-open door and into the room beyond, a small room, its walls lined with books, two elderly chairs by the empty fireplace, and a desk in one corner. Her brother was sitting behind it, a serious-looking man in his thirties, bearing the good looks which had passed his sister by. He smiled at her as she came in and she saw then that there was someone with him; a young man sitting easily in one of the chairs. He got up as she stood looking at him and smiled at her, and she, usually so calm and sensible, felt her heart lurch and thunder against her ribs. Here was the man, she told herself wildly, the one she'd been waiting for, tall and slim, with the kind of good looks one imagined and never saw... His eyes were the bluest she had ever seen and his hair, very dark, curled elegantly over his collar. She became aware that her mouth was a little open, so she closed it with a rush and smiled back at them both, once more her sensible self.

'I'm late,' she offered, 'sorry about that,' and waited to be introduced.

'This is Adam ter Brandt, he's over here to do a short course of anaesthetics—we met in Brussels last year at that seminar.' And as she held out a hand: 'Adam, this is Christina, my sister—she's Medical Ward Sister at St Athud's, and she housekeeps for me.' As he spoke Christina noticed a strange expression cross his face and wondered what it was. She must remember to find out later; George Henry was worried about something and she wondered what, but only for a second. Their visitor was speaking, asking her questions about her work in fluent accented English, looking at her with an obvious admiration which quite threatened to take her breath.

Presently she said: 'How about coffee? It won't take a minute.' At the door she asked: 'Supper, too, if you care to stay? Nothing exciting—macaroni cheese—the shops were shut.'

The coffee was accepted but supper declined on the grounds of a prior engagement. And if I'd been offered macaroni cheese, I'd have had a prior engagement too, thought Christina, getting coffee in the kitchen behind the stairs, and she fell to wondering about their visitor. He looked a lot younger than George Henry; probably younger than herself. She paused in measuring out the coffee to take a quick look in the small mirror over the wall cupboard. She looked every day of her twenty-seven years, in no time at all she'd have wrinkles and grey hairs. There wasn't time to have a good look now, but she would when she went to bed—there was that wildly expensive cream one of the older Sisters had been talking about, guaranteed to hold back the advancing years... But at least she was slim, although she could have wished to have been a little taller.

She made the coffee and carried it back to the study where she sat down and poured it out with a serenity she was far from feeling.

Adam ter Brandt went shortly afterwards, and because George Henry plainly had work to do at his desk, Christina collected up the coffee cups and went into the kitchen to get their supper. The receptionist had gone by now and the house was quiet as she started her cooking. With it safely in the oven she went upstairs to her room, tidied herself and then sat down before the dressing table again, to take down her hair once more and pin it in a different style so that the little curls had a chance to show themselves and she looked—she hoped—younger. She told her reflection that she was being silly as she did it, but all the same she left it like that and went on sitting, suddenly faintly discontented. The room, she decided, glancing round her, was nice enough, but it wasn't pretty. When she had first come to live with George Henry, he had already furnished the house and in the three years she had been with him she hadn't liked to change anything; it was his, and although she was his sister, she had no right to alter his home.

She had been glad at the time to join forces with him. Their mother had died so very soon after their father, leaving Christina lonely in the small Somerset cottage. She had been nursing in the nearby town then, going home very often, not bothering overmuch about the future, but left on her own there had been no point in staying there—besides, she had discovered that the house and most of the small amount of money which had been left had gone to George Henry. It had shocked her when he had told her that he was going to sell it, although she could quite see the sense in that; a young GP, just setting up on his own, needed money behind him. She had never let him see how much she had minded leaving the country, but had fallen in with his idea of getting a job in London and sharing his house. She had found a good job, too; going to and fro hadn't been all that difficult, there was a splendid little woman who came in to clean three times a week and she supposed that in time, if she really tried, she would get to like London; the London they lived in—in a road like thousands of other roads, where no one knew anyone else and all the houses looked alike. The birds couldn't be heard above the traffic and there wasn't much sky to be seen.

She had gone back to Somerset several times to stay with friends, not trusting herself to look at her old home, hating to come back, but she had said nothing to George Henry. He was content with his work, determined to get on and buy another practice in a better part of London, but only when he was ready for it. He was a good doctor and worked hard and he was a kind brother. At least she had someone.

She went downstairs and took a look at the macaroni cheese, then went into the dining room to lay the table. It was a small rather gloomy room and furnished in the modern style which Christina didn't really care for; she liked old pieces, not necessarily matching each other, and bits and pieces of china and silver lying around. Of course, she reminded herself loyally, that would never do for George Henry, for Mrs Tate wouldn't have the time to dust them. The sitting room led out of the dining room and always reminded her forcibly of a show window in a furniture shop; modern again and quite uncluttered. She wandered in and out of it again, not quite knowing why, her head regrettably full of Adam ter Brandt. It seemed a great pity that having actually met a man to stir her well-balanced heart, she should be forced to lose sight of him immediately.

She laid the table in a careless fashion and, reminded of supper by a strong whiff of cheese, went to the kitchen again.

George Henry wasn't working when she went to call him to his meal, just sitting staring in front of him, but when she asked if there was something the matter, he assured her that there wasn't, ate a hearty supper while he regaled her with his day's work, and then excused himself with the plea that he still had some notes to write up. 'So I'll say goodnight, Christina,' he finished as he hurried from the room—almost, she thought, as though he were avoiding her.

They met at breakfast, but only briefly—it was far too early in the morning to talk. She had to leave the house at a quarter to eight, and he had his surgery at half past eight. Christina cleared the table with speed, left the dishes piled up for Mrs Tate and left the house. It was a splendid autumn morning. She looked at the drab road and thought of the glowing trees and the wisps of smoke from bonfires and the hedges full of sloes and the cottage she still missed so abominably. In a few years, perhaps, when George Henry was well and truly established, they would buy a little house and spend their weekends there. He showed no signs of wanting to marry; she had asked him that so often and he had laughed and told her that he wasn't the marrying kind and weren't they perfectly content to stay as they were? And until now she had been. She quickened her pace towards the bus stop, telling herself sharply that it was ridiculous to allow a brief meeting with someone to unsettle her well ordered life.

Once at the hospital there was little chance of daydreaming. The changing room, a small dark room hidden away under the stairs which led up to the Medical Wards, was already occupied by Beryl Frith, the Women's Medical Ward Sister, and two part-time staff nurses who worked for her. They all exchanged brief good mornings and got on with the difficult business of putting on caps and getting into uniforms in as small a space as possible. Christina, sliding out of a jersey dress and into a navy blue cotton one, listened with half an ear to the other girls' gossip, while she mentally reviewed the day ahead of her. Nurse Trent had a day off, and one of the student nurses had a lecture at ten o'clock and it was Dr Robinson's round; they'd have to scuttle round to be ready by eleven o'clock… Her thoughts were interrupted by Beryl, who had been talking to her and hadn't got an answer.

'What I said was,' she repeated patiently, 'Freddy took me to that new restaurant in Greek Street last night—heavenly food, though I'm not sure what I was eating not that it mattered,' she went on dreamily, 'with Freddy there. You ought to try it some time, Chrissy.'

'It sounds great,' Christina agreed cheerfully. 'I must find someone to take me.' She bent to see into the tiny mirror and arrange her cap, and Beryl gave her a quick look. Chrissy was such a dear, always so calm and self-possessed and good-tempered a touch too matter-of-fact, though. And so capable and practical. Men liked a girl to be a bit helpless about things like unblocking sinks and changing electrical plugs and not knowing which bus to catch, but Chrissy could do all those things without fuss, taking them for granted in the nicest, most unassuming way, which probably was why the few men of her acquaintance, while liking her, tended to ask her advice and then go out with some feather-witted blonde.

Christina made her way upstairs to the top floor of the medical wing, exactly on time as she always was. During her training she had suffered long waits to go off duty in the morning because the Ward Sister had been late, and she had vowed then that if ever she became a Ward Sister she would make a point of arriving on the dot.

The two night nurses were waiting for her now, pale and heavy-eyed from eleven hours of duty. Christina bade them good morning, sat down composedly at her desk and listened to the night report without interruption. At the end of it she made one or two necessary comments, made a note or two and sent them off duty before her day staff nurse, Carole Pring, put her head round the door and was bidden to come in. Carole did so, bearing two mugs of tea and shutting the door neatly behind her with a foot.

'That new man, Sister,' she began at once, 'his BP's too low. Would you take a look presently? And young Tate is complaining about his head again.'

Christina cast her eyes over the report once more. 'Ah yes—

the night staff mention it too. I'll get Dr Fisher to have a look before Dr Robinson comes—he can take a look at Mr Truscott too. We'll alter his observations to half-hourly, don't you think?' She took a sip of tea. 'They're getting the patients ready for X-ray? Good, and there's Mr Soames's barium swallow at half past nine. You take Nurse Bates with you until she goes to lecture; the other two can make beds and get people up, that leaves Mrs Toms to take patients down to the departments.' She swallowed the rest of her tea while she sorted the post on her desk. 'I'll do my round.' She smiled at the girl opposite her, her grey eyes twinkling. 'Oh, and you'd better take Mr Soames down, Carole—Ken's on duty this morning.'

Carole blushed and giggled. She was twenty-one and pretty and she and the assistant radiographer spent all their free time together. 'I say, thanks awfully, Sister!' She added happily: 'He's taking me to see *Private Lives* this evening.'

Christina watched her go: that was twice in less than half an hour—first Beryl with her Freddy, and now Carole with Ken. She didn't know that she sighed as she got up and went into the ward.

It was a long ward of twenty-eight beds, not yet modernised, so that the beds faced each other in rows against the walls. There were two side rooms too where the very ill were nursed or occasionally a private patient, although they had a wing of their own in the centre block.

Christina went into the first of these now, to greet the old man sitting up in bed, glasses askew on his beak of a nose, reading *The Times*. He looked up as she went in and without saying good morning began a forceful summing up of what the government should do immediately. Christina listened quietly, her intelligent face very calm while she looked him over. He had been in hospital for more than a week with cardiac asthma and wasn't improving. It was a pity that he had no family to bother about him; his wife had died years ago and his two sons were both abroad and not in the least interested. She had tried once to get him transferred to the Private Wing, but he had objected so strongly that she had given it up; she supposed she would have him for a very long time, giving extra work to her nurses, wanting things they hadn't got, demanding attention while he read out long articles from *The Times* when there were a thousand and one jobs waiting to be done…

'I expect you're right,' she commented. 'These people can be so exasperating, can't they? Here are several letters for you, I daresay they'll make pleasanter reading.' She added: 'How do you feel today?'

'Not bad—couldn't sleep, though.'

She nodded. 'I'll get your pills changed. You shall have a good night tonight, Colonel.' She smiled and slipped from the room and into the next one. The young man with the headache was there. She saw that he looked ill and strained and when she spoke to him he answered drowsily. Not so good, she decided; the sooner Dr Fisher saw him the better. His pulse was too slow and although he hadn't been vomiting since his admission less than two days ago, she was prepared to bet her month's money on a cerebral tumour. He was due for X-ray that morning, but he wasn't fit to move. He'd been admitted for observation and it had been decided to give him a day's bed rest before starting on a number of tests, and although she had suggested an X-ray when he was admitted, Dr Fisher, who knew everything, had told her importantly that rest was far more important. Well, he had better think again, she thought as she whipped back into the office and asked the lodge to get him urgently.

He was inclined to be ill-tempered when he turned up ten minutes later. He had been up several times during the night and after a far too brief nap was about to sit down to a hearty breakfast, and instead of that here he was facing a calm-eyed young woman, telling him without heat to do something quickly. 'And I do mean quickly,' said Christina, not losing one ounce of her habitual serenity. 'Dr Robinson will be here at eleven o'clock and if he finds Mr Tate like this heaven knows what he'll do to you.' She urged him towards the bed, saying softly: 'It's just my guess, but do you suppose it could be a cerebral tumour?'

John Fisher didn't much like Christina. He respected her judgment, admired her cool which she never seemed to lose, and agreed with everyone else that she was a thoroughly splendid nurse as well as a loyal friend; perhaps it was because of these that he adopted a cocksure attitude towards her and why he said now: 'I've thought that all along. Get him to X-Ray at once, will you, and let me have his notes.'

She did both, forbearing to mention that beyond the bare fact of Mr Tate's admission there was precious little else written up. When she came back presently from seeing the patient safely to X-Ray, it was to find that Dr Fisher had filled a page with meticulous observations and added a query cerebral tumour at the end.

She finished her round after that before getting down to the task of having the ward ready for Dr Robinson, who had a fiend's temper concealed behind his urbane appearance. But the round went off very well. Dr Robinson had most of the beds and behaved rather as though he had all of them, making a kind of royal progress down the ward. But nothing could fault his manner towards his patients; he was pleasant, reassuring and listened patiently while they talked. Some of them rambled on at length, telling him things they had told him on the previous round, but he never said so. Christina rather liked him; his temper didn't worry her very much and since he had discovered that she wasn't in the least afraid of him, he seldom vented it upon her, and if he sometimes flew into a rage with one of her nurses, then she stood up for her with a cool determination which he had found difficult to dispose of. On the whole, the two of them got on very well. He was on the point of leaving the ward when he turned suddenly and addressed her. 'I suppose it was you who diagnosed Mr Tate for us, Sister?'

Her grey eyes were very clear. 'Dr Fisher was concerned about him,' she told him quietly. 'He told me when he came to examine him early this morning that he had suspected a cerebral tumour, sir.'

Dr Robinson nodded, swivelling his eyes behind their glasses to look at Dr Fisher, as red as a turkey-cock.

'That's what I thought you'd say. Well, he's got a chance now he's transferred to the surgical side. Thanks to you,' he added sotto voce.

The day was uneventful after that. Christina went down to her dinner presently, sharing a table with several of her friends, talking shop interlarded with clothes, boy-friends and holidays. Everyone seemed to be going abroad. She looked round her quite nonplussed when someone asked her where she was going for her winter leave.

She said slowly: 'Well, I don't know—I hadn't given it a thought. I expect George Henry will want to stay at home, and I might go down to Somerset. It's nice at this time of year, though I've no holidays until the beginning of October.'

She thought about it once or twice during the afternoon. It would be fun to go away, abroad, perhaps, even Scotland or Wales. Perhaps she could persuade George Henry to come with her, she was sure he hadn't made any plans.

She couldn't have been more mistaken. They had had their supper and for once he had followed her into their small sitting room instead of going to his study and it seemed an opportunity to bring the matter up, but before she could start he said with unusual brusqueness: 'Chrissy, I want to talk to you… I've been meaning to tell you for a week or two, but somehow…I'm going to get married.'

He paused to look at her and was reassured to see that she was looking at him with a serene face. The light was dim, so he couldn't see how pale she had gone.

'You know her—Hilary Woods. We've had an understanding for some time now and last week we decided to marry as soon as possible. There's no point in waiting—she'll give up her job, of course, and live here.'

Christina had the extraordinary feeling that she was having a dream. The room didn't seem quite real, nor did George Henry, talking away so earnestly about getting married—and to Hilary

Woods, a social worker with a puffed-up sense of her own importance. She knew, without her brother saying a word, that she would have to leave before Hilary put a foot over the doorstep. She said in her calm way: 'George Henry, how super for you! I'm so glad—Hilary will make you a splendid wife and she'll be so understanding.'

George Henry eyed her carefully. 'Then you don't mind? I've been worried—you know, wondering if you'd mind—I mean, finding somewhere else to live. Hilary said you'd be able to get a room at St Athud's without any trouble at all. I daresay you'd like it better—you'd be independent and have a great deal more time for your own amusement.'

Briefly, she wondered what she would do with all the extra time. Perhaps it would be better if she could find a bedsitter or a tiny flat, but there would be lonely meals to eat and no one to talk to. She wasn't going to feel sorry for herself but facts would have to be faced.

'Well, of course I can—the Sisters' rooms are pretty good, you know, and I can take up tennis again and I've always wanted to join the Social Club.' She uttered the thumping lie without blinking and saw George Henry relax. 'When are you thinking of getting married?' she asked.

'Well, actually, in a month's time. We've already been about the licence. It's to be a quiet affair—just a few friends and Hilary's parents. You'll come, of course, Chrissy.'

'I wouldn't miss it for the world! I'll go and see someone about getting a room. Hilary will want to make some changes here, I expect, and it'll be much easier if I'm not here.'

'We don't want to turn you out.'

'You're not, my dear, and I'm delighted for you both—when you see Hilary tell her that, won't you? I wouldn't like her to be worried on my account.' Christina got up and went to look out of the window into the dull street beyond, suddenly filled with the crazy desire to leave it all; go somewhere far away, start again in another job, perhaps meet someone who would want to marry her—someone like Adam ter Brandt.

She went the next day to ask about living in. There was a room free, she was told, and she went to look at it. It was nicely furnished in an impersonal way with a view over the streets around the hospital, but the idea of living there, probably for years, appalled her. It was sheer good luck that at dinner time Linda Soames, one of the Accident Room Sisters, announced that she was leaving in a month's time and did anyone want to take over her bedsitter. 'It's five minutes' quick walk from here,' she observed, 'and on the top floor. The street's fairly quiet and there's a kind of kitchen in a cupboard and you share the bathroom.'

When Christina said that she was interested, the entire table turned to stare at her.

'But you live with your brother,' exclaimed Beryl. 'Has he sold the practice, then?'

'No, he's getting married.'

'But, Chrissy...' someone started, and then stopped as she went on:

'I'm so glad, I was beginning to think that he was a confirmed bachelor.'

There was a little silence until someone else said: 'Who's the lucky girl?'

'Hilary Woods—she's a social worker.' She added: 'Ideal for a doctor's wife.'

She told herself that several times during the next day or two. Hilary came to dinner and Christina didn't allow herself to be annoyed at any of the remarks that young lady made. It was obvious that George Henry was very much in love and if he was happy that was more important than anything else. She listened with composure while Hilary made suggestions about her future, giving advice where none was sought, and to give her her due, unaware that she was being unspeakably bossy. Christina replied suitably to all the sensible suggestions put to her and offered no information, nor did she show her annoyance when Hilary criticised the way in which the beef had been cooked, the arrangement of the furniture in the sitting-room and the cheerful clutter of ornaments scattered round it. The latter Christina intended to remove when she left; most of them were hers, anyway, treasures from a happy childhood and bits and pieces which had belonged to her mother. As to the tables and chairs, Hilary was welcome to do what she liked with them, and that went for the beef too. She endured another half an hour of patronage while they washed up and then went thankfully to her room, on the plea that she had a long day before her.

Carole had gone off sick the evening before and the only way to get round that was to do an eight-till-eight herself; there was no one available to take over from her if she went off duty, and she didn't really mind. All the same, she was tired when she got home just before nine o'clock to find a note from George Henry saying that he had taken Hilary out to dinner. Christina went into the kitchen and looked in the fridge. She couldn't face the beef, not after Hilary's expert criticism. An egg, she supposed, and some toast. The front door bell rang as she was getting out the bread and she went to answer it—if it was a patient they would have to telephone Dr Howes who shared emergency calls with George Henry, after eight o'clock.

Adam ter Brandt was on the doorstep. In one smooth movement he had kissed her surprised face, come inside and shut the door behind him.

'Hullo,' he said with a devastating charm which left her speechless. 'Is George Henry in?' And when she shook her head, 'Good—pleased to see me? Where is he? On a case?'

She found her voice and she hoped it sounded as cool and matter-of-fact as usual. 'He's gone out to dinner with his fiancée.'

He pulled a face which made him look more devastating than ever.

'Going to marry? What about you?' He grinned at her. 'You'll never stay here as an uneasy third, will you?'

'Certainly not. I shall go into the Nurses' Home at the hospital or find a bedsitter.'

His blue eyes smiled into hers. 'But you don't want to, do

you? Tell you what—let's go and have dinner somewhere and you shall tell me all about it?'

'I was just going to...' she began feebly, aware that she was ready to fly out of the door at that very moment.

'Never mind that. Get a jacket and powder your nose—we'll go now.'

He drove a rather showy Mercedes Benz 450SL, and he drove fast, but Christina didn't mind. She was blissfully happy; Adam had turned up again, quite miraculously, and for the moment the future didn't matter a row of pins.

But in the little Greek restaurant, over kebab and a bottle of wine, she found herself telling him everything, something which astonished her, for she hadn't confided in anyone, not even her closest friends, for years. She ended abruptly saying in a shamed voice: 'I'm sorry, Adam, I've been boring on, why on earth didn't you stop me?'

'I didn't want to. Besides, I've just had a perfectly splendid idea. How about coming to Holland and working for six months or a year?'

'Me? But I can't speak a word of Dutch!'

'That won't matter—you will be given a crash course. Do you speak any languages at all?'

'Not fluently. I did French and German for A levels...'

He switched to French. 'Do you have a liking for languages? Are you a quick student?'

She answered him in rather hesitant but correct French. 'Yes, I think so, but how would I manage while I was learning?'

'Everyone speaks English, especially in the hospitals, and almost all the medical terms are the same, only pronounced differently. You would get help.'

'I think I might like it very much.'

He was speaking German now. 'And I think you would do very well, Chrissy. Will you do it? I would like you to come very much.' His blue eyes sparkled and she smiled back at him.

'I'll think about it,' she told him in German.

'And not too long.' They were speaking English now. 'It will be necessary for my partner—he's my brother, and the senior and Directeur of the hospital—to agree.'

'Oh, is he likely to object?'

Adam laughed. 'Not at all likely. He objects almost never—he is a calm man, so calm that sometimes one does not know what he is really thinking about, but I have no doubt that he will be glad to have you on the hospital staff. I shall be going to den Haag this weekend, I'll talk to him about it and let you know when I get back.'

She felt breathless. 'Yes, well—it does sound rather super.'

'Then that's settled. I shall be back in Holland in a few weeks now, but we'll see plenty of each other then, darling.'

Christina's cheeks pinkened, but she said with composure: 'Will you tell me something about Holland?' And while he talked she watched him, unable to take her eyes from his face. She was behaving like a teenage idiot, she admonished herself as they drove back, and she was enjoying it. And when Adam kissed her goodnight at her brother's door, she enjoyed that too.

CHAPTER TWO

THERE WERE three days until the weekend and Adam had said that he would return on the Mon day, but Christina didn't allow herself to get excited. She went steadily about her work, and if in the solitude of her room she spent rather longer than usual doing things to her face and trying out different hair-styles that was her business and no one else's.

She remained calm, outwardly at least, when Monday came and went and there was no sign of Adam. She reminded herself of all the very good reasons why he hadn't come and went home on the Tuesday evening, telling herself that he would be there when she arrived, or telephone or even write...

He had done none of these things. Moreover, Hilary was there, making it plain that Christina was making a quite unnecessary third, hinting plainly that there was a splendid film on at the Odeon and wouldn't she like to see it.

'Funny you should have said that,' said Christina in a bright voice. 'I'm meeting some of the others in an hour, we're going to eat first, there's just time before the second house.'

So she went to her room and changed, wished them a pleasant evening and left the house. The last thing she wanted to do; she was tired and depressed and hungry, and worst of all, supposing Adam came while she was out? She took a bus to Tottenham Court Road and sat through a film she wasn't in the least interested in, eating a packet of sandwiches in the dark, because she hated going into cafés by herself.

She could hear voices from the sitting room as she let herself in later, so she shut the door loudly enough for them to hear her and then went in. George Henry and Hilary were sitting side by side looking at patterns of curtain material; obviously there had been no visitors. Christina said she'd had a lovely evening, wished them goodnight and whisked herself out of the room to make herself a pot of tea and carry it up to her room, together with the remains of a macaroni cheese from the fridge. It was quite late by now and it seemed rather a waste to fuss over her face and hair, because Adam wasn't coming. Probably the senior partner had overruled him, probably too he himself had thought better of it. Life, she reflected, was full of small disappointments, but it didn't do to grieve over them. She got into bed and went to sleep almost at once.

She wasn't on until ten o'clock the next morning, which gave her time to rush out and do some household shopping before she went on duty. She had two days off, starting on the next day, and she occupied herself in deciding what to do. Usually she had spent a good part of them at home, keeping George Henry company at meals and quite often going out in the evening if he was free, but now he had Hilary… A day's shopping, she thought; something new would be good for her and she could lunch at one of the big stores. She hadn't been to Harrods for a long time; she could spend the afternoon there and have tea, and since Beryl's steady had gone to Scotland for a week, she might spend the evening with her. There was another day to plan, of course, but that would do for the present.

The day seemed endless. The ward was full and several patients were very ill, so it was long after eight o'clock when she got off duty. She had to wait for a bus too and it had begun to rain a little as she walked the last stage of her journey. As she put her key in the door she thanked heaven that Hilary had gone to see her parents in Highgate. George Henry would have had his supper long since; she would boil herself an egg and would spend half an hour with him. She closed the door behind her and crossed the hall to the study; the vague murmur of voices would be the television—George Henry had the habit of switching it on and then walking away and forgetting all about it. She opened the door and went in.

Adam was there; she didn't see anyone or anything else for a few moments. Her face lighted up with her delight and she cried 'Adam, I thought you weren't coming…' before she realised that besides him and George Henry there was someone else in the room.

He had risen to his feet as she paused at the door, a tall man, taller than Adam and, unlike him, heavily built. He had the same handsome face, but his mouth was firm and his nose high-bridged; moreover, although his eyes were blue, they were pale and very clear. Christina wasn't sure about his hair; it was so fair that it could have been grey or just flaxen. He wasn't all that young either, in his thirties, and dressed with a conservative good taste very much in contrast to Adam's rather flamboyant clothes. She had the instant impression of quietness before George Henry spoke.

'Chrissy, how late you are. Adam has brought his brother to visit us to see you, actually.' He frowned a little. 'You didn't tell me you were considering taking a post in Holland.'

She smiled at him. 'Well, love, it seemed a bit silly to say anything before I knew more about it.'

She shook hands with Adam and turned to the other man. 'This is Duert—I told him about you, and he decided he might as well come back with me and see you.' Adam was still holding her hand and she pulled it away gently, to be engulfed in a very large firm one.

'So much more satisfactory than writing letters and filling in forms.' His voice was deep and pleasant and he had a nice smile. He was looking at her in what she considered to be a vague fashion. 'I'm sorry we didn't give you a reasonable warning that we were coming perhaps we might meet and discuss this matter of a job?'

His straight eyebrows rose in faint query and she answered seriously: 'Of course. I have a free day tomorrow.'

'We can have lunch,' interposed Adam. 'I'll be free for a couple of hours.'

'Then perhaps you could spare me an hour in the afternoon?'

Christina gave him a long calm look. 'You mean there's a chance of me getting a job at the hospital?'

'There is a strong possibility, but we do need to talk about it.'

He gave her a lazy smile, friendly enough but not very interested. And she could hardly blame him; she must look pretty awful with damp hair and her face still wet from the rain. She said formally, 'That would suit me very well, Dr ter Brandt, if you would tell me where I am to meet you.'

'Oh, I'll pick you up directly after you've lunched with Adam.'

George Henry had been sitting back listening. Now he said: 'You're sure you want this, Chrissy? It's not just because Hilary and I are getting married? You said that you had the chance of a bedsitter or a room at St Athud's...'

'Oh, yes, I know,' she answered him with her usual calm air, 'but you see I wasn't sure, it was only a suggestion on Adam's part, but I really want to go, George Henry. A change will do me good—I'm getting in a rut.'

The three men looked at her, her brother with surprise because she had never before even hinted that she was dissatisfied with her job, Adam with lighthearted amusement, and Duert ter Brandt with a bland face and thoughtful eyes.

It was he who broke the silence with a casual: 'Well, we'll talk about it tomorrow, shall we?'

He held out a hand. 'I hope we haven't trespassed for too long upon your leisure. Goodnight, Miss Forbes.' He shook hands with George Henry too and Christina barely had the time to say goodbye to Adam before they went. Duert ter Brandt could at least have given them the chance to talk for a few minutes, instead of which he swept Adam out of the house with an authority, which although not apparent was nonetheless very real.

After they had gone she remembered that Adam hadn't told her where and when they were to meet for lunch. She was still digesting this when George Henry observed: 'I like him—Adam's brother, a nice unassuming chap.'

She answered him tartly: 'A bit too suave for me, but I'm not likely to see much of him if I get the job. He's the hospital director and presumably he does his directing from some office or other.'

George Henry fiddled with a pen lying on his desk. 'Have you any details of the job? The ward you'll be on, off duty, salary and so on?'

'None at all. Adam told me that there were vacancies at the hospital and that I might suit, but it was for Dr ter Brandt to decide. He wanted to know if I could speak French or German and he seemed quite satisfied with my efforts. It was really to see if I had any aptitude for languages, I think it seems you're given a crash course in Dutch.'

Her brother frowned. 'You really want to go, Chrissy?'

She turned an eager face to his. 'Oh, George Henry, yes!'

She was aware that her enthusiasm was largely due to the likelihood of seeing Adam again, and quite often too. She told herself sternly that she would have to be sensible about that, but that didn't prevent her, when she was getting ready for bed, from taking a long look at her face, close up to the dressing table looking-glass and with a bright light showing it up. Her eyes were all right, but the rest of her was mediocre; she had a creamy unblemished skin, but she didn't consider that that helped at all—and her teeth were good, but she couldn't be expected to smile all the time. Her nose was unimportant and her mouth was wide and her hair, inclined to curl if left to itself, had been pulled back severely for so long now that it had grown like it. She peered anxiously at herself and wondered what Adam saw in her, if indeed he saw anything at all. But he had squeezed her fingers when they had shaken hands and smiled at her in a way to make her wonder if he liked her a little. Perhaps she would know tomorrow.

'Well, what do you think of her?' asked Adam as he drove the BMW too fast away from the dull streets towards the West End.

His brother said slowly: 'She seems a sensible young woman.'

Adam laughed, 'And plain with it, but the most gorgeous eyes—but perhaps you didn't notice them. I bet she's never been chatted up in her life—and she's not so young either. Very rewarding material to work on.'

Dr ter Brandt said evenly: 'Do not make the mistake of thinking that she is like the rest of your girl-friends, Adam. She is unsophisticated, I grant you; she is also calm and matter-of-fact. Moreover, I have it from her brother that she is a very capable Ward Sister and thought highly of at the hospital. As you so ungallantly point out, she is neither very young nor pretty, and definitely not your cup of tea.' He added, still without heat: 'I think you should leave her alone.'

'Oh, don't worry, Duert, I haven't got designs on the girl, but she doesn't seem to have had much fun. A few dinners and an occasional evening out will do her the world of good. You'll consider her for a job?'

'Yes, I think I may. It rather depends on what experience she's had in the Accident Room and surgery.' The big man heaved his bulk out of the car as Adam stopped in front of Brown's Hotel and then turned to ask: 'Where are you taking her to lunch?'

'Oh, a little Greek place in Soho—' Adam gave its name and at the look of surprise on his brother's face added testily: 'Well, she's not used to the Ritz or Claridge's, she might feel awkward.' He looked away from the pale blue eyes staring at him so steadily. 'What time will you meet us?'

'I will be there at half past two. I think I may go back in the evening so see that you're punctual. What time do your afternoon lectures start?'

'A quarter to three.' Adam sounded sulky.

'In that case you had better be outside this place by two-fifteen.'

Dr ter Brandt turned on his heel and went into the hotel without looking back.

Adam telephoned quite early the following morning so that Christina had plenty of time in which to decide what she should wear. None of her clothes were very exciting, although they were good and in excellent taste. It was cool and cloudy so that she felt justified in wearing the suit she had bought only a few weeks earlier. It was grey flannel with a pleated skirt and a neat little jacket and she had a silk blouse in a pale silvery grey to go with it. She dressed with care, made sure that George Henry's lunch was ready for him, and left the house. Adam had said he couldn't fetch her, so she took a bus to Oxford Street and then walked the rest of the way through the crowded Soho streets.

The restaurant was small and faintly shabby as to paint, but it had tubs of flowers each side of the door and the net curtains at the windows were a pristine white. She was aware of a vague disappointment and the thought shot through her head that she need not have put on her new suit; she felt overdressed, what with the silk blouse and the patent leather shoes and handbag, when as far as she could see every other girl in sight was wearing jeans or some long flowing garment with a lot of bracelets.

But she forgot all that as Adam crossed the pavement to meet her and took her arm. 'What a punctual girl!' he greeted her. 'I was afraid you might be late, girls so often are—and I have to be gone again by a quarter past two.' He saw the look of doubt on her face and added: 'Oh, it's all right, Duert will be here to collect you and put you through your paces.'

They had gone inside and been given a little table at the back of the little restaurant, and when Christina put her hands on the table, Adam had covered them with his own so that all the questions she was going to ask him flew out of her head. All the same, she didn't allow herself to get carried away, although her heart was thundering in her ears. After a moment she gently withdrew her hands and looked around her. The place was a lot nicer inside than it was outside, she decided, and the waiter who served them was quick and attentive. She chose a fish salad and a fresh fruit salad and drank the wine she was offered without knowing what it was.

Adam didn't talk about the possibility of her getting a job, only discussed in a charming if vague fashion the various places he intended to take her to once she was in Holland. She was too sensible to believe quite all he said, although she would have liked to, but even if they only did half the things he was enthusing about, the future seemed to her to be an enchantment not to be missed. The time slid away too quickly and it was Adam who looked at his watch and said: 'Oh, lord—it's time we went.'

She put down her coffee cup in an unflurried manner. 'Very well. I'm going to powder my nose.'

'Must you?' He sounded irritable, but at her look of surprise he said: 'Sorry—I didn't mean to snap, but don't be too long, will you?'

The wine had flushed her cheeks a little, but otherwise she looked as well groomed as when she had left home that morning. She poked at her hair, put on more lipstick and rejoined Adam.

Dr Duert ter Brandt was standing on the edge of the pavement outside, his back to the restaurant. It was a very large back and very straight in its beautifully tailored jacket. He must have had eyes at the back of his head, for he turned round before they reached him, wished her a friendly good afternoon, said something in a soft voice to Adam and lifted his hand at a passing taxi. Once more barely given time to say more than goodbye to Adam, Christina found herself sitting back beside Dr ter Brandt.

'I thought that we might walk in Green Park,' his voice was quiet and slow after Adam's quick, accented English. 'You understand that there are a number of questions I must ask you? And if we are both satisfied I shall require references.'

She said yes a little breathlessly; funny to think that only a few days ago she had been contemplating a dull future in a bedsitter. But she hadn't got the job yet.

It was pleasant in the park; they strolled through its comparative peace while the doctor asked questions. A great many questions, thought Christina, answering them in her sensible manner, giving him facts and taking care not to boast or pretend about anything.

'And surgery?' he wanted to know.

'Not for the last two years, I'm afraid. I had the Women's Surgical Ward for two years before I got my present post, and before that I was in Casualty and the Accident Room, a year as Second Sister and previous to that about a year as a staff nurse.'

'You like accident work?'

'Yes, very much. I should have liked to have stayed on there, but I was advised that I should get all-round experience. I haven't been at St Athud's all the time, you know. I came to London when my parents died and took the job I have got now. Before then I was living near Yeovil. I worked at the hospital there, but I trained at Bart's.'

They had stopped to watch an old man feeding the birds and presently Dr ter Brandt said: 'The post I have to offer you is that of Third Sister in the Accident Department at the Theofilus Hospital. We operate three shifts in the twenty-four hours, and you would be expected to work each shift in turn. You would have two days off each week, six weeks' holiday in the year and for the first few months at least, attend classes in Dutch. You may live in the hospital if you wish or rent rooms or a flat close by.' He mentioned a salary which, changed into English money, seemed generous.

'But perhaps the cost of living is higher?' asked Christina, sensibly.

'About the same, I think.'

She said composedly: 'I may apply for the post?'

'Yes. I have an application form with me, which we will fill in presently. The post is vacant now, but of course you will have to resign—a month, I take it?'

The old man had gone and so had the birds. A cool wind rustled the trees around them and a few leaves fluttered on to the grass. Christina said in her sensible way: 'I have more than two weeks' holiday due to me, which means that I can leave in about ten days' time.'

'That would suit us very well.' He paused and added thoughtfully: 'But of course you would like to stay here until your brother's marriage?'

'No.' Her voice was level and quiet. 'That doesn't matter. I should explain that my brother and I are very fond of each other and we get on very well. I'm delighted that he's marrying, but his fiancée and I—well, we don't get on very well. I think it might be easier for all of us if I'm not at the wedding.' She added slowly, 'We haven't quarrelled or anything like that, but George Henry feels a bit mean because I'm having to find somewhere else to live and it would be a good thing if I'm not there to remind him...'

The doctor's smile was kind. 'I'm sorry, but thank you for telling me; I'm sure it's a sensible solution. These unfortunate occasions do arise, but I've found that time does much to improve them.'

'That's what I thought. By the time I get back to England it will be forgotten.' They had been strolling along, but now she stopped. 'I've taken up your afternoon, Dr ter Brandt. If there's nothing more I need to know, I'll say goodbye. I'm sure I can manage the form and I'll get the references and send them on to you.'

For answer he took her arm. 'A cup of tea, I think, and we can fill in the form at the same time.'

He walked her back across the park and into Piccadilly, crossed the street and ushered her through the splendid entrance of the Ritz. 'Tea here?' she asked uncertainly.

'It's the nicest place I know of for tea,' he told her as they were led to a table by the window.

Christina had gone past the hotel many times since she had been in London, but never been inside. It was splendid and elegant and everything she had imagined it would be, and she was glad that she was wearing the grey suit; there wasn't a pair of denims in sight, the atmosphere was peaceful and restful, and having taken it all in she said forthrightly: 'This is delightful. I've often wondered what it was like inside, and now I know.'

And when the tea came she poured it with a dignified self-assurance which gave the lie to Adam's theory that she might feel ill at ease in such plushy surroundings. The doctor, plying her with wafer-thin cucumber sandwiches, little iced cakes and tiny meringues, looked at her with approval. She was no fool, this rather plain girl with the lovely eyes; she had a delightful voice and nice manners and a sensible head on her shoulders.

And he liked the way she dressed too. She had a good figure and small, well kept hands. After a time, he mused, one forgot her lack of looks and probably, given enough incentive, she could improve on those.

He had an uneasy feeling that Adam was going to provide that incentive, and although, as he had said before, she seemed capable of looking after herself, she was too honest and nice a girl to be hurt. Of course, Adam might be serious about her; she was so very different from the usual kind of girl he fell in love with, it might be possible. Time would tell.

He asked casually: 'Are you meeting Adam this evening, Christina?'

She shook her head. 'No, he's got a lecture and he had to catch up on something he missed—and tomorrow he has a study day at Birmingham.'

The doctor sat back, his eyes on her face. 'I have to stay in London until tomorrow evening. Perhaps we might have lunch together, then if there are any snags or problems we can sort them out.'

'Thank you, I should like that.' Her gaze met his and she smiled. 'Should I fill in that form?'

They did it together, laughing a little while Christina tried to remember dates and how tall she was and the exact date upon which she had started her training. It was finished at last and she was surprised to find that they had been sitting over their tea for more than an hour. And she had enjoyed herself; her companion had turned out to be nicer than she had expected; rather reserved, perhaps, but he must be a good deal older than Adam. He would be comfortably married, of course; she had taken that for granted. She would have like to have asked him if he had any children, but she had already formed the impression that his private life was very much his own business.

They took a taxi back to George Henry's house after that, but the doctor, politely opening the door for her, refused her invitation to come in, pleading an evening engagement and wishing her a pleasantly impersonal goodbye as he went. Christina stood in the hall, listening to the coughs and murmurs coming from the waiting room, already stuffed with the evening surgery patients. She felt as though a door, briefly opened on to another world, had been gently but inexorably closed again.

'It's not my world anyway,' she reminded herself sensibly, and went upstairs to change the grey suit for a skirt and jumper and then went along to the kitchen to see about supper.

Hilary came that evening and displayed an unflattering amazement that anyone should want to take Christina to the Ritz for tea. She said, her rather prominent blue eyes narrowed: 'Well, really, whatever next? Was he trying to impress you?'

Christina considered the question. 'No—he's not that kind of man. I think it was because the Ritz was close by and it was tea time and I had to fill in a form. We had to have a table, you see.'

Hilary gave her a suspicious glance, but Christina appeared to be serious, so she gave a reluctant nod. 'Dead set on this job, aren't you? Supposing you hate it when you're there?'

Christina allowed herself a silent giggle. Hilary's face showed very plainly that she wished she hadn't said that; supposing Christina said that she would return home and expect to live with her and George Henry until she found another job to suit her? She said gently: 'Well, you know, Hilary, I'm a bit slow about making up my mind about places and people—other people know within seconds if they like something or someone, but not me.' She remembered very clearly that she had known within a second that she liked Adam, but of course there was always the exception to every rule... 'I shall enjoy the experience,' she finished.

Hilary agreed with eager enthusiasm and hardly concealed her pleasure when Christina mentioned that it wasn't likely that she would be at the wedding. George Henry, Christina decided, must be very in love not to notice, but that was a good thing. She was a firm believer in love, herself unloved.

'You won't come back,' observed Hilary in a satisfied voice.

'Probably not, and certainly not to London.' Christina beamed at them both. 'Have you decided what you would like for a present?' she asked.

Dr ter Brandt came for her at noon the next day, keeping the taxi waiting outside while he chatted amiably with George Henry, who had just come in from an emergency call. Which gave Christina time to take another quick look at herself in the old-fashioned wardrobe mirror. She was wearing the suit again because it seemed suitable in the elegant company of the doctor, and she wondered where they were to lunch.

She hadn't included Claridge's in her guessing. She got out of the taxi and looked up at its solid imposing front, then she looked at the doctor.

'Will I do for a place like this?' she asked simply.

He looked her up and down very deliberately. 'Very well indeed,' he assured her, and she said matter-of-factly:

'Oh, that's all right, then. I shouldn't like to let you down.'

They had a table by the window again, shown to it by the manager of the restaurant, who greeted the doctor with the smiling respect due to a regular visitor. There was a band playing softly somewhere and the restaurant was elegant and quiet. Christina sighed as she sat down.

'This is very delightful,' she observed, 'and a bit exciting to me. I expect you come here a lot?'

'From time to time. What would you like to drink?' And when she hesitated: 'A dry sherry would give us an appetite, if you'd care for that?'

'Please.' She added with disarming frankness: 'I don't know much about drinks.'

'Then you'll allow me to guide you.' He took the menu he had been offered and glanced across at her, already studying hers.

'I'm famished,' he told her placidly. 'I shall have a steak, but how about a starter? Avocado, perhaps?' and when she agreed, relieved to have some guidance through the enormous selection of food, 'If you like fish, I can recommend the salmon, or perhaps lobster?'

'Salmon, please.' She wasn't absolutely sure what you did with a lobster. She sat back and looked around her and the doctor looked at her. She had self-possession, that was evident, and no pretence. He had expected her to tell him that she didn't know what to do with a lobster and he was quite disappointed because she hadn't. She wasn't gauche, he decided, merely deprived of the usual opportunities most girls had of going out and picking up these useful pieces of information. He would warn Adam not to make the mistake of taking her to a second class restaurant again. She would be able to cope with Buckingham Palace if necessary because she had sense and natural good manners and an honesty which he found rather touching. He couldn't think of any of his women friends, offhand, who would have stopped outside a restaurant in order to ask if they would do.

He elaborated upon the job she had applied for while they ate their way through the most delicious lunch she had ever tasted, and watching the light-as-air profiteroles being piled on to her plate, she remarked: 'It all sounds quite splendid—but the thing is, I'm so taken up with this gorgeous food I don't think I'm appreciating it as I should.'

The doctor gave a great booming laugh. 'Then I shall have to send you a job description leaflet when I get back.'

Which reminded her to ask: 'You're going this evening?'

'Yes, I must.' He didn't tell her that he had stayed another day so that he might take her out to lunch. He had been sorry for her, but he wasn't any more. She was one of those calm, sensible girls who didn't allow themselves to become flustered. Adam would try and charm her out of that calmness, but Duert doubted if he would succeed. He would make sure that he didn't anyway; she was too nice a girl to have her heart broken by the carefree Adam. There were plenty of girls who could play his game and not get hurt. The doctor, whose own tastes ran to sophisticated women whose witty conversation kept him mildly amused and who were never surprised or excited about anything at all, glanced at Christina with puzzled eyes. There was absolutely nothing about this dab of a girl to interest him, so why had he taken her out to lunch? To save her from the disappointment of not seeing Adam, he supposed idly.

'Adam will be back tomorrow,' he told her, and watched her face light up. 'He has only three more weeks here; you will be quite at home in den Haag by then.'

She poured their coffee with a steady hand while she contemplated her exciting future. 'So I shall,' she told him. 'When will I know? I have to resign...'

'Oh, do that tomorrow, will you?' and at her look of surprise, 'I've recommended you for the post and I'm the director of the hospital, so the job's yours, Christina. Let me know when you can come and I'll arrange to have you met. You'll need a passport, of course; I'll see about your work permit. Have you enough money for your fare or would you like an advance?'

'I've enough, thank you.'

'Good—well, we'll see how you get on, shall we? If at the end of a month you're not happy, let me know.'

'And if I don't suit?' she prompted.

'Then I shall let you know.'

She wouldn't like that to happen. He seemed such an easy-going man, but she suspected that upon occasion he could be icy-tempered, venting his rage in a cold voice on whoever had been hapless enough to incur his displeasure. Christina hoped most sincerely that she would never be unlucky enough to do that, and anyway, she wouldn't see much of him once she was there. She didn't know much about hospital directors, but she hardly thought he would do anything else but administrative work.

There didn't seem much more to say after that. She finished her coffee, invented a meeting with one of the Sisters from the hospital, wished him a pleasant journey back home, thanked him for her delightful lunch and assured him that she really had to go. She wasn't surprised when he at once asked for the bill, paid it and ushered her out of the restaurant; indeed, she was a little worried as to whether she had lingered too long, which made her goodbyes rather brisk.

'I'll get you a taxi,' offered the doctor, and when she said no, thank you, she would walk as it was close by, and he asked where, his eyes gleamed with amusement when she said wildly: 'Oh, Piccadilly Circus,' which wasn't close by at all.

He stood on the pavement and watched her walk briskly to the corner and into Davies Street, on her way to the crowds and bustle of Oxford Street. He very much doubted if she was going to meet anyone.

Christina got on a bus when she reached Oxford Street and went home; it was mid-afternoon, George Henry was out on his afternoon visits and she had the house to herself. She sat down at the dining room table and made a list of all the things she had to do within the next few days, then she wrote a letter of resignation ready to hand in in the morning, made a cup of tea, washed her hair and then sat down again and allowed herself to indulge in daydreams just a little. Adam cropped up in all of them.

CHAPTER THREE

HALFWAY THROUGH the next ten days Christina took stock of her situation, not because she was having second thoughts or suffering from nerves but so that she might check on her preparations. She had had confirmation of her appointment at the Theofilus Hospital, together with a letter of businesslike brevity, telling her how, when and where to travel. She had also had rather a nasty interview with the Principal Nursing Officer, who took it as a personal affront that Christina should want to leave St Athud's, and she had borne with equanimity the endless questions and comments from her various friends and acquaintances, not to mention the rather anxious ones from Hilary, obviously terrified that she might change her mind at the last moment.

She had done some shopping too; a couple of dresses, one a soft green jersey the other a two-piece in silvery grey. These, reinforced by a handful of woollies and blouses from Marks and Spencers, last year's tweed skirt and some slacks would do very well for a start, she considered, and then after due consideration, went out and bought a long dark green velvet skirt and a very expensive silk blouse with lace insertions to go with it. She packed the lot together with undies, raincoat and a variety of footwear and declared herself ready.

Of Adam she had seen very little, but perhaps that was a good thing, for she had had quite a lot to do and the ward was full again. When he did telephone and suggest dinner she had had to refuse because her friends were giving her a farewell party, a rather noisy female affair which she had very much enjoyed. But on the following evening she was free and they had dined at a small French restaurant. On an impulse Christina had taken the new green jersey from her case and worn it, and had taken extra pains with her face and hair. Used to her brother's laconic praise of anything new, she wasn't too disappointed at Adam's casual: 'You look nice.'

She listened happily to his lighthearted account of his studies, what he intended to do when they were finished, and his plans for a holiday on Tenerife, and she was quite breathless with happiness when he suggested carelessly that she might like to go too.

'There'll be half a dozen of us,' he told her. 'We'll fly over, of course.' Luckily he didn't wait for her reply but rattled on about something else, which gave her time to reflect sadly that she hadn't a hope of going with him. But she didn't stay sad for long; after all, she would be seeing quite a lot of him when she got to Holland. The thought brought colour to her cheeks and made her eyes sparkle so that Adam paused in what he was saying to remark. 'You know, Chrissy, if you'd do something to your hair you'd be quite pretty.'

It was astonishing to her what an effect he had upon her usual calm. Her pink cheeks got a good deal pinker, although she tried to keep her voice light. 'I had it permed once, and I looked frightful, besides—I was quite hopeless at setting it.'

Adam looked surprised. 'Don't you want to make the most of yourself?' His smile was charming. 'For me, Chrissy? Buy some pretty clothes and have your hair done and use more make-up,' he coaxed her.

She said soberly: 'But then it wouldn't be me.'

He studied her with narrowed eyes. 'How old are you?' and when she told him: 'Three years older than I, but you've the naïveté of a girl of seventeen. I shall have to take you in hand.'

He said it lightly and laughed as he spoke, but he stretched out a hand and caught hers across the table, stroking it gently with a finger. Christina drew her hand away. 'It wouldn't be any good,' she told him matter-of-factly, 'I'm too old to change my ways.'

'If that's a challenge, I'll accept it,' he said at once. 'When you get to Holland, I'll take you to a really super hairdresser in the Hague; he'll do wonders for you, and a girl I know goes to a beauty parlour there. She'll take you along with her on a visit to a boutique and you won't know yourself, darling.'

It sounded too good to be true, and lying in bed later, she decided that it was. Even if she'd possessed the kind of money she would obviously have to spend to change herself into the kind of girl Adam admired, she was fairly certain that no amount of beauty treatment would turn her into someone glamorous everyone—and everyone was Adam, of course—would fall for at the first glance. All the same, she decided just before she fell asleep, she would go and have her hair decently cut and set and lay out what money she could spare on more make-up.

She went two days later—to a wildly expensive hairdresser her friends assured her was absolutely terrific. Not that the great man actually did more than spend a few minutes staring at her and then muttering instructions to the assistant. Probably he felt disheartened at what he saw, thought Christina, afterwards, for although her hair was trimmed it was still long and it had merely been washed and set so that the faint natural wave in it was given a chance to show itself, but at least the assistant had dressed it in a much softer style. Everyone agreed, when she displayed herself at supper that evening, that the astronomical sum she had paid had been worth it just for the new style alone. Christina, peering at herself in the glass, hoped so too.

She was to meet Adam once more before she left for Holland. He had no time, he explained on the telephone, but perhaps they could meet for drinks, just for an hour. She was free that afternoon, and encouraged by the visit to the hairdresser's, she rushed off to a beauty parlour, where a supercilious young woman examined her face from all angles, pointed out its defects with the remark: 'I always think it's best to tell the truth, don't you, madam?' and then went to work with a will. Christina was almost afraid to look in the mirror when she was finished, and when she did she gave a gasp. The face looking back at her was hers, all right, but now she had long dark eyelashes, a mouth which wasn't at all the same shape as it had been and a green eye-shadow which she wasn't sure that she liked. Indeed, she felt quite uneasy, and in half a mind to take the whole lot off, but the young woman, standing back to admire her handiwork, assured her that the improvement was quite fantastic, which wasn't really very flattering, and then sold her a lipstick and the eye-shadow she didn't like. Christina went on duty feeling extremely self-conscious and then was considerably heartened by a visit from Beryl, come to borrow some catheters, who declared that she looked quite super and on no account was she ever to go back to her old ways.

Christina laughed, 'Well, I'll not get much time to do all this every day,' she pointed out, 'but I'll do my best if you think it's really made a difference.'

And it must have done, for when Willie Fisher came to see his patients just before she went off duty he stared at her quite openly and muttered: 'You look different.'

It was a pity that Adam, when they met later that evening, said nothing at all, even though Christina had made a point of choosing a seat under a bright light so that she was clearly visible. He was full of some disagreement he had had with someone or other who was at the same course as he: he didn't make it clear who the someone was or why they had disagreed, only that he had been right and they had been wrong. She listened with sympathy, forgetting her disappointment, so that it was all the more acute when he said presently: 'Well, you're off in a couple of days, aren't you, darling? I'll be seeing you in Holland, and remember what I said about taking you to a good hairdresser and getting some decent clothes.' They were on the pavement waiting for a taxi to take her back to St Athud's, and before she could answer that, one had drawn up and Adam had opened its door, kissed her and popped her inside. 'Can't wait to see you again,' he said in a voice which sounded convincingly sincere. She treasured the words as the taxi bore her away.

The next day was the last one before she left London. She and George Henry and Hilary had dinner together, making the kind of animated conversation usual to such an occasion. Hilary, with the wedding only a week or so away, was disposed to be friendly, and annoyingly patronising too. Christina bore with it meekly because she didn't want to hurt George Henry's feelings. He was still feeling guilty, although she had been careful never to give him reason to do so. So the three of them laughed and talked and made little jokes about Christina having to learn Dutch, and Hilary observed with more than a touch of spite that probably she would meet some Dutchman or other and marry him and never come back to England.

She said it with a laugh, but Christina thought it was the one thing that Hilary would like to happen, at the same time making it plain that the chance of it happening was a remote one.

She left for Heathrow Airport the next morning, outwardly composed but inwardly wildly excited. Watching England disappear from under her, she had no qualms about leaving London. She would miss her brother and her friends, but if she had regrets it was for her home in Somerset. But even if she had stayed in London, her chances of returning there were small. Perhaps she would be able to return there for a holiday some time.

The flight was brief; she found herself in the reception hall at Schiphol, standing by the reception desk as she had been told to do, awaiting whoever it was who was to meet her.

She hadn't long to wait. A short stout man with a round cheerful face, dressed with great neatness in a navy blue suit, touched her on the arm.

'Miss Forbes? I am sent by Dr ter Brandt to meet you and take you to the hospital. My name is Corvinus—I am his butler.'

His English was good, although the accent was strong and a little difficult to understand, but Christina was so relieved to hear her mother tongue that she barely noticed that. She said, 'How do you do,' politely, and added: 'What do I call you? Instead of mister, I mean.'

He looked faintly shocked. 'Corvinus, miss.' He picked up her case and took her overnight bag from her hand. 'If you will follow me...'

He led her through the crowds and outside to where a Daimler Sovereign was parked. And very nice too, thought Christina. Dr ter Brandt must be doing very well for himself. The stout man opened the door with a flourish, but she said at once, 'Oh, no—if you don't mind I'd rather sit with you.' The idea of being driven, sitting in state on the back seat, to her new job didn't seem right at all.

He beamed at her, 'A pleasure, miss,' installed her into the front seat and got in beside her.

'Is it far?' asked Christina.

'No, miss, but the traffic is very great.' He drove smoothly away. 'Fifty-six kilometres only, and that on the motorway.'

Where the speed limit didn't matter overmuch, she decided a few minutes later; the traffic was going at a furious pace and her companion with it. She glanced around her. Motorways were the same the world over, she mused, cutting through the country, rushing past half-hidden villages and towns. She studied several distant church spires and wondered about them. As though he had read her thoughts Corvinus said: 'Den Haag is a beautiful city and the country round it is beautiful also.'

'Oh, good.' She turned to smile at him. 'Your English is very good. Have you lived in England?'

'Yes, for a time, and also for holidays. My wife is English.'

Just hearing him say that made her feel much more at home. She didn't suppose she would ever meet that lady, but nonetheless it gave her a comforting glow. 'Oh, that is nice,' she declared warmly.

Corvinus drove fast; they were approaching the outskirts of den Haag in no time at all. Christina looked around her with interest; this was going to be her home for some time and she was determined to like it. There was no sign of the beautiful country she had been promised, but Corvinus assured her that on the other side of the city, along the coast, there were wide avenues of trees and a good deal of wooded land. 'And Scheveningen,' he pointed out, 'that is also delightful, and also Wassenaar. They are to be reached with ease from den Haag. And even in the city there are great open...' he paused for a word and she helped him out:

'Do you mean a kind of park? Like Hampstead Heath in London?'

'That is it. They are beautiful, the woods, and there are walks there.'

She looked backwards over her shoulder as he drove past the Haagsche Bos. The woods did indeed look lovely, the leaves already turning red and gold, soon lost to sight as Corvinus turned towards the city centre. After a few minutes he drove slowly down a narrow lane, turned into a wide, busy thoroughfare and so to a wide sweep before the hospital. It was a modern building, nine stories high and built in a slender curve. Christina stared up at it with interest. It presented a challenge to her and while feeling nervous at meeting a lot of new faces, she was determined to make a success of the job. She thanked Corvinus as she got out of the car, and he said: 'I wish you happiness, miss,' and carried her bags up the shallow steps and into the enormous reception hall, where he went straight to the porter's lodge, handed her over to the dignified personage who presided over it, and with a quiet goodbye, went away.

She watched him go with real regret. He had been friendly and reassuring and it would have been nice to have had him by her for a little longer. The head porter recalled her to her surroundings with faint impatience.

'Come with me, miss,' he advised her, and led the way across the hall to a line of lifts.

'Where am I going?' asked Christina.

'The Directrice.'

The one bit she had been rather dreading, but better to get it over with. They went two floors up and then walked down a long chilly passage lined with doors. The porter knocked on the last one and when the green light above it came on, opened it and stood aside for her to go in.

The room was spartan and its occupant rather matched her surroundings. She was a tall thin woman of indeterminate age, with large bony features, greying hair drawn back from a high forehead and beautiful bright blue eyes. She was dressed severely in a dark blue uniform with an old-fashioned starched cap on her head and bows under her determined chin. Christina took one look and liked her.

Her English was good but not fluent as she greeted Christina gravely, bade her be seated and then looked her over without haste. 'Dr ter Brandt recommends you highly,' she observed in a pleasant voice, 'and we are happy to have you with us. There will be a trial period of one month, at the end of which time either side may terminate the contract. After which we would wish you to give three months' notice if you should want to leave.'

'Yes, he did explain that to me,' said Christina, 'and I agreed to that.'

She waited composedly for the Directrice to speak.

'You will report for duty tomorrow morning at eight o'clock. The senior Hoofd Zuster, Zuster Kaarsen, will show you your duties and arrange your free time. You will find your uniform ready for you in your room. Please come and see me if you wish help at any time.' She glanced at the clock. 'The midday meal is finished, but something will be brought to your room and you will be free to unpack and do as you wish for the rest of this day.' She smiled and nodded dismissal. 'I hope that you will be very happy here, Miss Forbes.'

Outside the door once more, Christina found a small round little lady waiting for her. She shook hands and said in a cosy voice, 'Hoofd Zuster Zande—no English.'

'Christina Forbes—no Dutch,' said Christina gravely, and allowed herself to be led back down the corridor and into a lift once more. This time it was the top floor they went to, where the nurses had their rooms, and they went up and down a number of passages and lobbies before her guide finally stopped before an open door leading to a wide corridor. '*Hoofd Zusters*,' she explained, and unlocked a door. The room was quite large and comfortably furnished with a view of the city below which was quite breathtaking. It was a pity that Christina disliked heights;

she took a brief glimpse out of the window and turned back to the room.

Zuster Zande flung open a door, revealing a small shower room, and then crossed to the built-in cupboard and opened it to show the uniforms hung tidily away. She smiled brightly, nodded her head, said '*Eten*,' and rustled away, leaving Christina to wonder what she had said. It was all very well to have a dictionary; she had learnt as many useful words as she had had the time for, now she suspected that the written word was a very different kettle of fish from the spoken one. She hoped that it meant food, and she was proved right, for a few minutes later there was a knock on the door and a young girl in a print dress and apron came in with a tray.

There were rolls filled with ham and cheese, a salad in a small bowl, and a large rosy apple, and better than all these, there was a pot of tea with sugar and milk. Christina, who had been warned by a friend who had holidayed in Holland that year that there was no milk served with the tea, heaved a sigh of relief, took off her jacket, and sat down at the little desk to eat her lunch. The tea was hot and strong and there was plenty of it; perhaps her friend had stayed in some remote place where tea wasn't easily obtainable. She drank the pot dry and turned to her unpacking and then to trying on her uniform. It fitted very well and she loved the starched caps with their brief muslin veils just covering the nape of her neck. The new hair-style suited them very well. She put everything ready for the morning and decided that she would go out.

She was getting into her jacket again when there was another knock on the door and two girls came in. They were about her own age, fair and pretty and blue-eyed and friendly. They introduced themselves as Leenie and Truus, and Leenie said as they shook hands, 'Our English is not good, but a little, you understand? We are now free and we wish to take you out.' She beamed at Christina, who beamed back,

'Oh, how very kind of you, I'd love that.'

'We go to change our clothes,' said Leenie. 'I am Hoofd Zuster of the Men's Surgical Ward, and Truus is Hoofd Zuster in the Accident Room—she works with you.' She added: 'Her English is not so good.'

Truus bearing this out, echoed, 'Not good,' and smiled.

'I must learn Dutch,' declared Christina, 'just as soon as I can. Is it difficult?'

'Not for us,' said Leenie, and went off into peals of laughter. 'You will have lessons.'

The three of them left the hospital presently, carrying on a lively conversation which involved a good deal of miming and hand-waving and laughter. Dr ter Brandt, pausing briefly at a first floor window as he took a teaching round in the Children's Unit, watched them go.

There were no other English nurses at the hospital, Christina learned at breakfast the next morning. She sat between Truus and Leenie at a round table for twelve and was introduced in turn to the other occupants, all of them *Hoofd Zusters* in wards or departments. They all spoke English too, although they assured her that once she started her lessons they would make a point of speaking Dutch to her. They were nice to her, friendly and helpful and full of hospital gossip, and she left the table with them, looking forward to her first day. The senior *Hoofd Zuster* in the Accident Room was a dragon, she had been told, but very good at her job; Christina would be the junior *Hoofd Zuster* under Truus and besides that there were four student nurses and several aides.

The Accident Room was vast, modern and magnificently equipped. Christina, having a quick look round before Zuster Bunsma arrived, approved of it all. There was already a sprinkling of patients waiting, but she had no time to investigate what Truus was doing, for Zuster Bunsma had arrived.

She was a large woman with big features, small dark eyes and grey hair, cut very short. She wore no make-up at all and her age could have been anything between fifty and sixty. She wished everyone a good morning in a brisk manner and turned to Christina.

'You come with high recommendations,' she observed without preamble. 'I hope you will prove them right.' She studied Christina slowly. 'You look a sensible young woman; I won't have anyone else in this department.' She added unexpectedly, 'I hope you will be happy working here, Zuster Forbes.' She nodded quickly and went on before Christina could say a word: 'We will go round the department and I will show you everything. You will be expected to remember all I have told you.'

Christina said calmly: 'I shall do my best, Zuster Bunsma,' and was wondering if she had said enough when one of the nurses came to whisper in her superior's ear. Zuster Bunsma frowned. 'You are to go at once to the *Directeur*'s office. This nurse will show you where to go. You will come to me when you return.'

The nurse spoke almost no English, which was a pity because Christina was dying to find out how it was that Zuster Bunsma's English was so good. She wondered if her Dutch would ever be half as fluent.

Dr ter Brandt had his office on the fourth floor, that much she discovered from her companion, which meant that they had to walk through a number of passages and take the lift. They stopped finally outside a door with his name on it, the nurse tapped and then stood aside with the air of someone who was glad she wasn't the one to be going inside, and Christina walked in.

The room was very large with two tall windows overlooking the courtyard below. It was close-carpeted and had panelled walls and a very large desk, behind which Dr ter Brandt was sitting. He looked up as the door opened and got to his feet.

'Ah, Zuster Forbes, welcome to our hospital.' He came round the desk and shook hands. 'All of us at the Theofilus hope that you will be happy working here.'

'Thank you, I'm sure I shall be, everyone has been very kind. The Accident Room looks splendid…'

'It is also very busy.' He offered her a chair and went to sit behind his desk again. 'You have met Hoofd Zuster Bunsma?'

He was being very formal, she decided, but now of course matters were rather different; she was in his employ. He was treating her with perfect courtesy, but his manner was so impersonal as to seem cold.

'Yes, I have. She was about to show me round when I was told to come here.'

'A splendid nurse, one of the best in the hospital. She has been at the Theofilus for something like thirty years.'

'Before your time,' observed Christina, for the moment forgetting where she was.

His face remained placid, but his eyes gleamed with amusement.

'I am thirty-seven, Christina.'

She had pinkened up to her hair. 'Oh, I do beg your pardon—I quite forgot who you were…'

His eyebrows rose. 'Surely not. It is only a matter of weeks since we last saw each other.'

'I didn't mean that,' she explained, 'what I meant was, I forgot that you're the director. You know, you have to be treated with respect and all that.' She saw him frown and added hastily: 'I've made it worse, but I didn't mean to. Oh, dear I should have been saying sir too. Please excuse me, I suppose I'm excited…'

He gave her a long thoughtful look. 'Ah, yes—Adam will be back in a few days. You must be looking forward to seeing him again.'

The pink which had almost faded returned even pinker than before. 'Well, yes I hope that is, it would be nice if we met again.'

'I'm sure you will,' his voice was smooth. 'Adam will be here for a few months; he didn't do very well on the course, he'll need more experience.'

'I'm sorry. Perhaps he found it more difficult taking it in London.'

The doctor didn't reply to this. 'If there is anything I can do while you are here, please let me know. You will find the Directrice very kind and understanding, but if at any time you should want to discuss anything with me, please do not hesitate to do so.' He got to his feet and she got out of her chair, bewildered by his change of manner. He opened the door for her and she went past him, making a conventional murmur. Finding her way back to the Accident Room, she supposed she wouldn't see him very often, perhaps never. She was a little surprised to find that the thought depressed her. But only for a moment; Adam would be back very soon now and life would be exciting once more.

And that was the last chance she had to think of him that day. Sister Bunsma was waiting for her when she reached the Accident Room and, mindful of that lady's words, Christina bent all her powers of concentration upon the task of learning as much as she could in the shortest possible time. And when she was released at last, she was told to accompany Truus for the rest of the day, watching her treatment of the various patients, learning if she could, the names of the equipment used and listening all the time. It sounded like nonsense, of course, but she had a quick ear and she was sensible enough to know that once she had got hold of the basic Dutch, she would learn quickly enough.

During the afternoon, she went to her lesson, given by a dry-as-dust elderly man, who without giving her a minute to think, plunged into a list of everyday words which, she heard to her horror, she was expected to repeat word-perfect on the following day. It was a relief to get back to the Accident Room, and because there was a sudden rush on, find herself helping one of the housemen with some uncomplicated arm plasters.

She was tired when she and Truus went off duty at five o'clock but she had enjoyed her day. Not wishing to incur her teacher's wrath on the following afternoon, she refused several friendly offers to go out and made herself comfortable in the sitting room with some of the Sisters and learned her homework, getting a good-natured girl sitting near her to correct her and finally hear her recite it. There was a good deal of friendly laughter over her pronunciation, but she was assured that she was doing remarkably well. She went down to her supper presently, quite pleased with herself.

The next day followed very much the same pattern as the first, only now she was expected to know where most things were kept in the Accident Room and, when it was possible without getting into language difficulties, treat some of the patients. She was elated that her teacher expressed satisfaction at her homework and ploughed her way through a dozen basic sentences, to be told that she was required to be word-perfect on the following day. 'You may think that I am working you hard, young lady,' said her mentor with an unexpected twinkle, 'but you have a natural gift for languages, I think, and if you work hard you should have a good knowledge of our language within three months, perhaps less.'

On the following morning during breakfast she was told to report for duty at once, to find the cubicles occupied with stretchers, dazed people sitting around, and a good deal of noise and bustle. Zuster Bunsma was already there and beckoned her over. 'There is an accident between a touring bus and a car.' She paused to wave two ambulance men towards an empty cubicle. 'Some are not seriously hurt, so far eight are badly injured. It is an English bus, so you will be of great use. Go now to the cubicle in the corner and prepare the patient for examination.' She smiled suddenly. 'Forget that you are in this hospital and think that you are in England. In that way you will work faster.'

There was an elderly woman lying on the couch in the far cubicle. Her face was cut and bleeding and so were her hands, but her extreme pallor might be caused by some more serious damage. Christina said softly: 'Hullo, I've come to get you ready for the doctor. Does anything in particular hurt? I can see your face and hands are cut, we'll see to those, but I must get your shoes and dress off so that we can take a good look.'

'You're English,' mumbled the woman. 'What a blessing! It's my chest, dear such a nasty sharp pain...'

Christina said soothingly: 'Don't worry, Mrs... Burrows, is it? I'll take a quick look, the doctor will be here in a moment.'

There was no injury to be seen; she took the BP, felt for a pulse so faint it was barely perceptible and noted the woman's grey face. A coronary, and the quicker she could get a doctor the better.

She smiled reassuringly at the woman and pressed the alarm buzzer by the side of the couch.

Dr ter Brandt's quiet voice behind her was unexpected, but she didn't waste time on that. She said quietly: 'Mrs Burrows, cuts of face and hands, severe pain in chest, no visible wound there.' She added the startlingly low blood pressure and the almost total absence of pulse, and then raised her voice a little so that the patient could hear her.

'Here's the doctor, Mrs Burrows, you'll be all right now.'

He wasted no time and yet he gave the impression that he was unhurried. Mrs Burrows was examined, sedated and borne away to the Intensive Care Unit in the minimum of time, leaving Christina to clear the cubicle in readiness for the next patient.

Dr ter Brandt had gone within seconds of Mrs Burrows, but before he went he said: 'That was quick thinking, Sister. I congratulate you.'

She was kept busy after that; cuts and concussions, broken bones and shock, but always she was aware that Dr ter Brandt, far from sitting in his office directing, was striding around in a white coat, working twice as hard as anyone else and still looking placid.

Things quietened down slowly. By midday those who needed further treatment had been warded and the rest sent to their hotel. Christina, drinking coffee with Truus while the nurses cleared up, heaved a sigh.

'All those poor souls—what a wretched end to their holiday! What happened to the driver of the car, Truus?'

Truus opened her mouth to tell her and then closed it again, her eyes looking at someone or something over Christina's shoulder. Christina turned round to look too as Dr ter Brandt came further into the office. He spoke to Truus, who got up and went out. 'To fetch me some coffee,' he explained placidly, 'and

I cannot think why you should always look so surprised when we meet. Perhaps you will tell me?'

Christina put down her mug. 'Well, you're not at all what I expected.' She said rather crossly because it was difficult to put into words. 'I thought a director would stay in his office...'

His eyes narrowed. 'Indeed? I wonder where you got such a strange idea?' His voice held mockery. 'I have a practice too—but I feel sure that Adam will have told you that already.'

'Yes, he told me that you were the senior partner.'

'Ah, I've disappointed you—naturally you expected someone middle-aged and pompous. Probably going bald...'

If the note of mockery hadn't been there she would have laughed, as it was she said seriously: 'As a matter of fact, I did...'

Truus interrupted her, carrying a tray with fresh coffee, and he sat down on a corner of Zuster Bunsma's desk and drank it.

'I hear you are showing an aptitude for our language.'

How fast the hospital grapevine worked! 'I've only had two lessons.'

He nodded carelessly. 'Mijnheer Beek is a splendid teacher, especially when he has an eager pupil. By the way, you had better ask for a day off on Friday.'

She asked him why, although she had guessed already. A little colour came into her cheeks and her heart doubled its beat.

He started at her with a faint smile which she didn't care for. 'Did you not know? Adam is coming home.' He turned to speak to Truus and bidding them a rather curt goodbye, went away.

Truus collected the mugs and the pair of them went back on duty again.

'He is splendid, the doctor,' said Truus admiringly. Christina agreed absentmindedly, her head deliriously full of Adam.

CHAPTER FOUR

THERE WERE two whole days before Friday, but if she wanted to be free on that day she would have to ask Zuster Bunsma as soon as possible, something Christina wasn't too keen on doing. She had only just arrived and a request for a day off so soon was likely to be frowned upon. If she had been in Zuster Bunsma's place, she would have frowned it down too, and probably Dr ter Brandt had been testing her just to see how keen she was on the job. She went to lunch with Truus, went back for an hour's work in the Accident Room, which she was fast discovering was almost always busy, and then went to her lesson without seeing Zuster Bunsma, still thinking about Adam. So much so that Mijnheer Beek pulled her up quite sharply with the reminder that she would get nowhere at all unless she applied herself to learning at least some of his language. She was sensible enough to see this for herself; for the rest of the hour she was an exemplary pupil.

It was time for their tea break when she got back, but she saw at a glance that they weren't going to get one. The place swarmed with small children, weeping and howling in concert. Zuster Bunsma sailed from her office as Christina went in, with: 'Zuster Forbes, these children were on a school picnic, and one of them was foolish enough to stir up a swarm of bees. The stings must be removed and antihistamine given. You will take the end cubicle and treat the children in it. There is a nurse already there.'

It seemed strange, after several years of telling others what to do, to be given orders oneself. But logical enough, Christina told herself sensibly as she made her way to her patients. She was new, foreign and needed to prove that she could cope with the job. She pulled back the curtains and joined the howling mob of little people inside.

It was no good trying to stop them. She didn't know what to say. She caught a small boy, sat him down in a chair, gave him a reassuring smile and a hullo and picked up the dirty little paw, its back red and swollen.

'Oh, we'll have this out in no time,' she assured him, and began gently to clean it, talking all the time. He didn't understand her, of course, but her voice was soothing and held authority, so he stopped howling to look at her, and she picked up the forceps laid ready and whisked out the sting, handed him over to the nurse for further cleansing and began on the next child. There were six children in all, although it seemed twice that number, and she was removing a clutch of nasty stings from the last small leg when Dr ter Brandt came quietly in.

'Last one?' he wanted to know.

'Yes—' she hesitated and added 'sir', and didn't see his grin. 'But I haven't given the antihistamine yet.'

He went across to the trolley and began to draw up the drug, at the same time saying something to the nurse who was with her. The girl went away and he said placidly: 'We should be able to manage this little lot between us—I've told Nurse to help at the other end.'

He was good with children, waiting patiently while Christina caught and held each child, and keeping up an endless stream of talk while he gave the injections so that half the children were screaming their heads off in anticipation of his treatment and the other half were shrieking with laughter.

Finally, with a good deal of giggling and squealing, they were returned to one of the two teachers with them and Christina began to tidy the cubicle, very aware of the doctor sitting on the couch, swinging one leg and watching her. At last, everything done to her satisfaction, she said briskly: 'Thank you for your help, sir. I'll find Zuster Bunsma and see what she would like me to do.'

'Time enough. Did you ask for your day off, Christina?'

Her 'no' was faintly defiant.

'Afraid of the dragon? I imagine not. Ah, I have it—you're new here and you don't think you should ask favours.'

'Something like that,' she answered composedly.

'Very commendable.' His voice was dry. 'But unless you do so you won't be able to see Adam.'

She said with calm: 'It's kind of you to bother yourself about me, Dr ter Brandt, but Adam knows where I am if and when he wants to see me.'

The placid expression on his face didn't alter. He got up from the table, ready to leave. 'You're very sure of yourself, and of Adam. I wonder? He favours pretty girls, you know, and you aren't pretty, Christina.' With which outspoken remark he went away, leaving her white-faced with fury.

She spent the rest of the day thinking up stinging remarks to make to him when they met, only they didn't. And the next morning, going on duty, when she met him in a corridor, unfamiliar in slacks and a sweater, she had been surprised enough to answer his good morning with no trace of coldness. 'There has been much business,' observed Truus, hurrying to catch her up. 'A fire and people injured.'

'Is that why he's up?' asked Christina.

'Naturally Dr ter Brandt is there when there is work,' said Truus a little coldly.

Christina ignored the coldness. 'Does he live here, then?'

'No, no. He lives at Scheveningen. There he has a practice in—how do you say?—rooms…'

'Consulting rooms,' supplied Christina.

'That is so. Also he has a house there.'

Even though she disliked him so much there was no reason why she shouldn't know something about him. There were several questions on the tip of her tongue, but they were already going through the door into the Accident Room, and it was, she saw at a glance, a hive of activity.

It was astonishing the number of people who damaged themselves on the way to work in the morning. Christina, examining the cut hand of a girl who had fallen over clutching a milk bottle, forgot all about Dr ter Brandt, forgot about being angry and just a little anxious in case Adam had forgotten her completely, forgot that she was twenty-seven, and on the best authority not a pretty girl; she became absorbed in her work and the busy day ahead of her.

She didn't know whether she was pleased or not when she saw the off duty book later that day. She had her day off and the day following it too. But it was impossible to tell whether it had been Zuster Bunsma's own idea or whether Dr ter Brandt had arranged it. In any case, she had heard nothing from Adam. She went to bed that night feeling despondent and looked the next morning at the post pigeonholed for the nursing staff. There was nothing for her.

She was kept too busy to brood over it during the day. She had found her feet by now and after three lessons was in possession of a handful of useful Dutch words. Besides, she had an ear for languages; unable to understand most of what was said around her, she could still guess the gist of it, and Truus or Zuster Bunsma were never far away. She was left quite often now to carry out the Casualty Officer's instructions and the patients, once they grasped the fact that she knew what she was doing, weren't unduly disturbed. She went off duty a good deal later than usual because there had been a sudden rush of patients in the late afternoon and she had offered to stay on. As she pointed out to Zuster Bunsma, she wasn't doing anything that evening and she was free to lie in bed in the morning if she wanted to.

So it was almost time for first supper as she left the Accident Room and began the walk through the hospital which would bring her to the lift taking her to the top floor and her room. As she went she wondered how she would spend her free time. Adam, she decided sadly, wasn't going to telephone or write; probably he had scores of interesting friends to visit. She would turn herself into a tourist—there was a tremendous amount to see; the Ridderzaal, the Mauritshuis, the Costume Museum and the Royal Library. They would do for a start, and as for a meal,

Truus had told her to go to de Bijenkorf, a big department store in the centre of den Haag, or if she was short of cash, there was a good snack bar in Hema, which as far as she could make out was a mixture of Woolworth's and British Home Stores.

She was almost at the lift when she paused. Perhaps there was a letter for her; it wouldn't take a minute to retrace her steps and look. She was half way there even while she was thinking it.

There was nothing. She stood looking at the empty compartment for a moment and then turned round. She had been silly to come, she told herself.

Adam was behind her; she almost fell against him and he flung his arms around her, laughing at her surprised face. And not just surprised, it glowed with sudden delight, her grey eyes sparkled and her mouth curved into a wide smile. 'Adam!' she cried in a small breathless voice. 'Adam!'

He kissed her lightly. 'Hullo, Chrissy. Are you glad to see me?' and then, 'Lord I'd forgotten what glorious eyes you have.'

'Oh, Adam, it's lovely to see you again!'

'So you did miss me.' He looked down at her with a smile to charm the heart out of her, which became a little mocking as he stared at her.

'You look very severe in that outfit, and years older than you are. For heaven's sake, why have you dragged your hair back like that, and your nose is shining...'

She was too happy to mind. 'I'm only just off duty and we've been busy.' She remembered where they were and looked round the entrance hall; there was no one there and she was conscious of relief. Dr ter Brandt, she felt sure, wouldn't approve of Adam's arm round her.

'Well, go and pretty yourself up, we're going out for a meal.' He put his other arm round her and bent to kiss her once more.

'Not here,' Dr ter Brandt's voice sounded weary, or bored or both. 'Adam, I must ask you to remember where you are.'

He had come in through the swing doors of the hospital and was standing looking at them with an expressionless face. After a moment he continued on his way with a polite, 'Good evening, Christina,' as he went.

She murmured, 'Good evening, sir,' her face red, but Adam didn't look in the least put out. His brother had barely disappeared when he said, half laughing, 'Good lord, darling, you don't call Duert sir, do you?'

'Yes, of course I do. I'm working for him and he's the director.' She raised troubled eyes to his. 'I wish he hadn't seen us, Adam.'

He shrugged his shoulders. 'Surely you don't mind? He's a good chap, but he's got out-of-date ideas. He's not above kissing a girl himself, but only in the right place, certainly not here.' He laughed. 'We must get him to change his views, mustn't we? Now do go and change, there's a dear girl—I'm famished.' And when she still hesitated: 'Don't let him worry you, for heaven's sake, Chrissy—he won't dismiss you; as long as you do your work well and we're discreet, he won't be in the least interested.'

She went then, her pleasure at going out with Adam tempered with a strong wish that Dr ter Brandt hadn't arrived just when he did. He must think her a cheap sort of young woman; he had wished her a very civil good evening, but his eyes had swept over her as though she hadn't been there.

She showered and changed into the green jersey dress and a velvet blazer and took care to do her hair in the new style she hadn't bothered with since she had come to Holland. It was disappointing to be greeted with Adam's: 'There you are. You've worn that dress before.' He saw the look on her face and added: 'Its pretty, that's why I remember it.'

His smile stilled the small stab of uncertainty. 'I'm glad you like it.' She kept her voice calm with an effort because just to be with him again was so wonderful.

He took her to the restaurant at the end of the pier at Scheveningen, driving his car with a reckless speed with rather took her breath, and parking it on the boulevard before walking her along the pier. The restaurant was attractive and the food good, although Christina hardly noticed what she was eating. Adam had set out to charm her and was succeeding; she had always been possessed of a sound common sense, now she had none. She listened to his outrageous flattery and believed it because she wanted to, and when he embarked on plans for their future amusement she agreed to them all. He was to work at the Theofilus, he told her, getting experience in both surgery and medicine, and when she asked him eagerly for how long he grinned disarmingly at her and told her for as long as she wanted him to. The evening flew by, and at the end of it she bade him goodnight rather primly, mindful of his brother's capacity for turning up unexpectedly. But the entrance hall was empty and quiet, only the faint murmur and quiet footsteps of the night staff and the squeaking of an occasional trolley emphasised the stillness. Christina went soft-footed to the lift, gained her room and went dreamily to bed. She woke in the night, blindingly aware that she was behaving like a schoolgirl in love for the first time. But what did that matter if Adam loved her too?

He was taking her out to lunch the next day. She got up late, dressed with care, with the resolve to get some new clothes with her first pay packet and went out of one of the side doors to where his car was parked. She had to wait a little while and when he came, ten minutes later, he was carelessly apologetic. 'Duert kept me,' he told her, 'wanted to talk about my future. I told him I was happy enough with the present.'

He opened the car door and she got in as he settled himself beside her.

'Are you free too?' she asked him.

'Good lord, no. I'm supposed to be going to do a round with Dr van Tripp at two o'clock.'

Christina searched her memory. 'The senior physician? So you like medicine?'

Adam belted along the road in the direction of Scheveningen. 'Can't stand it, but Duert says I must do six months with van Tripp. I don't intend to, of course.'

'What will you do then?'

He said airily: 'No idea—surgery, I suppose. I need a holiday—Duert seems to think I'm a man of iron as he is. Always got his nose to the grindstone, poor chap—a pity he didn't marry.'

'Well, there's nothing to stop him, is there?'

'Oh, yes there is—unrequited love, darling. He fell in love years ago with a girl—a beautiful dolly who threw him over for a millionaire. Duert's rich, but he's not that rich.'

She felt a pang of pity. 'Oh, the poor man! I'm sorry.'

Adam chuckled. 'Don't waste your pity on him, Chrissy, he's able to take care of himself.'

They were in Scheveningen now, going down the Badhuisweg. 'I thought we'd eat a *nasi goreng* at the Bali.' He glanced at his watch. 'No time to talk much, I'm afraid, but we can meet again later.'

They ate their meal a little hurriedly and Adam left her without ceremony at the end of it. 'You'll enjoy looking round the shops,' he told her airily, 'and there are trams to take you back when you feel like it. I'd drive you back, but I mustn't upset old Duert by being late for van Tripp's round.'

Christina was left standing outside the restaurant, feeling at a loss, but making excuses for Adam. It had been sweet of him to take her out to lunch when he had so short a time in which to do it, and he was quite right, she would enjoy looking at the shops. She ignored the small nagging thought at the back of her mind; that Adam held his brother in wholesome awe even though he derided him so wittily, and there had really been no reason why he shouldn't have driven her back with him.

She spent a pleasant enough afternoon, admiring the expensive clothes and trifles in the shop windows, deciding what she would buy when she had some money and having tea at an elegant little tearoom. The bill staggered her when she saw it; she would have done better to have gone back to den Haag and found Hema. She boarded a tram presently and went back into the city because the shops were shut now and she had nowhere else to go. Then she went back to the Theofilus and, much to her discomfiture, came face to face with Dr ter Brandt as she crossed the courtyard.

His 'Good evening, Christina,' was deliberately spoken, and just as deliberate was his pause as he reached her. Short of ducking round him she couldn't avoid him, so she said, 'Good evening, sir,' with something of a snap and a decidedly heightened colour.

He didn't seem to notice either. 'You have no need to call me sir when you are off duty,' he told her mildly. 'I hope you enjoyed your day with Adam?'

She frowned a little. 'Well, it wasn't a day, actually. He took me to lunch, but he had to get back to do a round with Dr van Tripp.'

Her companion's face didn't alter its placid expression, but his eyes beneath half-closed lids were suddenly alert. 'Ah, yes,' he said smoothly, 'I'd forgotten that, but there is still this evening.'

'You've forgotten that you recommended him to attend that lecture at the...' she frowned again, 'I've forgotten the name, but it's at Leiden.'

He said unsmilingly: 'I become increasingly forgetful. The place you mention is the University, close to the Hortus Botanicus gardens. Leiden is a charming place, you must visit it some time.'

He didn't seem to expect an answer and she couldn't think of one anyway. After a little pause she said awkwardly: 'Goodbye, Dr ter Brandt I expect you're on your way home.' For answer he caught her gently by the elbow, turned her round and walked her back the way she had come. 'No,' he said pleasantly, 'I have someone to see presently. I came out merely for a breath of air and a cup of coffee. Perhaps you will join me? I should like to hear what you think of den Haag and the hospital. First impressions are always interesting.' And when she didn't answer at once: 'Unless you have other plans?'

'No, I haven't,' said Christina baldly.

'Splendid. You don't mind if we walk?'

'No—no, of course not.'

They crossed the busy street and plunged into a succession of small streets and narrow lanes, coming out surprisingly quickly into Langue Voorhout where the doctor turned almost immediately into a small restaurant. Christina just had time to read the name—Le Bistroquet—as they went inside.

It was small and, she judged, expensive, and hardly the place in which to drink coffee. Even as she thought it Dr ter Brandt murmured, 'I missed lunch—would it be asking too much of you to join me in a meal?' And at her look of enquiry: 'Yes, I know I could eat at the Hospital, but as we are here...?' His raised brows asked her a question.

'Thank you,' she said composedly, 'I should like to.'

Which was true enough. Since she couldn't dine with Adam, anyone or anything would do to help her pass her solitary evening. Besides, she didn't particularly want to go to supper at the hospital.

The doctor appeared to be well known. She accepted a drink and studied the menu, secretly appalled at the prices. She searched for the cheaper dishes, reading the French carefully, unaware of her companion's eyes upon her face. When she said that she'd have an omelette fines herbes and nothing else, his firm mouth curved into a faint smile.

'Oh, you must have more than that,' he begged her. 'I'm famished, but I can't eat while you nibble at a snack. How about avocado vinaigrette, sole Véronique and one of their hot soufflés? I'm sure Adam gave you a splendid lunch, but you must have some sort of an appetite by now.'

His voice was casual, but his eyes were intent.

'Oh, yes—it was lovely.' She sounded forlorn without knowing it.

'The forerunner of many more, I daresay,' he observed easily. 'And now, tell me what you think of the Theofilus.'

Christina was surprised, thinking about it afterwards, to find that she had enjoyed her evening. Dr ter Brandt had been amusing, pleasant and a good host. She was quite sure she didn't like him, but that was largely because he had Adam under his thumb. Poor Adam, she thought as she brushed her hair and got ready for bed, having to spend his evening at some stuffy lecture.

She went to sleep almost at once, happily unaware that Dr ter Brandt, having returned to the hospital with her, was waiting patiently in his office for his brother. He had to wait quite a while and when at last Adam was ushered in he wasted no time.

'I should like to know why you missed the teaching round this afternoon, Adam, and why you saw fit to lie to Christina?' He sat back in his chair and studied his brother through half-shut lids. 'I seem to remember telling you that Christina wasn't quite the same as your usual girl-friends. I suggest that you leave her alone.'

Adam scowled. 'Look here, I took the girl out to lunch, that's all. I can't help it if she's got some silly ideas into her head, can I?' The scowl changed into an ingratiating smile. 'Look, Duert, I just want to give Christina a bit of fun. Once she's found her feet and made some friends, she'll forget all about me.' His eyes narrowed. 'Not keen on her yourself, are you?' and then at the cold stare he got, added hastily: 'All right, I was only joking!'

His brother remained silent and Adam rattled on: 'Tell you what—I'll take her to the Annual Ball and introduce her to as many people as I can. You surely won't object to that?'

'No, provided that Christina wishes to go. And now you're here, Adam, be good enough to take your job seriously, or there'll be trouble.'

Adam, with a lighthearted goodnight, strolled off, leaving Duert sitting behind his desk, staring at the writing pad on it with a thoughtful look.

Christina didn't get up until everyone along the corridor had gone on duty. There was no hurry, the day was before her and she had nothing to do. She bathed and dressed slowly, made herself coffee in the tiny kitchenette near her room, and prepared to go out. It was a pleasant enough morning, the pale, wide sky with small clouds scudding across it before the wind, hinted at rain later, but as she had the half-formed plan to spend most of her day in museums and the larger shops, that wouldn't matter. It was a pity that Truus was on duty all day, otherwise they might have spent the afternoon together. She was already on good terms with several of the Sisters, but most of them went home for their days off and those that didn't were on duty.

She gained the entrance hall, wished the porter in his little box good morning and made for the entrance, glancing at the post in its pigeonholes as she went.

There was quite a pile under F and the porter, seeing her stop, went to look through it. Two letters, one from George Henry, and the other unstamped, her name scrawled right across the envelope.

She put her brother's letter in her pocket; she could read that presently, over a cup of coffee. The second envelope she tore open eagerly; she felt sure it was from Adam, and she was right.

His writing was large and flourishing so that what was really only a brief note seemed like a long letter covering two pages. He was free that afternoon, he told her, and would take her out to tea. Would she be at the Pier Restaurant again at half past three? He was hers, Adam.

Of course she would be there. She didn't pause to wonder what would happen if she refused, nor did it enter her head that he was taking her very much for granted. She wandered out into the watery sunshine with a head full of dreams.

But half past three was a long way off. She found her way to the Mauritshuis and, once there, forgot all the other places she intended visiting. She left it two hours later, her head a happy jumble of Old Masters, and had her coffee at a snack bar while she read George Henry's letter. He was happy and relieved that she had settled in so well. The wedding was to be the following week and Hilary sent her love. Christina made a mental note that she must get a card to send, and then, because it was already noon, had another cup of coffee and a *kaas broodje* with it.

Refreshed, she set out for the shops, lingering from one window to the next. It was a pity that a sudden downpour left her bedraggled and damp, but by then there was no time to do more than smooth her skirt and run a comb through her hair. If she was to reach Scheveningen by half past three, she would have to hurry.

Adam was waiting for her and her glow of delight at seeing him was a little chilled by his sudden frown. 'Didn't you have an umbrella?' he asked after a perfunctory greeting.

'It was dry when I came out this morning,' she reminded him. 'Do I look awful?'

There wasn't much make-up left on her face and her hair was less than perfect, but her grey eyes were lovely. 'You look gorgeous, darling—you always do.'

Adam uttered the compliment with the smoothness of much practice, caught her arm and hurried her into the restaurant. Sitting at a table overlooking the sea, her make-up repaired and her hair re-done, she smiled at him happily. 'Have you a half day?' she asked.

'Not quite—that would be too generous of Duert. I'm on duty again at six o'clock, but I wanted to see you. Has anybody told you about the Annual Ball?' he added. 'Well, you've hardly been here long enough, I suppose. It's held at the Theofilus in two weeks' time. Will you come with me? It's great fun. Of course, you'll have to do something about your hair and you'll need a decent dress. I know several girls who'll love to take you round the shops.' He put out a hand and covered hers with it. 'Say you'll come, otherwise I won't go.'

Common sense told her to ignore that; of course he'd go whether she was there or not, but it was nice to hear him say it. 'I'd like to come with you,' she told him, careful not to sound too excited. 'I'd rather buy my own dress, though, if you don't mind, and I'll find a good hairdresser.'

'Splendid!' Adam took the tea she had poured out and began an amusing account of his morning's work. He didn't take his work very seriously, but she had no doubt that he was clever at it. He was already a junior partner with his brother, although there were two other doctors who shared the practice as well. Christina would have liked to have known where his home was, although he had to live in at the hospital. Somewhere close by, presumably, since Dr ter Brandt spent a good deal of his day at the Theofilus, but she couldn't quite bring herself to ask Adam. It was a funny thing, but although she was so hopelessly infatuated with him she wasn't quite sure of him as a friend. She thought with surprise that she had told Dr ter Brandt a whole lot of things she would never tell Adam—he would have been bored. She wondered what miracle had caused him to single her out from all the much prettier girls he must know. One day she would ask him.

They walked along the boulevard when they had had their tea. The rain had stopped, but grey clouds were piling up over the cold looking sea. Christina found it exhilarating and urged Adam to take her to the far end where the fishing harbours were. But when she would have stayed to look at the moored fishing boats and all the paraphernalia that went with them, he showed signs of impatience. It didn't matter, she told herself, she could come again on her own or with one of the Sisters, and next time she would walk along the promenade or even along the firm sand at the water's edge.

Now she was content to remain almost silent while Adam talked—he was an amusing talker and she listened with pleasure to his racy comments about people he knew, but it was over too soon. Presently he drove her back to the hospital and this time there was no Dr ter Brandt to invite her to drink coffee with him. Not that she minded; she didn't give it a thought, she was glad to find the Sisters' sitting room empty, so that she could mull over her afternoon and everything Adam had said, and dwell happily on the prospect of going to the dance with him. She was so deeply engrossed in thinking up a suitable outfit for this event that she almost missed her supper.

CHAPTER FIVE

CHRISTINA HEARD all about the dance at breakfast the next morning. Someone mentioned it and at once there was a burst of talk, laboriously translated for her benefit. Everyone was going, as far as she could make out, and when one of the girls at the table suggested kindly that a partner must be found for her, and she told them briefly that she had been invited to go by Adam ter Brandt, there was a sudden silence, instantly covered up by an outburst of talk. The talk was so animated that she fancied that she must have imagined the tiny pause, and she quickly forgot it in the ensuing discussion about clothes. One dressed, it seemed, in one's very best. The *burgermeester*, a sprinkling of foreign consuls and all the upper crust of den Haag society would be there. 'Beautiful dresses, jewels,' declared Leenie dramatically. 'We do not, how do you say? compete, but we look nice.' She beamed at Christina. 'You have a dress?'

'No,' said Christina, 'I haven't—I thought I'd get something…'

'Blue,' observed Truus, and was instantly contradicted by half a dozen voices. All the colours of the rainbow were suggested, but Christina laughed and shook her head. 'It'll be a secret,' she told them.

And there the matter rested. The Accident Room was as usual bursting with patients all the morning, and in the afternoon, when there was a lull, she had her lesson. She rather enjoyed it because she persuaded her sober teacher to instruct her on how to buy clothes.

She was on the point of going off duty when she heard the ambulances clamour. She had turned back to join Zuster Bunsma before it had stopped at the wide doors, and was surprised when that lady said abruptly: 'You are off duty, Zuster Forbes.'

'Yes, I know,' said Christina, 'but Zuster Felman has just gone to X-Ray for you and Zuster Keizer's busy with that fractured clavicle.'

Zuster Bunsma shot her a look and then nodded. 'I shall be glad of help.'

She had never spoken a truer word. The first ambulance, containing two young men who had been hit about the head with a blunt instrument, was followed by a second and a third. The policeman who roared up on a motorbike had a short discussion with one of the Casualty Officers, who told Zuster Bunsma, who in turn found time to tell Christina.

'A gang fight,' she said in her fluent, accented English, 'wild boys who will perhaps make difficulties here. You do not feel frightened?'

'No—at least, I haven't so far.'

'I have asked for male nurses—Zuster Keizer and Zuster Felman are young and pretty, so they can go to one of the wards.'

Zuster Bunsma sailed away to cope with a belligerent youth with a cut head, leaving Christina to wonder if she really was as plain and elderly as that lady had implied.

Most of the patients were quiet enough, anyway. They must have had frightful headaches, judging from the cuts and bruises, but a handful of them were proving difficult to manage. Christina, doing her best to make a gangling youth sit down while she cleaned up a nasty knife wound on his check, was taken off guard when he put up a hand and caught her wrist, twisting it painfully. He laughed when she said, 'Let go,' not understanding her, and she struggled to think of a suitable phrase from one of her lessons which might suit the occasion. There wasn't any; she had been taught to ask for the salt, enquire the time, ask if there was pain, was there a headache and a dozen other useful sentences, but none of them met her requirements. She gave her wrist a sharp tug and winced with the pain. Her other hand still held a swab firmly to his cheek, she would have to drop it and slap his face or would that be assault? She said calmly: 'You really are a silly twit,' then dropped the swab as a large hand grasped her shoulder.

'Trouble, Christina?' enquired Dr ter Brandt in a mild voice. The mildness was only for her, though. She had no idea what he said to her patient, in a cold abrupt voice which caused him to drop her wrist as though it were a hot coal, but it was instantly effective. The boy remained silent and unmoving while she cleaned the wound and then held his head steady while the doctor stitched the cut under a local anaesthetic, and when he had been handed over to one of the waiting policemen, Christina began clearing the trolley. There was another ambulance coming and everyone else had their hands full at the moment. She wondered what it would be this time and was startled when the doctor lifted her hand from the couch she was changing and examined her wrist.

'You'll have a bruise, I'm afraid. I'll take a look at it later. We'll have whatever this is in here, please.'

So Christina went to meet the ambulance men with the stretcher with: '*Hier, alstublieft*,' and watched while they deposited their burden on her newly cleaned couch.

Quite a different kettle of fish; a not so young woman, poorly dressed and grubby. Christina had taken a quick look at her and said urgently: 'Shall we get her to Maternity at once, sir?'

'No, I don't think there's time. Get some clothes off her and I'll scrub.' He said something to one of the ambulance men and went across to one of the telephones. 'I've asked Maternity to send down a couple of nurses and a stretcher.'

The woman opened her eyes for a moment. 'You're English!' Two tears trickled down her cheeks. 'It's like a miracle!'

Christina was peeling off clothes and arranging blankets. 'Yes, dear—they do happen. Could you tell us your name—and should we tell anyone? Your husband?' She glanced at the wedding ring on the woman's finger.

The woman sounded hopeless. 'He's gone. He worked here and when he sent for me I came to Holland, but they told me that he'd gone to somewhere or other—the Middle East—he works on those oil rigs.'

'No one else?' enquired Christina softly.

'No,' she sighed. 'The name's Brown, Liz Brown.'

Christina stood aside as Dr ter Brandt bent over his patient. 'This isn't your first?'

Mrs Brown had shut her eyes again. 'No, doctor—I've two more. They're with my sister in Nottingham.'

'You hadn't the money to get home?' It was more a statement than a question.

'That's right.' Her voice came out on a sigh. 'Can't believe my luck coming here.'

Dr ter Brandt glanced across at Christina. 'Got the blanket ready?' he wanted to know, and then to his patient, 'Everything will be all right now, Mrs Brown, you and the baby will be in bed in no time at all.'

Which was quite true. Ten minutes later Mrs Brown was studying the small bundle in her arms. 'I always wanted a daughter,' she said, and fell instantly asleep.

Dr ter Brandt was giving instructions to the nurse who had come down from Maternity, and presently Mrs Brown and the baby were whisked away. Christina, clearing up yet again, asked in a troubled voice: 'What will happen to her? The poor soul!'

'We'll keep her in for a couple of weeks, get her on her feet again and in the meantime I'll see what I can do to get her back home. We might even trace her husband.'

'The villain!' said Christina with feeling, and then: 'Do you always come down to the Accident Room when there's a rush on, sir?'

'If I'm free. Are you disappointed to find that I don't spend the day behind my desk?'

'No—oh, no.' She spoke too quickly because somehow Adam had given the impression that was just what his elder brother did do. She added: 'You can't have much time at home.'

He didn't answer and she went pink; he had every right to snub, of course, she had been too inquisitive. It was a relief when there was a sudden influx of patients and Zuster Bunsma called her to take over a small snivelling girl who had been bitten by a dog. By the time the small creature had been dealt with, there was no sign of the doctor. Back in his office, presumably. Christina cleared up and longed for her supper. Probably she wouldn't get any, it was long past the time for that meal, the night staff already on duty. She supposed she would have to go out to one of the snack bars close to the hospital and get coffee and something to eat. Perhaps one of the other girls would go with her. Adam was away, so there was no hope of seeing him. Christina said goodnight to Zuster Bunsma and started off in the direction of the canteen; there was a chance that it might still be open. It wasn't, and she was retracing her footsteps when she met Zuster Bunsma again.

'I am looking for you, Zuster Forbes,' said that lady at once. 'Dr ter Brandt wishes to see your wrist—it was injured this evening, is it not so? Kindly to come with me.'

Christina thinking longingly of food, went meekly enough. Zuster Bunsma wasn't the kind of person one argued with.

She was led to Women's Surgical, where she found Leenie, still on duty and talking to Dr ter Brandt in her little office. Christina, feeling rather a fool, paused in the doorway and he looked up to say: 'Ah, yes, I think I should take a look at your wrist, Zuster Forbes—hospital rules, you know. You have had your supper?'

She felt like telling him that since he seemed to have a finger in everyone's pie, why Women's Surgical at nine o'clock in the evening? Surely there were surgical housemen on duty? he must know she had missed that meal. She said stonily: 'The canteen is closed, but I intended going out for a meal, thank you, sir. I was on my way…'

His blue eyes held hers for a brief moment. He said something to Leenie and then came over to Christina, picked up her hand and examined her wrist. There was an ugly bruise already and it was painful, but that was all; she said so in a matter-of-fact voice and he agreed with her coolly enough, adding: 'If you will go with Zuster Bunsma, she will see that you have your supper.'

It was on the tip of her tongue to refuse, but something in his face stopped her. She said. 'Very well, sir,' and added a quiet goodnight as she followed the older woman out of the office.

The canteen door, which had been shut, was now open. Zuster Bunsma sailed through it and sat down at one of the smaller tables, waving to Christina to sit down too. The supper they were served was excellent and her companion, unbending now that she was off duty, proved to be entertaining and informative, only she wasn't informative about Dr ter Brandt. The discreet questions Christina put about him were ignored. Of course, she told herself, getting ready for bed later, Adam had told her a good deal about his brother, but always jokingly—that tale about unrequited love, for instance. She got into bed and lay wondering about that. Somehow the doctor didn't give the impression of being a man with a broken heart; on the other hand, his manner gave nothing away—that annoying placid expression... She went to sleep.

She sensed a subtle difference in Zuster Bunsma's manner towards her after that particular evening. She was left to get on with it now, floundering about in her sparse Dutch but on the whole coping very well. Injuries were the same all over the world, a broken leg was a broken leg whatever it was called, during the next few days she increased her vocabulary, not bothering with long sentences; learning essential words as fast as she could, greatly encouraged by her teacher who had the sense not to bother her with too much grammar.

She was beginning to enjoy her job and she would have been quite happy if she could have seen more of Adam. But he, his days filled with work on the wards, had no time to do more than send her scribbled notes. They all began 'Darling' and ended 'your Adam', and Christina cherished them, reading them over and over again, and although she was much too busy to think about him during her busy days, she allowed her sensible head to be filled by daydreams during her leisure. Not that she had much of that; she had made friends quickly enough, and if it wasn't Leenie or Truus taking her on a tour of den Haag, one of the other Sisters would take their place. Christina learnt a great deal about the city during the ensuing days, but when one morning she met Adam in the hospital and he told her that they would be going to the ball in a week's time, she cried off accompanying anyone for a day or two, explaining that she wanted to buy a dress, promising that if she got into difficulties she would ask for their help.

So, armed with her dictionary and a great deal of good-natured advice from her friends, Christina made her way to the shopping centre.

She hadn't a great deal of money, but what she had she was well prepared to spend. It didn't take her long to discover that the big stores were beyond her purse, and the cheaper, popular shops had nothing quite right for the occasion. She took to the arcades and small side streets, and in one of the boutiques found what she sought. It was a simple dress, well made and a perfect fit, its grey chiffon cleverly cut to fall in folds over a silk slip. She bought it, although it left her purse almost empty, but she was quite reckless by now. Pay day wasn't far off and she need spend no more money until then; there was just enough for a pair of evening shoes if she could find them. It seemed a hopeless task. There were gold and silver sandals in abundance but none in pale grey satin. By a stroke of luck, just as she was about to give up the search, she found a pair of white satin sandals, shop-soiled and therefore cheap. She bought them and, after some difficulty with the language, bought a pale grey dye.

It was on her way back that she realised that she hadn't enough money to go to a hairdresser. She would have to do the best she could with Truus's electric rollers…

The dying was fairly successful. Christina eyed the faint streaks with some misgivings and made a mental note not to let her feet be seen more than was absolutely necessary. She tried the dress on that evening before an admiring audience, who agreed that it was just right. 'Although jewels would be nice,' observed Leenie, 'pearls or gold chains…'

'Silver!' exclaimed Christina. 'I've got two.' They were produced and put on and declared to be perfect.

'And now your hair,' said Truus. 'We will have a *repetitie*.'

'A what?' Christina thumbed through her dictionary. 'Oh, a rehearsal.'

She sat patiently while several pairs of hands wound her hair round the rollers and presently unwound it. It was Truus who brushed it out, letting it hang almost to her shoulders and then brushing the ends up into a thick bouncy roll. Christina, studying the result, was taken aback. She looked younger and less ordinary; all the same it didn't seem quite her. But it was a change. She turned to Truus to thank her, but that young lady already had the brush in her hand once more. 'I am wrong,' she cried, 'it must be others…' She went to a drawer and rummaged around and came back with a narrow velvet ribbon. 'This,' she said. 'You will sit still, Christina.'

She tied the ribbon round Christina's head and then rolled her hair round it, brushing the front high and letting it wave softly round her face. The result was entirely satisfactory. It might lack the sophisticated elegance of a hairdresser, but it suited her. Highly delighted with themselves, her friends took themselves off to their respective rooms and Christina hung her finery away and brushed out her hair. She hoped with all her heart that Adam would find her appearance even half as nice as her friends had done.

She had brief glimpses of him during the next few days and on one evening he took her to Scheveningen for a drink after they had come off duty, declaring that he had missed her beyond anything and that Duert was working him far too hard. 'It's all very well for him, sitting behind a desk all day', he declared. 'He's forgotten what it's like to be young.'

Christina made the mistake of disagreeing with him. 'Well, he doesn't sit behind a desk all day,' she pointed out reasonably. 'He came down to the Accident Room last week and worked as hard as the rest of us. I don't know how he manages a practice as well as the hospital.'

'Oh, he lives for his work,' said Adam sulkily. 'I told you he hasn't any use for women; he's not the marrying kind. I daresay it would have been all right with that first girl.'

Christina hoped that he would go on, but disappointingly, he didn't.

She saw very little of Duert ter Brandt and only once to speak to. He was standing outside the Surgical Ward entrance as she was passing, talking to two housemen, but he paused when he saw her, and with a word to them deliberately stopped her.

'Good morning, Christina,' his voice was as placid as his face. 'Are you going to the Ball with Adam?'

She forgot to say good morning. 'Yes, yes, I am.'

He stood towering over her, staring down at her. His, 'Good, good,' was casual and after a moment, a little bewildered, she inched away. 'Don't let me keep you,' he begged her, leaving her to wonder why he had stopped her in the first place. She was left with the feeling that she had been dismissed from his mind absolutely, but there was so much more to think about that she thought no more about it.

She was working hard at her lessons now and making progress, and she was enjoying her work too. Answering Hilary's rather acid letters, she was able to say with perfect truth that she had never been so contented with her lot. And there were the preparations for the ball to fill her spare time. She had practised her new hair-style under Truus's friendly eye and there was a constant coming and going between rooms to admire dresses and borrow things.

The ball was to be held in the lecture hall at the back of the hospital and Christina was to meet Adam in the foyer there. She dressed slowly, made up her face with anxious care and started on her hair. It went up like a dream. Truus, coming to make sure that she had got it right, was delighted.

'And the dress is pretty,' she declared. 'You look nice.'

'And so do you,' said Christina. 'But you're so pale, Truus. Don't you feel well?'

Truus made a face. 'I have eaten something that is not good, I think. It will pass.'

Several Sisters went through the hospital together and Christina with them. She looked calm and serene, but her insides were in a terrible turmoil. Suppose Adam wasn't there?

But he was, looking rather impatient, but perhaps that was a good sign. She chose to think so, and then felt suddenly apprehensive because the dresses around her were so lovely, making the grey chiffon which had looked so right and elegant in the boutique quite insignificant. Adam's 'There you are, you look like a mouse,' didn't do much to raise her self-confidence either, but he smiled at her with such charm that she decided that he had meant it as a compliment and beamed at him with delight.

'Isn't it super?' she demanded of him. 'And everyone looks so marvellous.'

He laughed and squeezed her hand. 'What a kid you are! I think it's all a bit of a bore, but it's been done for years and Duert is the last one to go against tradition.'

'Does he think it's a bore too?'

He shrugged. 'I haven't any idea, but even if he did, he would never allow anyone to know. Let's go in.'

The lecture hall had been lavishly decorated with flowers and blazed with lights and up at the other end a band was playing to a floor already nicely full. There was a group of people standing just inside the big double doors—the Directrice, almost unrecognisable in plum velvet, a rather stout lady in mauve brocade, a distinguished-looking elderly man wearing a heavy gold chain over his evening dress, and Duert ter Brandt. Christina thought he looked magnificent in his white tie and tails, completely at ease, bending a little to listen to something the Directrice was saying.

'This is all a bit silly,' muttered Adam as they paused to shake hands, first with Duert and the Directrice and then with the Burgermeester and his lady, but Christina found it rather nice to be treated as a guest and greeted as such. She smiled rather shyly at the Directrice, and was passed to the doctor and was disappointed to be given a pleasant and quite impersonal greeting, for all the world as if he wanted to get it over with as quickly as possible. She flushed a little as he introduced her to the Burgermeester and his wife. Perhaps he hadn't approved of her going with Adam. But when he had asked her whether she was going to be at the Ball with Adam and she had said yes, he had said, 'Good, good,' in rather a strange way. She pulled her wandering wits together and replied to the Burgermeester's carefully spoken Dutch with her painstakingly learned conventional sentences, appreciating the compliment he was paying her. He could just as easily have addressed her in English, she was sure of that.

The band was playing a conventional foxtrot and she and Adam took to the floor at once. 'It's a bit staid to start with,' he told her. 'When the Burgermeester goes, we let go a bit.' He added with surprise, 'I say, you dance well.'

Christina glowed at his praise. She wasn't all that good, actually, but she was light on her feet and quick to respond. They circled the hall, while Adam greeted his friends, pausing every now and then to speak to one or other of them. Some of the girls were lovely and he appeared to be on excellent terms with them. 'I shall have to dance with one or two girls presently,' he told her, and made a funny face at her. 'Distant cousins and daughters of members of the Hospital Board.' He sounded as though he disliked the idea. 'I'll introduce you to a couple of chaps—they'll look after you until I get back.'

Of course he had to circulate, she told herself sensibly. He must know almost everyone who was there, and there weren't only hospital staff, there were dignitaries from den Haag, a sprinkling of officials from the Consulates and all the local doctors and their wives, so she agreed cheerfully enough, and presently when there was a pause in the dancing she was introduced to a group of girls and young men. The group changed every few minutes as couples left it to dance or joined it, and presently one of the men, a houseman on the medical side, asked her to dance. When they rejoined his friends there was no sign of Adam. The second man Adam had introduced her to swung her on to the floor before she had time to look around her. He wasn't dancing as far as she could see, but his brother was, with an exquisitely turned out young woman who was laughing a lot as he talked. Christina wondered if anything ever shook that placid look from his face. It was impossible to read his real thoughts, but he must be enjoying himself, for his partner positively sparkled.

Her musing was brought to a stop by her companion's rather stilted English. 'I leave you here,' he said formally. 'Adam returns soon, I think. I have to dance with others.' He waved an expressive hand, taking in half the hall. 'You will sit here, please.'

Perhaps Adam had arranged for her to be parked in the alcove half hidden behind a great bank of flowers and ferns. Christina said goodbye to her partner, quite glad to see him go, for he danced badly, and settled down to wait. There was still no sign of Adam, but it would be easy to miss him on the crowded floor. Several of the Ward Sisters she knew danced past and waved, and she waved back, and presently Duert came into view, this time with a tall blonde girl. She didn't think he had seen her, and hoped he hadn't, although she was not sure why.

She sat through that dance and the next. Probably if she had gone on to the dance floor she would have found herself a partner, but she was shy of doing this—besides, Adam might come to look for her. She had a splendid view of the dancers although she wasn't easily seen herself, only by Duert ter Brandt who kept her under his eye without appearing to do so.

Christina was getting a little impatient and was on the point of making up her mind to leave her alcove when she was surprised to see Truus creeping along the wall towards her. She got up and went to meet her, putting an arm round her and sitting her down in the chair she had just left. 'Truus, you're ill,' she said urgently. 'What is it?'

'A pain—here.' Truus put a cautious hand on her stomach. 'And I feel so strange—I think I want to be sick.'

Christina looked round her. The dance floor was packed and no one was looking in their direction, nor was there anyone she knew in sight. There was a door behind her, if she could get Truus through it and back into the hospital itself… She turned back to her friend and was alarmed to see that her white face had taken a greenish tinge. 'Truus—' she began, and was gently interrupted by the doctor's deep voice.

'Something's wrong?' He bent over Truus for a moment. 'If you will open the door, Christina, I'll carry her back to the surgical floor.' He added as an afterthought, 'You might come with us.'

She hurried ahead, opening and shutting doors and then waiting at the open lift door. Truus was moaning softly and the doctor spoke to her in a comforting murmur. As the lift stopped he said: 'Straight into the side ward on the left, Chrissy—get the bed turned down and then fetch the nurse on duty.'

She was turning to obey him when Truus put out an urgent hand. 'Don't go,' she whispered, and caught Christina's dress in an urgent hand. The gathers were ripped, but Christina didn't notice, and when she did she tucked the torn flounces into her waistband and forgot about it.

'Now telephone Night Sister, my Registrar and the Directrice, in that order,' Dr ter Brandt ordered in his calm voice.

She did that too and went back to find that Truus was lying on the bed being examined. Presently the doctor straightened up. 'Appendix,' he said to no one in particular. 'I want her up in theatre in ten minutes.'

His eye fell upon Christina hovering at the open door. 'You had better stay with her until she's anaesthetised,' he suggested, and turned away to speak to the Directrice, who, despite the plum velvet, was already in command of the situation. Someone brought a gown for Christina and she bundled into it, and as soon as Truus was ready, went with the trolley on the brief journey to the theatre block. Night Theatre Sister was already there, so was her nurse. Christina could see them through the glass porthole in the anaesthetic room, laying up a trolley. She smiled down at Truus, now dozing under the influence of the drug the doctor had given her, and when she opened a hazy eye, squeezed her hand.

They took her away presently and Christina started to take off her gown. She didn't feel like going back to the dance, but she would have to in case Adam was looking for her. She was half-way to the door when one of the nurses came out with a message from Dr ter Brandt. Would she be good enough to wait in Sister's Office until he was ready—about twenty minutes.

She sat quietly in the little room thinking of nothing, feeling tired now. She looked up in surprise when Duert came in; the twenty minutes had gone very quickly. He was still wearing his green theatre gear and she realised with surprise that he must have been operating.

'Is Truus OK?' she asked.

'Yes—I'll be ten minutes,' he told her, and opened the door wider to allow the Directrice to enter. Christina stood up, but was waved back into her chair, while her companion, once more in the plum velvet, went to the small mirror and examined her hair and face.

'You will say nothing, if you please, Zuster Forbes,' she remarked. 'It is not likely that we have been missed and Dr ter Brandt does not want the evening spoilt for his guests. No one saw you?'

'Only the doctor—everyone was dancing and Truus was against the wall and I was half hidden by some flowers.'

The Directrice nodded, satisfied. 'That is good. As soon as Truus is conscious we will return to the dancing.'

'Poor Truus,' said Christina, 'I hope she gets well quickly.'

The Directrice went away then and Christina sat on, not thinking about anything much. After ten minutes both the Doctor and the Directrice came back together. 'She's conscious—just,' said Dr ter Brandt. 'Will you take a look, I daresay she will want to see you.'

Christina went back to the side ward. Truus was nicely round and on the point of dropping off to sleep. She smiled a little at Christina and muttered: 'Thank you,' before she closed her eyes, and after a minute or two Christina said goodbye to the night nurse looking after her and went back into the corridor. There seemed little point in going back to the theatre block, and no one had suggested that she should. She began to walk slowly towards the swing doors which would lead her to the stairs and dance hall.

She hadn't reached the doors when Duert came through them. He looked so cool and elegant that she was hard put to it to remember that ten minutes earlier he had been wearing a green theatre shirt and trousers and wellington boots. He said at once in a brisk no-nonsense voice: 'I've asked the Directrice to go on ahead. We'll go in a few minutes, my Registrar will stay for a while to make sure Truus is all right.' His eyes surveyed her. 'You're a bit untidy, and your dress is torn.'

Christina was suddenly angry. 'Well, what do you expect?' she snapped. 'There wasn't much time to mend my dress or do my hair, was there?'

He put out a hand as she made to pass him, holding her with an arm round her shoulders. 'My poor girl—what a thoughtless fool I am! You shall have time to stitch your gown and do whatever you need to your hair—what is more, we will have coffee before we return.'

He swept her through the door, still with an arm round her, took a lift to the ground floor where he guided her through several narrow passages and opened a door into a large apartment, used apparently as a board meeting room. 'Sit down,' he invited her kindly, and pressed a bell, and when a porter came, ordered coffee and a work basket, and when the astonished man had gone, told her to go through the door at the other end of the room. 'There's a cloakroom there with a mirror and so on,' he said. 'Do you need a comb?'

Christina said no, thank you in a surprised voice and did as she was bid. The cloakroom was well lighted and it had a good mirror. She did her face, and because her hair was in danger of falling down, unpinned it and swept it into a knot low on her neck and went back to the doctor.

The coffee had arrived and smelled delicious. Her nose twitched with pleasure and Duert, looking at her from half closed lids, smiled faintly.

'You be mother,' he invited. 'They've brought sandwiches too, thank God; I'm famished.'

And so, thought Christina, am I. She drank her coffee and ate her share, then almost choked when he remarked casually: 'Your hair looks much nicer like that—you didn't look like you with all those loops and things.'

She gazed at him in astonishment. 'Like this?' she repeated. 'But I do it like this every day.' She went on: 'Adam says...' and then went pink.

'Ah, yes, of course. Well, don't let an out-of-date old fogey like me influence you.' He sounded serious, but she thought that he was secretly amused.

'I don't intend to, Dr ter Brandt.' She had pulled the sewing basket to her and was searching for a needle and thread. There was only one needle, a thick thing which would mark the delicate fabric of her dress. She sighed a little thinking of all the money she had spent and now it wouldn't be fit to be worn again. There was black cotton and white and nothing else; she chose the black and mended the gathers as best she could. It looked a botched-up job when she had done, but the doctor assured her that no one would notice, and she took comfort from his words. He got up to go when she had replaced her sewing things and she was conscious of regret. They had hardly spoken to each other, but she had found his company restful.

They slipped back into the hall through a small side door and Duert at once gathered her into his arms and danced her off into the centre of the floor, and since he was greeted by a number of people in a perfectly normal fashion it seemed likely that no one had missed him. They wouldn't have missed Christina; she didn't know many of the people there and she was hardly a conspicuous figure in the grey dress.

The dance went on for quite a long time and she began to enjoy herself. Duert danced very well, nothing startling, but he was nicely up-to-date with the newest steps. When the band stopped playing her took her arm. 'There's Adam,' he pointed out. 'I'm sure you must be anxious to get back to him.'

Adam was angry, she saw that at once, and she would have liked Duert to stay talking for a few minutes, but he merely thanked her politely for the dance and disappeared into the crowd of dancers.

'And where have you been?' asked Adam. There was a nasty edge to his voice.

'Oh, dancing,' she said quite truthfully, 'and I sat over there in that alcove for a bit. One of your friends told me to until you came back. Only you didn't.'

He frowned. 'Well, I got held up. And what have you done to your hair?' His eye fell on the mended dress. 'And your dress...you're not fit to be seen!'

It was a pity she had been told to say nothing about Truus, but even so Adam didn't need to be so bad-tempered. She said coolly: 'You mean to be seen with you, don't you, Adam?'

She turned on her heel and slipped through the dancing couples. Safely on the other side of the hall, she whisked through a door and started along the passage, intent on getting away. Her room, she fought fiercely, a pot of tea and her bed...

'And where are you off to?' asked Duert ter Brandt. He had come out of another door further along the passage and was waiting for her.

She stopped in front of him. 'My bed,' she told him in a quiet little voice.

'You're leaving Adam? It's barely midnight—we dance until the early hours, you know.'

She couldn't think of anything to say; just lately, she thought wearily, she had lost her cool composure completely. Not so long ago she would have dealt with such a situation with calm and dignity, but then until she had met Adam, she hadn't been in situations such as this one.

'He upset you?' The question was quietly put and she had nodded without thinking. 'Shall we go back and put it right?'

'No—no, thank you. You're very kind. It's all so silly...'

He smiled. 'Tomorrow you will see each other and laugh together about it.'

'Yes—you don't mind if I go to bed? I've enjoyed my evening...'

His eyebrows rose. 'Now that is a fib, Chrissy. Never mind, we must make it up to you one day. I'm very grateful for your help with Truus—you're a sensible girl too.'

It would have been so nice if he could have said beautiful instead of sensible. She smiled politely and wished him goodnight and went on her way. The stitches in her dress had given way again, and the torn flounce trailed forlornly behind her as she went.

CHAPTER SIX

CHRISTINA HAD TOLD Duert ter Brandt that she was tired, but in actual fact, once she was in bed she had never felt so wide awake. Perhaps, she thought uneasily, she shouldn't have left Adam like that; he had invited her to the ball in the first place and probably he had been delayed. Tomorrow she would beg his pardon and everything would be right again. And then there was her dress; she would have to get some matching thread and mend the tear properly. She wasn't very likely to go out again, but just supposing she did, she had no chance of buying a new one. She closed her eyes; tomorrow was a day like any other and she would need her sleep. She must remember to get flowers or something similar for Truus. She might go and see her before she went on duty in the morning—she could eat her breakfast quickly…

That meal was taken up almost entirely by excited talk about the ball and poor Truus. The news had already spread around the hospital, and Christina found herself the centre of interest and a good deal of sympathy.

'Such a splendid ball,' declared one of the Sisters, 'and you had so distinguished a partner.' There was a little silence and Leenie said quickly, 'I saw you dance with Dr ter Brandt—is he not splendid?'

'Oh, yes,' said Christina composedly. 'He looked very handsome. The dresses were beautiful—there was a white dress with sequins…'

The conversation took a lighter tone and lasted until she rose from the table. 'To see Truus before I go on duty,' she explained.

Truus was awake; she looked pale and tired but declared that she felt fine. 'You were kind,' she said gratefully. 'I think I would have fainted if you had not seen me. Why were you not dancing?'

'Adam had to dance with some people he knew.'

Truus looked as if she was going to say something and then thought better of it. 'The work in the Accident Room, who is to do it?' she wanted to know.

'Someone called Nanda Staal.'

Truss sniffed. 'Her—she is *trots* and will not work.'

'What's *trots*?' queried Christina.

'Proud—she does not like to make her hands dirty or spoil her nails. She has many boy-friends.'

'Then you must come back as soon as you can,' said Christina. 'Now, I must go or I'll be late and Zuster Bunsma will be cross.'

'Oh, no, she will not—I heard her tell Dr ter Brandt that you were a good nurse.'

Christina had the urge to ask if the doctor had had anything to say to that, but instead she said cheerfully: 'How kind of her. I'll come and see you when I'm off duty—everyone's coming when they've got a minute.'

If she didn't hurry she was going to be late. She nipped along to the lifts; all three were miles away on other floors, and it would be quicker to take to the stairs. She was tearing down the first flight when she found herself stopped by Duert ter Brandt, very correctly dressed in sober grey, mounting the stairs in a leisurely fashion.

'Fire or haemorrhage, Sister?' he asked evenly.

She had stopped dead in her tracks for the simple reason that there was far too much of him to pass. She said breathlessly. 'I'm late, sir,' and since he was looking at her gravely with no sign of a smile: 'The lifts were engaged, I thought it would be quicker if I used the stairs. I'm sorry I was running.' She stopped, much struck by a thought. 'Aren't nurses allowed to run in Holland either?'

'I imagine nurses are not allowed to run in any hospital. You didn't sleep.' It wasn't a question, and she flushed.

'I expect I was over-excited.' It sounded a tame excuse and Duert looked down his handsome nose at her. 'After your hilarious evening? Two dances with my brother, a couple more with junior doctors and then hidden away behind the flowers...'

Her grey eyes flashed. She said icily: 'You forget, I danced with you—enough to turn any girl's head.' She added for good measure: 'I hate you!'

He stood aside and she rushed past him, going at a great rate, running at top speed, expecting to hear his voice reprimanding her. Instead she heard him laugh. She was almost at the Accident Room door when she paused, bewildered. She had behaved like a stupid idiot at utter variance to her usual calm. Dr ter Brandt had spoken the truth, but there had been neither mockery nor scorn in his voice; he had simply stated a fact in that calm voice of his—and she had been abominably rude. Her cheeks flamed remembering her schoolgirlish outburst. Of course she didn't hate him. She opened the door and went in, wondering if he would tell her that she wasn't suitable after all, and suggest in that pleasant voice which betrayed nothing that she should return to England.

She had to stop thinking about it then, because the Accident Room was teeming...old ladies who had fallen down and fractured a femur, small children with cut heads, bigger children who had fallen into one of the many canals in the city, elderly gentlemen with cardiac trouble...they were all there and seemingly in greater strength than usual. Christina set to work with a will. She had learned most of the necessary words by now and her eyes told her as much, sometimes more, than her ears. Zuster Bunsma, after a brisk good morning, assigned her patients and marched away to deal with a particularly nasty heart attack. Christina worked on her own, barely noticing Nanda Staal, although she did notice that she herself had far more patients allotted to her than usual. She was glad of it, actually, for the morning passed quickly and midday dinner was a snatched meal because Nanda was off duty for the afternoon.

It became quieter as the day wore on and Christina had time to wonder if she should apologise to Duert ter Brandt, but the question was when? She wasn't off duty until five o'clock and she would barely have time to change and go along to her lesson. Perhaps tomorrow morning, she decided, and realised that all day she had been expecting a call to the office.

She had seen nothing of Adam, and in a way she was glad, although she hoped they might meet as she went off duty, but by the time she left the Accident Room she was tired and so didn't much care whether she saw him or not. Nanda had proved as tiresome as Truus had warned; never where she was wanted and far too careful not to get involved in the messier cases. Christina aware that her normal calm was ruffled, hurried to shower, change, gather together her lesson books, and start on her short walk to Mijnheer Beek's house. The entrance hall was full of people armed with plastic bags and flowers, waiting impatiently for the visiting hour to begin, and she wormed her way through them and reached the door. It was being held open for her and she darted through with a breathless '*Dank U wel*' to discover that it was Dr ter Brandt propping it open. The sight of him put her in mind of what she had to do; never mind if she was late for her lesson, here was the opportunity she hadn't hoped to have. She stopped on the top step.

Not waiting to plan her speech, she spoke quickly, wanting to get it off her chest. 'I meant to come to your office,' she told him earnestly, 'to apologise, you know, but we had rather a busy day and I have a lesson this evening and there wasn't time.'

'And what were you going to apologise for?' asked the doctor. He was leaning against one of the double doors which was impeding the passage of those going in and out, and she put out a hand and twitched his sleeve.

'You're in the way,' she said matter-of-factly, and then: 'I was abominably rude to you. I do beg your pardon, and if you think I'm saying it because I'm afraid you might give me the sack, I'm not.'

His mouth twitched faintly. 'No, I would never think that, Christina. So you don't hate me?' and when she shook her head, 'But you're not sure if you like me, either, are you?' He laughed, and she thought how very good-looking he was. 'Neither was your head turned, was it? Your so sensible head, it's already been turned by Adam, hasn't it?'

She stared up into his blue eyes and wished she could think of something dignified and crushing to say, only she couldn't. What she did say was: 'You don't like Adam and me being friends, do you?'

'No—at least, I have no objection to you being friends, Christina.' He sighed. 'You're on your way to Mijnheer Beek? I'll walk with you, I have to see him about a small matter.'

She stood her ground. 'There's no need,' she told him in her calm way, and he agreed with her readily; too readily for politeness, she considered, and then he added surprisingly:

'But I feel that no opportunity should be lost in getting to know each other.'

He started down the steps, and she, mindful of the fact that she was already late for her lesson, went with him. 'Why?' she asked.

They crossed the forecourt and started along the pavement outside.

'Because I feel sure that we shall have a good deal to do with each other in the future.'

She blushed which made her really rather pretty; he glanced sideways at her and then quickly away again. 'Oh—because of Adam and me...but you don't approve.'

He took her arm and crossed the street. 'My dear girl, does that matter? You're old enough and wise enough to know your own mind.'

She said quickly: 'But Adam isn't?'

Her companion grunted, which could have meant anything at all; he wasn't going to continue the conversation. Christina enquired after the woman whose baby had been born in the Accident Room and was told that she was doing well; so was the baby. 'And I've managed to fix up her return to England,' observed the doctor. 'In a week's time, when she's fit to travel.'

Christina made some noncommittal reply and was glad when they reached Mijnheer Beek's house, a narrow building, squeezed in between two larger ones. The ground floor was a baker's shop, and Christina sniffed appreciatively as they went in at the side door.

The inner door, leading to the upstairs rooms, was a solid affair with a glass spyhole and an old-fashioned bell which the doctor tugged with some vigour. The door, worked by mechanism from the floor above, opened at once and a testy voice boomed down the steep staircase:

'You are late—I shall wish to know why, Christina.'

The doctor propelled Christina up the stairs and followed behind. 'My fault,' he shouted cheerfully, 'I delayed her: she is not in the least to blame.'

They emerged on the landing above, to find Mijnheer Beek waiting for them at his door. He said something in Dutch to the doctor and they laughed together before he said: 'We shall say no more about it, but there will be no English spoken, if you please.'

'Oh lord!' moaned Christina, and Mijnheer Beek gave a great rumble of laughter.

The doctor had made himself comfortable in one of the old-fashioned overstuffed armchairs. 'Coffee?' he asked mildly.

So they had coffee, brought by Mijnheer Beek's meek-looking wife, and Christina made stilted conversation with her teacher while the doctor listened. It vexed her rather that he should do this, but on the other hand it put her on her mettle. She considered she was doing rather well when Mijnheer Beek observed dryly: 'She is good, Duert, she learns fast and she has a large vocabulary, but she avoids her tenses—everything for her is in the present.'

Duert smiled. 'So I fear for myself, but later she will understand the future perfect—it has such possibilities.'

Christina muddled her way through saying that she found the past tense much harder, and he smiled again, a small secret smile as though he were enjoying a joke.

He walked back with her presently, and it wasn't until he had wished her a grave good evening as they reached the hospital that she remembered that he wanted to see Mijnheer Beek about something or other. She turned to look at his broad back disappearing round the side of the hospital and decided against going after him; she had the nasty feeling that he had forgotten all about her.

It was two days before she saw Adam. He was waiting for her as she came off duty after her dinner, catching her arm and drawing her into a narrow passage where no one could see them. 'Angel!' he exclaimed. 'I've the rest of the day free—how about you?'

Christina smiled widely at him, delighted that he was so glad to see her.

'I'm only off until five o'clock—Nanda has days off and Zuster Bunsma thought I'd better be on this evening—as many as possible of us because there's some sort of competition on at the Kursaal for teenagers and she thinks they may start a fight.'

Adam shrugged his shoulders. 'Trust that old crow to expect the worst!'

'She's not!' cried Christina. 'She's severe, but she's marvellous when we're busy—and I daresay she's right.'

He gave her a charming smile. 'Don't let's quarrel about it. We'll go down to Scheveningen and have tea, I promise I'll bring you back in time.'

It was a day left over from summer. It was only when they got out of the car and started along the boulevard that they met the full force of a chilly wind. But it was exhilarating walking arm in arm along the hard sand, and Adam was at his most amusing and in a high good humour. Christina wanted very much to talk to him about the ball, but his mood could change so quickly and she wanted her lovely afternoon to go on for ever.

They turned back presently and had tea and oversized cream cakes, then because she was getting a little worried as the time was getting short, Adam drove her back to the hospital, sulking a little because she couldn't spend her evening with him. Determined to be sensible, Christina said cheerfully: 'Well, there must be dozens of girls you can spend the evening with,' and was a little daunted at his instant: 'Oh, yes—and I did promise a girl at the ball…'

He didn't say any more, which was infuriating. Christina reminded herself that she had no special claims upon him; if she had fallen in love with him that was her business. She bade him a cheerful goodbye and hurried away to get into her uniform. She had a scramble to get on duty punctually, sliding in through the door just as Zuster Bunsma came from her office. There was little to do for the first hour or so, a few minor casualties dealt with swiftly by the Casualty Officer and despatched home to their own doctors. Christina filled in her overtime concerning equipment and the contents of the drug cupboard, and was just thinking of her supper when the telephone rang. Zuster Bunsma, going over instruments with the student nurse on duty, lifted the receiver with the air of someone who had expected it to ring anyway. She listened in silence, murmured a reply and looked at Christina.

'I am right—the Directeur warns me that there is a fight at the Kursaal and already the ambulances are collecting those who are hurt.'

Christina whisked into action. They were always ready, but it was possible to be readier than ready, and if several patients came in together it helped to have everything exactly so; forms laid out, a good supply of instruments, dressing packs, gowns, rubber aprons…she advanced to the doors as the first ambulance drew up and the crew opened its doors to haul out a stretcher. A girl, she couldn't have been more than fourteen, her head roughly bandaged. Zuster Bunsma cast an experienced eye over her. 'You take her, Zuster Forbes; Dr Timmerman is on his way.'

Dr Timmerman was nice; quiet and rather shy and capable. He arrived just as Christina had her patient ready to be looked at. It was a scalp wound, not severe although it had bled a good deal, he dealt with it swiftly, with Christina handing things and then clearing up quickly ready for the next patient. The girl, in the care of a policeman, was driven home to bed; Christina wondered about her, but the place was full of teenagers by now and there was no time to speculate about her patients, only clean their cuts and bandage and give injections and hold their heads while they were sick. She had been busy for an hour or more when she found Duert ter Brandt beside her. One of the housemen had just stitched a small cut on a boy's hand and she was putting on a dressing and giving him an anti-tetanus injection. Duert stood without speaking until she had finished, but when she would have begun to clear up he stopped her. 'Let someone else do that,' he said abruptly, 'I need you over here.'

The patient was a very small girl, brought in with the rest, although how she came to be there in the first place was a mystery. Her mother had been sent for, the doctor explained, luckily she had known her name and where she lived, and her injuries weren't severe. 'Get her on to your lap,' he instructed Christina. 'There's a small cut on her shoulder I must stitch, but she's a wriggler.'

The moppet was plump and pretty with a tearstained face and round blue eyes. She climbed on to Christina's lap without demur and the doctor standing, prudently behind her, produced the local anaesthetic spray, warning her jokingly that it would be as cold as ice cream. The child made no objection, although she twisted round to see what the doctor was going to do next, which would never do. Christina held the small head close to her shoulder and began, rather desperately: 'Once upon a time there were three bears...'

The child was diverted, staring open-mouthed, drinking in every word even though she couldn't understand one of them, while the doctor, sewing daintily on the small shoulder murmured: 'Definitely one of my favourite stories. And here, if I mistake not, is Mum.'

He spoke quietly to the rather wild-eyed young woman who had been ushered into the cubicle, put on the dressing, wished the moppet the time of day, thanked Christina for her help and disappeared. Christina saw him later, bending over an unconscious boy, and when she had time to look around her again, there was no sign of him. It was disconcerting when Zuster Bunsma said dryly: 'Dr ter Brandt has gone—you were looking for him?'

'No, no, not particularly. I was just wondering...' Christina felt her cheeks grow warm; as though she cared where he had gone!

Zuster Bunsma added severely: 'He works too hard; he has no life of his own.'

'Well, he could have,' observed Christina reasonably. 'I mean, if he ever married and had a wife and children...'

She was unaccountably depressed when her companion said: 'And that, I think, will be soon.'

The last of the teenagers went and there was only the clearing up to be done. The night staff came on duty and Christina went thankfully to her supper. It had been a tiring evening, she reflected, but she had enjoyed it too, she reminded herself, and she had had a delightful afternoon with Adam. She had a day off on the following day too, perhaps they would go out again. He didn't know that, of course, but if he wanted to find out when she was off duty, there were ways of finding out. She dismissed the thought in case she might be disappointed.

Most of the other Sisters were at supper. Christina, eating cold meat and cheese on slices of bread and following them with more bread spread lavishly with jam, joined in the conversation as best she could. She used a mixture of English and Dutch words with no grammar to speak of, but helped out with a bit of arm waving and a good deal of laughing, managed very well. Several of them went to visit Truus after their meal. It was a week since the ball and her operation and she was up and about again, with the promise of a return to her own room the next day before a couple of weeks' holiday. It was almost ten o'clock by the time they left her and as they started off to the lift, Leenie said suddenly: 'I am not tired, I will go for a walk, just for half an hour. Who comes with me?'

Four or five voices agreed at once, and when Christina hesitated, Leenie cried: 'You too, Chrissy, you are free tomorrow and can sleep all you wish to in the morning.'

So they fetched their coats and went out into the late evening. The lovely day had been swallowed up into a cloudy evening and before the night was out it would rain. They turned towards the centre of the city, declaring that a good walk would do them all good and they could get a tram back. It wasn't a very great distance, as they knew all the short cuts and presently came out into the Plaats, the hub of the pedestrian shopping centre, with its cafés and enticing showcases of jewellery and scarves and handbags. They wandered from one to the other, taking care that Christina wasn't left out of their chatter, and then, after a cup of coffee at one of the small coffee shops, began their walk to the nearest tram halt. It was while they were waiting at it that Leenie clutched Christina's arm and exclaimed: 'There is the Directeur—there, in his car. The girl with him—is she not beautiful? They say that he may marry her, but I do not think so. She is not—how do you say?—sympathetic to his work.' She added wistfully: 'But she has most lovely clothes.'

Christina said hearteningly: 'You're pretty too, Leenie,' and allowed her eyes to wander to Dr ter Brandt's car, waiting at the lights. The girl was stunning, staring straight ahead of her, looking cross, and as for the doctor, he looked as placid as he always did—he also looked tired. The lights changed and he drove on and the girls clambered on to their tram. It was later, when she was back in her room, sitting on the bed brushing her hair, that Christina fell to thinking about the doctor. He couldn't be quite such a dull stick as Adam had made out. Dear Adam, laughing and teasing, making her feel beautiful. At least, for most of the time, she amended honestly, but perhaps he only criticised her because he wanted her to look her best. The thought sent her to the dressing table to stare at her reflection. There wasn't much comfort for her there, her eyes were all right and thank heaven her eyelashes were long and curling, but her nose was nondescript and her mouth too large. If I were a man, she thought, I'd not look at me twice. The only consolation was that she didn't look anything like her twenty-seven years; no frown marks, no turned-down mouth, no grey hairs, but only little laughter lines at the corners of her eyes. Her skin wasn't too bad either. She slapped on some night cream for good measure and got into bed. Tomorrow she was free to do as she liked, anything could happen. She went to sleep and dreamt of Adam.

He telephoned while she was still pottering around in her dressing gown. He had a half day and how about a drive to Amsterdam and a meal there? 'We'll get back here about six o'clock,' went on Adam, 'and go out to dinner and dance if we feel like it.'

Christina said yes in a breathless way and rushed to borrow the electric rollers. She had washed her hair only the day before, but she hadn't bothered to curl it, and now, even though she had the entire morning in which to get ready, she got down to the business of making the best of herself. It would have to be the grey suit, she hadn't anything else suitable, but what about the evening? The grey two-piece would have to do, she hadn't worn it yet and she wasn't sure if Adam would like it. It was plain and what her mother would have called neat; certainly not the height of fashion, or at least not what Adam would consider fashion, but it would hold its own in an unspectacular way.

She spent a leisurely morning doing her nails, her face, and then her hair. The rollers had done their work well, and her thick brown hair bounced nicely around her shoulders. She put on the suit and prayed fervently that it wouldn't rain.

They drove the fifty-odd kilometres to Amsterdam along the motorway, going very fast. Adam was in tearing spirits and although he had said nothing about her suit, he admired her hair. 'That's better,' he had observed with careless charm. 'You know, you'd be a pretty girl if only you spent a little more time on yourself.'

But time was something she didn't have much of in the usual way, and how could she go on duty with her hair hanging round her neck? Zuster Bunsma wouldn't like it. She said so and Adam laughed. 'Don't tell me that you worry what that old dragon says about you—she's as old-fashioned as Duert.'

'He's not old-fashioned,' declared Christina strongly, and instantly regretted it, because Adam looked sulky and muttered something under his breath, so that she made haste to ask him where they were going and how she was looking forward to the rest of the day together. It took a few minutes to coax him back to sunny spirits and after that she was careful to keep their talk to trivialities and to listen with the proper amount of interest to amusing accounts of his work on the medical side.

He knew Amsterdam well, which was a good thing, weaving his way through a number of narrow streets until they reached a canal where he found a place to park the car.

'We'll do the boat trip first,' he told her gaily, 'everyone does, you know. We'll sit at the back, so that you can listen to me and not the guide—I'm much more interesting!'

And so he was. Christina was shown the patrician houses bordering the Singel, the narrowest house in Amsterdam, the noble mansions on the Keizers Gracht and the Heren Gracht, the narrow waterways leading from one gracht to the next. She was entranced, asking questions as fast as Adam could answer them. She left the boat reluctantly, and if truth were told, perfectly willing to repeat the trip there and then, but Adam whisked her along Damrak, pointed out the Royal Palace and the war memorial in Dam Square and crossed into the Kalverstraat, a narrow street full of shops, some very fine, some surprisingly tatty. Not the best of the shops, Adam pointed out; the boutiques were in the PC Hooftstraat or the Leidestraat. They walked to the end so that she could see the Munttoren and then Adam declared that he had had enough of sightseeing and wanted his tea. Christina, her head turned in all directions so as to miss nothing, would cheerfully have missed her tea in exchange for a visit to a museum, but that was something she could do on her own later. Adam took her to a café on the Leidesplain where she drank milkless tea from a glass and ate a cream cake. She could have eaten two, as she had had no lunch and only a cup of coffee and she was hungry, but Adam was already talking about leaving the city in good time.

He drove back to den Haag fast, talking little, but when they reached the hospital he leaned across her to open the car door and dropped a kiss on her cheek at the same time. 'I'll be here in an hour,' he told her. 'We're going to have a wonderful evening.'

All the while she was dressing, her hair in the electric rollers again, she was worrying as to whether Adam would like her dress. It had looked charming in the shop when she had bought it, but now she wasn't so sure. But there was nothing to do about it now; she draped an angora stole around her shoulders—one she had had for several years but still flattering in its softness—and went down to the entrance.

Adam was in the car waiting. He opened the door as she reached it and she saw that he was wearing a blue velvet suit and an open-necked ruffled shirt; her dress looked staid and dull beside it and just for a moment she felt hopeless and dowdy and out of her depth. But beyond telling her laughingly that she looked like a grey mouse, he said nothing, only asked her if she was hungry.

Her spirits lifted at once, and she assured him she was as he drove into the heart of the city, parked the car and ushered her into the Chalet Suisse.

It was a pleasant restaurant and very crowded; they had a leisurely meal and Christina, her doubts lulled by Adam's charm, began to enjoy herself. When he suggested that they might go somewhere and dance she agreed happily, and it wasn't until they were seated at a small table in a dimly lit night club that she realised where they were. The floor show was just ending and she hoped fervently that it wouldn't come on again, although Adam had enjoyed it, laughing at her and teasing her light-heartedly. 'What a good thing we met, Angel,' he told her, 'for you would have become a real old maid otherwise. You're only twenty-seven, you know, and it seems to me that you've missed a good deal of fun until I came along.'

She laughed with him and when he suggested that they should dance, got up at once. He was easily the best looking man in the room, she decided, and thanked heaven silently that at least she could dance, even if she fell short of his expectations in other directions.

It was one o'clock when they left and raining hard as they reached the street. Christina hesitated in the doorway; she had nothing with which to cover her hair and the rain would play havoc with it, but Adam took her arm and began to walk rapidly down the street. 'The car's not far,' he pointed out, 'it's not worth getting a taxi. What a splendid evening, darling, though you really must get yourself some pretty clothes.'

They reached the car soon enough, but not soon enough for Christina's hair; it hung damp and straight round her face, and the mohair wrap hadn't been improved by its wetting either. She slipped into the seat beside Adam and thanked heaven for the dim light; she must look frightful. She would get him to drive to the side door where it was almost dark…

But for some reason he didn't want to. He pulled up with a screeching of brakes and got out with her into the brightly lighted entrance. They were inside when he turned to look at her. 'Good God!' he exclaimed. 'You look…' He stopped himself as he caught her calm eye. 'Well, you must see for yourself your hair's ghastly—you really must go to a decent hairdresser—suppose we'd met any of my friends?'

She felt sick, but she wasn't going to let him see that. She said quietly: 'Thank you for my lovely evening, Adam, I did enjoy it. Goodnight.'

She went quickly before he could answer her, half running through the quiet passages. There was no one about, which was a good thing because she was crying just a little, too unhappy to know why, not wanting to think about it. The lift whined to a halt and its door opened as she reached it and Duert ter Brandt stepped out. His sharp eyes took in the tears at once and he said vaguely, not looking at her: 'Good evening, Chrissy, you've got yourself very wet.' He took the stole from her shoulders and gave it a vigorous shake. 'That's a pretty dress you're wearing. I hope you've had an enjoyable day.'

'Yes—no,' sniffed Christina, trying to sound normal and failing utterly. 'It rained and—my—my hair's gone straight.' She was aware that she was being ridiculous, but she couldn't stop herself.

'So it has,' the doctor sounded casually interested. 'Straight hair suits you, though.' He added gently: 'You had better make yourself a hot drink before you go to bed.' And when she sniffed again, he handed her a spotless handkerchief, wished her goodnight and closed the lift doors.

He was a very comforting man, she thought as the lift soared upwards. And that was funny, for he was almost a stranger to her, and yet whenever they met he made her feel...she paused, at a loss for a word. Important? Attractive? as though she mattered...?

She slipped into her room and went to look at her ruined hair in the mirror. It was frightful. It struck her that she hadn't minded in the least that Duert should see her looking so awful, and yet she would have given anything to have been able to hide from Adam's eyes when they had reached the hospital. Surely it should have been the other way round?

CHAPTER SEVEN

IT WAS THE BEST part of a week before Christina spoke to Adam again. True, she had encountered him several times in the hospital, passing him with a serene nod in a corridor, or wishing him a calm good day on the several occasions when she accompanied a patient for admission to a medical ward. And indeed, there had been little opportunity of doing more than this; the whole hospital was busy and the weather had given up any pretence of a fine autumn, with nothing but rain and grey skies, offering no inducement to explore the surrounding countryside.

It was just such a morning, gloomy and wet, as Christina got ready to go out on her day off. She had decided to spend it at the Costume Museum, have lunch and then browse through the shops and explore the covered arcades, and in the evening she could catch up on her letter writing in the Sisters' sitting room, sitting cosily by the big stove, listening to the talk round her and doing her best to understand it. She tried not to think about Adam too much. Her common sense told her that she would never be able to change into the kind of girl he admired; either he must learn to love her as she was or she must let him go.

The museum was all she hoped for. She came out of its doors at midday into a downpour of rain and the first person she saw was Adam, standing just inside the porch, staring out into the street. She almost turned and went back inside, only he turned round and saw her and the teasing smile on his face drove all her sensible plans from her head.

'Hullo,' he said, and tucked an arm into hers. 'They told me this was where you'd be! Let's go and have lunch and decide what we'll do with our afternoon.'

She forgot her resolve to treat him with cool dignity, and exclaimed with delight: 'Oh, Adam, are you free for the rest of the day?'

'Lord no, only until six o'clock. Let's go to the Pier. There's a taxi rank just across the street.'

'Didn't you bring the car?'

He hesitated so briefly that she didn't notice. 'No—I left it in the hospital forecourt.' He tucked an arm into hers and walked her briskly to the taxi and threw an arm round her once they were in it. He kissed her too, lightly on a cheek, and told her that she looked pretty and where had she been hiding for the best part of a week?

'Me? Nowhere. I saw you several times, but there wasn't a chance to talk. We've been busy.'

'So have we. I shall be glad to move to the surgical side—I loathe medicine. The appointment's only for six months, thank heaven.' He started to talk about his plans and didn't stop until they arrived at the Pier at Scheveningen. Apparently he wasn't going to allude to their last meeting or apologise to her. Christina found herself making excuses for him as he took her inside, gave her a drink and discussed what they should eat. Adam was in high good humour, laying himself out to entertain her, and presently he began to talk about the holiday he was planning. 'We'll fly there, of course, there'll be half a dozen of us—we'll go just before Christmas and stay for a couple of weeks.'

'Will you be able to get leave from the hospital?'

'Certainly—and you must too, Chrissy.' He put a hand over hers and added wheedlingly: 'Darling Chrissy!'

It cost her a lot to refuse; her tongue longed to say yes, but she didn't hesitate. 'I simply can't. Truus is getting engaged at Christmas and will be on holiday, the part-time nurses are both married with children, and I can't go and leave Zuster Bunsma with two student nurses—it wouldn't be fair.'

He took his hand away and his smile held a sneer. 'Don't be such a prig, my dear. The Accident Room managed very well before you came; you're only a junior Sister and easily replaceable.'

She flushed a little. 'Yes, I know that, and I'm sorry if you think I'm a prig but I'm not going to change my mind—besides, I can't afford a holiday like that.'

Adam said carelessly: 'Don't let that bother you, if you come it will be all expenses paid.'

Christina shook her head, and he hunched a shoulder and stared out of the window at the wide expanse of sea and sky, a uniform grey and the rain still pelting down. After a minute she said: 'We quarrel a lot, don't we, Adam? Perhaps it would be better if we didn't see each other…'

She kept her voice steady by a great effort and met his look with a straight gaze, and then was totally disarmed by his low voiced: 'My darling Angel, don't ever say that again! You're the most wonderful girl I've ever met, surely you know that by now?' He smiled dazzlingly at her. 'A future without you is unthinkable.'

Good sense warned her not to listen, but good sense had no chance. She smiled uncertainly and was lost, not seeing the flicker of triumph in his eyes. He caught her hand again and squeezed it gently. 'Let's look at the shops,' he suggested, 'and never mind the rain.'

She couldn't have cared if it had snowed or blown a gale. She was entirely happy—well, perhaps not entirely; right at the back of her head there were doubts, so vague that she was almost unaware of them. She forgot them entirely presently, peering into the shop windows while Adam pointed out the kind of clothes she should wear and lingered before a jeweller's window, begging her to choose the largest diamond ring there…

They had tea later and took a taxi back to the centre of the city, where Christina elected to get out, saying that she was going to meet some of the Sisters and go to a cinema. It wasn't true, and she hated lying about such a trivial thing, but she wanted their lovely afternoon to end now, not in five minutes' time in the glare of the entrance lights in full view of anyone and everyone passing. She thanked Adam for her lunch as he kissed her goodbye, a rather absentminded salute, but then she excused him. His mind was probably on the evening's work ahead.

She walked briskly away, going up Noord Einde until she judged the taxi to be out of sight before turning and retracing her steps. She didn't hurry; the rain had stopped and the streets were filled with people on their way to the cinema, the theatre or a restaurant. She stopped to look in the shop windows and then had a cup of coffee in a snack bar before making her way to the hospital. She was crossing the forecourt when she saw Adam coming down the steps from the main door. He was wearing a dinner jacket under his coat and had an arm round the shoulders of one of the prettiest girls Christina had ever set eyes on.

She stood still watching them get into his car and drive away and then she walked on quietly, her mind an icy blank, to go to her room, take off her outdoor things and go down to supper with the other Sisters.

When one of them remarked that she looked pale, and did she feel all right, engendering an anxious little chorus that perhaps she had started a cold, she agreed in a wooden little voice.

'It is better that you go to bed early,' said Leenie sympathetically, 'for you eat nothing. I bring you hot coffee presently.'

Christina hardly slept, but she hadn't expected to. She sat up in bed in the dark, stripping away her dreams from hard facts. She had been behaving like a foolish schoolgirl, and she a grown, sensible young woman who should have known better, allowed herself to be flattered, imagining that Adam, handsome, carefree Adam, was in love with her. She recalled what he had said to her over lunch—that he couldn't face the future without her. She put her hands over her face, stony with misery, and began to cry.

She fell asleep as it was getting light, and when she woke, thanked heaven that she had another free day. She would go somewhere, anywhere, and walk and walk until she was too tired to think. It had stopped raining, but thick clouds were racing across a dull sky, chased by a brisk wind. Christina made herself some tea, got dressed, put on her raincoat and a headscarf, and went down to the entrance. It was almost one o'clock by now and there weren't many people about—it was too early for the visitors and those of the nurses who weren't at second dinner would be on the wards or off duty. She looked round her quickly; there was no one who knew her in sight. She nipped smartly across the expanse of marble flooring and actually had a hand on the swing door when a large well kept hand caught her gently by the wrist and turned her round. Duert ter Brandt hadn't said a word; now he studied her face, so carefully made up to mask puffy lids, white cheeks and a pinkened nose.

'Oh, dear, dear,' he observed slowly, and when she tried to free her arm: 'No, my dear, it won't help matters by running away. Have you had lunch?'

She was angry now. 'No—I don't want any. Will you kindly let me go?'

'No. Did you have any breakfast?' His voice was quiet, but it expected an answer.

'No.' She drew a deep breath. 'Will you please let me go? I'm only going out.'

'In that case, we'll go together, because I am going out too.'

His hand upon her arm prevented her from doing anything else. She was walked across the forecourt to where his Rolls stood, popped into the front seat, had her seat belt fastened and driven away before she could frame a single rational sentence. She sat silent for a minute, fighting a strong wish to put her head on the enormous shoulder beside her and howl her eyes out. Presently she said in a wooden little voice: 'I have no idea why you're doing this or where we're going, but I want to get out of the car at once.'

'Tantamount to committing suicide,' observed her companion placidly. 'As to why I'm doing it, it is my business to enquire into obvious signs of unhappiness among the hospital staff, and where better than a quiet café over a cup of coffee?'

He was driving away from den Haag, along the motorway to Leiden, but at Wassenaar he turned off towards the sea and presently when the road narrowed with fields on the one side and the dunes on the other, he stopped at a small wayside café, ushered Christina into its dim interior and ordered coffee. She hadn't heard him order anything else, but the plump goodnatured woman behind the tiny bar brought *Kaas broodjes* too. The bread smelled delicious and the cheese and butter looked mouth-wateringly fresh. Christina gave a small, involuntary sniff and the doctor remarked: 'Drink your coffee and eat up like a good girl, an empty stomach plays havoc with the emotions.' He smiled at her so kindly that she caught her breath like a small child on the verge of tears so that he said quickly: 'Drink your coffee, Chrissy,' and this time his voice was one which would brook no refusal.

She drank the fragrant brew and then, under his eye, began on the *broodje*. He ordered more coffee for them both, sitting back easily on the small hard chair, making conversation about nothing at all. But presently when they had finished he paid the bill and with the air of a man with a job to do, stowed her back in the car and drove on.

'We're going the wrong way,' said Christina as they passed a signpost pointing the way to den Haag behind them.

'No—we're going somewhere where we can walk.'

He didn't say any more, but turned off once more, down a lane which led through the dunes to the sea. Presently they passed a house or two and then an occasional villa, set well back from the road in a well laid out garden and then, surprisingly close, a church spire above the dunes and a cluster of rooftops around it, and a moment later the road curved and they were in full sight.

The town was small, tucked in behind the sea dyke and between the dunes. It had a long narrow main street lined with typical seaside shops, small and old-fashioned, most of them closed now, since the season was over. Duert parked the car on the short promenade, ushered Christina out of the car and led her down a long flight of shallow wooden steps to the beach itself. It stretched, wide and white, on either side of them, as far as the eye could sea, a choppy sea worrying away at its edge. There was a wind blowing, quite strong and cold, but the doctor didn't seem to notice it. He turned Christina round to face him, buttoned her raincoat under her chin and then took her arm and started off along the beach. She went reluctantly, for she had no wish to walk into a fierce wind, nor did she wish for his company. To be left alone to cry in some quiet corner would have suited her mood very well.

Presently when she had got out of breath she began: 'I don't really want...I mean, I'd rather be alone—I know you're very kind...'

He didn't give her the chance to stop walking. 'At the moment you don't know what you want, Chrissy, so allow me to decide what's good for you until such time as your head is clear of what might have been and your cracked heart is mended—as indeed it will be. And I'm not being kind; patients who come to the Accident Room don't want to be met by a long face and puffy eyes—they feel like that themselves.'

'You don't know anything about it!' Her voice was quite savage because she was so unhappy.

'Oh, but I do. I was standing at my office window when you saw Adam leaving yesterday evening.' The doctor added with a curious intentness; 'And why should you be so sure that he doesn't love you any more just because he was taking a girl he has known for years out to dinner?' He paused and stood looking out to sea, not looking at her.

Christina smiled sadly. 'He told me he was going back on duty—he must have known.' She said, suddenly fierce: 'You've known all the time, haven't you, that he was only—only amusing himself. I must have made a nice change from that lovely girl...a b-bit long in the t-tooth and as p-plain as a pikestaff...'

'I have often wondered,' observed the doctor, 'exactly what a pikestaff was.'

'Why, it's the shaft of a pike, of course,' she told him impatiently, and made an effort to snatch her arm away, without any success. 'Oh, why can't you just leave me alone?' she asked him in a high voice which she strove to keep steady. 'I daresay you think I'm a fool, you'll be telling me presently that I should have had more sense, being taken in by all that romantic nonsense, but of course how could you possibly understand—you don't know what it is to love someone!'

He gave her a quick look from under half shut lids. 'I'm sorry you think that.' His voice was abrupt. 'I won't say any more; you wouldn't believe a word of anything I said at the moment, would you?'

He turned her round and walked her back, silently now, the wind howling and bowling them along at a fine pace, and back on the promenade he ignored the car and crossed to one of the hotels that lined it and which was still open. It was warm inside but quite empty. They walked through the restaurant to a small tea room at the back and Duert let go Christina's arm at last and said: 'Go and tidy your hair,' he sounded kind and impersonal, 'and I'll order tea.'

She went obediently to comb the tangle of hair into something like smoothness and powder her still pink nose, and presently found herself in the deserted tea room again, drinking her tea while her companion embarked on a gentle conversation which required no answering, let alone much attention on her part. But the tea had revived her and the walk had tired her nicely. When he suggested that they should go she got up quite briskly and went with him to the car, already thinking of what she would say to him when they were back at the hospital. He had been kind, she supposed, in an impersonal way, but quite indifferent to her feelings, only intent on getting her back to normal as fast as possible so that she would be the same as usual when she went on duty in the morning. He was callous, and it would relieve her feelings to tell him him so.

In fact, she decided, as she settled in the seat beside him, she wouldn't wait until she returned to the hospital, she would tell him now, very politely, of course, and she would tell him too that he had no need to worry that she wouldn't carry out her duties in the proper manner and that there was no necessity for him to concern himself with her private affairs as she was well able to manage them. He started the car and they went back through the sleepy little town, past the shops and the church, along the narrow road leading back to the main road. It was almost dark by now. Christina stared ahead of her into the brilliant path made by the car's lights. Too brilliant; she closed her eyes against it and went to sleep. Presently her head lolled sideways on to the doctor's shoulder.

He glanced down at her pale sleeping face, slowed the car and slid on to a patch of grass between the trees at the side of the road, slipped an arm around her and pulled her gently against his shoulder, then settled back in his seat. It was quiet and dark, and after a little while, despite the car's comfort, chilly, but he made no movement, his face so calm that he might have been sleeping too.

It was more than an hour before Christina woke up. She yawned and opened her eyes and then closed them again, only to sit up a moment later with them wide open. Before she could say anything Duert spoke quietly. 'You've been asleep. You will have missed your supper at the hospital—we'll go to my house and have a meal before I take you back.

Unhappiness had flooded over her like a choking mist. She cried impatiently: 'I'm not hungry—I'd like to go back, I'm tired...'

'You'll be even more tired if you don't pull yourself together,' he spoke without a trace of impatience. 'Where is your pride, Christina?'

She began furiously: 'What do you know...' and then stopped. He was right, of course, hatefully so. She had been completely out of character ever since she had met Adam, carried along on a wave of make-believe. She swallowed back her rage and said in a toneless voice: 'It's very kind of you to offer me a meal, the walk made me quite hungry.' And then as he started the car: 'How dark it is, autumn turns to winter so quickly, doesn't it?' She didn't wait for his reply, but once embarked on the weather, she kept up a steady flow of chat, delivered in an over-bright voice, determined to let him see that she had plenty of pride still.

She didn't look at him at all, or she would have seen a look on his face which would have stopped her in mid-sentence, pride or no pride.

They were in Scheveningen by now, but instead of taking the main road leading to the centre of den Haag, he turned the car into a wide tree-lined Avenue, lined with massive houses, each in its own grounds. Halfway down it he turned the car once more into a similar avenue, but much quieter, with houses, even larger, standing well back from the road. Even in the light of the street lamps they looked impressive, and Christina, relieved at being able to stop talking, fell silent, looking around her.

Presently she asked: 'Do you live here?'

His, 'Yes,' was almost curt as he ran the car through an open gateway guarded by stone pillars with stone lions sitting on them, and up a smooth drive, to stop before a great porch, reached by steps and leading to a massive door.

This was opened as they got out of the car and Christina saw Corvinus standing there. The doctor spoke to him as they went up the steps, and he answered gravely and then wished her a polite good evening and closed the door.

Christina looked around her with interest. The hall was rectangular, with several doors on either side as well as one beside the curving staircase on one side, leading up to a gallery above. The walls were panelled in wood painted white and hung with pictures and portraits, and the floor was black and white marble, strewn with silk rugs. Duert threw off his car coat, then unbuttoned her raincoat and took it from her before ushering her through a double-arched doorway.

The room rather took her breath. It was large and lofty and furnished with grandeur, and yet it had a few homely touches which reassured her; there was a stack of newspapers cast down on a small table near the great open fireplace where a fire burned brightly, a squash racquet leaning against one of the velvet-covered armchairs, a large shaggy dog curled up before the flames and a cat, obviously of humble ancestry, sitting on a small chair, washing itself. It paused to look at them as they went in and the doctor said: 'Hullo, Gertrude,' and whistled to the dog, who leapt to his feet and came tearing to meet them. 'And this is Thomas, rather elderly and getting deaf. Sit here by the fire. Corvinus has gone to fetch Sally, his wife.'

Christina sat down, accepted the glass of sherry he offered her, and looked about her while the doctor sat down in a large wing chair opposite her with the dog's head on his knee. At last she asked: 'Do you live here all alone?'

'Well, not quite that—there are Corvinus and Sally, two maids and the gardener who lives in a cottage behind the house. If you mean am I unmarried, then yes, I am alone.'

She blushed, because of course that was what she had meant, although she wasn't really interested. The door opened and Corvinus came in, accompanied by a small round dumpling of a woman, with a still pretty face and a nice smile. The doctor got to his feet. 'This is Sally, Christina, she will take you upstairs to tidy up. Come down when you are ready.'

Christina got up too and shook Sally's hand and murmured something or other, then followed her out of the room and across the hall, up the lovely staircase to the gallery above. For something to say, she asked: 'What part of England do you come from, Sally?'

The little woman paused to look at her halfway, smiling broadly: 'Somerset, near Castle Cary—Middle Netherton, miss.'

Christina's wan face lighted up. 'Oh, how nice! I—my home was just outside Yeovil—Little Stanisford.'

Sally beamed. 'I know it well, miss. My sister and her husband went to live there when he retired a couple of months ago.' She shook her head. 'I never did—such a small place as the world is, to be sure!'

They had been walking along the gallery as she spoke and now she opened a door at the far end and ushered Christina into a large, airy room with tall windows overlooking the side of the house. The furniture was large, old and beautifully polished, and the hangings and bedspread were in a rose-patterned chintz which exactly suited the mahogany's gloss.

'What a charming room,' observed Christina, and went to look out of the window.

Sally opened a door, indicating the bathroom beyond. 'It's a nice house,' she stated in her soft country voice. 'Much too big for the doctor—that is until he marries and has a family. His brother—you'll have met him I daresay, miss—he lives in den Haag, likes the noise and bustle, I suppose. He comes here quite a bit, though.'

'I—I heard that he was a partner...?'

'And so he is, miss, but the consulting rooms are in den Haag and he doesn't do much at the practice at present because he's working at the hospital.'

'Oh, I see. I—I have met him.'

Sally shot her a shrewd glance. 'You look tired, miss, and here's me standing gossiping. You've not been ill, might I ask?'

'No, oh no—just tired.' Christina smiled brightly at Sally as she went away, leaving her to wander into the splendidly equipped bathroom and wash her face and then make it up carefully before doing her hair. She would have liked to stay longer in the room, it was restful there and the garden below was a delight to the eye with its stretches of green lawn and beds of chrysanthemums; it would be a picture in high summer. There were trees too and a high brick wall, so that there was nothing to be seen of any other house. She looked her fill and then went reluctantly, downstairs.

The doctor met her at the bottom of the staircase. 'I usually have my meals in the morning room at the back of the house,' he greeted her casually. 'The dining room is rather overpowering for one or two—my great-great-grandfather, who built the place, had twelve children and probably needed all the space he could get.'

He was leading the way to the back of the hall and opened a small door into a fair-sized room with doors leading on to a terrace. Its walls were panelled in wood, painted pale green and the rug on its polished wooden floor was silk Persian. The colours of the silk brocade curtains matched it exactly. The table in the centre of the room was oval with cabriole legs and the four chairs arranged around it were upholstered to match the curtains. Christina thought they might be early Georgian, but she wasn't sure. The table was laid with silver and glass with a bowl of late roses in its centre, and looking at it, she was struck with the thought that Duert must be a rich man—it was strange that she hadn't thought of that before, but then she hadn't thought of him, only of Adam.

The doctor, watching her, had a very shrewd idea of what she was thinking; he said with unwonted briskness: 'Sally is a splendid cook. I hope you will manage to eat something.'

Christina took her place at the table and assured him in a composed voice that she had no doubt that she would do justice to Sally's cooking, and during the delicious meal which followed, she kept up a steady flow of conversation about everything under the sun, repeating herself frequently. Her companion, making suitable replies in a placid voice, made no attempt to check her, only when they had finished their meal and had returned to the drawing-room for their coffee and she had fallen silent did he say: 'You don't have to try too hard with me, Chrissy.'

She gave him a smouldering glance. 'You told me to pull myself together—well, I have.'

'Indeed yes. And now you will go back to the hospital and go to bed and sleep, and in the morning, if and when you see Adam, you will ask him about this evening and probably discover that you have been breaking your heart for no reason at all.'

She put down her coffee cup on the little piecrust table beside her. 'It's nice of you to say that, but you know it isn't true. I've been a fool, but that's no reason why I should go on being one.'

'All the same, I think you should give him the chance to explain.'

She gave him a suspicious look. 'You won't see him...tell him?'

He raised his eyebrows. 'My dear girl, why should I interfere?

Did I not explain to you that my only interest was in bringing you to your senses so that your work won't suffer?'

Christina got to her feet. She wanted very much to say something scathing, something that would take that look of calm self-assurance from his face, but she couldn't think of anything at all. She said stiffly: 'Thank you for my supper—if I could have my coat?'

He jerked the old-fashioned bell pull on the wall and Corvinus came trotting in. When he had gone again the doctor said pleasantly: 'You will forgive me if I don't drive you back? I have an engagement very shortly. Corvinus will take you.'

He held her raincoat for her and put it on and tied the scarf viciously over her head. 'I can go by tram,' she told him coldly.

'Don't be tiresome,' said her host in a patient voice which made her grit her teeth. He ushered her into the hall where Corvinus was waiting. 'Goodnight, Christina.'

The drive to the hospital only took a few minutes, and Corvinus, engaging her in conversation, kept her mind occupied. There was no one to see her getting out of the Daimler as he drew up in the forecourt, and it wasn't until after she had gained her room that she realised that she might have had some explaining to do if they had. It struck her forcibly then that perhaps the doctor had sent Corvinus with her for the same reason.

She was getting ready for bed when Leenie tapped on her door to enquire after her cold and offer coffee. They were joined by several others and it was late when Christina finally got into her bed. She had been sure she wouldn't sleep, but she had reckoned without her long walk and the claret the doctor had discreetly plied her with that evening. Despite her wish to remain awake so that she might think about Adam, she felt her eyelids drooping. It was strange that instead of Adam she found herself remembering very clearly Sally saying, 'Much too big for the doctor—that is until he marries and has a family.' As she dropped off she had no idea why the thought of Duert ter Brandt marrying should make her feel sad.

CHAPTER EIGHT

CHRISTINA WAS coming out of Mijnheer Beek's little house after her lesson the following afternoon when she ran headlong into Adam. For a moment she imagined that he had come to find her and then when she saw the look of uneasy surprise on his face, she knew she was mistaken. She felt the colour leave her face, but she said in what she hoped was a normal voice: 'Oh, hullo, Adam.'

She had had the impression that he was going to rush past with some urgent excuse, but now his face relaxed into the familiar charming smile. 'Hullo, Angel,' his voice was warm and smooth and she had to steel herself to ignore it. 'Did you enjoy the film? I thought of you while I was slaving away in Medical.'

She eyed him gravely. 'Did you really, Adam?' She wanted him to confess—she would have forgiven him a lot if he had done so, but he didn't. He laughed and ran a finger down her cheek, making it a caress. 'You're on my mind day and night,' he told her.

It was a pity that they were standing in a busy street, because there were a lot of things she wanted to ask him, but she doubted if her temper would stand the strain and the last thing she wanted to do was make a scene. She said hurriedly: 'I can't stop—Mijnheer Beek kept me and I've only just time to get back on duty.'

Adam caught her hand. 'How about tonight?' he asked.

She took her hand back. 'Oh—is it my turn?' she asked coolly, and hurried away, choked with a mixture of feelings—misery because he'd lied to her, triumph at her parting shot and a distinct nervousness at the idea of meeting him again. Her elation didn't last long, the thought of the months ahead damped it down so effectively that by the time she reached the Theofilus nothing short of running away seemed to fill the bill. She was halfway across the entrance hall when the head porter stopped her. She was to go to the Directeur's Office at once please.

She glanced at the clock; it was barely ten minutes before she should be on duty in the Accident Room. She racked her brains for the right words and told him that haltingly, but he shook his head and repeated his message, so she went up the main staircase and along the corridor to the office and knocked on the door.

The doctor told her to come in—in Dutch—and she did so, to find him sitting behind his desk, piled high with a conglomeration of papers and books and forms. He swept them carelessly aside as she went in and got to his feet. He wished her a good evening with remote pleasantness and begged her to sit down, and before she could speak: 'Yes, I know you're on duty at six o'clock and you'll be late—I've told Zuster Bunsma not to expect you for the next twenty minutes or so.'

Christina sat and looked at him, behind his desk once more, and wondered why she had been sent for, but apparently he was in no hurry to tell her; he sat frowning down at the papers before him. Perhaps he was going to give her the sack and found it difficult. She said, to help him: 'You wanted to see me—I expect you would like me to go back to England...'

'Now why in heaven's name should you think that?' he asked in astonishment.

She said with a kind of despairing calm: 'Well, I behaved very badly yesterday, didn't I? And—and anyway, I think I'd like to go if that's possible, but I don't suppose it is—it would mean breaking my contract...' And when he didn't say anything, she went on: 'I met Adam just now—just bumped into him outside Mijnheer Beek's house. You were wrong, you know.' She turned her head and stared out of the window and the doctor stared at her.

'Did you give him a chance to explain?' he asked placidly.

'No.'

'I think you should. A storm in a teacup?' His voice was mild.

She turned to look at him. 'No.'

'Then perhaps this is the right moment for me to offer you a job outside the hospital.' He put up a large hand. 'No, don't start babbling, Christina, just listen.'

'I never babble!' she cried indignantly.

'Er—normally, no. Mijnheer Beek has cancer of the lung; he will be operated on in three days' time, here, in this hospital. He has asked that you should be his nurse.' The doctor permitted himself a faint smile. 'He is of the opinion that his chances of recovery will be much greater if he has some sound reason for staying alive, and feels that correcting your rather sketchy Dutch grammar—for of course you would be expected to speak Dutch at all times—and encouraging you in the art of conversation in our language, might furnish him with the required energy to recover. He will return to his own home after ten days and you would go with him. There is no reason why he shouldn't make a complete recovery; fortunately he will be able to carry on with his teaching after a period of rest. Will you do this, Christina?'

Her wide grey eyes were on his face. 'Will I go back to the Accident Room?'

'You will have several weeks in which to decide what you want to do. If at the end of that time you wish to return there, we shall be delighted to reinstate you, otherwise I am perfectly willing to release you from your contract.' He smiled at her, a kind, understanding smile, and she felt strangely comforted by it.

She took a deep breath. 'Very well, I'll nurse Mijnheer Beek. When am I to start?'

'He will be admitted the day after tomorrow to a room in the private wing, he will go to theatre on the following day and you will accompany him there and after that to the ICU until such time as we decide that he is able to be returned to his own room. There will, of course, be a night nurse, who will take over from you at nine o'clock each evening. You will be relieved each day for your off duty, but I should be obliged if you would postpone your days off for the first week.' He stood up. 'I think that is all, Christina, unless there is anything else you would like to know?'

'No—no, thank you. I'll do my best for Mijnheer Beek. I didn't know he was ill.'

'It would annoy him very much if anyone knew.' He opened the door for her, then half closed it again. 'Christina, would you like me to arrange a meeting between you and Adam? Should you not be quite sure? There might be some good reason why he went out...'

'Thank you, I wouldn't want that.' She added with some spirit: 'I'm surprised that you should say that, Dr ter Brandt. If I remember aright, you objected to Adam and me being friends.' She frowned. 'Why are you so persistent?'

'I have my own good reasons. But I'll not meddle. Goodnight, Christina.'

She had no opportunity to think about the interview. She changed and went to the Accident Room as quickly as she could, to find it busy, too busy for her to spare even a thought for her own affairs. Later, when they were quieter and waiting for the night staff to come on duty, Zuster Bunsma told her rather severely that she would be missed and that it was to be hoped that she would return when Mijnheer Beek was recovered.

Christina was surprised and touched, for Zuster Bunsma wasn't given to praising people; she murmured suitably, wished the lady goodnight and took herself off to her room. She had told no one of the Directeur's request, but all the same, she was met by several of her new friends, only too anxious to discuss it with her. Over innumerable cups of coffee they talked until late, so that she went at last to bed and at once to sleep.

Mijnheer Beek, presenting himself at the appointed time, showed a cross face to Christina when he was ushered into his room in the Private Wing, but it wasn't only cross, she saw at once that in the clear light of the clinical little room, it looked a nasty colour and drawn. Of course, she had always seen him in the dim light of his curtained study and had never suspected that he was ill. But she knew better than to sympathise with him; she answered his caustic remarks with polite and faulty Dutch, and suffered his testy comments with calm. It took some time to get him settled because he made a point of doing exactly the opposite to what was required of him, but at last he was ready, sitting up in bed and glaring at her.

She glanced at her watch. He was to be examined at noon, she had been told, and it wanted only a minute or so to that time. She tidied the room with all speed and was straightening the quilt, oblivious of her patient's irascible mutterings, when the door opened and Dr ter Brandt came in. He wished her good day, speaking in his own language, and then addressed himself to Mijnheer Beek. Christina didn't quite catch what he said, but it had the effect of improving the old gentleman's temper, so that presently he submitted quite cheerfully to a lengthy examination. He even addressed a few remarks to Christina, and when she answered him with tolerable correctness this time, observed to the doctor that she had, on the whole, done him credit.

They both looked at her then, but she refused to be discomposed by it, standing there by the bed; waiting patiently until Dr ter Brandt thought fit to continue his work. Which he did presently without answering, which for some reason, put her out.

The operation was a success, which considering Mijnheer Beek's determination to do exactly the opposite of what was asked of him, was surprising. By the time he was back in his own room, Christina was tired out, what with coaxing him to wear the garb suitable for a patient going to theatre, explaining a dozen times why he couldn't eat his breakfast the same as he usually did, trying to keep him quiet after he had had his premed, and then escorting him to theatre, where she watched Dr ter Brandt perform a neat piece of surgery before going with her patient to the Intensive Care Unit; the day was well advanced by the time he was back in his own bed and she longed for a breath of fresh air, but she had promised Mijnheer Beek that she would stay with him, so she did, dealing calmly with his tubes and bottles, making her observations with meticulous accuracy.

It was almost half past nine when she finally handed the now sleeping old man over to the night nurse. She would have her supper and go straight to bed, she decided, but halfway to the dining room she changed her mind. She needed exercise; she would go for a brisk walk—she could always make coffee when she got in. She didn't bother to change but put a raincoat over her uniform, bundled her hair into a scarf and then left the hospital. She was walking briskly along the pavement outside the hospital forecourt making for the pedestrian crossing when Dr ter Brandt's voice made her jump and let out a squeak of surprise.

'And where are you going at this hour, Christina?' he wanted to know.

She came to a halt at the crossing. The light was red and she had perforce to stand still. 'For a walk, sir. I need some exercise.'

The light turned green, so she said a hasty goodbye and crossed the street to find him still beside her. 'You've not had your supper?'

'No.'

'Good, we'll eat somewhere. Where did you intend to walk to?'

She stood still, looking up at him. 'Just anywhere, and I don't want any supper, thank you.' She added composedly: 'Don't let me keep you.'

He said coolly, taking her arm: 'You're not, but doesn't it strike you as absurd that two solitary people should eat alone when they could keep each other company? We don't have to talk,' he told her kindly. And when she didn't answer: 'We could walk through the park—I wouldn't advise you to do so alone at night, though. There's a café of sorts on the other side.'

Christina was still wondering how to refuse politely when he marched her through an open gate and set off along a path between rough grassland. It was lighted, not very adequately, and it was difficult to see her surroundings by reason of the dark night around them. There was a blustery wind too, making conversation difficult. They had walked for several minutes when she ventured: 'I don't think we ought to…that is, you're the Directeur and it really doesn't do.' She paused and went on awkwardly, 'Do you take the other Sisters out?'

He said silkily: 'My dear girl, is this your idea of being taken out? I happened to meet you and what could be more natural than to drink a cup of coffee together?' He added deliberately: 'Of course, I know I'm a poor substitute for Adam.' He took no notice of her sudden gasp. 'Do not imagine that I have singled you out for special attention, I would enjoy equally well walking with Zuster Bunsma or Leenie, or even that redhaired girl who works in Out-patients.'

Christina checked the laughter bubbling up inside her. 'You have a very catholic taste,' she told him severely.

He grunted something and walked her briskly forward again and within a few minutes came out of the park within yards of a small café, very bright and clean and almost full. The menu was a simple one, but the soup was delicious, and invited to try an *uitsmijter*, Christina found it to be delicious too; two generous slices of beef on bread, topped with fried eggs and a salad on the side. She ate it all and drank two cups of coffee besides, comparing it silently with the dinner she had eaten in the splendour of her companion's house.

She had been taken aback to find that he lived in such comfort—perhaps luxury was the better word. She stole a look at him now; his suit was of impeccable cut, his shirt was silk and his tie, sombre-hued though it was, was silk too. It was borne in upon her suddenly that he was a handsome man, his mouth was firm and his chin even more so. Why hadn't she noticed that before? Perhaps because his habitual placid expression masked them.

He looked up and she looked away, pinkening because she had been staring. Just as though he had been reading her thoughts, he observed mildly: 'You've never really looked at me before, have you, Chrissy?'

She put down her coffee cup. Something in his voice made her answer truthfully. 'Not—not to see you. I mean, I've looked at you, but not...' She came to a stop and he nodded gently.

'I understand.' He added casually: 'Have you seen Adam?'

She said quite fiercely: 'No, and I don't want to.'

He nodded again and called for the bill. 'Shall we walk back the way we came?' he wanted to know. And on the way back he kept the conversation firmly in his own hands, wishing her a quiet goodnight as they reached the hospital.

She saw him the next day, of course, and on the succeeding days too: several times a day when he came to visit Mijnheer Beek, but beyond giving her instructions about his patient and listening gravely to her reports, he had nothing further to add. All the same, Christina found herself looking forward to his visits even though his manner towards her was impersonal. Perhaps, she decided, he felt he had done all he could to settle matters between her and Adam, although she wasn't at all sure whose side he was on. She remembered very clearly that he had told her he didn't like the friendship between her and Adam, and yet he had done his best to put his brother in a good light, even made excuses for him.

In a way it was a relief when Mijnheer Beek was pronounced fit enough to return to his home, and she with him. The transfer was accomplished not without difficulty. Mijnheer Beek, as usual, took exception to everything, snapping away at Christina in his beautiful Dutch and sneering at her efforts to answer him in the same language. It was pleasant at last to see him sitting in his chair in the dark little sitting room tut-tutting over the various items of news Mevrouw Beek was entertaining him with. It left Christina free to go to her severely furnished bedroom and unpack her things. A fortnight, Dr ter Brandt had said, just to make sure that her patient did nothing foolhardy and to allow his wife to impose the routine the doctor had suggested. She welcomed it; she had been hard put to it to avoid Adam in the hospital. Indeed, he had on several occasions waylaid her, producing a charm to send any girl's heart beating fast, but although she could hardly bear to do so she had resisted it. She supposed she should feel pleased about that; she felt nothing but a kind of emptiness.

Duert called each day, but never at the same time. Sometimes he stayed only long enough to take Christina's report and take a quick look at Mijnheer Beek, sometimes he would stay for an hour, drinking coffee and eating the light-as-air biscuits Mevrouw Beek fetched from the baker's shop below, and Mijnheer Beek made a point of keeping Christina there, so that he might demonstrate to the doctor what capital progress she was making.

It was during one such visit, about a week after Mijnheer Beek had returned home, that Christina, having helped her patient to undress and dress again after his examination, settled the old man in his chair once more and helped Mevrouw Beek fetch in the coffee, obediently sat down to drink her own, the signal for Mijnheer Beek to fire questions at her about this, that and the other thing, to be answered in correct Dutch.

'She'll soon be fluent,' he observed grudgingly, 'although her English accent is marked.'

The doctor stretched his legs before him. 'I like it,' he said. He looked across at Christina. 'Let's hope that it won't be a wasted accomplishment,' and seeing her puzzled look: 'When you return to England.'

She stared at him. His blue eyes met hers guilelessly and he was smiling faintly, but she didn't smile back. She didn't want to go back to England, she wanted to stay in Holland, here in den Haag, at the hospital, because if she didn't she would never see him again. It wasn't Adam, she thought confusedly, it was Duert all the time, only I didn't know. She became conscious that both men were looking at her intently and mumbled something, and the doctor said smoothly: 'But that, of course, won't be just yet.'

Christina collected the coffee cups and carried them away to the kitchen where Mevrouw Beek was getting their lunch, and stayed there until she heard the doctor's measured tread in the little hall. He put his head round the door to wish them goodbye, passed the time of day with Mevrouw Beek, told Christina to be sure and see that her patient confined his activities to what was allowed, and took his leave. Christina put down the drink she was preparing for Mijnheer Beek and slipped on to the landing. There was a small window facing the street at the head of the stairs, and she peered out. The Rolls was below and Duert was getting into it. It was annoying that he should look up, just as if he knew that she would be there, and wave.

It was time for Mijnheer Beek's pills. She handed them to him and when he spoke to her, answered him absentmindedly, and what was worse, in English, so that he choked over them and had to be patted on the back.

As soon as he had his breath he said snappily. 'Where are your wits, my girl? You must speak Dutch at all times. You behave like someone in love!'

Christina blushed. She wondered what Mijnheer Beek would say if she told him that she was; suddenly, unexpectedly and head over heels. And so unsuitably too. And what would anyone, and by anyone she of course meant Duert, think of a young woman who, having given up a good job so that she might be with the man she had fallen in love with, switched her affections to someone else and that after demonstrating in no uncertain manner that her heart had been broken?

She went through the rest of her day, outwardly as composed as usual, even addressing her patient in a meticulously correct Dutch which earned his grudging praise, but behind her calm face her head was like a pot on the boil. To go back to England and never see Duert again was unthinkable, but on the other hand she wouldn't know where to look when she met him again. She thanked heaven that on the following day she was free in the afternoon, and she had heard him tell Mijnheer Beek that he would probably come about three o'clock. She could be out; she would stay out until the last possible moment too; that would give her a day in which to sort herself out.

Mijnheer Beek took longer than usual to settle for his after-lunch nap the next day. Christina flew into a skirt and sweater and since it was raining again, her raincoat and headscarf. It was barely two o'clock, but she wasn't going to feel safe until she was well clear of the house. She poked her head round the living room door, bade Mevrouw Beek a hurried goodbye and started down the narrow stairs. She was halfway down when the street door opened and Duert came up them, two at a time. He came to an unnerving halt on the same step as she was, so that they were squashed together, her face within inches of his chest.

'Oh dear,' said Christina, and uttered the prosaic words with so much feeling that he flung an arm round her as well.

'It's raining,' he said, laughing down at her, 'and you're going out.'

She leaned back a little and looked at him and then quickly away again. 'Yes—yes, I don't mind...'

'You're early—you don't usually go until three o'clock.' He stared down at her, his eyebrows raised in question.

'No—I... That is...'

He watched the colour steal into her face and grinned suddenly. 'Running away again?' he asked softly, and kissed her suddenly. The next moment he had released her and gained the top of the stairs and opened the Beeks' door.

Christina nipped smartly down the stairs and out of the door, intent on getting as far as possible in the shortest possible time. She didn't stop to wonder why she was doing this, even though she wanted very much to linger by the Rolls drawn up to the pavement in the hope that Duert would return. She saw that the lights by the pedestrian crossing were green and once across the street she could go into the park. The lights changed to red as she reached them and she stood fuming with a dozen other people, watching the stream of traffic. It seemed an age before the lights changed again and she actually had set a foot on the street when she was neatly hooked back on to the pavement.

'Beek's asleep,' observed Duert cheerfully. 'We'll take the car somewhere we can walk.' And when Christina made a small rebellious noise: 'We can't possibly tramp the streets of den Haag for the rest of the afternoon.'

She was bustled into the car and driven away while she was still forming and discarding polite refusals.

They hadn't gone any distance at all when she realised the road they were on. 'We came this way...' she began.

'That's right. It's pleasant by the sea even on a day like this,'

Duert said mildly. 'What do you think of Mijnheer Beek, Christina?'

He kept the conversation on their patient, ignoring her small efforts to change the subject, until they were within sight of Noordwijk aan Zee, when he asked abruptly: 'You are feeling better, Chrissy, about Adam? You've seen him?'

'No, I haven't, and I feel quite all right, thank you.'

He glanced down at her with an expressionless face. 'Yes? Ah, here's the sea. We'll walk the other way this time, shall we?'

He parked the car just where he had parked it previously and they went down the steps in the pouring rain, to stand on the beach and look at the grey, tumbling sea. 'Nice,' observed Duert, and took her arm.

They walked a long way, not speaking because the wind was blowing in their faces, taking the words from their mouths. They went quite a distance before he turned her round and started back again, the wind this time bowling them along at a fine rate. By the time they reached the steps Christina's face was glowing and dripping with rain, her scarf plastered to her head, but she didn't care how she looked, they raced to the top and ran across the promenade and into the same hotel where they had been only a few days ago, only now everything was different. Just for a little while she was happy because she was with Duert, who didn't seem to notice if her hair was falling down or the rain had washed away her lipstick, who somehow, without saying a word, made her feel beautiful. Nonsense, of course, she told herself as she left him to do what she could to repair her hair and face. He seldom looked at her anyway. But he had kissed her, she reminded herself, so perhaps he liked her a little, perhaps he was sorry for her, trying to heal her hurt pride, and yet he had asked her if she had seen Adam…

She raked the comb through her still damp hair and went back to the tea-room, and when presently, Duert suggested that they should return to his house for dinner, she raised no objection. She had always been honest and she wanted to go. It never entered her head to refuse; probably he thought her a fickle creature, but that didn't really matter, in a little while she would have to go back to England because he had so plainly expected her to, and she would never see him again.

Belatedly she asked: 'What about Mijnheer Beek? I'm supposed to be back by six o'clock, but I forgot...'

'I told him I'd see you home this evening.' He smiled at her gently. 'Shall we go?'

At his house, she was taken to the same room as before and only then deplored the fact that she was wearing such a sensible outfit, with no glamour to it at all. She busied herself with her hair and achieved a tidy head and then turned her attention to her face, making up with care although she was sure that the doctor wouldn't notice. But he did. In the drawing-room over drinks he remarked casually: 'I like your hair like that—you're not a girl to wear curls and waves.'

She wasn't sure if that was a compliment or not as she thanked him politely.

No one had shown surprise at her coming again so soon. Corvinus had welcomed her with dignified pleasure and Sally had taken her upstairs with every sign of satisfaction—almost as though she had been expected. The lovely old house and the people in it had welcomed her. When Duert married, as one day he would, his bride would be a lucky girl indeed. Christina, exchanging small talk with her host, fiercely suppressed a longing to be that girl.

They dined presently—watercress soup, lobster thermidor and a light-as-air soufflé, and all the while the doctor kept the conversation away from any personal subject. Christina, relaxing under his calm, amusing nothings, drank the wine he poured for her so that the future, for the moment at least, receded and only the delightful present remained.

They were having coffee round the fire in the drawing-room when the door opened and Adam came in. Christina put her cup down very carefully into its saucer and looked at Duert. He didn't look in the least surprised and certainly not annoyed; he greeted his brother pleasantly and told him to draw up a chair and ring for another cup, then began a conversation into which Christina was drawn willynilly.

Adam stayed for an hour, charming and amusing as ever, and it seemed to her that Duert was encouraging him. She was stiff with rage when at length he got up to go and walked deliberately over to her chair, saying: 'Well, goodnight, Angel—we must make a date very soon.' She just managed to turn her head away in time so that his kiss fell on her cheek.

After he had gone she sat silent for a minute or so, looking down at her hands lying quietly in her lap. When she stole a look at Duert she found he was looking at her with a faint frown.

'Did you know that Adam was coming?' she asked him quietly.

'Oh, yes—I asked him to. Am I right in thinking that he doesn't matter very much any more?'

She said steadily: 'Yes, you're right.'

He nodded. 'Good. One must look not once, but twice, Christina. It isn't just good looks and charm and a gift to amuse—one only sees those the first time, it's the second look which counts.'

'You must think me an awful fool,' she muttered.

'We're all fools at some time or other, you less than most, I suspect, that's why you found it so hard.' He glanced at the grandfather clock, a magnificent thing of bronze and marquetry. 'You don't need to go back before ten o'clock, do you? Would you like to see round the house?'

She welcomed it, because to sit there and make cheerful conversation with him was going to be beyond her. She didn't see his smile as she jumped from her chair, eager to have her thoughts drowned in a conducted tour.

There was more than enough to engage her attention; lofty rooms with splendid plaster ceilings and high windows draped in brocades and velvets, furnished with beautiful pieces, the wood gleaming with age and polishing.

'Of course, I seldom use these rooms,' observed Duert, guiding her into a small, cosy apartment beyond a vast dining room, 'but being a bachelor I seldom entertain as much as I should. Come and look at these portraits…'

They went upstairs presently and along the gallery, while he opened doors on to an endless succession of bedrooms and then took her down a number of narrow passages to where the smaller rooms in the older part of the house were. It was more than an hour before they went back to the drawing-room again and Christina, seeing the time, said almost at once: 'Oh, that was splendid, it's the most beautiful house and so enormous, only I simply must go, Mevrouw Beek might be wondering…'

He made no effort to detain her. Her things were fetched and she was helped into them, bidden goodnight by the attentive Corvinus and led outside to the car. It was still raining, but she didn't notice. She hadn't felt so happy for years. It wouldn't last, of course, but she was going to make the most of it all the same. She thanked Duert quietly for her dinner when they reached Mijnheer Beek's door, and he said nothing at all, only bent to kiss her gently.

She went to bed in a glow of happiness, her thoughts so vague that she hardly heeded them, but there was one thing she was certain of. She loved Duert.

CHAPTER NINE

CHRISTINA DIDN'T SEE Duert the next day; he telephoned for a report on Mijnheer Beek, telling her in a businesslike way that he would be away for two days and if she was in any difficulty, to telephone his Registrar. He hung up briskly, leaving her feeling flat. She wasn't sure what she had expected to happen, but she hadn't thought of him going away.

There was no reason why he shouldn't, she agreed to herself as she attended to Mijnheer Beek's many wants. He had taken pity on her once more, that was all. The sudden thought that he didn't want to see her again was so sharp that she dropped the glass in her hand and spent the next few minutes picking up the splinters while Mijnheer Beek, in the prosiest of Dutch, told her off for being careless.

But moping wasn't going to help matters; it was a cold day after the rain and a good walk would help to bring her back to good sense. Life had become a mess for the moment, but she had only herself to thank. She sallied out into the street and began to walk, without realising it, towards the hospital.

She turned the last corner, and saw it, looming above everything else, at the end of the street and the sight of it was very comforting, for was that not where Duert worked? She stopped in her tracks, struck by the absolute necessity to go and look at his home; only to look, because that was where he had been born and had lived all his life, where he ate and slept and entertained his friends.

She got on the next tram and sat impatiently while it rattled its way from the centre of den Haag to its elegant outskirts. The sea was close now, she could smell it as she got off and walked through the quiet, tree-lined avenues until she reached Duert's house. It was clearly visible from the pavement now that the trees had shed their leaves and it looked larger. One would call it a mansion, she supposed, or a gentleman's residence. She strolled along, peering into the grounds, and when a gardener came round the corner of the house with a rake in his hand, she crossed the road and walked slowly back again still looking. Looking at its dignified front, one would never guess at the comfort and treasures within. She stopped, remembering for no reason at all the girl who had been sitting in the doctor's car; perhaps he had gone away with her, perhaps she was staying in the house. Christina had had no idea that jealousy could be so painful. She just stood there, wishing in a silly fashion that something lovely would happen; if Duert were to come out of his house and see her and invite her in; or come along in his car and stop right beside her and call her name…

Her ridiculous daydream became reality. A car stopped with a squeal of brakes right beside her and a voice said, 'Christina,' and then, mockingly: 'Angel!'

She blinked and looked into Adam's smiling face as he got out of the car. 'Inspecting the ground?' he asked, and laughed gently, 'like a good general before the battle.' And when she gave him a bewildered look:

'You don't have to give me that innocent touch, Angel,' his eyes narrowed. 'You're a plain girl, sweetheart, but no fool. Transferred your affections, haven't you? And why not? Duert's the head of the family and very, very rich, with the family house and all its treasures, and he's made a name for himself besides. He could buy you anything you ever wanted and keep you in luxury for the rest of your calculating little life. Clever, clever girl!' He put out a hand and caught her arm in a painful grip. 'Shall I let you dream on, Angel, or shall I warn you that Duert spends his life being kind to those less fortunate than himself? The odd avuncular kiss means less than nothing…'

Christina reddened and he laughed again. 'Don't tell me that you're so naïve that you supposed he was falling for you? A couple of kisses and the odd meal? You amused me when we met, you were so unlike any other girl I'd ever known, but you're no different.'

She felt sick and ready to explode with anger, but she managed to take a calming breath so that her voice came out quite steadily even if rather high. 'It doesn't matter what you think, Adam—none of it is true.'

He said lightly: 'Probably not, but who's to know? And if you succeed in capturing old Duert, and God knows he'll probably marry you out of sheer pity; even he might not know either, he might wonder…after all, you made a splendid show of being in love with me…but you'd never discover what he felt about it. He's never been one to show his feelings.'

He dropped her arm and flung his own round her shoulders. 'Imagine being with him for the rest of your days and never being quite sure if he believes you married him for his money.'

It was outrageous; it didn't even make sense. She wanted to go somewhere quiet and think about it, but Adam didn't give her the chance. He was standing facing the house now and his arm tightened as he looked over her shoulder to watch the Rolls coming round the side of the house. Duert was driving; he turned smoothly into the road and drove past them slowly, his face impassive as he saw them. The moment he was out of sight Adam took his arm from Christina's shoulders. 'Oh, well, I must be off—my half day, you know, and I'm taking a rather special girl out this evening.'

She hardly heard him, and she certainly didn't see him drive away. After a minute or two she retraced her steps to the nearest tram stop. A great deal of what Adam had said was sheer malice; all the same there was truth in it too. Right at the back of her mind the hope had been growing that Duert was beginning to like her, and that might have been the beginning of something more, but now she might even find herself wondering if she really loved Duert or whether it was his wealth. But it wasn't, she told herself fiercely. If he were penniless she would love him, but Adam had sown a tiny seed of doubt in her mind. He had made her feel cheap too. His words would pop into her head each time she saw Duert.

Tending her patient for the rest of the day she wasn't her usual calm self at all, mangling her Dutch so that Mijnheer Beek pulled her up on every sentence she uttered, listening to her strangely meek apologies with disbelieving snorts.

It was a good thing that Duert was still away the next day, it gave her time to pull herself together, which was a good thing, for when he paid his usual visit on the following morning his placid face had an icy inscrutability which froze her bones. And it was made worse because she had no idea why—not that he kept her in suspense for long. He examined Mijnheer Beek, declared him to be fit enough to do without a nurse, suggested most strongly that he and his wife should take a short holiday and then present himself for a further check-up, refused the coffee offered him and invited her coldly to step into the dark little sitting-room with him.

'You will report for duty—er—let me see, tomorrow afternoon at three o'clock. Zuster Bunsma will be informed.'

It was obvious to her that he had no intention of saying more. She asked bleakly: 'What have I done?' and since the occasion seemed to demand it, added: 'Sir.'

'Oh, you have done well with Mijnheer Beek; it is a pity that your common sense doesn't extend to your private life. I had rather formed the opinion that you had had a change of heart about Adam.'

'Well, I have,' declared Christina, very much on edge, so that her voice came out too loud.

'Indeed?' he sounded almost lazy. 'And yet I saw you yesterday afternoon, in front of my house, of all places, standing with Adam's arm round you.'

Christina went very red, then white, so that her ordinary face looked plain and pinched. 'Oh, no!' she whispered.

'Oh, yes, Christina.' He gave her a small mocking smile. 'You should be more careful where you meet.'

'But I didn't—I wasn't—I only went there because...'

'You hoped Adam might be at the house?'

She shook her head. 'I didn't know he lived there.'

Duert said pleasantly: 'He doesn't. I'm surprised that you didn't know that, but he must have told you that this is the one afternoon in the week when he helps with the practice.' He gave her a long look.

'Why were you there if it wasn't to meet Adam?'

She stared back, wondering what he would say if she told him that she had gone there just to look at the house, because he lived there and it made him seem nearer. Not now, though. He had never seemed so far away. She clamped her mouth shut; there could be nothing worse than telling him.

When she didn't speak he said with the calm coldness which was much worse than an angry shout: 'You will be good enough to be more discreet with your personal affairs, Christina, although you are to be forgiven, I suppose, because you won't be seeing him for a long time.' His voice became expressionless. 'Unless he intends to take you to New York with him?'

Her mouth had gone very dry; it was quite difficult to speak. 'No,' she said finally.

He opened the door. 'Tomorrow afternoon, then, and I trust that when he goes you will have your feelings under control.' He was gone, which was as well. If he had stayed a moment longer she would have picked up the first thing handy, and flung it at his head.

It was quite difficult to carry on as usual, but she managed it. Mijnheer Beek, rather to her surprise, expressed regret at her going, although he was quick to point out that just as soon as he returned from his holiday he would expect her to resume her lessons and, what was more, study hard while he was away. Christina, a dozen plans milling around inside her head, assured him, with no truth at all, that she would and went to pack up her things, joined presently by Mevrouw Beek, quite tearful at parting with her. 'For you've been like a daughter to me,' she declared, 'and you aren't afraid of my husband, either.' She added: 'And your Dutch is now so good. You will stay in Holland?'

Christina wedged a pair of shoes into her case and slammed the lid. 'It's delightful here,' she said evasively, 'and Mijnheer Beek has been such a splendid teacher, I feel quite at home in Holland now.'

Zuster Bunsma received her back with a brusque warning that two of the nurses were off sick and they were short-staffed. 'And you do not look very well yourself,' she remarked tartly.

'I'm very well, Zuster Bunsma, and I'm glad to be back. Shall I take Zuster Smit with me and see to that young woman with the compound fracture?'

Zuster Bunsma nodded. 'Yes. They have just telephoned to say that there is a car accident on the motorway, and we must expect casualties.'

It was good to be back, thought Christina, gently easing denim slacks off her patient. She had had to slit the seam to expose the injured leg and then cut off the striped woollen sock. It was a nasty fracture and the student nurse, who had only just started her training, winced at the sight of it so that once the Casualty Officer had arrived Christina sent her to her tea; the girl would need it if there was a bad crash coming in.

The first of the victims arrived ten minutes later—an elderly woman with head injuries, her hair full of fine splinters of glass, and hard on her heels came an old man, his cuts and bruises not nearly as bad as his state of shock. Christina set Zuster Smit, back from her tea, to make him comfortable, take his temperature and BP, and search gently for injuries, while she turned her attention to the glass splinters.

Three more people arrived in quick succession. Zuster Bunsma sent the second nurse to relieve her and waved her urgently towards the Casualty Officer, already bending over the first of them. A young woman this time, pale and unconscious. Blood was coming slowly through the front of her sweater and Christina whipped out her scissors and began to cut the garment loose, to expose a round jagged wound.

'The driver?' she asked, and nodded at the bruises already changing from redness to purple. 'Shall I get this skirt off—I'll have to cut it.'

She bent to her task, vaguely knowing that Zuster Bunsma was busy close by and that there were several housemen there now. She was hardly aware of Duert taking the place of the Casualty Officer, she was fully occupied doing her own work, handing things to him without looking up. It wasn't until she heard his quiet voice say in English: 'I want this girl in ICU, at once, the left lung is perforated and heaven knows what else besides,' that she realised he was there.

She organised the porters and trolley and then, obedient to the doctor's calm order, accompanied the girl to ICU. She stayed to help for a short time and when she got back to the Accident

Room, the doctor was with Zuster Bunsma examining the last of the patients, another elderly woman. Christina began to clear up. The two younger Zusters were already busy. Even with the three of them working flat out, they were barely finished by the time the woman was warded. Christina was checking the apparatus beside each couch as Duert went away. He wished her a courteous good evening and added his thanks as he went past her.

She went to bed late that evening. The other Sisters wanted to hear about her stay at Mijnheer Beek's house and Leenie was back on to light duties. One of the girls had got engaged while Christina was away, so that there was a good deal of laughing and teasing. She joined in the chatter, glad to do so because she didn't have to think.

But in her room later, in bed and very wide awake, she let her thoughts roam. She wouldn't be able to stay. Duert despised her, and to encounter that polite, cool gaze each time they met was more than she could endure. He had told her that if she wished to break her contract he would allow her to do so, and that was what she must do. Go back to England and start again, she supposed, but not London. She wouldn't be able to bear Hilary's thinly veiled dislike or George Henry's worried questioning. She would go back to her home; perhaps there would be a place for her in Yeovil Hospital. She thought with sudden longing of her home. Life had been uncomplicated then and surely could be again.

But having made up her mind, it was another thing to carry out her decision. Duert proved singularly elusive, and it was another three days before she could get an appointment with him in his office, and when she finally got there, already slightly off balance by reason of a hectic morning's work and Zuster Bunsma's nasty mood, she found it almost impossible to take the chair he so coldly offered and repeat the calm and collected speech she had rehearsed far too often over the last few days. It came out in a hotchpotch of half-finished sentences and far too many reasons as to why she wished to terminate her contract. She floundered on for quite a few minutes while Duert sat back in his chair, watching her, his face inscrutable, his eyes gleaming with amusement. Presently he took pity on her.

'You need not make such heavy weather of it, Christina,' he pointed out placidly. 'I told you some time ago that you were free to go if you should wish.' He turned over the papers on his desk. 'As a matter of fact, I have an application from a nurse who trained here, for a post in the Accident Room. She is anxious to start work as soon as possible if there should be a vacancy.'

Christina felt as though he had, ever so politely, poured a bucket of cold water over her. She said stiffly: 'Then I wouldn't be upsetting anyone if I go quite soon.'

'As to that, I have no doubt that you are upsetting quite a number of people. You have made a good many friends while you have been with us.' He half closed his eyes. 'But none of us is indispensable, or so we are told.'

'No—well, will you please tell me when I can go?' She felt empty. She had expected him to be angry, argue with her, point out what a mess she had made of things, and here he was telling her in the pleasantest manner imaginable that she could go.

'And what is quite soon?' enquired Duert conversationally. 'Today? Tomorrow? Next week?' He sat looking at her thoughtfully. 'It would suit me very well if you were to leave in a week's time—a Tuesday. What do you intend to do?'

'Go home. I can get a job at the local hospital—I worked there before.'

'Ah yes. Well, Christina, I'll arrange for your salary and so on to be given you when you leave.' He added casually; 'Adam leaves for New York on the same day.' He glanced up at her under his lids.

Christina looked back at him and didn't say a word. It wouldn't matter what she said, he wasn't likely to believe her. She got to her feet and said: 'Very well, sir,' and went out of the room. Probably he had had a mind to say more, but she wasn't going to wait to hear it.

She hardly saw him during the next week, and as each day flew by she longed for it back again so that she might have a chance of meeting him. She packed her case, bore unhappily the surprised protests of her friends and still more unhappily Zuster Bunsma's pithy remarks about young women who should know better than to give up a good job where they were appreciated. 'And what is more,' continued that lady, 'you have taken the trouble to learn our language—you are by no means fluent and your grammar leaves much to be desired, but in time you would have done very well. A great waste.'

She had arranged to leave after breakfast, and although it had been taken for granted that she was returning to England she had done nothing about booking a flight. She said goodbye to everyone, ordered a taxi to take her to the station and then, although she hadn't intended to do it, went along to the Directeur's Office. There was something she had to say to him. It was unlikely that he would believe her, but since they wouldn't see each other again that wouldn't matter much; at least she would have got it off her chest.

It was fortunate that his secretary offered the information that he was free. Christina marched in in her sensible raincoat, a woolly cap pulled well down against the chill outside, her face white with the effort to remain matter-of-fact.

Duert got to his feet. 'Good morning, Christina. You are about to leave? I am sorry to see you go, but I hope that in a little while we shall meet again.'

'No,' said Christina quite violently, forgetting to be matter-of-fact, 'I don't want to see you again ever. You don't believe a word I say and you're glad to be rid of me, aren't you? You couldn't send me away fast enough. I just wonder what would have happened if I hadn't asked to go. And I'll tell you something—I thought I loved Adam, but that was because I—haven't met many men who took any notice of me, but it wasn't love at all—I don't care if he goes to Timbuctoo. But he liked to think that I was still in love with him.' She moved a little nearer to the door, ready to bolt. 'And I wasn't meeting him outside your house—he saw me there, and I'll tell you why I was there. I wanted to look at it again, just because you live in it—it's your home—I wanted to remember it...' She opened the door. 'That's funny, isn't it?'

She banged the door shut and flew along the passage and

down the stairs and out to the taxi. When she got to the station she left her case at the luggage office and with her tote bag slung over her shoulder, went to find the bus station.

There was a bus on the point of leaving. She got into it, thankful to get inside away from the cold raw wind, and sat looking out at the passing traffic, not seeing any of it, certainly not noticing Sally, waiting to cross the road, staring at her in surprise.

The bus seemed to take an endless time, stopping frequently, its passengers in no haste to get off or on. After the Rolls it was unbearable, but it stopped finally and Christina got out at the end of the narrow street and started to walk down it towards the sea. Halfway down there was a café open, and she went inside and drank a cup of coffee before going on again through the almost deserted little town. The boulevard was deserted too, not to be wondered at on such a bleak morning. The wind was boisterous and cold, stirring the grey sea into angry waves. Christina shivered as she went down the steps to the beach; her raincoat was too thin and she thanked heaven that she had her woolly cap and gloves. She was totally mad, she told herself, a sentimental idiot, making a useless pilgrimage just because she had walked here with Duert.

If it hadn't been for the urgent buzz of his intercom, Duert would have caught Christina up easily enough before she left the hospital. As it was he was immediately involved in matters which held his attention for the next half hour, by which time he rightly judged that she would be gone—a fact verified by the head porter. He sat down at his desk again and sighed. How like Chrissy to make a statement to alter a man's whole life and then disappear. He rang his secretary, told her to book him a seat on the afternoon flight to Heathrow, trod through the hospital to the Directrice's Office, where he spent some time, leaving that lady in something of a flutter, had a brief discussion with the deputy Directeur and then returned to his own office to map out the shortest route to Christina's home. He had warned his colleagues that he might be away for at least four days, but he had to bear in mind the fact that Chrissy might not have gone to her home after all. Presently he got up from his desk, left instructions with his secretary and went out to his car.

Corvinus took the news of the doctor's sudden departure with his usual goodnatured calm, merely enquiring if he would be away for any length of time. The doctor paused on his way to his study. 'I have no idea—it rather depends on how long it takes me to find Miss Forbes.'

Corvinus hid a grin of pleasure. 'Yes, indeed, doctor. Lunch is ready when you want it.'

'Lunch?' asked his employer vaguely. 'Oh, I suppose so.' He went inside and shut the door, and Corvinus, walking fast for such a comfortably stout man, hotfooted it to the kitchen. Sally was straining soup with meticulous care, but she stopped doing it when Corvinus told her the news.

'But I saw Miss Christina this very morning—not two hours ago, on the bus going to Noordwijk. She didn't see me—she was looking out, but I doubt if she was noticing anything. Very unhappy she looked.'

Corvinus picked up the tray and went along to the small dining room, where he set the plate of soup before the doctor. He watched him sample it before observing thoughtfully: 'You'll excuse me, doctor, but you said you were going to England to fetch Miss Forbes back,' and when Duert growled an assent: 'Maybe Sally made a mistake, but she's sure that she saw Miss Christina on the bus going to Noordwijk, not two hours ago.'

The doctor put down his spoon. He had gone a little white, but he said in a steady voice: 'Ask Sally to come here for a minute, would you, Corvinus?' And when she came, a little breathless and excited at being caught up in what she privately believed to be romance with a big R: 'Are you quite sure, Sally? It's important…'

'Certain sure, doctor. She was wearing a green woolly cap and I thought as how it didn't suit her.'

'You're quite right, it doesn't. Did she look…how did she look, Sally?'

'White and worn down. She was looking out of the window, but she wasn't seeing anything, if you know what I mean, doctor.'

He smiled at her. 'I'm sorry, Sally, I'm not going to eat my lunch, I haven't the time, but you can make up for it by cooking something really delicious for our dinner this evening.'

'You'll want your car coat?' said Corvinus. 'I'll fetch it. Is there anything you wish us to do, doctor?'

Duert was already in the hall, getting into the jacket his devoted servant was holding out. 'No, I think not—yes, there is. Make sure that the guest room Miss Christina used is ready for her.' He grinned at Corvinus. 'And thanks to both of you!'

Christina walked northwards into the teeth of the wind, glad of the exercise, although after half an hour or so her steps slowed, because it was hard going. She turned round once to stand and stare at the little town, already some way away, dwarfed by the sea and the sky, turning from a uniform grey to an ominous black. Presently it would rain, but she had no thought of turning back, not yet at any rate. The blustery wind made thinking impossible and she didn't want to think for a bit. Already horror at what she had said to Duert was creeping through her head; even with no one in sight for miles around, she got red in the face just remembering. She tramped on, a lonely figure in a lonely landscape.

The first time she heard a whistle she didn't bother with it. It was so faint above the sound of the wind, it could be a seabird or even the wind itself. But when it persisted she stopped and looked around her. It wasn't until she had turned right round to look behind her that she saw Duert, coming towards her at twice her speed. She dismissed the instant idea that she would run; there was nowhere to run to and he would overtake her. She stood still, wondering how on earth he had known she would be there and what he would say.

He fetched up in front of her, breathing easily, as though he were in the habit of walking miles in a half gale. 'Are we going to the North Pole?' he asked pleasantly. 'Or are you by any chance running away, my darling?'

She opened her mouth to speak and then closed it again. Presently she mumbled: 'How did you know I was here?'

'I didn't. Sally saw you in a bus, which was fortunate, because I had arranged to fly to England this afternoon and fetch you back.' He came a little closer and put his arms round her. 'If you had waited just one minute—but no, you go rushing off, telling yourself that you're unloved and unwanted.'

Two tears trickled down her cold cheeks. 'But I am,' she wailed. 'You sat there like an iceberg, t-telling me that it suited you if I left as soon as possible...'

'Well, I could hardly marry you while you were still working at the hospital, could I?'

She glared up at him. 'Don't you say things like that to me!'

'It slipped out,' declared Duert meekly. 'I'll start again.' He held her a little more closely and pushed the unbecoming cap back from her face. 'I fell in love with you the very first time we met, only I thought that you and Adam...so even when you quarrelled with him, I had to encourage you to make it up, didn't I? I wanted very much to tell you that although he's my brother he's not quite ready to settle down yet—that he falls in and out of love just for the fun of it. I thought at first he was serious about you and then I wasn't sure, and when we came here that first time I longed to tell you, but you wouldn't have listened, would you, my little love? And then when I saw you both—I did my best to hold you at arm's length, for it seemed to me that if you went back to England and Adam was in America, then I stood a chance later on.' He lifted her chin so that he could look into her face. 'Do I stand a chance, my love?'

Christina smiled shakily. 'Oh, yes, I think I love you more than anyone else in the world. I don't know what I'd do if you didn't love me too.'

'That question won't arise.' He kissed her hard and then again slowly. 'We're going back home,' he said softly, 'our home now. We'll be married just as soon as the law allows and I shall buy you a new hat, because I can't like this one.' He turned her round and began to walk back towards the town, but presently he stopped and wrapped her tightly in his arms again and kissed her until she was breathless.

Christina kissed him back. 'We ought to hurry,' she told him. 'It's going to rain.'

'There are some things which cannot be hurried,' said Duert, and bent to kiss her again, just to prove it.

A GIRL NAMED ROSE

by

Betty Neels

CHAPTER ONE

THE EARLY summer sky, so vividly blue until now, was rapidly being swallowed up by black clouds, turning the water of the narrow canal to a steely grey and draining the colour from the old gabled houses on either side of it. The two girls on the narrow arched bridge spanning the water glanced up from the map they were studying and frowned at the darkening sky. The taller of the two had a pretty face, framed by dark curly hair, her blue eyes wide with apprehension; the smaller of the two, with unassuming features, straight pale brown hair piled into a too severe topknot and a pair of fine brown eyes, merely looked annoyed.

"It's going to rain," she observed, stating the obvious as the first slow, heavy drops began to fall. "Shall we go back if we can, go on, or find shelter?" She added in a matter-of-fact way, "I haven't the faintest idea where we are." She began to fold the map, already wet, but before she had done so the rain came down in earnest, soaking them in moments. Worse, there was a sudden flash of lightning and a great rumble of thunder.

The pretty girl gave a scared yelp. "Rose, what shall we do? I'm soaked."

Her companion took her arm and hurried her off the bridge. "I'll knock on a door," she said, "perhaps there's a porch..."

The brick road they were on was narrow and the houses lining it were solid seventeenth and eighteenth century town mansions built by wealthy Dutch merchants, their doors massive, their windows symmetrical, presenting an ageless calm in this backwater of Amsterdam, and not one of them had a porch. A second flash of lightning sent the smaller girl up the steps of the nearest house, to bang resoundingly on the great brass door knocker.

"You can't," objected her companion; she didn't answer, only knocked again.

The door opened and she found herself staring into an elderly bewhiskered face; it belonged to a stout man, almost bald except for a fringe of hair with a stern expression and pale blue eyes. She swallowed and drew a breath.

"Please may we stand in your doorway?" she began. "We're wet and lost."

Before the man could answer a door behind him opened and shut and a voice asked, "English, and lost?" and said something in Dutch so that the man opened the door wider and stood aside for them to go in.

The hall they entered was very impressive; its black-and-white tiled floor partly covered with thin silky rugs, its white plastered walls hung with paintings in heavy frames; the man who stood in its centre was impressive too, well over six feet tall, with great shoulders and the good looks to turn any girl's head. Any age between thirty and forty, Rose guessed, wondering if his fair hair was actually silver.

She hung back a little; this was the kind of situation Sadie could cope with admirably; her pretty face and charming smile had smoothed her path through three years of training at the children's hospital where they both worked; they could certainly turn things to her own advantage now.

"Come in, come in." The blue eyes studied them sleepily. "Very wet, aren't you? Give your cardigans to Hans, he'll get them dried for you and come into the sitting-room while I explain where you are."

He smiled at them both, but his eyes lingered on Sadie's glowing face, damp with rain, her curls no less attractive for being wet, whereas Rose's hair hung in damp tendrils, doing nothing to aid her looks.

He held out a large hand and shook their proffered ones firmly. "Sybren Werdmer ter Sane," he said briskly. It was Sadie who answered him. "I'm Sadie Gordon and this is Rose Comely." She smiled bewitchingly at him as he opened a big double door and ushered them into the room beyond.

It was a large lofty apartment, its ceiling was plaster with pendant bosses, and a central recessed oval with a border of fruit and flowers. The windows were large and draped with heavy swathes of plum-coloured velvet, and the same rich colour predominated in the needlework carpets strewn on the polished wood floor. The furniture was a thoughtful mixture of the old and the new. Vast display cupboards flanked the steel fireplace with its rococo chimney-piece and mirror, a pair of magnificent seventeenth-century armchairs, elaborately carved and velvet-cushioned, stood on either side of a small table inlaid with mother-of-pearl. A pair of William and Mary winged settees were on either side of the fireplace and there were a number of lamp tables and small comfortable easy chairs.

A delightful room, Rose thought, but Sadie said at once, "I say, what a simply heavenly room—you'd never guess from the outside..."

"Er—no, I suppose not. Do sit down; I've asked Hans to bring you some tea and in the meantime tell me how I can help you."

"Oh, Rose will explain; we're hopelessly lost—my fault, I wouldn't stop to look at the map."

"Where are you staying?"

Rose answered him in her quiet sensible voice. "At a small hotel called 'De Zwaan', it's close to the Amstel Hotel, down a narrow side street. We got here yesterday, quite late in the evening, and we're leaving again in the morning. We're on a package tour; six of us, but the other four didn't want to explore. We were all right to start with, but these small streets are all alike, aren't they? Besides, they are so picturesque we just walked on and on..."

"It is so very easy to get lost!" commented their host. "But you aren't too far out of your way. Will your friends worry?"

"They went shopping and they won't be back at the hotel until the shops close. We have a kind of high tea at half past six."

"Ah yes, of course," murmured Mijnheer Werdmer ter Sane; he had never eaten high tea in his life and indeed was a little vague as to what it was, but there was no need for him to comment further for Sadie, who had been frankly staring around her, wanted to know if the large painting of a family group wearing the stiff clothes of a couple of hundred years earlier were any relation to him. He led her over to take a closer look and when Hans came in a few minutes later with the tea tray, paused only long enough to ask Rose to pour out. "What is it you say in England? 'Be Mother'."

She poured the tea from a silver teapot into paperthin china cups, reflecting that no one had ever called her motherly before; homely, plump, dull, uninteresting—all these, repeated so often that they no longer hurt; indeed anything her stepmother said to her now had no effect at all, and even though she was aware that there was truth in what she said, she enjoyed the friendship of a large number of people who didn't seem to notice her unassuming looks. The others sat down presently and she handed cups and as she did so admired her host's good manners, and when he turned to her and asked her what she thought of Holland, she answered him unselfconsciously in her pleasant voice. After a few moments she noticed that he was asking apparently casual questions, all of which she answered with polite vagueness, completely wasted from her point of view for Sadie broke in to give him chapter and verse about St Bride's, with a wealth of unnecessary detail about their training and how they had passed their exams not six months previously and now held Staff Nurses' posts. "Rose is the gold medallist," she informed him, "she's the only one of us with any brains; anyway she studied and we didn't. There were always other things to do in the evenings when we were off duty." She added ingenuously, "You know, housemen and the senior medical students."

Mijnheer Werdmer ter Sane's blue eyes rested fleetingly on Rose's face; what he saw there caused him to say kindly, "I imagine that a gold medal is worth at least half a dozen housemen, your family must be very proud of you."

This tactful remark didn't have the effect he expected; Rose's face flooded with colour and then went pale and she mumbled something, luckily lost in Sadie's chatter. "That's why we're here,'' she explained, ''we've been saving up for months to have a holiday—to celebrate, you know. Only a week.'' She sighed dramatically. ''Back to work in two days' time.''

She turned blue eyes to him. ''You speak perfect English. Have you been in England?''

His voice was smooth. ''Yes, from time to time. We are, of course, taught it in school; Dutch is a difficult language so we need to be proficient in the more widely used tongues.''

''You sound like a professor,'' declared Sadie.

''Oh, I do hope not. Now shall I explain your street map to you?''

A nicely worded hint that they should think of leaving; Rose got to her feet at once and followed him to the table between the windows and handed him her map, and he took a pen from his pocket, marked a cross on it and then inked in their return route. ''So that you will know exactly where you had got to,'' he pointed out, ''but I hope you will allow me to drive you back to your hotel—there's always the chance that you will get lost again.'' He handed Rose the map and tugged an embroidered bell-rope by the fireplace and when Hans came, spoke to him in his own language.

Hans came back almost at once with their cardigans and their host said easily, ''It's a bare ten minutes drive; Hans will fetch the car round.''

He helped Sadie into her cardigan and answered her light-hearted chatter good naturedly and then turned to Rose. But she was already buttoned neatly into hers, standing quietly with the map in her hand.

''We are very grateful,'' she told him gravely. ''It's quite frightening, being lost—and then the storm...but there's no need for you to drive us back, now we know how to follow the map we can walk quite easily.''

''I am sure that you could, you seem to be, if you will forgive me for saying so, a very practical young lady, but I should prefer to take you back; besides I have enjoyed the company of both of you—the gratitude should be mine for helping me to pass a dull afternoon in my own company.''

Oh, very polished, thought Rose, even if he doesn't mean a word of it.

They went out into the hall and before Hans opened the front door, she had time to have another quick look round. The staircase was at the back of the hall, thickly carpeted, with barley sugar balusters, curving up gracefully to the floor above; there was a massive chandelier above their heads and a great carved oak table against one wall. It was tantalising to have a glimpse of such a fine house before they were out on the narrow pavement and being ushered into the dignified dark grey Rolls-Royce motor car standing there.

Sadie slid into the front seat, exclaiming prettily that it had always been her ambition to travel in a Rolls, and Rose got into the back, quite content to do so, only half listening to her friend rattling on about one thing and another while she looked out of the window, trying to see both sides at once; she wasn't likely to come to Amsterdam again for some time, indeed if ever, and she wanted to see as much as could be crowded into their brief stay.

At their hotel they bade their host goodbye, thanked him once more, and Sadie said, ''I hope you come to London and we see you again; don't forget where we are—St Bride's.'' She gave him a beguiling smile as they shook hands. ''I think you'd be much more fun to go out with than any of the housemen I know!''

He made some laughing reply and opened the hotel door for them.

Inside Rose said doubtfully, ''Sadie, weren't you a bit—you know...? After all he is a complete stranger...''

Sadie laughed. ''Look who is talking—who knocked on his door, then?''

''Well, we had to get in out of the rain and I didn't know he was living there, did I?'' They began to climb the steep stairs to their rooms on the top floor. ''The others will be back and I'm famished.''

The rest of the party were milling around the small, plainly furnished rooms gossiping about their day. As Rose and Sadie reached the top landing they surged out of doors, full of questions.

''Where have you been?'' demanded a lanky girl with a long face. ''We've been getting worried; after all, Rose, you've got all the plans for tomorrow and the money for the hotel...''

Rose began mildly and was cut short by Sadie's exuberant voice. ''We walked miles and got lost and then there was that awful storm so Rose knocked on the door of a simply huge house and we had tea there and came back in a Rolls-Royce.''

The lanky girl goggled at her. ''You're making it up.''

''It's quite true,'' said Rose composedly. ''We did get lost, Alice. Did you have a good time shopping?''

''I'll say,'' a girl with red hair interpolated, ''a good thing you've got the money to pay the bill here, Rose, I'm skint.''

''I'll pay this evening, we don't leave until after lunch, so if there's any money over we'll share it out.''

The little group dispersed to tidy for the evening and Rose went into her own room and changed her damp dress for a cotton jersey and did her hair again. Which done she made up her face and then stood peering into the very small looking-glass which hung on the wall. She was undoubtedly a plain girl; not, she conceded, hopelessly so, her skin was good, she had nice eyebrows and her eyes were passable, only her nose was too short and turned up very slightly and her mouth was too wide, and as for her hair...fine and silky reaching to her waist but most uninterestingly pale brown. She pinned it severely to the top of her head and went to join the others. There was no point in her being sorry for herself and indeed she seldom was, but today it had struck her forcibly that no man, certainly not one as handsome as Mijnheer Werdmer ter Sane, would bother to look at her twice. Not that he had ignored her; his manners had been beautiful but she thought that they would have been just as beautiful if she had been an elderly aunt or a chance acquaintance he wasn't likely to see again.

They trooped down to their high tea and joined the other members of the coach party in the basement dining-room; they were mostly elderly couples with a sprinkling of middle-aged ladies on their own who treated the six of them with a guarded friendliness and greeted them now with looks of mild reproof.

"We spent a delightful afternoon doing the canal trip," one of the single middle-aged ladies told them. "It's something you shouldn't have missed. Most instructive." She began to enumerate the various sights they had seen, and they, making formidable inroads into the cold meat and ham on the table, murmured and muttered in reply.

"And what did you do?" asked a cosy matron kindly.

"Went to the shops—they are super." Alice took another slice of bread and buttered it lavishly. "But Rose and Sadie went for a walk and got caught in the storm. They came back in a Rolls-Royce..."

Sadie looked daggers at her but Rose answered composedly enough, "Yes, we were lucky enough to be offered shelter by someone who kindly drove us back here."

"But you didn't know him?" one of the single ladies, a wispy faded blonde, asked with faint excitement.

"Not then, we didn't," explained Rose in her sensible way, "but we do now. We were lost you see and had to take shelter."

An old man with glasses pronounced it his opinion, that foreign parts, while interesting, were unreliable. A remark which closed the conversation for the simple reason that it was difficult to answer.

They weren't to leave until directly after lunch on the following day and since there was enough money over after Rose had paid their bill, the six of them voted to take a trip along the city's canals. They prudently packed their bags before going to their beds; there would be ample time in the morning for sightseeing, but much as they had enjoyed their brief stay they had no wish to be left behind with almost no money in their pockets.

They got themselves up early, had the coffee and rolls and cheese the hotel provided and made a brisk beeline for the Central Station from which the boats left.

There weren't too many people about at nine o'clock in the morning; they got on to one of the first boats to leave and settled down to enjoy themselves.

It was a splendid morning and the old houses, viewed from the water, looked at their very best. They viewed the smallest house in the city, the Munt, and the patrician houses lining the canals, with suitable interest while the guide, switching from English to German to French with enviable ease, pointed out the highlights of the trip. They were back again soon after ten o'clock and trooped down Damrak to the Dam Square, intent on coffee before they went back to the hotel. They were waiting to cross the square, thick with traffic and noisy little trams when Sadie caught Rose by the arm.

''Look,'' she cried loudly. ''There he is, over there...''

Too far away for him to see them, Rose judged, watching the Rolls slide between two trams with Mijnheer Werdmer ter Sane at the wheel. Besides, what would be the point, even if he did? They weren't going to meet again.

They lunched at the hotel, cheese rolls and coffee because the hotel didn't cater for cooked meals at midday, and then they boarded their coach. Rose felt a twinge of regret as they were driven through the city's heart and its suburbs; streets of neat houses and flats, all exactly alike and not in the least resembling the lovely old houses in the centre of the city. At least she had investigated the inside of one of them, and very nice it was too. She allowed her thoughts to dwell on the pleasures of living in such a house, lapped around with comfort, no, not comfort, luxury. She said out loud, ''I wonder if he was married?''

Sadie, sitting beside her, chuckled. ''Well, of course he would be—I daresay he had a handful of children too, on the top floor with Nanny.''

Rose was surprised to find that the idea quite upset her.

The coach kept to the motorway, giving her little time to do more than glimpse the villages to be seen on either side of it. "Next time I come, if I ever do," she told Sadie, "I shan't go on a single motorway; I'm sure there is heaps to see."

"Well, I don't suppose you'll come again," said Sadie comfortably; she sounded faintly smug; more or less engaged to a solid young man with his feet firmly on the first rung of banking, her own future was already cut out for her. She added, "I mean, you are sure to get offered a sister's post—there's Sister Coutts on children's medical due to retire, and the junior night sister leaving to get married at Christmas."

Rose resolutely brushed away the vague daydreams floating around inside her head. She didn't much care for medical nursing and nor did she like night duty; she would like to work on the children's surgical ward, but chance was a fine thing; the ward sister there was young enough to be there for another twenty years, and certainly had no intention of marrying. Rose consoled herself with the thought that she might be going there as a staff nurse. Perhaps when she had more experience she would look for a sister's post at another hospital, as far away from her home as possible. Not that it was home any more. Even after two years it hurt to think of her father; they had lived so happily together after her mother died until quite out of the blue, just after she had started training, he had told her that he was going to marry again.

Her stepmother was still quite young, a well preserved forty, with a pretty face and a charm which she lavished on Rose when there was anyone there to see it. They had disliked each other on sight, but Rose had done her best to understand her father's remarriage and had tried hard to like her stepmother. It wasn't until her father died suddenly and her stepmother married again within six months of his death, that Rose admitted to herself that she didn't like her and never would. She couldn't stand Mr Fletcher, a tall thin man, who doted on her stepmother but treated Rose with cold severity. It was like having two strangers in her home and during the following year she had gradually stopped spending her days off and holidays there, feeling an interloper each time she went to the village near Tunbridge Wells. Instead she had answered her mother's elder sister's invitation to visit her and now she felt more at home there in Northamptonshire. Her aunt lived at Ashby St Ledgers, in a comfortable little house, a rather sterner version of Rose's mother, but kind and affectionate and ready to welcome her niece. She was an enthusiastic gardener, a staunch supporter of the church and had a finger in every village pie and was looked after by a little dumpling of a woman Rose remembered from her childhood when she had been taken on a visit to Aunt Millicent. Both ladies, in their way, made much of her, her aunt in an off-hand manner which didn't quite conceal her very real affection, and Maggie with a cosy warmth made apparent by the nourishing meals she dished up and the hot milk she insisted Rose should take to bed each night.

"I'd like to see more flesh on your bones," she would mutter, pressing the nourishing drink into Rose's hands when she went to bed, and each time Rose went to stay, she would return with a large cake in her case; devoured with gratitude by Rose and her friends the moment it was unpacked.

She thought of her aunt now; she would be going to see her in a few weeks' time but first she would have to settle down on whichever ward she was sent to. Hopefully back on children's surgical, she had been there for three months as a student nurse and loved it. She turned to say something to Sadie but that young lady was asleep, her pretty mouth slightly open, her curls, rather untidy now, framing her charming face. No wonder the Dutchman had been so taken with her, thought Rose, quite without envy.

The bus stopped just before they reached Zeebrugge and they all got out and had tea and a biscuit; the tea—a teabag in a saucer with a glass of almost boiling water, and no milk, was refreshing but not at all like the dark strong brew they shared in each other's rooms when they came off duty. They were off again within fifteen minutes and shortly after went on board, where they left everything in the bus and climbed the stairs to the upper decks. They knew the journey would take four hours and there was still the drive to London from Dover; they wouldn't be at the hospital until midnight at least. Luckily none of them were on duty until one o'clock the next day. Their main thoughts were now centred on food. Lunch had been light and hours ago; Rose counted what was left of the money and then shared it out between the six of them. There wasn't a great deal, not enough to go to the restaurant with the other travellers in the coach, but there was a cafeteria on board. They trooped along its counter, getting value for their money, spending it on rolls and butter, cheese, hard-boiled eggs and cups of tea.

It had been great, they all agreed, sitting round a table, munching, for the most part the food had been good and generous; they had seen a lot and their fellow passengers had been friendly.

"But next time I go," declared Sadie, "I'll travel by car and eat all the time at those heavenly restaurants we saw and never went into. I'd like to spend at least a week in Amsterdam, wouldn't you, Rose?"

Rose drank the last of her tea. "Oh, yes—but I'd like to see a lot more of Holland too. But Amsterdam was smashing."

Alice said slyly: "I bet you'd like to meet that Dutchman again..."

"Yes I would." Rose spoke readily enough in her composed way. "One meets someone and wonders about them and that's as far as it goes. Shall we go on deck for a bit? We'll have to sit in that coach presently."

It was most fortunate that the coach went within a hundred yards of St Bride's and the driver, being a kind man, took them almost to the door. They tumbled out, exchanging goodbyes with the other passengers, collected their cases, thanked the driver, handed him the tip Rose had been jealously guarding, and hurried across the street from the hospital to the Nurses' home. The warden on duty let them in with a good deal of shushing and requests to be quiet, and rather dampened in spirits, they went softly up the stairs to the second floor where the staff nurses had their rooms. They did not linger over getting ready for bed; there was a brisk to-ing and fro-ing in competition for baths, quick good nights and then sleep. Rose, laying her head in a cloud of soft brown hair on her pillow, spared a thought for the Dutchman and then resolutely shut him out of her mind. The last few years had taught her to make the best of things and try to improve on them if possible, and never, never, to waste time on wanting something she couldn't have: to see him again. She closed her eyes and slept.

There wasn't much leisure in the morning; they got up for breakfast for the simple reason that if they didn't they would be hungry, but it was a cheerful rather noisy meal, for everyone wanted to know about their trip. Besides there was the hospital gossip to catch up on, and once they were back in their rooms, there was the unpacking to do, clean caps to make up and another pot of tea, made in their own little pantry, and by then it was time to go to the office, one by one, to be told where they were to go on duty.

There were no surprises for Rose; staff nurse on children's surgical and she was to report to Sister Cummins at one o'clock. As an afterthought she was asked if she had enjoyed her holiday, to which she made a suitable reply before getting herself tidily out of her superior's presence.

Sister Cummins seemed pleased to see her; she was a big, vigorous young woman, quite wrapped up in her work and a splendid nurse. She had no use for nurses who weren't prepared to work as hard as she did, and made a point of saying so, so that she wasn't popular, but Rose got on well with her, going calmly about her work and refusing to take umbrage at some of Sister Cummins' more caustic remarks. And as for the children, they got on splendidly together; she settled down quickly into the chaotic routine of the ward, and if, just now and again, her thoughts turned to the lovely old house and its handsome owner in Amsterdam, she shook them off briskly.

The ward was very busy, for the hospital did a good deal of major surgery in the paediatric wing; very small patients with heart conditions, cystic hygroma which had become infected and needed surgical treatment, pyloric stenosis, club feet, hydrocephalus. Rose, trotting quietly to and fro between the cots, had her heart wrung a dozen times a day and yet her days had their lighter moments too. The convalescent children, full of good spirits, were as naughty as she could wish and Sister Cummins, once they were on the road to recovery, didn't believe in checking them more than was necessary. There was a play-room where they were taken each day under the care of two of the nurses and they screamed and shouted and played together and more often than not, fell asleep. Rose never had much time to spend in the play-room, there were so many ill children to nurse, but it pleased her to hear the normal racket even if it did give her a headache by the end of a busy day.

She was to have a long weekend in a week's time; the two weeks she had already done on the ward had flown and although she had had days off she hadn't gone away. She hadn't heard from her stepmother but she hadn't expected to, she sensed that she wouldn't be welcome if she went to her home. Besides, there was nothing for her there any more. It would be nice to see Aunt Millicent and Maggie again; she would help in the garden and take her aunt's old dog, Shep, for gentle walks and eat huge meals.

It had been more than a full day; three operations and a street accident. Rose, going off duty over an hour late, looked as tired as she felt. A long hot bath, and never mind supper, she decided, she could make tea for herself and there were some biscuits in the tin and perhaps if one of her friends felt like it she would nip down the street to the fish and chip shop and get a bag of chips.

Head well down, she ran down the wide stone staircase leading to the front hall; there wasn't anyone about; those who had an evening off had gone long ago, those on duty were busy seeing to suppers, hurrying to be ready in time for the visitors in half an hour. She jumped the last two steps and ran full tilt into the man standing at the foot of the stairs.

She had butted him in the waistcoat and her head shot up.

Not, for heaven's sake, one of the consultants. It wasn't, it was the Dutchman, quite unshaken, smiling down at her.

"Well, well," he said pleasantly, "Nurse Comely, literally bumping into me."

She blushed, hating herself for doing so, unaware that the colour in her cheeks made her almost pretty. She said nervously: "Oh, hullo, Mijnheer Werdmer ter Sane. What a surprise. Have you come to visit someone?"

He was smiling a little. "Yes, are you going off duty?"

It was silly of her heart to leap so violently, and even sillier that she had thought even for a split second that he was going to ask her to spend the evening with him. She must be mad. She said soberly, "Yes, I am. Very late. We're busy today." She added succinctly: "Children, you know."

"Ah, yes." He stood for a moment, not speaking, and she saw that he wanted to go but didn't want to be too abrupt about it.

"Well, I must hurry," she told him brightly. "I'm supposed to be going out." She held out a hand. "It was nice to see you again, goodbye."

He shook her hand gently and said just as gently, "Indeed, a pleasant surprise for me, too, Nurse."

She gave him a quick smile and crossed the hall very fast and went out of the door to cross the road to the nurses' home. Now if she had been Sadie she would have managed better; turned on the charm, made some amusing remarks...only she wasn't Sadie. She went to her room and not allowing herself to brood, undressed, lay in the bath until impatient thumps on the door got her out of it, drank her tea in the company of such of her friends as were off duty too, and went to bed early, pleading a headache.

She wasn't allowed peace and quiet for long. Sadie, coming off duty a couple of hours later, burst into her room with an excited, "Rose, Rose, wake up, do. He's here—our Dutchman, I've just met him in the hall and guess what, he's a surgeon and knows old Cresswell"—Mr Cresswell was the senior consultant at the hospital, an elderly grumpy man who somehow became a magician once he had a scalpel in his hand—"I asked him why he was here."

"You didn't," expostulated Rose in horror.

"I did. Why not? And he said I'd know soon enough. What do you suppose he wants?"

Rose sat up in bed and hugged her knees. "Sadie, I don't know. Probably to consult with someone, or give a lecture or borrow something."

"He remembered me," said Sadie, ignoring this remark. "He said, 'Ah, my charming visitor.' He told me he was delighted to see me again. I hope he's here in the morning. He might ask us out to lunch or a drink or something."

Rose eyed her friend soberly. "You perhaps, not me, and anyway, it might not be quite the thing; he's much more likely to have lunch with old Cresswell and the other consultants."

Sadie grinned at her. "The trouble with you, Rosie, is that you have no romance in you, not one ounce."

Rose curled up in bed. "Well, let me know what happens. We'll both be at first dinner tomorrow."

It was half way through the morning when Sister Cummins came down the ward to where she was bending over one of the cots, adjusting an intravenous drip. "Staff, will you go to the office? Now. Miss Timms wants to see you."

"Me, heavens, whatever have I done?"

"Your guess is as good as mine. I'll take over here. Leave your apron in my office and tidy your hair."

Two minutes later Rose, hair smoothed beneath her muslin cap, went as fast as she dared without actually running through the labyrinth of passages to the centre of the hospital where Miss Timms had her office, tucked away behind an outer office, guarded by her two assistants. There was another door to her office too, opening directly on to the passage Rose was racing along. As she reached it she skidded to a halt. Miss Timms had a loud voice. "I'm sorry that I must disappoint you, Mijnheer Werdmer ter Sane, Nurse Gordon is a very good nurse and I agree with you that she has a pleasant manner, but she isn't very skilled in the nursing of children and toddlers. Now Nurse Comely is our gold medallist and is at present staffing on the acute children's ward; she has already spent some months there during her training and is absolutely trustworthy and highly skilled.''

Rose was standing like a statue; quite forgetful that it was a most reprehensible thing to eavesdrop; moreover, listeners never heard good of themselves, a fact borne out by the Dutchman's remark. His voice wasn't as loud as Miss Timms', but it was deep and very clear; she didn't miss a syllable.

''Then I must bow to your good advice,'' he was saying. ''I am sure that if you recommend her so highly, Nurse Comely will suit the case very well. But it seemed to me that she lacks a certain light-heartedness—she is a very quiet girl, is she not?''

Miss Timms didn't answer at once, and Rose held her breath and beat down her sudden rage. Quiet was she, lacking in light-heartedness, was she? Why didn't he go all the way and say that she was plain?

''Not a girl that one would notice,'' pursued Mijnheer Werdmer ter Sane blandly, ''but of course she will spend a good deal of time with her patient. You see, Miss Timms, I had hoped for someone who would be able to cheer up the child's mother—distract her thoughts and so on, and it seemed to me that Miss Gordon filled the bill.''

Rose ground her splendid little teeth and let out a breath as he went on, ''But I bow to your wisdom—if I might have a few words with her?''

''She should be here by now.'' Miss Timms' voice held a faint triumph at getting her own way. It also sent Rose soft-footed past the door, to tap on the outer office and be admitted, to be urged into Miss Timms' office without more ado.

After living for several years with her stepmother, she had learnt to hide her feelings. She was slightly pale and she was breathing rather fast but that could be put down to her sudden summons. She said politely, ''Good morning, Miss Timms, you wanted to see me?'' and then, ''Good morning, Sir,'' in a colourless voice. Her glance was so quick that she didn't see his sudden sharp look which was perhaps a good thing.

CHAPTER TWO

MISS TIMMS SAID, "Ah, Staff Nurse Comely," in a voice which suggested that she was about to pronounce judgment on Rose's head. "I must explain why I have sent for you."

Rose sat, inwardly seething. She looked the picture of composure with her pretty hands folded tidily on her lap and her dark eyes upon Miss Timms' face. Mijnheer Werdmer ter Sane sat down too, to one side and a little behind her, very relaxed in his chair although he was watching her from under hooded lids. He still watched her as Miss Timms began to speak in her most impressive voice.

"Mijnheer Werdmer ter Sane is a surgeon, a friend and colleague of Mr Cresswell and he has come to me with a request which Mr Cresswell begs me to grant." She paused, inflated her massive bosom with a deep, dramatic breath, then went on. "Doctor ter Brandt, who lives in The Hague, is a friend of both Mr Cresswell and Mijnheer Werdmer ter Sane. He is married to an Englishwoman, a trained nurse from St Athud's, they have a two-year-old son and Mrs..." she glanced at the man sitting quietly listening and said coyly, "I suppose one calls her Mevrouw?"

"It would be quite suitable if you were to refer to her as Mrs, indeed I would suggest that you address me as Mister."

Miss Timms bowed her head in majestic acknowledgement. "Thank you. As I was saying, Mrs ter Brandt is expecting her second child within a few weeks and is therefore unable to deal with the painful situation which has arisen." She paused again and if her listeners were impatient they gave no sign.

"Two days ago the little boy fell and before his mother could pick him up, had rolled down stone steps leading to the garden. He has sustained a depressed fractured skull and is in the children's hospital in Amsterdam where Mr Werdmer ter Sane is a consultant. His mother is most anxious that he should have an English nurse since she is unable to do much for him herself. Mr Werdmer ter Sane got in touch with Mr Cresswell who kindly suggested that a nurse from St Bride's might be borrowed. I have recommended you for the case, Staff Nurse, you will leave this afternoon. That will be all."

Not quite all, however. Mr Werdmer ter Sane got to his feet and observed blandly, "Perhaps I might ask Nurse Comely if she will accept. She may not wish to take the case although I hope that she will."

She looked at him then. "Yes, of course, I'll come," she told him without fuss. She added silently, even though I'm quiet and not light-hearted and not pretty either. She added out loud this time, "If you are sure that there isn't a nurse who would suit you better?"

His eyes were suddenly intent on hers. He said smoothly, "If Miss Timms recommends you so highly, I feel sure that the matter is entirely satisfactory. Would you be able to leave at three o'clock this afternoon? We can go by hovercraft from Dover and be in Amsterdam late this evening."

He glanced at Miss Timms. "That could be arranged, Miss Timms?"

"Certainly, Staff Nurse may go off duty now and pack what she will need." She nodded at Rose. "Very well, Staff Nurse, you may go. Have you enough money to tide you over?"

"No," said Rose baldly. "Payday is next week."

"As I am aware. Come to the outer office in an hour's time and you will receive an advance in cash."

"Thank you, Miss Timms." Rose turned to the door and found it being opened for her; her thanks were wooden.

It was well past eleven o'clock; she sped back to the ward, gave Sister Cummins a brief resumé of her interview, listened with sympathy to that lady's opinion of foreigners who came borrowing the best nurses in the hospital without so much as a by-your-leave and was bidden to have her coffee before she left the ward. "I'll have mine too," said Sister Cummins gloomily, "and just whisk through the routine—how far had you got? I suppose I'll be sent some feather-brained idiot…I could strangle that man."

She thumped the coffee-pot down on her desk as there was a tap on the door and called "come in" in a grudging voice.

Mr Werdmer ter Sane came in, completely at ease. "Sister Cummins? I've come to apologise for taking your staff nurse away. Believe me, only the urgency of the situation drives me to such a drastic step." He shot a glance at Rose's calm face. "I dare say Nurse Comely has already explained to you…"

Sister Cummins' wrath was oozing away under his charm. "Well, it is most inconvenient but I can see that it is urgent." She waved him to the padded office chair in a corner that no one ever had time to sit in. "Have some coffee while you tell me about it…"

Rose fetched another mug and poured the coffee as he eased himself into the chair and began his explanations; much more succinctly than Miss Timms had done and in half the time. He drank his coffee with every sign of enjoyment too, although by now it was lukewarm and tasted frightful. "And if I might take up a few more minutes of your time? It would be useful to explain to Nurse Comely what she should bring with her."

He glanced across at Rose; he looked kind and impersonal. "Your passport, money, uniform, for you will be at the hospital for some time, I imagine, and whatever you wear out of uniform. Enough for three or four weeks, but I'm sure that if you forget anything Christina ter Brandt will see to it."

He got up and smiled charmingly at Sister Cummins who smiled back, quite won over. When he had gone she turned to Rose, collecting mugs and putting them on the tray. "You know, I quite envy you—he is really rather nice. We could do with a few like him in this place." As Rose reached the door, she added, "You'd better get cracking, you don't want to keep him waiting." Just for a moment she looked wistful. "I wouldn't mind being in your shoes. Bye."

Rose balanced the tray, kicked the door open with one foot

and said, "I hope I'll come back here, Sister. I'm happy on this ward. I don't suppose I'll be gone for more than a few weeks at the outside."

She had half an hour before her dinner time; she went to her room, got her case from the depths of the wardrobe and started to pack. Uniform and caps, tights and undies, dressing-gown and slippers and a cotton skirt and a handful of tops as well as a plain linen dress, sandals, make-up and a sponge bag and her rain coat. It was time by then to go to the office and collect her money; most of her month's salary so at least she wouldn't be penniless. She put the envelope in her pocket and went along to the canteen, collected her shepherd's pie, potatoes and beans, and bore her plate to the table where her friends were already sitting.

Sadie greeted her excitedly. "I say, Rosie, I saw him again coming out of the office—he seemed in a hurry, but he waved. I wonder why he's here."

Rose speared some pie and added mustard. "Well," she said slowly, "he's here to borrow a nurse—a friend of his with an English wife; their small son has got a fractured skull, I don't know any details, I suppose I'll get those later..."

"Later? What on earth do you mean?" She had the attention of the whole table now.

"He's borrowed me. Mind you, he didn't want me particularly, only Miss Timms seemed to think I'd do. It's for a week or two and I'm going at three o'clock this afternoon. Back to Amsterdam."

"Rose, how absolutely marvellous. And you'll see him every day."

"I don't know about that, Sadie, I'm going to look after a toddler, not accompany Mr Werdmer ter Sane to nightclubs."

There was a little burst of laughter and then a spate of questions between gobbling their dinners with one eye on the clock. Milk pudding and strong tea brought their meal to an end and they got up to go back on duty. Only Sadie lingered. "Have fun, Rose, I wish it was me..."

Rose smiled at her friend. ''I'm sure he wishes it was you, too, love. But Miss Timms didn't give him a chance.''

Sadie brightened. ''Keep reminding him about me,'' she urged. ''I know I'm going to marry and settle down but I wouldn't mind one final fling.''

Rose finished her packing, showered and got into a cotton jersey shirtwaister; not high fashion, but very simple and suitable for a journey, then she went to phone her aunt.

Aunt Millicent took the news calmly, merely hoping that her little patient would make a good recovery and voicing the opinion that travel broadened the mind and would Rose be sure and keep her money in a safe place. ''And let me know how you get on, my dear,'' she finished. ''We shall both be glad to hear from you; here's Maggie.''

Maggie disliked the telephone; her voice, faintly apprehensive, came over the wire hesitantly. ''Take care now,'' she begged Rose, ''and don't eat too much of that nasty foreign food. Come back soon, love.''

Rose put the receiver back; they were dears, the pair of them, the moment she got back when she had days off she'd go and see them. She pondered the problem of ringing her stepmother and decided against it. There was little point in it, neither she nor her new husband took any interest in her, nor she in them.

It was getting on for three o'clock; she went along to the pantry and made herself a pot of tea and sat drinking it, checking over in her mind that she had everything she might need with her. She tidied the tea things away, went to her room and collected her case and shoulder bag and crossed the street to the hospital. She was early but the Rolls was there in the forecourt with Mr Werdmer ter Sane at the wheel. As soon as he saw her he came to meet her, took her case and put it in the boot and ushered her into the front seat.

''I don't intend to stop on the way,'' he informed her, his tone so friendly that she found herself agreeing at once. ''We can get a sandwich and coffee on the hovercraft. You've had lunch?''

''Yes, thank you.'' The shepherd's pie and milk pudding still felt solid inside her. She settled herself without fuss and sat back in the comfortable seat; she had little intention of talking and remembering his remarks to Miss Timms, she imagined that he probably felt the same. And indeed, he had nothing to say until they were clear of the last suburbs and racing towards Dover.

"This case," he began, "I'll fill in a few details. The little chap's name is Duert, he's two and four months, a healthy specimen and being sensibly brought up. He's lively and big for his age...his father's a big man. He has a posterior fossa fracture and there is a good deal of swelling of the brain. I have operated to relieve this but there was a CSF leak and I'm worried that there might be a latent infection. He is in the children's hospital in Amsterdam; his parents live in The Hague, but I can keep a closer eye on him if he's on my ward. He's in a side ward and you will be doing day duty, probably your free time will be curtailed for a few days; it will be made up to you later. His father is the director of a hospital in The Hague but he visits whenever he can spare a minute. His mother expects their second child within a few weeks; she's a level-headed girl and realises that there is little that she can do at the moment. That is why she begged for an English nurse; she feels that she can phone you and talk about Duert. She visits him each evening with her husband and she is convinced that he will recover..."

"And you? What do you think?" asked Rose.

"He has a very good chance but it depends largely on good nursing now. You have nursed similar cases?"

"Oh, yes. Won't there be a language difficulty?"

"No. At least not in the hospital, the night nurse is English-speaking and so is the ward sister. I doubt if you could hold a general conversation with them, but you will find that they understand medical terms. My registrar speaks excellent English. You will have a room in the nurses' hostel and when Duert goes home I hope that you will be able to go with him until such time as Christina has got things organised."

"Christina?"

"His mother. They have a splendid nanny, not a trained nurse though, but able to take over from you once Duert is out of danger.''

After that he was silent, leaving her to her own thoughts. She couldn't help but reflect that if it had been Sadie sitting beside him, he might have found something to talk about. He was treating her pleasantly enough but with, she suspected, indifference. To be expected, she told herself philosophically, after all, she was a nurse, being driven to a case by the patient's doctor; and the patient was all that they had in common.

She hadn't been on a hovercraft before; she found it exhilarating. She ate the sandwiches and drank the coffee offered her and sat composedly while Mr Werdmer ter Sane studied the papers he drew from his brief case.

It was still light when they landed, and since the land was flat and the sky wide, she was able to see around her. She longed to ask what this was and that was, but her companion, beyond making sure that she was comfortable, had little to say. Only as they slowed to go through the lighted outskirts of Amsterdam, did he observe, ''A very restful travelling companion—no girlish exclamations of delight, no endless questions about windmills and clogs, no demands to know when we should arrive. I must congratulate you, Nurse Comely.''

To which she made no reply at all.

Once through the suburbs, the city took on the enchantment she had remembered from her brief visit. The sky was clear and starlit, silhouetting the gabled houses against the deep blue above, and once they were away from the main streets, there were only the street lamps reflected in the canal water.

She hadn't asked where they were going; she hoped just for a moment that they would go to his house first, but she was to be disappointed. They left the quiet old streets presently and turned back into the main part of the city. A short cut, she guessed, and knew that she was right when they turned into a wide courtyard with the hospital, quite unmistakable, beyond. Mr Werdmer ter Sane switched off the engine. ''Well, here we are,'' he observed quietly, and got out to open her door and usher her through the wide entrance.

There was no waiting about; he lifted a hand to the porter on duty and led the way to a row of lifts. They got out on the second floor and Rose followed silently as he trod unhurriedly a long wide corridor and through swing doors.

It was very quiet; there were wards on either side, their doors open and night lights burning and the shadowy figures of nurses going to and fro. Mr Werdmer ter Sane tapped on a door at the end of the corridor and went in.

There was a cot in the room, barely visible in the dim light, surrounded by all the impedimenta of post-operative equipment. Sitting side by side in chairs drawn up to the cot were two people. They turned their heads as Rose and Mr Werdmer ter Sane went in and the man got up. He was a big man, heavily built and tall, and he looked tired and very anxious.

''Sybren—you've made good time.'' He looked at Rose and smiled. He was good-looking and his eyes were very blue. ''And this will be our English nurse.'' He put out his hand and then he put a hand on his wife's shoulder. ''Chrissy, now you will be able to sleep.''

The girl took her eyes from the small figure in the cot. Mrs ter Brandt wasn't pretty, but her eyes were a lovely grey in a white face. She smiled at Rose.

''Thank you for coming.'' She got up and offered a hand. ''You're from St Bride's, aren't you? The best nurse they have got, Sybren says. Little Duert will be all right now.''

Rose said comfortingly, ''I'm sure he will and I promise you I'll look after him, Mevrouw ter Brandt.''

The two men had turned aside to talk but presently Doctor ter Brandt said, ''We're going home now, darling—Sybren will take a look at Duert and explain things to...'' He glanced over to Rose. ''May I call you Rose? She will come on duty in the morning and you can phone her then and come and see Duert later in the day. And I promise you we won't pull any wool over your eyes, darling.''

Rose saw the look which passed between them; loving and trusting and very understanding. It must be awful, she thought, as she wished them a calm good night.

Mr Werdmer ter Sane closed the door. "Now, before we find Night Sister and get you settled, let us go over the notes..." He gave her a sharp glance. "You are not too tired? There will be a meal for you presently, but this is too good an opportunity to miss."

He went and looked at the unconscious child, examining him gently. "He's no worse, but he's by no means out of the wood. I want every smallest change noted and I want to be told at once. I'll give you a phone number and you are to ring me without waiting to report to the ward sister. Tell her, of course, but I want to know first. You understand?"

Rose nodded. She was tired and hungry but since Mr Werdmer ter Sane didn't appear to be either, she supposed she would have to forget that for the time being. He began to go over the case papers with her in great detail, and when he had finished, "You understand all that, Nurse? Have you any questions?"

"No, not at present," she told him and he turned to ring the bell by the cot. "Night Nurse," he told her, "while Duert and Christina are here she isn't needed."

The girl who came in quietly was big and fair-haired and pretty. She said something to Mr Werdmer ter Sane and smiled at Rose, who said "Hullo", and offered a hand.

"Wiebeke—Rose," he said briefly. He went on in Dutch so that Rose couldn't understand but when he had finished he said, "I was telling Wiebeke that you will be on duty at seven o'clock in the morning. She speaks English but if you have any hang-ups for heaven's sake give me a ring." He turned back to the night nurse, saying over his shoulder, "Wait a minute, will you? I'll introduce you to Night Sister."

It was five minutes before he had talked to Wiebeke and taken another look at the child. Rose said good night to the other girl and followed him back the way they had come and into a small office. Night Sister was a large bony woman with a calm, middle-aged face. She got up from the desk as they went in, smiled at them both and asked in English, "This is our English nurse?" She shook hands and listened while Mr Werdmer ter Sane talked and then said, "We will go at once to the hostel, you must be tired, and tomorrow morning at seven o'clock we will see you here on duty. We are glad to welcome you, Nurse Comely."

She glanced towards their companion. "You are going home, Doctor?"

"No, not just yet. I'll wish you good night." He nodded to them both and walked back the way they had come.

"He is anxious," explained Night Sister, "he is—how do you say?—godfather to the little Duert. We go this way."

Rose hardly noticed where they were going; she was famished and wanted a bed and a bath more than anything else in the world. It was several floors down and any number of passages before they went through a door and up more stairs leading to silent corridors lined with doors. Night Sister opened one. "Your room, Zuster Comely."

Rose went past her into a small, nicely furnished room, very clean and bright. "I'm not a sister," she said shyly. "Only a staff nurse."

Night Sister laughed. "Ah, but here we call all nurses 'Zuster' and the sister is 'Hoofdzuster'. The bathroom is at the end of this passage, there are six—but first someone will be coming very soon with your supper. And in the morning a nurse will show you where to go. You will be called at six o'clock." She smiled again. "I hope you will be happy with us. Good night."

Left to herself, Rose unpacked and then since her supper hadn't arrived, undressed and got into her dressing-gown. She was brushing her hair when there was a tap on the door and a young woman came in with a tray. She nodded and smiled and put the tray on the writing-desk under the window and when Rose asked, "What shall I do with the tray?" giggled gently, shrugged her shoulders and went away.

The supper was all that she could have wished for: soup and savoury pancakes and a bowl of yoghurt and a jug of piping-hot coffee. Rose disposed of everything and crept down to the bathroom past the silent rooms. The water was hot and she lay for a while going over the events of the day, then mindful of the early start in the morning she got out reluctantly and presently was back in her room. A rather nice room, she thought drowsily, putting out the bedside light.

It seemed that she had only just shut her eyes when she was being gently shaken awake. A girl was bending over her and she sat up in bed, not sure where she was for the moment. The girl smiled. ''You get up,'' she said, and ''I fetch you.'' At the door she paused, clutching her dressing-gown about her. ''Okay?''

''Okay,'' said Rose and jumped out of bed.

She was fetched by a whole bunch of girls who shook hands in a friendly fashion and exclaimed over the old fashioned uniform St Bride's nurses still wore. They bore her along with them, back down the stairs and into the hospital and then underground. The canteen was large and cheerful with tables for four or six and a long counter along one end. Rose, who was hungry again, was disappointed to see that there was only bread and butter and slices of cheese and great urns of coffee. Perhaps just as well, she decided, catching sight of the clock, there wouldn't be time for any more.

Conversation was sparse but friendly at the table, because eating and drinking were more important than gossip and presently they swept her along once more and left her at the children's unit.

Rose went in through the swing doors to the familiar sounds of shouts and cries and the general din made by a number of toddlers even if they weren't so well. The office she had been taken to was close by, she tapped on the door and went in.

Night Sister was there, still on duty, and there was another, younger woman with her who got up from the stool she was sitting on.

''Nurse Comely. I am glad to meet you. I am the hoofdzuster of the ward and presently I will explain your duty times to you, but now I think it best if you go to relieve the night nurse, please.

Mr Werdmer ter Sane will be in presently and he will wish to see you also.''

Rose went along the corridor and opened the end-room door. Wiebeke was sitting at a small table filling in the charts, but she looked round as Rose went in and beamed at her. ''You have slept? Yes? We have had a good night. Duert is still unconscious. I tell you the report now?''

Wiebeke's English was sometimes quaint, but understandable, besides the treatments and feeds and charts were the same as she was used to at St Bride's, only in another language. When she had made quite sure that she had understood Wiebeke's report, Rose bade her goodbye and set about her day's tasks.

She had just finished giving Duert a nasal feed when Mr Werdmer ter Sane came in. His good morning was quiet and he went at once to look and having seen the child sat down to read through the reports and charts.

When he had finished he asked: ''Have you anything to report, Nurse Comely?''

''Nothing more than is written there, sir.''

He got up and went over to the cot. ''Let's see now...'' He went over the small body very carefully, looking for some sign of awakening consciousness, and found none. Presently he straightened up. ''I'll be back presently,'' he told her. ''Mevrouw ter Brandt will be coming in this afternoon. I'd be obliged if you will be here when she comes; it will make things easier for her if she can talk to you.''

There wasn't a great deal to do but she needed to keep the little boy under constant surveillance. She was relieved briefly for her midday meal and soon after she returned Christina ter Brandt arrived. Her husband and Mr Werdmer ter Sane came with her. They went to bend over the cot until Dr ter Brandt said quietly: ''Sit down, darling, he's doing as well as we hoped. Sybren and I are going to have a talk in Sister's office. Shall I get someone to send in a pot of tea? You two girls can have a chat while we are gone.''

He laid a large comforting hand on his wife's shoulder and smiled at Rose.

Left to themselves, Rose brought her stool close to the cot so that she could watch little Duert. ''He's a lovely boy,'' she said in her pleasant voice. ''Has he blue eyes?''

''Like his father's.'' Christina patted herself. ''This one's to be a girl with grey eyes like mine. I don't mind what colour they are but Duert has set his heart on it.'' She looked away for a moment. ''You haven't seen any sign at all?''

''Not yet,'' said Rose gently, ''it's always a long business, isn't it? We've had several like Duert at St Bride's; they took their time but they all went home fit and well.''

Christina ter Brandt smiled rather shakily. ''Bless you, what a comfort you are. You think he'll—he'll be none the worse?''

''Yes, I think that. I think Mr Werdmer ter Sane thinks that too.''

''He's a tower of strength. You met him when you were on holiday?''

''Well, yes. I banged on his door because we were lost and there was a fearful storm and he very kindly gave us tea.''

''Who's us?''

She wasn't sure if her companion was listening, her eyes were on her small son, but Rose went on talking comfortably, anything was better than sitting in silence. ''Sadie—one of my friends. She is a dear and very, very pretty—she is marvellous with children too. She and Mr Werdmer ter Sane got on awfully well...''

''And you don't?''

''Oh, yes, of course.'' Rose remembered his opinion of her and went a delicate pink and Christina gave her a second look. ''He's not very easy to know,'' she said casually, ''plenty of girl friends when he has the time for them, but no sign of getting married. Did he fall for your friend Sadie?''

''Well, I think he might have done if they had seen more of each other.''

''I am glad it's you...may I call you Rose? I think you are

the sort of person who won't get impatient if I burst into tears or have sudden hysterics.''

''Indeed I won't.'' Rose got up and eased the small body gently from one side to the other, took the pulse in the flaccid wrist, charted it and sat down again. A tray of tea was brought in then and Rose was asked to pour out.

''This is fun,'' said Christina ter Brandt, taking her cup. ''We've heaps of friends but I haven't wanted to see any of them since—since...'' She took a sip of tea. ''But it's great to be able to sit here with Duert and have someone to talk to who understands what's happened to him.''

In a little while Dr ter Brandt came back, took another look at his little son, passed a gentle time of day with Rose and took his wife away.

They met Sybren in the corridor. ''She's a darling,'' said Christina to him. ''Do you know I feel quite different now she is here. She's so sure he's going to get better and so—so sensible and kind. When Duert is well enough to come home, she must come too, just for a bit,'' and at his look of doubt, ''don't say it can't be done because between the pair of you, you can do anything you've set your heart on.'' She looked at her husband. ''Duert, dear, please...''

He had an arm round her shoulders. ''Provided Rose will agree, we'll get her by hook or by crook.'' He looked at his friend. ''Well, what do you say, Sybren?''

''She is a good nurse and if you want her, we'll arrange things.''

Christina said thoughtfully, ''Would you rather have had her friend—what was her name—Sadie? Very pretty, Rose tells me. And a good nurse too.''

He smiled down at her. ''Very pretty, but I don't think we could better our Rose; unflappable and sensible and somehow slides into place without any fuss.'' He bent to kiss her cheek. ''We'll have good news for you, Chrissy, just be patient.''

Rose was patient too; perhaps the small child's life depended on her regular frequent observations, the careful taking of pulse, checking the slow breathing, the level of consciousness. She was relieved for her meals but that was all, but she had known that already; when she went off duty in the evening she had her supper and then went for a brisk walk, sometimes by herself, more often with one or other of the nurses. They were friendly girls but she had little time to get to know them. Wiebeke she saw morning and evening, but beyond giving each other the report they wasted no time. Little Duert's life depended on constant observation until he regained consciousness and they both knew it. For the next few days nothing else mattered.

Christina ter Brandt came each day to sit by her little son's cot and hold his hand while she talked to Rose. That she was happily married was evident, just as it was evident that she was whole-heartedly loved. Rose, after a few days, found herself liking her very much, just as she liked Dr ter Brandt. Two people such as they were deserved a miracle.

Mr Werdmer ter Sane came twice a day to study the charts carefully and examine his small patient. He had little to say to Rose although he was always pleasant and careful to enquire as to her welfare, enquiries she brushed aside just as pleasantly. She was beginning to feel the lack of exercise and change of scene but she had no intention of saying so.

It was on the fourth day, half way through the morning, that she noticed the faintest of movements and the little boy's breathing changed slightly from slow and shallow to a steadier rhythm. She went to the phone in a flash and asked for Mr Werdmer ter Sane to come at once, and then whisked back to the cotside, taking another look before ringing Sister's office. Only there was no one there to answer. Rose went back to the cot, took down the side and perched close to the small form. It seemed to her that the level of unconsciousness was lighter even in those few minutes. She stroked the little hand she was holding and began to sing very softly: nursery rhymes, one after the other, and was rewarded by the flicker of an eyelid. When the door opened and Mr Werdmer ter Sane came quietly in, she flapped a hand at him and went on singing "Hey diddle diddle, the cat and the fiddle''. She had a small high voice a little breathless now with excitement. ''The cow jumped over the moon,'' she went on, aware that he was standing behind her.

The cherub in the cot opened two astonishingly blue eyes, said sleepily ''lickle dog'', and closed them again.

''Oh, my goodness me,'' said Rose in a whisper. She took the large hand on the counterpane beside her and gave it a squeeze, quite unaware of what she was doing. But only for a moment; she dropped it like a hot brick and stood up, to recite very accurately exactly what had occurred.

Mr Werdmer ter Sane grunted and bent over the little boy who stirred under his gentle touch and then opened his eyes again. He said something in Dutch and straightened to his great height again. ''I do believe we're coming out of the wood, Rose.''

Very much to her surprise he bent and kissed her cheek. ''Good girl.'' He went to the phone and made several calls and very soon Sister was there as well as his registrar. The three of them talked quietly and then the two men examined the child very gently. Rose stood a little apart. Sister was there, handling things and dealing with their needs and there was nothing for her to do. Sister and the registrar went presently and Mr Werdmer ter Sane asked her to stay by the cot while he phoned and then presently he gave her careful instructions and went away too.

There was little enough to do; only watch carefully and carry out the usual nursing chores. It was half an hour later that he came back and this time he had the ter Brandts with him.

Rose didn't say anything; indeed they weren't aware of anyone else except the little boy in the cot. She slid away to the desk at the window and turned her back and was surprised when Mr Werdmer ter Sane joined her.

There wasn't anything much to see; a variety of gabled roofs and an enormous number of chimney pots and above them, a wide pale blue sky. She stared out at them and wished she could think of something to say and presently he went away again without having uttered a word, back to the cot at the other side of the room and now it was Christina beside her.

"Rose, oh Rose, you don't know how happy I am. Oh, my dear, we're so grateful and thankful." She turned a tear-stained face to her. "We'll never be able to thank you enough."

"But I haven't done anything," said Rose, feeling awkward.

"Oh, yes, you have. You'd made up your mind that little Duert was going to get better and you've had no off-duty and you've had your eyes on him all the time. That was clever, singing the nursery rhymes. Sybren says he's not out of the wood yet but it's time and careful nursing. You'll stay, won't you? I can't nurse him myself, but I know he is safe with you."

"Of course, I'll stay. I am so happy for you and your husband, you must be in the seventh heaven. And I'll take great care of him, I promise you, and Wiebeke is wonderful, you know. You'll be able to sleep at night now."

"Yes, oh yes." Christina looked up at her husband who had just joined her. He smiled a little at her and then looked at Rose. "We are in your debt for the rest of our lives, Rose."

When they had gone she took up her station by the cot again. Perhaps there would be days ahead when not much progress would be made, but it was a start. She took Duert's hand in hers once more and started to sing "Ride a cock horse" in her soft little voice.

Mr Werdmer ter Sane, coming back up the corridor, paused to listen outside the door. He frowned heavily, aware of annoyance because Rose, that most uninteresting of girls, disturbed him. A pity that Christina had set her heart on having her back home when little Duert was well enough to leave hospital. Hopefully, she wouldn't need to stay long.

CHAPTER THREE

THERE WAS a steady improvement in little Duert; he slept for the greater part of the day, but the intervals of wakefulness lengthened and by the end of a week he could be lifted carefully on to his mother's lap when she came to see him. No permanent brain damage, Mr Werdmer ter Sane assured her, little Duert was going to be perfectly all right. Even now, he pointed out gently, he was smiling at his mother and father and talking a little. Time and patience, he counselled Christina. Rose wasn't sure if he was quite so hopeful with Doctor ter Brandt although there was nothing in the men's manner to betray their thoughts; she knew it was important to keep Christina happy and at the same time no attempt was made to pull the wool over her eyes; the little boy was indeed making progress but he still had a long way to go and she didn't relax her watchfulness one particle.

It was at the end of a sunny afternoon, when the ter Brandts had gone home, that Mr Werdmer ter Sane came back to talk to her. Rather to her surprise he wanted to have her opinion of little Duert's progress.

She didn't hurry to answer; he wanted facts, not guesses and too-hopeful opinions. "He's going ahead, but very slowly. Well, I know progress is slow in these cases but I dare say it seems slower because we're all so anxious to see him well again. However, he's beginning to enjoy his food, he listens when I talk and sing to him and he loves his parents' visits." Rose paused and looked up at the grave face. "What are you afraid of, Sir?"

"Ah, discerning Rose, meningitis, so keep your intelligent eye open, will you, for the next week. After that we should be all right. No sign of vomiting? No twitching?"

"Fits?" said Rose. "No, none at all. After fourteen days he should be safe, shouldn't he?"

"Yes, three, no, four days to go. Are you getting tired? You are not getting your proper off-duty, but you do realise that

Christina trusts you completely.'' He smiled suddenly. ''So do I, Rose. Bear with us for a few more days, then you shall have time to yourself.''

The smile had shaken her; she had glimpsed a man she hadn't known, quite different from the austere politeness she had come to expect.

''I'm quite all right,'' she assured him. ''I go for a walk every evening and I wouldn't know what to do with myself even if I were free.''

''It's nice of you to say so, but I find that hard to believe; you knew how to make the most of your stay here when we first met.''

''Yes—well, Sadie was with me, she wanted to see everything too.''

He cast a quick look at the sleeping child in his cot. ''Ah, yes, Sadie. And how is she? A very pretty girl, I was sorry I had no time to see more of her when I came over to St Bride's.''

''She was sorry too.'' So he had fallen for Sadie after all, perhaps not all that deeply, but it would have been nice for them both if they could have got to know each other better. ''It was such a pity,'' went on Rose rather recklessly, ''that Miss Timms insisted on me; Sadie would have loved to come and I'm sure you would have liked to have had her here...''

''You preposterous girl,'' he exploded with a force whose very quietness was blistering. ''What an extraordinary thing to say to me. And how, now I come to think about it, did you know that Miss Timms urged you upon me?''

Rose kept her eyes on his face, quite petrified inside although she looked her usual calm self. ''I heard her. The office door was open as I reached it and she has a very ringing kind of voice. I heard you too.'' She tried a conciliatory smile and met a bleak stare. ''I didn't mean to listen. I'm sorry you had to have me when you wanted Sadie.''

He said in an even voice: ''You were brought here to nurse little Duert: something which you are doing admirably. You can have little leisure to, er—take an interest in my own wishes, Nurse Comely. I suggest that we confine ourselves and our conversation to the needs and treatment of the patient.''

Rose went a very bright pink but she met his bland look; it wasn't only bland, there was amused mockery there too, which made it much worse. She sought worriedly for something to say and drew a blank; Providence came to her aid in the shape of his bleep which sent him to the telephone and then, with no more than a nod, out of the room.

Left with her patient, Rose bustled quietly about her duties. Duert was sleeping and there wasn't a great deal to do for another hour other than the regular observations. She sat down by the cot where she could watch him and went over her conversation with Mr Werdmer ter Sane. A most unsatisfactory one, she thought sadly. Her stepmother had never made any bones about her inability to interest even the most ordinary of young men; she could see how right that lady had been, for not only did Mr Werdmer ter Sane have no interest in her whatsover, he appeared to dislike her as well. She reminded herself that she didn't like him either but the thought didn't give her the uplift in spirits she expected; it left her gloomier than ever.

But she was a sensible girl; moaning would get her nowhere, and little Duert was showing signs of waking. She went and sat on the side of his cot and began on the string of nursery rhymes he enjoyed and was rewarded presently by his chuckles.

Mr Werdmer ter Sane brought his registrar with him that evening and it was after the pair of them had examined the little boy and checked the charts that the registrar paused beside Rose to enquire if she was going anywhere that evening?

''Me, no,'' said Rose surprised.

''Then perhaps you will come to my home and have supper with my wife and me? My wife would like to meet you.''

Rose pinkened with pleasure. ''Oh, would she? How nice. I'd love to come.''

''You go off duty at seven o'clock? I will be outside the hospital at eight o'clock. We have a flat not far away.''

''That's awfully kind of you. I'll be ready.'' Her eyes sparkled with excitement; the other nurses had been friendly and gone with her for walks in the evening or made rather laborious conversation round the TV but this was something different. She beamed at him and then stopped smiling as she caught Mr Werdmer ter Sane's eye. The mockery was there again. Well, let him mock. Her "good night, Sir", was uttered with a light-heartedness which sent his eyebrows up.

It was well past seven o'clock by the time she had given Wiebeke the report and detailed little Duert's progress; by now she had learnt her way around the hospital and skipped along its corridors and down its stairs intent on getting to her room. She had reached the bottom of the last staircase before she saw Mr Werdmer ter Sane watching her from a few feet away.

"You are late, Nurse Comely?"

"There is the report to give," she pointed out, "and Wiebeke and I spend a minute or two talking to Duert so that he knows I'm going and she is coming." She didn't wait for his answer but skipped past him, along the passage to the nurses' home and through the door. He stood where she had left him and a look of faint surprise was on his face and presently a reluctant smile tugged at his strong mouth.

Some hours later, lying in her bed, comfortably sleepy, Rose reviewed her evening. It had been a delightful one. Wim Becke had been waiting for her and had driven her in his old Citroen to a quiet little backwater of narrow streets where he had a flat. The house was tall and thin and, like most of the old houses, extended back from the street to a depth of several rooms. He lived on the second floor and they mounted narrow twisting stairs to reach it. The landing was small but once inside the tiny hall opened out into a long narrow passage with all the rooms on one side. Wim's wife had welcomed her warmly in an English not to be compared with his own rather pedantic speech, and they had all spent some time admiring the small girl, already asleep, before sitting down in the pleasant, low-ceilinged living-room to have their supper. And after the meal they had sat and talked and plied Rose with advocaat, and Marijke had suggested that when Rose was free again, she might like to spend a few hours with her. "We can go to the shops," she offered, "they are not too far away and perhaps you wish to buy."

Rose hadn't left too late, Wim worked a long day now and was on call for a good deal of the time. "But of course, Mr

Werdmer ter Sane is also always available unless he is out of the country. He is splendid with children as you have seen.''

''He is also Wilma's godfather,'' interpolated Marijke proudly. Rose had murmured suitably. Obviously he was thought of very highly in Wim's small household.

The next few days went uneventfully by; little Duert, now that he was fully conscious, was going ahead by leaps and bounds. Mr Werdmer ter Sane came and went, often accompanied by Doctor ter Brandt and Christina, but whether he was accompanied or alone, he had little to say to Rose. On one evening, out for her usual brisk walk before bedtime, she had seen him driving his Rolls. There had been a girl sitting beside him, a sparkling dark creature, laughing and gesticulating. That much Rose had seen as they went past. Mr Werdmer ter Sane had been looking ahead, faintly smiling, and of course he hadn't seen her standing on the pavement.

Only of course he had.

The crucial two weeks were up the following morning; he examined the little boy even more thoroughly than usual before turning to Wim.

''I do believe that there will be no after effects; he should go ahead fast now, but we must take care for another few weeks. I'll talk to Duert about getting him home—the sooner the better now, you agree?''

He glanced across the cot to where Rose was standing. ''You have done a good job of work, Rose. I must remember to tell Miss Timms when next I see her, perhaps it will compensate her a little for the inconvenience of borrowing you.''

He and Wim spoke Dutch after that and she set about settling little Duert for his nap and presently they wandered away with brief nods. At the door Sister appeared to ask for Wim's advice about something and led him away and instead of following them Mr Werdmer ter Sane turned back into the room.

''Do you always go walking alone in the evenings?'' he wanted to know.

Rose fastened the cot sides and gave him a brief glance. ''Yes.'' And then, ''Not quite always; if there is someone off duty who isn't going out they go with me.''

"You are not lonely?"

She had been lonely for some years: she had plenty of friends, everyone liked her but no one loved her. Of course she was lonely. "Not in the least," she assured him.

She was glad to see him go.

Christina and Duert ter Brandt came the next morning. "Sybren's busy," explained Duert smoothly. "He told me last night that we could have little Duert home next week."

"That is marvellous news," said Rose. She sat Christina down in a chair by the cot where the little boy was having his morning nap. "He's made such strides." She glanced at Christina who looked happy but tired. "You have a nanny, don't you? Isn't the baby due next week?" she added hastily, fearful of sounding as though she was prying. "Won't he be pleased to have a baby sister…?"

Duert ter Brandt agreed pleasantly. "Only there is a snag. Christina would like you to come back with us, just for a couple of weeks while she is getting back on her feet. Nanny's a treasure, but she's not a trained nurse."

Rose said at once: "Oh, I should have loved that—to see little Duert really fit again, but I'm supposed to go back to St Bride's—Sister Cummins was quite annoyed at me coming here, you know."

"Ah yes! the militant gorgon on children's surgical—I've met her. Rose, if I could manage to persuade her and your principal nursing officer to let you stay another couple of weeks, would you come back with little Duert? I know you've had no off-duty, but once he's settled in, you shall have your free time made up to you threefold." He took a look at his wife. "Chrissy, it's your turn, darling."

"Please come, Rose," Christina begged. "If you are there looking after him, I can have the baby in peace of mind. Please say you'll come?" She paused. "Then if anything should go wrong you'll be there to look after him."

"Nothing's going to go wrong," declared Rose, "and if Miss Timms will let me, I'll come."

Little Duert woke up then and was sat carefully on his father's knee. "We are eternally grateful," said Duert ter Brandt. "I'll set about seeing everyone concerned."

Hoofdzuster came in then, followed by a ward maid with a tray of coffee, and Doctor ter Brandt suggested with a gentle authority which no one would have dreamt of querying that he and Sister might have a little chat while Rose and Christina sat apart. "There must be an awful lot you want to know," he concluded kindly to Rose.

He was a dear, mused Rose, going to sit by Christina, and she, who had taught herself not to be envious because it was such a waste of time, was envious of Christina. To be loved like that; for no reason at all Mr Werdmer ter Sane's face rose before her eyes and she shied away from it. "What will Mr Werdmer ter Sane say?" she asked before she could stop herself.

"He'll agree," said Christina instantly. He had agreed on the previous evening when he had gone to The Hague to dine with them, indeed, more than that, he had suggested it in the first place. "He thinks very highly of you as a nurse, Rose. And so do we. I'm so glad you'll come. Now I'll tell you something of where we live."

Which took some time; Hoofdzuster went away presently and then the ter Brandts, and Rose was on her own again with the sleeping child. Little Duert woke presently and they embarked together on the childish games which delighted him.

The week slid away, the weather got warmer, little Duert became increasingly active and Mr Werdmer ter Sane paid him frequent visits, coolly polite to Rose, merely enquiring if she was content with the details she had been given by Christina and bearing a message from Dr ter Brandt that he had arranged everything satisfactorily. It only remained for her to write to Aunt Millicent explaining the situation and assuring her that she was perfectly content to remain for as long as was required.

Aunt Millicent wrote back by return; a sensible, no-nonsense letter pointing out that Rose should take full advantage of her stay in Holland and whenever possible see all that there was to see. Moreover, she should be thankful that she had been trained in a profession which was doing some good in the world. This rather tart missive ended with the hope that Rose would pay a visit as soon as possible when she returned to England for both she and Maggie were missing her. It made no mention of the letter which Aunt Millicent had received from Mr Werdmer ter Sane, explaining Rose's extended stay in his country, and pointing out that it was largely due to her devoted care that his small patient had recovered. Aunt Millicent had read the letter several times and become quite thoughtful over it.

When the time came Rose was quite sorry to leave the hospital; she had made some friends there in her limited free time, she had liked the Hoofdzuster and she got on well with Wim. She had even begun to have a limited knowledge of Amsterdam, exploring rather gingerly on her short evening walks. Now she would have to begin all over again in The Hague, but that might be fun for Christina had told her that it was a charming place with a great deal to see, near the sea and with some splendid shops. "And heaven knows you haven't had a chance to buy so much as a newspaper," she had declared. "I promise you that just as soon as we are organised at home you shall have your lost free time made up to you."

Dr ter Brandt came to fetch them, explaining in his quiet way that Christina had chosen that very day to start the baby. "It won't be just yet," he added, "and nothing would do but that I should collect you as we had arranged. I would have asked Sybren to bring you but he's in Brussels for a couple of days."

So Rose wasted no time in getting her patient into the car with all his bits and pieces, together with her case, and then she got in beside him. "How long does it take to get to The Hague?" she asked anxiously.

"It's forty miles more or less. About thirty minutes on the motorway."

They did it in twenty-nine and Rose guessed that under Dr ter Brandt's calm he was on edge to get home just as fast as he could. All the same, when they arrived at the substantial mansion on the outskirts of The Hague he took time to introduce the short stout man as Corvinus his butler and told her that he would assist her in any way he could, before he asked a quick question in his own language. Apparently the answer was satisfactory for the doctor carried his small son indoors and upstairs, bidding

Rose follow. The staircase was wide and led to a gallery above, lined with doors and with several passages leading from it. A door was flung open as they reached the head of the stairs and a small plump figure bounced out.

''Nanny,'' said Dr ter Brandt. ''Forgive me, Rose, but I must go to my wife.''

This left her smiling uncertainly at Nanny with little Duert, crowing with delight in her arms.

Nanny smiled back. She said something in Dutch and held out a hand and Rose proffered her own, rather awkwardly because of little Duert. Then she handed the little boy over to the other woman and was rewarded by her sudden smile. ''I'll fetch the things in,'' said Rose, and trotted off downstairs again to find Corvinus making his way across the hall, burdened by all the impedimenta they had brought from the hospital.

He gravely refused help. ''And if you will come with me,'' he begged her, to her great relief speaking a quite tolerable English, ''I will show you the nursery and your room. I understand that Nanny will be looking after the baby. Little Duert is in the night nursery and your room is next to it.''

''The baby?'' asked Rose quickly.

''Very shortly, nurse. So my wife tells me. She is the housekeeper here. She is English and her name is Sally and I'm sure she will be glad to help you in any way.''

Rose beamed at him, feeling at home. ''Nanny doesn't speak English?''

''No, nurse. She is from Friesland. But she is a most friendly person and very glad that you will be here to look after little Duert while she helps Mevrouw with the baby.''

She followed him across the hall and up the staircase then across the wide landing and into a passage leading from it. There were three doors, and he opened the middle one. ''Your room, Nurse. As soon as Sally is free she will come to welcome you. We are at the moment rather—rather…''

''At sixes and sevens?'' asked Rose helpfully and was rewarded by his ready smile. ''Don't bother about me, I'll unpack and then go and see Nanny.''

Unpacking didn't take long; she tidied her person, explored

her charming room and the splendid bathroom leading from it, took a look at the nursery and went through the passage to the landing once more. Nanny had come out of a door on the other side of it; Rose tapped and hearing a voice answer went inside. Little Duert was sitting in his high chair, playing with the teddy bear which went everywhere with him, and Nanny was getting ready for the baby. They smiled at each other and Rose dropped a kiss on the little boy's cheek, wondering how on earth they were to communicate.

It wasn't difficult after all; Sally came into the room, she was a plump little woman, her round face beaming. ''Just fancy, Nurse, Mevrouw ter Brandt has just had a little girl. Ever so quick and the doctor was just in time.'' Her eyes fell on little Duert. ''And here's our dear boy back home. My goodness, what a happy day. Now if you like to tell me how you would like things arranged I'll see to it. Nanny can't speak a word of English, but she's a dear soul; we're all very pleased to have you here, I can tell you, knowing how you've nursed him well again. I dare say the doctor will be along presently to talk to you. I'll send up some coffee and whatever you want for little Duert.'' She paused for breath and Rose said, ''You're awfully kind, I do hope I shan't make any extra work.''

''Lor, no, Nurse, there's enough of us and to spare.'' She trotted away and Rose went to look at the little boy. He seemed perfectly happy and had settled down just as though he had never been away from home. He would have dinner shortly and then have his nap, just as he had in the hospital; Mr Werdmer ter Sane had made it very clear that he was to be kept quiet, but she saw no difficulty there; he was as placid as his father.

She was piling bricks for him, hoping that Nanny, sitting and knitting at the table, wouldn't be jealous, when Dr ter Brandt came in. He had a bottle under his arm and three glasses in his hand.

''A daughter,'' he told them, ''a darling little girl who will be as beautiful as Chrissy. They're both asleep, Rose. I'm so sorry that you should arrive into such a disorganised household. Will you drink the baby's health—and Chrissy's, and forgive us?''

He turned to speak to Nanny who chuckled and shook his

hand and embarked on quite a speech. When she had finished Rose said, "Oh, that's marvellous news. Is your wife all right?"

"Wonderfully so." He smiled at her and she found herself wishing that some day a man would look like that about her. "Champagne, Rose..."

He picked up little Duert in one great arm. "You have a very small sister, if she's anything like your mother, she'll twist us all round her thumb."

The three of them drank their champagne before Dr ter Brandt said, "Now as to your days, Rose..."

He had it all worked out, telling her first and then explaining to Nanny in Fries. "Nanny doesn't mind in the least if you share the nursery; she will look after the baby and leave you to deal with little Duert; get him out of doors as much as you can and check his progress. Chrissy will be about in a day or so, and once she is, we both want you to have a day to yourself. We've grossly overworked you and intend to put that right." And when Rose murmured politely, he said, "I'm going to take this young man to see his mother and sister; if you'll give him his dinner when we get back while Nanny has hers, she'll keep an eye on his rest while we have lunch."

Later with little Duert fed and already asleep in his cot with Nanny keeping an eye on him, Rose went downstairs for her lunch, a meal she took with Dr ter Brandt. "Christina's still sleeping," he explained, "when she wakes I'm sure that she will want to see you and show you our daughter."

He glanced at her briefly. "I've phoned Sybren—he's delighted. He'll be back in a day or so; he'll be keeping an eye on Duert for another week or so. You're quite happy about the boy?"

Rose said that yes she was, and savoured the chocolate mousse Corvinus had served her.

"And we thought," went on Dr ter Brandt smoothly, "that you might like a free day on Saturday. I'll be home, Chrissy will be up and around and Nanny can take over for a while. We owe you so much, Rose—never-ending thanks for all you have done... We can never pay our debt."

Rose blushed. "I've liked looking after little Duert and I've been quite happy. I'd love to have a day off—I'll go to Amsterdam, there is such a lot I've got to see there.''

''A delightful city,'' agreed her host, ''but very changed I'm afraid. The smaller streets away from the centre haven't altered but the Dam Square and Kalverstraat have. Once Christina's back on her feet I'm sure she'll want to show you something of The Hague before you leave us.''

Later that afternoon she went to see Christina, sitting up in bed, a pretty colour in her cheeks. ''Isn't it marvellous?'' she demanded. ''A daughter, just what we wanted. Little Duert liked her too. Come and look at her.''

A darling baby, Rose conceded, and thought how super to have a baby in your own home with a midwife to look after you and Nanny and a doting husband to fill your room with flowers. She went away presently to fetch her little charge and sat him on the bed, where he stayed until it was time for his tea.

Rose had her dinner alone. Dr ter Brandt had his with his wife so that Rose, once she had settled little Duert for the night, went down to the dining-room where she sat in solitary state at a vast table while Corvinus looked after her. His manner towards her was fatherly so that she was emboldened to talk to him which stopped her feeling lonely.

She settled quickly enough into the routine Dr ter Brandt had mapped out; a very easy routine as it turned out, with nothing else to do but care for little Duert, keep an eye on his progress and play with him in the large garden around the house. And in a couple of days, Christina quite often joined them, lying on a chaise longue in the shade of an old mulberry tree in the centre of the vast lawn, the baby in her pram close by and Nanny keeping an eye on all of them. It was very pleasant; the idea of going back to St Bride's was by no means welcome but had to be faced. Another week, Rose decided, and little Duert would be fully recovered and there would be no more need for him to have her there.

Dr ter Brandt was away for most of the day, although he came home to lunch. There had been no sign of Mr Werdmer ter Sane. Rose kept faithfully to his instructions, made a careful report to

Dr ter Brandt each evening and wondered if she would ever see Mr Werdmer ter Sane again.

He came unaccompanied and soft-footed into the nursery, on Friday evening. Rose was presiding over her small charge's supper and had her back to the door. It was little Duert's crow of delight which made her turn round.

She spooned in the next mouthful; her good evening was pleasant and a bit cool which was a waste of time for he came to stand beside her chair and laid a large hand on her shoulder. He said chattily, ''How splendid to come back to such a contented household: Christina with her new baby, Duert like a lord of the earth, Nanny in transports, this little chap almost fit again…and you, Rose?''

''I'm very well, thank you,'' she said, and shovelled in another spoonful.

''Duert tells me that you are to have a day off on Saturday. What are your plans?''

She said a trifle tartly, ''I shall spend the day in Amsterdam, there are places I want to see…'' Before he could speak, ''I'm going by train because I want to.''

She wasn't looking at him which was a good thing because he was smiling. ''A splendid notion, you will be glad to get rid of us for a few hours. I suppose you wouldn't consider a companion—Amsterdam is sometimes a little dicey for a solitary stranger.''

''I don't know any companions,'' said Rose frostily, ''and I'd like to be by myself.''

''You know me,'' observed Mr Werdmer ter Sane surprisingly.

''I'd rather be by myself.'' She added belatedly, ''Thank you.''

''You are a stubborn girl, aren't you, Rose? Never mind, but oblige me by not going to the Dam Square and loitering there. It's the gathering place of any number of strange types these days.''

''I'll bear it in mind.'' She wiped little Duert's face and got up.

''You have no need to bother about me,'' she told him. ''I

expect you feel that it's your duty, but I'm quite sensible, you know. Being a plain girl has its advantages.''

He had taken his hand from her shoulder and turned away. Just as though she hadn't spoken he observed, ''I am responsible for you, you will be good enough to do as I ask.''

He went away without waiting for her to answer, which was a good thing because she had made up her mind then and there that the Dam Square would be the high spot of her day. She was a little muddled as to why she had decided that.

He came back later with Dr ter Brandt, and examined the little boy. Rose answered his pleasantly impersonal questions in like tone, agreed quietly that his patient was making splendid progress and listened with disquiet to the doctor telling his friend that of course he would stay to dinner. His invitation was repeated by Christina who had come to join them. ''And don't dare refuse,'' she begged him, ''this is my first dinner party since I had the baby, I shall dress up and so shall Rose.''

Dress up? thought Rose wildly, the only faintly suitable dress was the linen one, very plain even if a pretty blue. Second thoughts calmed her though; no one was likely to notice what she was wearing, the three of them would have a lot to talk about and Christina would be the centre of interest.

Once little Duert was in his cot and Nanny had come back into the room from her supper bearing the infant and begun on her preparations for the baby's comfort, Rose got ready for her evening. She had had her meals with Dr ter Brandt and now that Christina was about again, with her too, but they had been informal meals; true, the table had been set with silver and beautiful glass and the food had been cordon bleu, but Christina had worn housecoats—luxurious and glamorous, but nonetheless housecoats, so that Rose hadn't found her cotton skirts and tops too out of place. But this evening, she suspected, was to be more of a social event. She got into the blue linen, dressed her cloud of hair in the neatest possible fashion, took a quick look at her charge, and went downstairs, pausing to carry on one of the peculiar conversations with Nanny. It was surprising how well they understood each other and managed never to get into each other's way. Corvinus was in the hall, hovering to open the drawing-room door for her with a friendly smile. He liked Rose, she reminded him of Mevrouw ter Brandt, quite unlike the midwife, a haughty piece, even if she was good at her job, ordering him and Sally around and wanting her meals at all hours. He had been delighted to see her go. He held the door wide and thought that Rose looked very nice in her blue dress.

She was the last one down. Christina, in a silk dress which Rose instantly coveted, turned to smile at her as she hesitated just inside the door and the two men got up, the doctor to offer her a chair, making her feel instantly at ease with some gentle remark, while Mr Werdmer ter Sane went over to the drinks table and asked her what she would have.

After that it was all right, they absorbed her into their light-hearted talk until Corvinus appeared to tell them that dinner was served and Christina took Rose's arm and led her across the hall to the dining-room.

They dined superbly; asparagus salad with shrimps, *sole meunière,* roast partridge, followed by meringue tartlets, a glorious concoction of strawberries, meringue and whipped cream, all washed down by the doctor's best champagne, saved for such an occasion. They toasted the baby, little Duert, Christina, and then to her embarrassment, Rose. And afterwards they had coffee in the drawing-room before Rose excused herself on the plea that little Duert would need her attention. "And I'll be up to say good night to him presently," said Christina ter Brandt. "I know he's asleep and I've said good night once all ready...besides I have to feed the baby..."

Rose nodded understandingly; even with a faithful Nanny, Christina kept a very motherly eye on her children.

"And then you'll go to bed yourself, darling," declared her husband. "Good night, Rose. It has been a pleasant evening."

Mr Werdmer ter Sane opened the door for her with a casual "Good night, Rose." Her "good night, Sir" was uttered with a cold politeness and she heard him draw in his breath sharply. On her way upstairs she wondered if it annoyed him that she hadn't succumbed to his undoubted charm, despite the clear fact that he had no time for her.

She left the house soon after breakfast the next morning having given a careful report to Christina before she went. The doctor would be at home all day and Nanny was there too, she could enjoy herself without worry.

True to her plan, she took a train to Amsterdam, admiring the orderly countryside and the bright clean stations and once at the Central Station she got out and made her way without haste into the busy streets. She had a map with her and she knew where she wanted to go; Damrak first then the Palace, and despite Mr Werdmer ter Sane's warnings, the War Memorial in the Square. There was a large café on the corner of Damrak; she had her coffee watching the busy streets and the crowded pavements before crossing the road to the Palace, paying her entrance fee, and touring its grand but chilly interior. Not a place to be cosy in, she decided and went thankfully back into the sunshine. The square was crowded. She stopped to admire the patterned cobbles of its pavement and began to make her way towards the memorial. She didn't hurry; there was a street organ playing near the palace and she paused to look and listen before she sauntered on once more. There was a constant coming and going in the square; people going from Damrak across to Kalverstraat, Rokin or in the opposite direction to Raadhuisstraat. But as she reached its centre she saw that there was a small crowd round the memorial, young people mostly, good naturedly pushing and shoving and shouting to each other. They were sitting on the steps so that it was almost impossible to get through the mass of them. Rose walked round towards the back of the memorial until she thought she saw a gap. There was a man standing on the steps, making a speech though nobody much seemed to be listening and for the first few yards nobody impeded her progress. But then she was brought up short. A small wiry youth, grubby and dressed in jeans and a shirt, blocked her way.

Rose wished him a good morning politely, and asked him to let her pass. ''Just to see the war memorial,'' she explained politely, and then, ''do you understand me?''

''Cors I do. What's a pretty girl like you doing 'ere, anyway?''

''I've just told you,'' said Rose patiently.

''Nothing ter see.'' He glanced round at the youths around them. ''Is there, men?''

They had formed a ring round her. They meant no harm, she told herself, she was in the middle of a public square and she had only to shout…

She turned to make her way out of the crowd again but the circle had closed in on her, bent on teasing her.

Mr Werdmer ter Sane, driving slowly up Rokin towards the square, looked casually across to the crowds as he slid the car towards the outer edge of it. The usual lot, he thought idly, and then looked again. He had glimpsed a small figure in a blue dress standing very still.

He wasn't supposed to stop the car there but he did, to cross with quick strides to the fringe of the milling crowd. He clove his way through it, parted the ring of young men with a sweep of his arms and took Rose's arm. He didn't leave immediately, but delivered a short, pithy speech in his own language which his audience answered with sheepish mutterings before they melted sideways to allow him to urge Rose away.

It wasn't until they were crossing the square towards the car that he spoke.

"I am not a man to say 'I told you so'," he declared with a snap, "but you are behaving like a tiresome child, Rose. I told you not to get mixed up with that disreputable lot. Did I not make myself plain?"

"Oh, yes you did—that's why." She gave him a clear look and added soothingly, "You have no need to get cross. They wouldn't have bothered me."

He shook her arm. "That's where you are wrong. Oh, they wouldn't harm you, I dare say. They would have stolen your purse perhaps, or walked you off to one of the houseboats they live in…"

She came to a halt by the car. "I'm sure you meant well," she told him kindly. "Thank you. Now I'm going to the Rijksmuseum."

His grip didn't slacken. "Miss Timms must have been out of her mind," he observed bitterly. "She said that you were utterly trustworthy and sensible."

"Well, I hope I am when it comes to being a nurse. But today

I'm just me, doing what I want to do.'' She took his hand gently from her arm.

''Goodbye, Mr Werdmer ter Sane.''

She walked briskly away, happily unable to hear or understand his softly muttered Dutch swearwords. She would have to go soon, he thought, watching her small straight back disappearing down the street. She was a disturbing influence in his life and he wished whole-heartedly to be rid of it.

CHAPTER FOUR

ON HER WAY back to The Hague that early evening, Rose told herself that she had had a lovely day; she had spent hours looking at the paintings in the Rijksmuseum, had a snack lunch there and then hurried to Rembrandt's house, taken a quick look at the seventeenth-century Munttoren on the way there and then doubled back to go down the Kalverstraat to the Begijnsteeg, leading to the Begijnhof. She stayed there, looking at the fourteenth-century houses encircling the old church, given long ago to the English Reformed community in the city, and then presently wended her way back towards the station. She had seen almost all she had wanted to; the unhidden thought that she would have liked to take another look at Mr Werdmer ter Sane's house was one she didn't choose to contemplate.

Dr ter Brandt had suggested that she should take the particular train she was on and she had to admit that he had judged the time very nicely; she was pleasantly tired and although she had had a cup of tea in one of the many coffee shops, she had had, for the time being at least, quite enough. She would catch a tram from the station and be back at the ter Brandts' house in good time to shower and change her dress.

Corvinus was waiting outside the station and at the sight of him her heart leapt into her throat; something awful must have happened; little Duert—the baby... She should never have gone. She almost ran to him.

"Corvinus—is there something wrong? Little Duert...?"

"He's grand, Nurse. The doctor asked me to meet this train—he thought that you might be tired."

She could have hugged him. "Oh, how very kind. I was going to catch a tram."

"That's what Mevrouw thought." He beamed at her and ushered her into the car. "You have enjoyed your day, Nurse?"

"Yes, thank you—just roaming round looking at places I'd read about."

Which was true, she thought suddenly, but she had been escaping too, only she wasn't sure from what; surely not the kind household she was in? Certainly not little Duert. She stopped thinking then and remarked brightly about the charm of the city streets.

She was crossing the hall when Christina opened the drawing-room door and poked her head out. "There you are," she declared comfortably. "If you're not too tired come in for a minute and tell us what kind of a day you've had. The baby's not due for a feed for half an hour and little Duert's being bathed by Nanny—there's nothing for you to do."

The doctor was there too, and if he noticed Rose's quick glance round the room to see if anyone else was there, he gave no sign. He pulled a chair forward, pulled the bell-rope when his wife suggested that Rose might like a cup of tea, and invited her to tell them about her day.

She enlarged upon the Palace, skipped briskly over the little episode with Mr Werdmer ter Sane and plunged into a detailed account of the visits she had paid to the Begijnhof and Rembrandt's house. "I loved every minute of it"—she ignored the tiresome exchange with that gentleman—"I wish I'd had more time to potter through the smaller streets..."

"Oh, where Sybren lives," said Christina cheerfully, "the very best part of town, my dear—you must get him to take you on a stroll—the houses are lovely and all those funny little bridges." She smiled widely and turned her head as the door opened and he walked in. "We were just talking about you," she told him as he bent to kiss her cheek. "Rose wants to explore the streets in your neighbourhood."

He straightened and glanced across at Rose, sitting like a poker, her face very pink. "It's charming certainly," was all he said, and then, "I hope you enjoyed your day, Rose?"

"Very much, thank you." She got up. "I think I'll go and

tuck little Duert up, I dare say Nanny wants to do things for the baby. Thank you for the tea.''

Christina had seen the blush. ''That would be sweet of you. I'll be up presently then he can go to sleep and you'll have plenty of time to change.''

Dr ter Brandt had gone to open the door for her; Mr Werdmer ter Sane was lounging at the window. Rose slid thankfully away.

The moment the door was shut, Christina said, ''Now Sybren, just what happened in the Dam Square? Rose skated over whatever it was, terrified that we would ask questions. Now, give?''

He came and sat down opposite her and Dr ter Brandt sat beside his wife, idly taking her hand in his. ''I asked her not to go poking around the war memorial, oh, a day or so ago. I was driving through this morning and there she was surrounded by a gang of layabouts. I hauled her away and offered to drive her around in the car. She refused, of course.''

Christina said demurely, ''Well, yes. I expect you gave her a piece of your mind...''

''I pointed out that she had been foolish.''

''Naturally.'' Her voice was still demure and she avoided her husband's eye. ''She wasn't hurt or frightened?'' She glanced at his face, blandly calm, hiding his true feelings. ''She made light of it...''

''Neither.''

''Oh, good. Perhaps if she goes out again before she leaves us you could spare the time to show her some of the *grachten*.''

''Oh, I would have been delighted, Chrissy, but Mies van Toule is in Amsterdam for a couple of weeks—we haven't seen each other for some time...''

''Oh, Mies,'' observed Christina brightly, ''she's so pretty—beautiful really, is she here already? You're not going to back out of dining with us?''

He laughed. ''Of course not. And she doesn't get in until tomorrow, I'm going to pick her up at Schiphol.''

Very much later, when Sybren had gone and Rose had gone to bed and the house was quiet, Christina sat brushing her hair while the doctor pottered to and fro, pausing patiently to listen to her comments on the evening.

"They were so awfully polite at dinner," she mused out loud. "Darling, I thought that perhaps they were getting a bit interested in each other, didn't you? Sybren is such a dear, he ought to get married and be happy like us. Now he's going to get tangled up with that frightful Mies woman. And Rose—doesn't know she's in love with him, she only knows that he's there, if you see what I mean. Do you suppose she should go back to England before she discovers that? And will he miss her if she does?"

"My love, Sybren is a life-long friend but I would hesitate to guess at his intentions. I agree with you that Rose is probably in love with him and once she's discovered it for herself she will have the greatest difficulty in hiding it from anyone, and that includes Sybren. She's very vulnerable, I think, and I would hate to see her hurt. But Sybren is a dark horse; I think we'd better leave matters to sort themselves out."

The next day, being Sunday, it was Nanny's day off and since Christina was quite her old self again, that lady consented to be driven to the station to catch her train to Delft, where she visited her brother. It was heavenly weather, they took the children into the garden and sat about chatting and playing with them while the doctor, who had had a busy week, stretched out on his beautiful lawn and closed his eyes. Corvinus brought their coffee out to them and lunch was a delicious cold meal taken on the patio at the back of the house. Rose, nicely tired with so much sun, happy to see little Duert quite well again, and nicely stimulated by the ter Brandts' light hearted talk, didn't give Mr Werdmer ter Sane a single thought until she was on the point of sleep and then it was only to remember that his name hadn't been mentioned once all day.

He didn't come for two days and when he did, he was politely aloof, wanting to know how his little patient did and nothing more than that. He looked tired, Rose thought, carefully giving him chapter and verse and then waiting for any instructions.

They weren't quite what she had expected. "Well, Rose, I think we've done what we set out to do. This young man is as good as new; there's nothing more you can do for him; Nanny is quite capable of looking after him and of course Christina is a splendid mother."

He was standing quite squarely in front of her, staring down into her face. She said questioningly, "When would you like me to leave, Sir?"

"When the ter Brandts can arrange things. I shall look in on the boy whenever I visit. I'll go and see Christina now and drive down to see Duert at the hospital. I must thank you for the real help you have been both to myself and the ter Brandts. I dare say you will be glad to get back to St Bride's. Life has been quiet for you here."

She looked no higher than his top waistcoat button. "I've been happy here."

"I'm glad." He sounded kind in an impersonal way. "But you'll be glad to see your family again?"

"Oh, yes." She couldn't understand why she felt so utterly miserable; she had guessed that she would be leaving very shortly and it had been no surprise. She put out a hand. "Good-bye, Sir."

He took her hand and bent to kiss her cheek. He said on a sigh, "I suppose I shall always be Sir to you, Rose. I wish..." He was interrupted by Corvinus coming into the nursery with the information that a Juffrouw van Toule wished to speak to him on the telephone. He went away at once and left Rose wondering who she was. Well, she wasn't likely to know; she picked up little Duert and carried him off for his dinner; there was nothing like work to take one's mind off things.

It was arranged that she should leave in three days' time. She had no need to bother with the details, Dr ter Brandt told her in his calm way; if she would say what time of day she would like to travel he would book her flight and Corvinus would take her to Schiphol. He would also, he told her, telephone Miss Timms and perhaps Rose would like to phone later, and of course she was to phone her aunt as soon as possible.

It was super having everything settled for her; the ter Brandts were the nicest couple and she thought they were so happy and so sure of each other. She doubted if there were many devoted couples such as they were. Rose paused in the middle of a game of ball with little Duert and allowed herself to day-dream just for a moment—to have a husband who loved you and spent all his life making you happy—it would be wonderful

There was to be a farewell dinner too. ''Such a small return for your kindness and all you have done for us,'' declared Christina, ''and look—we're coming over to England in a month or so and we shall come and see you. We're coming on our own, I mean without Nanny—she'll go to her brother's. Duert's a dab hand at changing nappies and listen, Rose, when we get back home again, we want you to come and stay—as our guest, so please say you will. We'll let you know the dates as soon as we can and you can get leave. Please say you will.''

''Oh, I'd love to and thank you for asking me. When will that be?''

''About the end of August. Good, I'm so glad. Now do you want to do any shopping? I'll have little Duert this afternoon and you can go into town. Corvinus can take you and drop you off by the shops, and do take a taxi back.''

So Rose got into the blue dress again and was driven to the main shopping centre and after Corvinus had begged her to be careful and to be sure and get a taxi back, she set off; Noordeinde and Hoogstraat and Lange Voerhout, she explored them all thoroughly, the money she had had no chance to spend burning a hole in her pocket. Finally she found what she wanted; a soft pink crepe dress, very simply cut with a lower neckline than she had ever had before, long sleeves and a calf-length swirling skirt. It was rather more than she had expected to pay but she was feeling reckless and it would do very nicely for the hospital ball next winter. Very satisfied with herself she found six Delft blue coffee cups for her aunt and a silk scarf patterned all over with little Dutch figures for Maggie, and by then it was time to find a taxi and go back to the ter Brandts.

She felt sad on her last day as she packed her case; she had been happy and she had made friends who would remain her friends, not just disappear after a few months. Even if she never saw them after the promised holiday she would know that they were there. As for Mr Werdmer ter Sane, she wouldn't see him again, something which didn't matter at all, she told herself. The feeling of something lost must be because she was sorry to be leaving Holland.

She put little Duert to bed as usual on her last evening, had her usual amicable exchange with Nanny and went to dress. The pink was just as pretty in her own room as it had been in the shop. She pinned up her hair, did her face with care, and then went downstairs. The ter Brandts were in the drawing-room in all the elegance of black tie and silvery chiffon and pearls. ''Oh, very nice,'' observed Christina, ''pink suits you and such a pretty dress—where did you get it?''

They swept her along between them and got into the car and somehow between them made her feel confident that she didn't look so bad after all.

They went to the Royal in Woorhout, long established, fashionable and very, very expensive. It was almost full and they had a table in the window with a splendid view of the restaurant around them. Rose, drinking the dry sherry the doctor suggested, looked around her. It was an elegant place and being a Saturday evening there would be dancing; hence the black ties and well-dressed women, she supposed. She ate her way happily through spinach tartlets, chicken à la King, an enormous confection of ice cream, chocolate and whipped cream, and drank the champagne in her glass. The evening, as far as she was concerned, was nothing short of heaven, with the three of them skimming over any number of subjects in a light-hearted manner. They were drinking their coffee when she glanced across the restaurant and saw Mr Werdmer ter Sane sitting at a table quite close by. There was a girl with him; a beautiful girl with dark hair curling around her shoulders, wearing a red dress with one sleeve and the other shoulder bare. She was laughing a lot but Mr Werdmer ter Sane wasn't: he was smiling certainly but he looked, even at that distance, tired and withdrawn. He looked up and saw Rose and stared at her, unsmiling, so that she went very pink. The doctor, happening to glance at her, saw the look on her face and followed her gaze. His own remained impassive as he lifted a hand in greeting. Christina had seen him too by now.

"Sybren's here," she declared, "with that Mies girl." She caught her husband's eye and went on brightly, "This place is full tonight, isn't it? It's lovely at Christmas time, Rose, and at New Year, everyone wears their very best dress and we dance for hours. Do you go to many dances in London?"

Rose was forced to answer her; she had got her blush under control and said in her quiet way, "Well, not many—the hospital ball of course, but you see, I'd need a partner..."

The doctor steered the talk away from the pitfalls ahead. "Well, will you get a few days leave?" he asked kindly. "I did mention to Miss Timms that you hadn't had anything like the off-duty you're entitled to..." He led the conversation back to trivialities and presently when they got up to go called a casual greeting to his friend as they passed their table. Christina greeted him too although she didn't stop and Rose summoned a stiff little smile, puzzling as to why she should feel so shaken at the sight of Mr Werdmer ter Sane; after all they had bidden each other goodbye; it was a pity he hadn't been able to finish what he had been saying when he was called away. And he had looked at her so strangely across the restaurant, as though he was annoyed to see her again. Perhaps he was, she reflected soberly, after all, he had never really liked her as a person even while he had conceded that she was a good nurse.

In the car she said wistfully, "What a beautiful girl that was..."

"With Sybren—very beautiful." Christina's voice was dry. "She's to be seen in all the best places..."

Saying goodbye the next day was difficult; Rose kissed little

Duert's chubby cheek, kissed Christina, was kissed by Dr ter Brandt, bade farewell to Nanny and Sally and got into the car with Corvinus. She felt as though she were leaving some of herself behind, although she told herself robustly that it was no more than an episode which in a few months would be forgotten.

Going through the gate to the plane she told herself that she would start forgetting now, only it wasn't as easy as that; Mr Werdmer ter Sane's face, with that look of annoyance, superimposed itself on her more prosaic thoughts about Miss Timms, St Bride's and the likelihood of holidays.

She had chosen to take a morning flight; she reached St Bride's just as first dinner was over so that several of her friends were crowded into the staff nurses' sitting-room, drinking tea. They fell upon her with gratifying pleasure, plying her with strong tea and a flurry of questions: there was no time to answer them all; they rushed back on duty and she was left to unpack, get her uniform ready for the next morning and then go down to the office to report to Miss Timms.

She was surprised to find that lady unusually gracious. ''You have done well, Staff Nurse,'' she was told. ''Both Dr ter Brandt and Mr Werdmer ter Sane have spoken highly of you, indeed Mr Werdmer ter Sane has written to Mr Cresswell in glowing terms and has asked me if I will allow you to make up the off-duty you have had to give up while you were in Holland. I think I can see my way to allowing you four days' leave, Staff Nurse. If you will go and see Sister Cummins and tell her that you will be back on Thursday at one o'clock, there is no reason why you should not be free as from now.''

So Rose flew back to her room, packed a bag once more, phoned her aunt and dashed out to catch a bus to the station. She caught a train to Daventry with minutes to spare and spent the hour-long journey thinking of the things she would do in the next four days.

She was in time to catch the late afternoon bus to Ashby St Ledgers. It was packed and she knew most of the passengers by sight so that they chatted and the short journey passed quickly.

The bus was a local one and the driver obligingly stopped whenever anyone wanted to alight, so that progress through the village was slow. They passed the church and the Coach and Horses and the Gate House where the Gunpowder Plot had been hatched, and finally drew to a halt on the corner of a narrow lane. Aunt Millicent's cottage, standing aslant to the village street, looked peaceful and picture-book pretty, its thatched roof in perfect order, its stone walls whitewashed. Rose bade the driver goodbye, picked up her case and went the few yards down the lane to the gate. The path to the cottage was brick with not a weed in sight, and bordered by a lavender hedge along its entire length. There was a wide stretch of grass to one side of the cottage leading to the kitchen garden at the back and Rose had no doubt that the beans and peas and potatoes were growing in an orderly manner; they wouldn't dare to do otherwise under Aunt Millicent's eye.

She was suddenly happy and ran up the path to the door and pushed it wide open. ''I'm here, Aunt Millicent—Maggie...''

Both ladies came into the narrow hall to welcome her, each in her own fashion. ''Nice to see you,'' said her aunt. ''You look tired, my dear, I'm glad they let you come home...''

Rose hugged her, it was nice to hear Aunt Millicent say that; she felt a sudden urge to burst into tears, luckily prevented by Maggie's urgent, ''Now you sit down this minute, the pair of you. I'll bring a nice tray of tea and you can sit for half an hour. Worn to the socket you must be—all very well that man praising you to the skies, a lot of good that does if a body's worn to a thread.''

She bustled away to the kitchen and Rose asked, ''What man? And do I look so awful?''

''Tired—I said so,'' observed Miss Curtis. ''Mister Werdmer ter Sane wrote to me—he seemed very impressed with your work; said you'd been invaluable and regretted the loss of your free time. I had a charming letter from Mevrouw ter Brandt too.'' She smiled as they sat down opposite each other in the low-ceilinged room. ''You've earned your holiday, Rose.''

Maggie came in with the tea then and since she was almost one of the family, she fetched a cup for herself and listened while Rose told them the more interesting bits about her stay in Amsterdam and The Hague.

Presently she went away, albeit reluctantly, to see about supper and Rose sat back in the shabby armchair that was so comfortable, nicely filled with tea and several slices of Maggie's lardy cake.

''Were you homesick?'' asked her aunt.

''No I didn't have time for that and by the time I did everyone was so nice that I felt almost at home. The ter Brandts were so kind...''

''And Mr Werdmer ter Sane?''

''Kind?'' She thought about it. ''Well, yes in a way. You see, I was the nurse there to do as he asked; I don't really think that he thought of me as a person, if you see what I mean.''

''Married?'' Aunt Millicent's voice was casual.

''No, but he's got a girl friend, I don't know if they are engaged yet—she'd been away but she came back to Amsterdam while I was there, she's like a fashion-plate—very, very pretty and not a hair out of place and when I saw her she was wearing a way-out dress—everyone was looking at her.''

Aunt Millicent gave a snort. ''What does she do for a living?''

''Do? Oh Aunt Millicent, girls like her don't work. I expect she has loads of money, anyway.''

''There's no accounting for tastes,'' observed Miss Curtis, a remark which might have meant anything.

The weather was heavenly; Rose in a rather faded cotton dress which had luckily been found in a cupboard in her bedroom, gardened under her aunt's stern guidance, helped around the house, and strolled through the lanes and fields round the village. Days had never gone so fast, the idea of St Bride's and the narrow busy streets round the hospital filled her with a longing to stay where she was, but at least, she told herself, she would be coming back again; the cottage would still be there for years to come and she was sure of a welcome. It was a pity she felt so unsettled though; she tried to get to the bottom of it as she hung out the sheets for Maggie before breakfast on her last day. She had almost finished when the gate creaked.

She whipped round to see who it was, struck with devastatingly final clarity by the knowledge that just for a split second she had hoped that it was Mr Werdmer ter Sane. Of course, it wasn't; Henry, the boy from the village shop, was clomping up the path with the day's news. He shouted a cheerful greeting and she answered him in a rather wispy voice, shocked at her own thoughts. She pegged the last sheet and then stood looking at it. All these days she had been wanting to see him again only she hadn't admitted it, even to herself. It was extremely foolish of her to wish it; even if they did meet again no good would come of it. Just for a moment common sense fled from her sensible head and day-dreams took over; supposing, just supposing, they were to meet again and he was glad to see her; looked at her as he had looked at the beautiful Mies, told her that he had missed her. Rose stood in the bright morning sunshine, lost in her dream.

It only lasted a minute or two; she picked up the washing-basket and started back to the kitchen door. ''You are daft, Rose.'' she muttered, ''you think you've fallen in love with him; ten to one if you met him again you'd turn and run.'' A lie if ever there was one.

She hated leaving the next morning, the village lay peaceful under warm sunshine and lovely blue skies, it didn't seem possible that she was in the same world when she got out of the taxi at St Bride's; the sun wasn't warm, it was hot, piercing the motionless air laden with petrol fumes, even the blue sky seemed to have shrunk. Rose went over to the nurses' home and unpacked and got into her uniform and went down to dinner in the canteen. All her friends were there and she cheered up under the warmth of their greetings, and regaled her with the latest hospital gossip. But half way through a particularly spicy titbit about the new surgical houseman and Mr Cresswell, Sadie stopped and said, ''Rose, you're not with us—what's the matter? You're *distraite*—not just fed up at coming back.'' She started to say something else but the look on Rose's face stopped her. She finished lamely, ''Oh, well, I dare say you are hating it all—it's beastly coming back... Let's all get together over a pot of tea after we're off duty and then we can hear all about Holland.''

Rose cast her a thankful look. ''Okay, Maggie gave me a super cake, we can have that with the tea.''

Sister Cummins was glad to see her back and there were still several small patients left from before Rose had gone to Holland. There were a lot of new little faces too and she plunged straight into the busy routine. Half way through the afternoon Miss Timms sent for her.

''You enjoyed your leave, Staff Nurse?'' she wanted to know.

Rose said that yes, she had, thank you.

''I am told,'' said Miss Timms with dignified geniality, ''by Dr ter Brandt, that he and his wife wish you to pay them a visit later in the summer. This may cause some inconvenience on Sister Cummins' ward but I feel that an effort must be made to accede to his request. You will let Sister Cummins know the date as soon as possible, Staff Nurse, so that things may be arranged satisfactorily.''

She nodded her rigidly coiffed head and Rose made a speedy exit before Miss Timms could have second thoughts. The ter Brandts weren't coming to England for at least a month and they had asked her to go after that...a lot could happen in that time and Miss Timms could change her mind.

The afternoon and evening seemed endless but at last she was off duty, her shoes off, comfortably dressing-gowned, cutting Maggie's cake while mugs of tea were handed round. The cake eaten, and mugs refilled, someone asked: ''Well, what happened in Amsterdam or wherever it was Rose? Did you meet anyone groovy? What were the housemen like? And what about that super specimen who came over here to fetch you?''

''Mister Werdmer ter Sane,'' said Rose; she was amazed how calm and indifferent her voice sounded while her heart thumped and thudded at the mere mention of his name. ''Yes, of course,

I saw him—every day at first—little Duert was very ill and no one quite knew what would happen.''

''Did he take you out?''

''Heavens no. I was the nurse, remember. Besides he's got a steady—a simply ravishing girl...''

It was Sadie who said in a disappointed voice: ''Oh, has he? I suppose he'd forgotten all about me—us, calling at his house?''

''No, as a matter of fact, he hadn't—he spoke of you—he certainly hadn't forgotten you, Sadie.''

There was a burst of laughter. ''Good old Sadie, competing with the Dutch glamour girl.'' A voice from the back cried, ''You should have gone instead of Rose.'' Everyone laughed again, but it was kind laughter; they all liked Rose. They were a little taken aback at her fervent, ''Oh, I wish you had, Sadie.'' She wouldn't have fallen in love with him then, would she? She would have remained heart-whole, content to carve a career for herself in the nursing world, her simple sensible head clear of silly dreams about a handsome, aloof Dutchman, who she was pretty certain had already forgotten all about her.

But the ter Brandts hadn't forgotten her; the even balance of her busy days was disturbed by a letter from Christina ter Brandt; they had decided to come to England earlier than they had planned; they would be staying in London for a few days, and would she come to see them? Dinner, suggested Christina, or failing a free evening, lunch and she would phone as soon as they arrived during the following week, so that they could plan something. The baby flourished and little Duert was as good as new and they all sent their love, and that included Nanny, Corvinus and Sally. There was not one word about Sybren Werdmer ter Sane.

Rose wrote back cautiously: she would love to see them all again but it depended on whether she was free; Miss Timms had already offered her leave when she wanted it and she wasn't going to spoil her chances for that. It was madness, she told herself over and over again, to see Mr Werdmer ter Sane again, but nothing was going to stop her. She was sensible enough to know that it would do her no good; the quicker she forgot about him the better, only she was finding it singularly difficult to shake him off. Going round the ward, taking temperatures, adjusting drips, feeding the small creatures who couldn't for the time being, feed themselves, his face rose before her eyes a dozen times a day. It was most inconvenient, and such a waste of time, he would have consigned her to oblivion.

He might have wished to do so, but unwillingly enough, he had thought of her a good deal on a number of occasions. Why, he asked himself irritably, should a small plain girl, unfashionable as to dress and lacking in witty conversation, remain so persistently in his head to annoy him? And why, in heaven's name, did he cancel everything when Mr Cresswell phoned him and asked him if he would be good enough to cooperate with him on a particularly tricky operation at St Bride's and accept with alacrity?!

He arrived at St Bride's quite early in the morning and joined Mr Creswell there, and the first person he saw, probably because he was looking for her, was Rose.

She had not known that he was coming; Sister Cummins had told her that the toddler with cancer of the leg was to be operated upon by Mr Cresswell but she hadn't said a word about anyone else taking part in it. Rose knew that it was a difficult operation; very few had been attempted so far but if it were successful it should be a miraculous recovery for the child. Rose, who had been specialing the little girl, had just bathed and fed her when the two surgeons arrived. Mr Cresswell's "Good morning, Rose" was genial, Mr Werdmer ter Sane gave her a tight-lipped greeting which instantly quenched the glow of delight which had enveloped her at the sight of him. She muttered something in reply, aware that she must appear gauche, the very last thing that she would wish to be, so that at once she became the very epitome of professional perfection, answering Mr Cresswell's questions in a colourless and correct voice, which made him exclaim, "Good God, Rose, have you swallowed the poker?" A remark which brought her down from the heights of correctness to her usual sensible manner. She even replied to several of Mr Werdmer ter Sane's civil remarks in her usual calm manner and sat on the side of the cot with the toddler on her lap while they gently examined her. Mr Werdmer ter Sane had to bend very close so that his handsome features were only inches away and she could see the grey hair which grew as thickly as the fair. She closed her eyes so as not to see it, and he, looking up for a moment, stared at her face; she might not be pretty but the dark lashes sweeping her cheeks were some of the longest and curliest he had ever seen. He frowned quite fiercely so that when she opened them again it was to meet his beetling brows. She met his look with a calm she didn't feel; he disliked her even more than she had thought. No, dislike wasn't the word, indifferent described the stare he had given her.

They would operate in two days' time; there were tests to be carried out first and the parents had to be told of the risks and the chance of success. "And you will bring the child to theatre," said Mr Cresswell, "and special her afterwards, that'll knock your off-duty for six, but you must be used to that by now, Rose. I'll see Sister Cummins when she comes on duty and get things fixed up. We'll operate at eight o'clock and it'll take all of seven hours—perhaps more. What do you say, Sybren?"

"Seven with luck on our side."

The two men wandered off down the ward, and Rose, nicely thoughtful of their needs, sent the third-year student nurse after them to see that they had the coffee they would almost certainly expect. It had been a shock seeing Mr Werdmer ter Sane again but she had no doubt that by the time they met again in theatre she would have come to terms with the situation. Two days would be ample time in which to pull herself together.

CHAPTER FIVE

ROSE WORKED very hard at getting herself into a rational frame of mind, helped considerably by not seeing Mr Werdmer ter Sane during the next two days. He came on to the ward but always while she was off-duty, so that she received his and Mr Cresswell's instructions through Sister Cummins. But while she was on duty at least she had little time to think about him, the toddler was ill, would indeed die if the operation wasn't successful, and over and above that, there were other ill children in the ward in need of constant attention. The student nurses worked hard but there were some treatments they weren't able to do so that Rose and Sister Cummins had more than enough on their hands. On the evening before the operation Sister Cummins, giving the report to Rose before she went off-duty for the evening, remarked that she would be glad when it was all over. "I know we cope with all kinds of surgery, but this is going to be an all-day affair and even after that, Shirley will need to be specialed...I know Mr Cresswell wants you to do that, but leaves us very short-handed." She frowned. "I did suggest to Mr Werdmer ter Sane that the specialing could be done by a third-year nurse, even a qualified nurse from another ward if I could borrow one, but he was adamant. You or no one. Well, I can't blame him, you're a good nurse and it'll be a feather in our caps—yours especially, if Shirley pulls through." She went to the office door on her way off duty. "Your time off may have to be shelved for a day or two but you know that, don't you, Staff? I'll see it's made up to you."

There were two student nurses on with Rose until the night staff arrived. They went softly round the ward, settled the little ones for the night and she checked dressings and the very ill children. Shirley was already in a side ward and asleep, too young to bother about what was to happen next and too ill to mind. Rose was taking her temperature when Mr Werdmer ter Sane came quietly in.

Rose finished what she was doing, aware that her heart was behaving badly again and thankful that in the darkened ward he couldn't see her face.

His "Hullo, Rose", was quiet and devoid of expression. She murmured back at him, fastened the cot side soundlessly and waited for him to speak.

She had no idea what he was going to say and was taken aback when he said, "Christina and Duert send their love and so does little Duert. You know they are coming over soon?" And at her surprised nod, "I'm to tell you that Christina will phone you at the end of the week. She knows about Shirley and realises that you won't be free until then."

Rose said, "Oh, yes. Well..." and found her head empty of words. The two days hadn't been enough, she doubted very much if two years would be enough either, even two hundred.

Mr Werdmer ter Sane eyed her narrowly across the cot. Even in the dim light she looked rather plain for she was very tired and hungry for her supper. The thought passed through his mind that his strange wish to see her again must have been born of imagination, she was just about the least glamorous girl he had ever set eyes on. "Well, shall we go over your instructions for tomorrow?" he asked briskly, amazed that he had had some vague idea of inviting her out to supper.

They parted presently with polite good nights, he to go to the consultants' room to have a final brief talk with Mr Cresswell and his registrar, and she to the office where the night staff were waiting impatiently for the report. It took longer than usual for there were all the extra instructions for Shirley's pre-op treatment. By the time Rose got to the canteen, suppers were over and the counter was bare. The night cook and her companions in the kitchen were getting the night nurses' midnight meal ready. Rose went over to her room and then joined her friends in Sadie's room to drink tea and eat biscuits. But she was still hungry. There was a coffee stall down the street from the hospital where one could buy hot baked potatoes and pies. She fetched her purse and nipped out of a side door, bent on buying hot potatoes for herself and various of her friends. It was just unfortunate that on her return she should run full tilt into Mr Werdmer ter Sane crossing the forecourt to his car. He stood her upright and looked at the bag of potatoes she was clasping with both hands, and although he hadn't said a word she felt compelled to speak. "So sorry, Sir—I was in a hurry..."

"Supper?"

"Yes, I was too late for the canteen." She gave him a disconcertingly clear look from her brown eyes and slipped past him and through the side door again. Mr Werdmer ter Sane, bidden to dine with friends at the Savoy, angrily spurned the feeling of positively tender compassion which seized him. The ridiculous thought that he would like to see her smile, hear her laugh, take the pins out of her severe bun of hair and buy her more flowers than she could hold in her arms, received the same severe treatment.

He muttered a few telling phrases in his own language, got into his car and drove to his hotel to change for the dinner party. The friends he was dining with had a charming daughter, pretty and witty and always dressed in the forefront of fashion. Undoubtedly she would dispel the extraordinary ideas he had; he had known her for some time and was aware, without conceit, that she would marry him if he asked her. He didn't love her and he was sure that she didn't love him, but they had similar interests and he had the money which she found essential to her way of life. He had come to the conclusion some years ago that there was to be no ideal woman for him; for one thing, he wasn't sure what she would be like.

The dinner party was delightful, Charmian, the daughter, wittier and prettier than ever, the food delicious. Half way through the *boeuf bourguignon,* he found himself wishing that he was eating baked potatoes with Rose. The thought merely made him more attentive to Charmian, nonetheless he left early with the pretext that he was operating early the next morning.

Rose, gobbling her potato with a healthy appetite, listened to the chatter around her without hearing it. She was thinking lovingly of Mr Werdmer ter Sane, blissfully aware that she would see him for hours on end the next day even though they wouldn't exchange a word. But just to be there, watching him operate was something she recognised as a bonus. He would go back to Holland almost at once, she supposed, for he was a busy man but in the meantime she would see him again. It was a pity that they had met on her way back with the potatoes... She was roused from her thoughts by someone wanting to know if she intended to apply for the post of junior night sister which was unexpectedly vacant at the end of the month. No one seemed to want it—night duty was never popular, but as Sadie pointed out, it was a useful stepping off ground for a day sister's post if one became vacant. "Not that I want it," said Sadie, tossing her curls, "I dare say we'll get married next year. Rose, you are going to be a bridesmaid so don't go deciding on any holidays until I know the date."

Rose went on duty early so that she could do all the last-minute chores for Shirley before she took the child to the theatre. The small leg had already been prepped; she sat the drowsy child on her lap and tied the theatre gown down her back, and sat quietly then with Shirley cuddled up to her own theatre gown. Shirley opened a sleepy eye and Rose beamed down at her. "Beautiful moppet," she said softly, "you'll grow up to be a gorgeous princess and a handsome prince will come along and marry you and you'll be happy ever after and your leg will never hurt again, so just you close that eye and go to sleep again and when you wake up I'll be here to tell you more about that prince."

Mr Werdmer ter Sane, on the ward earlier than expected, paused in the doorway and listened to Rose's soft voice, staring at her small straight back and neat head crowned by the stiffly frilled cap the staff nurses wore. He was sure, without conceit, that if any one could save Shirley's leg, he could, at the same time he was glad that Rose would be there in theatre; she was just as sure as he was and two determined people were so much better than one. He retreated soundlessly and then retraced his steps, and made just enough noise for her to hear him come.

His "Good morning, Rose", was pleasantly civil, he bent over Shirley for a moment, remarked that he would see them in the theatre very shortly, suggested that Rose should carry the child there instead of using the usual trolley, and went away again.

Shirley didn't rouse as Rose wrapped her in a blanket and carried her the short journey to the theatre wing. The anaesthetist grunted at her as she laid the child carefully down; he was a dour Scot who had a marvellous way with children but wasted few words on anyone else. Rose said good morning cheerfully in answer to the grunt and began her various duties without fuss. She liked theatre and the surgeons liked to have her there; she was quiet and did what she was told at once and had a tremendous capacity for staying on her feet for hours at a stretch. Mr Cresswell, coming in to take a look, said: "Hullo Rose, ready for a hard day's work, I hope," and went away again and presently they were all in theatre, ready to start.

Mr Werdmer ter Sane was operating; nobody had attempted that particular surgery in England, although he had had success with two cases in Vienna, so that he would take the lead, inaugurating a new technique which Mr Cresswell would continue with further cases. It was daring, but Shirley was going to die if nothing was done and the previous patients were doing well. He bent his great height over the table and started his work.

It was long, tedious and painstaking work; the two men with the registrar and one of the house surgeons assisting, cut, sawed, dissected, trimmed, pinned and plated with controlled patience, muttering to each other from time to time, pausing momentarily to assess their work. Theatre Sister, known throughout the hospital as Clean Kate because of her obsessive cleanliness, stood stolidly passing instruments and swabs for the almost six hours which the operation took, although the scrubbed staff nurse backing her up was replaced half way through by a second. The theatre nurses did the same, but Rose stayed where she was by the anaesthetist, with a short break for a cup of coffee towards midday. The operation was going well; when she wasn't attending to the anaesthetist's wants, Rose watched Mr Werdmer ter Sane's large hands fitting things together with the precision of a skilled needlewoman making a patchwork quilt. She found it fascinating, hardly noticing the hours slipping away, until at length he and Mr Cresswell stood back leaving the registrar to the final stitching. After a moment they stripped off their gloves, thanked everyone there for their help and left the theatre. Rose pictured them swallowing hot coffee and devouring sandwiches in Sister's office; they must be famished, and come to think of it she was famished too.

It was another hour before she was relieved for her own meal. First there was Shirley to escort to intensive care where she would remain for the rest of the day and the following night and in the morning she would be transferred back into Rose's care.

Midday dinner had been cleared away for an hour or more by the time she got to the canteen but cold meat and pickles and a bowl of lettuce had been left for those who had been in theatre. Rose ate this sustaining but unexciting meal in the company of the theatre staff and then went back to the ward, for there were still two hours of duty to get through.

Not that she had time to grumble about that; the room in which Shirley was to be nursed had to be prepared, the equipment, and there was a lot of it, tested and put in place, the panic trolley positioned so that it could be got at in seconds, and when Rose was at last satisfied that everything was as it should be, there were a couple of dressings to do on the ward before Sister Cummins came on duty for the evening. By the time she had given the report, gone over the operation in detail, conned the off-duty with her so that there would be sufficient staff to cover the next day, it was half past five.

Too late for tea and too early for supper. She went to her room, had a shower and got into a cotton dress, tied her hair back and looked at her clock. There was still almost an hour before the canteen would be open and she was too tired to get on a bus and go to one of the cheaper restaurants in Oxford Street. She lolled out of the window; it was such a lovely evening that even the shabby roofs and chimney pots around the hospital looked different. Then someone tapped on the door and she said "Come in" without looking round. "Don't ask me to go out," she began and saw that it was the home warden, a middle-aged bony lady of uncertain age who gave the strong impression of disapproving of anyone under the age of forty. She said now in a severe voice, "There's someone in the visitor's room to see you."

"Not me," said Rose instantly, "I don't know anyone...I expect it's Staff Nurse Chumley you want, she's got dozens of boy friends."

The warden gave her a nasty look. "I don't make mistakes in names," she observed chillingly. "Staff Nurse Comely I was told to fetch, and that's what I'm doing."

"Do you know who it is?"

"No, I do not. Nor is it my business to ask." She turned such a basilisk stare upon Rose that she said, "Oh, well I suppose I'd better go down."

She skipped past the warden who warned, "Not the Sister's lift, Staff Nurse."

So of course Rose felt compelled to do exactly what she was told not to do.

The visitor's room had been designed to damp any ardour felt by the nurses' men friends, it smelled of polish and the linoleum floor struck chill into their hearts as well as their feet. The chairs were tubular steel and imitation leather and gave no comfort to the sitter. There was a plain wooden table in the exact centre with a rubber plant upon it.

Rose opened the door slowly, wondering who she would see. The sight of Mr Werdmer ter Sane sitting on the table with the rubber plant was rather more than she had expected. Her "Oh, heavens above, it's you," was spontaneous if unflattering. She paused inside the door and he got to his feet making the small room even smaller.

"In person, Rose. We've had a hard day; I wondered if we might enjoy one of your high teas together?"

She goggled at him. "High tea?" she repeated unnecessarily. "They don't have high tea in the sort of restaurant you'd go to."

"Something which must be remedied. The porter tells me that there's a small restaurant opposite Charing Cross station. I don't know about you but I'm famished."

She stayed where she was, her hand still on the door knob. "Why do you want to take me?" she asked. "There's Sadie...I know she's off this evening."

He said patiently, "That was quite a job we did today, I'd like to mull it over with someone who knows what I'm talking about."

She nodded her head, it wasn't exactly a flattering reason and it didn't do much for her ego, but she understood how he felt.

"Yes, it's not fashionable but the food's good and they don't rush you."

"Let's go then?"

She hesitated. "My hair—and I haven't got my purse."

"The hair's fine." Like a small girl's, he thought, very clean and shining. "And you won't need a purse, will you? I've a handkerchief with me and small change." He added kindly, "Your face doesn't need any fussing over."

She didn't answer, well aware that no amount of fussing would turn her into a beauty. "Then I'm ready," she told him quietly.

He ignored his car in the park. "Nowhere to leave it," he explained, "we can take a taxi."

Which they did, not speaking much as they were driven from the East End along the Commercial Road and Fleet Street and into the Strand. The restaurant looked welcoming as they stood looking at it from the pavement.

"It's not in the least like that marvellous place the ter Brandts took me to," observed Rose doubtfully.

He didn't answer her, but swept her inside and sat her down

at a table for two in the window, and then handed her the menu and said, ''Now, choose our high tea.''

The place was brightly lit even though it was barely dusk and the smell of food was delicious. Besides it was almost full of customers, eating and drinking and talking and laughing. Rose was aware that it was hardly her companion's scene but since he wanted high tea he was going to get it.

''Tea for two,'' she told him, ''a pot of tea—bacon and egg and sausages and tomatoes, toast and butter, jam and a plate of cakes.'' She cast a quick look at him but not a muscle of his face moved. ''Scottish high tea has scones, baps and soda bread,'' she explained.

''It sounds delightful but we'll make do with the English version, shall we?'' And when the waitress arrived he ordered everything she had suggested, and when the tray of food arrived he ate it with an enjoyment which was much enhanced by the sight of Rose, obviously enjoying every mouthful. And if he would have liked something else to drink other than the strong tea he was offered he didn't say so, and throughout the meal he talked of this and that and in such an undemanding way, and it wasn't until Rose had polished off a Danish pastry and poured the last of the tea, that he spoke of the operation that day. He hadn't meant to do more than make some light reference to it although he had told her otherwise, but that, he had to admit, had been because he wanted an excuse to take her out. A meal at Lyons was hardly his idea of taking a girl out, but then Rose wasn't his kind of girl. He couldn't call to mind any of his girl friends who would have listened to him boring on about pins and plates and shortening of the bone. But Rose wasn't bored. What was more, she asked sensible questions and listened to the answers. He paused presently. ''Am I boring you?''

She gave him the clear look he found so disquieting. ''No, I wanted to ask all sorts of questions in the theatre. It was a splendid operation, the first of many I hope. Just think, Shirley will grow up and be able to dance and run...''

''Her leg will be almost three inches shorter.''

"It's surely possible to get a special shoe. And she'll be alive..."

"You don't think that will prevent her from marrying?"

"Why ever should it? If someone falls in love with her—and she's going to grow into a very pretty girl, you know—do you suppose he'll care about that? If he loves her? Look at the thousands of plain girls who get married..." She stopped and the colour rushed into her face. But she didn't look away.

"Beauty is in the eye of the beholder," his voice was very kind but not in the least pitying. "And I don't believe that there is a living soul who is completely plain. A girl with a plain face may have beautiful legs or a lovely body or magnificent eyes, sometimes all three. Most fortunately, as you observed, Shirley is a pretty child and will grow into a pretty woman, probably clever enough to know how to conceal her damaged leg to her best advantage."

"You've given her that chance."

"Yes, but I couldn't have done that without help from other people, you for one." He smiled suddenly and her heart rocked. "Shall we have another pot of tea?"

With the coming of the fresh pot came fresh conversation. She wasn't quite sure how it had all started, but she found herself telling him about her stepmother and Aunt Millicent and Maggie, only at the last minute did she remember not to let him know where Aunt Millicent lived. She had no idea why she wanted to keep that a secret but it seemed important that she should. And presently their talk swung back to St Bride's which reminded Rose to say, "Sadie hopes she'll see you again before you go away. She's one of the nicest people I know—we've been friends from the first day we started training."

"A charming girl," was all he was going to say. "I shall be in London for a few more days, just to see Shirley turn the corner and at the same time look up a few old friends."

"I expect you have a great many?" Rose put down her cup. "Would you mind if we went back now? I'm on duty at half past seven tomorrow morning."

He lifted a finger for the bill. ''Until when?''

''Oh, just for a couple of days I'll be on all day except when I go to a meal. It's much better if there are just two of us on a special case like Shirley.''

They went out into the summer evening and he hailed a taxi. ''I hope you will be free to spend some time with Christina and Duert.''

''Oh, I expect so. It will be nice to see little Duert and the baby.''

She sat rather primly beside him and he glanced sideways at her. She was tired now and a little pale, her mane of hair looked too heavy for her neck. Her hands, too, lay neatly clasped in her cotton lap. She turned her head suddenly, her lovely eyes thoughtful. ''Will you tell me why you asked me to come out with you? I'm not your sort of a companion, am I? And I don't suppose you have ever been inside such a lowly restaurant before or eaten high tea?''

He answered her slowly, ''I'm not sure myself, Rose. Shall we put it down to a sudden urge to do something different? I've enjoyed our evening.''

She mused sadly that probably he thought of her and a place like that small restaurant in the same breath; she was quite sure that the beautiful girl she had seen him with would never have gone there. For that matter, he would never have suggested it in the first place. When the taxi stopped she thanked him again, but he got out with her. ''I'm going to see Shirley,'' he told her and waved away her repeated thanks. ''A pleasure, Rose.'' He looked down at her. ''You're tired, aren't you?''

She said that yes, she was; she was unhappy too, but that was her secret.

She saw him often enough during the next few days; he came several times a day to take a look at Shirley, sometimes with Mr Cresswell, sometimes by himself, and he had nothing to say to her other than matters concerned with the toddler. And on the third day he paused long enough to say: ''She'll do. Thank you, Rose.''

Mr Cresswell came alone or with his registrar after that and Rose tried very hard to believe that she didn't mind not seeing Mr Werdmer ter Sane again. After all, she told herself sensibly, no good would come of meeting him. He had been kind, taking her out to a meal, but then he would be kind to a stray dog or an old lady who had fallen down in the street. She was aware that a good doctor or surgeon had a degree of compassion tucked away out of sight which perhaps the ordinary man in the street didn't possess. She had no wish to be pitied, she told herself firmly, and redoubled her efforts to get small Shirley on to the road to recovery again.

It was little short of a miracle that the child should make such a splendid recovery for the operation had been a severe one. Of course there would be frequent check-ups to make sure that there were no secondaries, and it would be some weeks before she would take her first few steps, but the leg—its sound parts neatly put together again, the cancer cut away—encased in plaster, was healing just as it should.

It was almost a week before Rose heard from Christina. They were in London, staying at the Connaught Hotel and would Rose have dinner with them one evening soon? She would phone, said Christina's note and Rose could tell her on which evening she would be free.

Sister Cummins allowed her a half-day and the promise of a long week-end at the end of the following week; she added graciously that since Rose had been so cooperative about her off-duty during the last few days she might choose which evening she would like. So she phoned Christina and agreed to have dinner with them in two days' time, which gave her the time to wash her hair and do her nails and make sure that the crepe dress she so seldom had the opportunity to wear was quite pristine.

She would be fetched, Christina had said, and it was nice to find Duert ter Brandt waiting for her in his own car when she got to the hospital entrance. He greeted her with his usual calm, gave her news of his small son, enlarged on the beauty of his little daughter and observed that both he and Christina were delighted to have the chance to see her again. And by then they were at the hotel.

"We're on the first floor," explained the doctor. "We need to spread ourselves as the children are with us."

Rose wasn't quite prepared for the delightful sitting-room into which she was ushered. She glanced round her at its comfort; her experience of hotels was slight but it seemed to her to be the height of luxury. There were doors on either side, one of which was opened as they went in and Christina came hurrying in, and behind her, not hurrying at all, Mr Werdmer ter Sane. The last person she had expected to see.

Christina greeted her warmly and hugged her. "How lovely to see you, Rose," she exclaimed, "and what a pretty dress." She nodded carelessly in Mr Werdmer ter Sane's direction, "Sybren's here too—just to cast an eye on little Duert, you know."

Rose said "Hullo," in a calm little voice while her heart thudded against her ribs. Surely he could have done that while they were in Holland? After all he only lived half an hour's drive away. Why come to London?

Christina answered her unspoken thought. "It gives him a chance to enjoy the bright lights. Come and see the children..." She whisked Rose away to admire them in their respective cots. "I do love Nanny," confided Christina, "but it's rather fun to have them all to ourselves and Duert is so good with them. Of course we couldn't do that in The Hague, Duert's days are so busy and it's quite a large house to manage." She smiled at Rose. "Will you come and spend a week with us soon? Sybren says he had to come over here again in two weeks' time and he'll give you a lift. Do say you'll come?"

Rose was bending over the baby's cot. "I'd love to come; I'll have to see if I can get a week off. But there's no need for Mr Werdmer ter Sane to give me a lift; I can get a plane so easily."

Christina gave her a quick glance. "Yes, of course, but let us know when you can come, won't you? We shan't be going back home for ten days—you can fix something up before then?"

"Oh, yes. Will you be here—in London?"

"We're going to spend a day or two with friends of Duert's but not until next week." She tucked her small son in cosily. "Doesn't he look sweet? I'll never thank you enough, Rose."

Rose said gruffly: "My goodness, I didn't do much, it was Mr Werdmer der Sane..."

"Isn't his name a mouthful, why don't you call him Sybren?"

"Well...I don't know him very well and anyway I don't think he'd like it."

To which Christina said nothing but led the way back to the sitting room where they were given drinks and were absorbed immediately into undemanding conversation.

Presently the floor waiter brought dinner and they sat around the table with its snowy cloth and gleaming glass and cutlery and ate a delicious meal in a leisurely fashion. Rose, very conscious of Sybren sitting opposite her, was quite unaware of what she ate.

It was a warm evening; they had their coffee on the balcony outside the sitting-room, and London, veiled in the summer twilight, looked lovely and mysterious too. Well, amended Rose to herself, that particular bit of London; she doubted if the streets round St Bride's could look lovely even if one employed the liveliest of imaginations. Which reminded her that it was time she left. She caught Christina's eye. "If you don't mind, I must go—I'm on duty early in the morning..." She added: "It's been a lovely evening, thank you..."

"We've enjoyed having you, Rose." It was Dr ter Brandt who spoke. "Before you go will you promise to phone us here and tell us when you can come and see us?"

"Yes, of course. I'll see about it tomorrow, and thank you for asking me." They were all on their feet and Sybren said, "I'll run you back."

"No—no, there's no need, I can get a taxi." Rose's pleasant voice was so sharp that they all looked at her. It was Sybren who said easily, "I've not had a chance to ask you about Shirley—I thought you might bring me up to date on the way back to St Bride's."

Rose blushed and felt foolish. ''Of course—I'm sorry. But I didn't want to break up your party—you must want to talk.''

Christina said gently, ''Sybren's spending the night here; we've all the time in the world to talk. It's been a lovely evening and don't forget to let us know when you can get that week off.'' She put an arm round Rose and kissed her lightly and her husband did the same while Sybren looked on with an expressionless face. Perhaps he'll kiss me when we say goodbye, thought Rose, and went a very bright pink at the idea, unaware that her face was an open book to be read by anyone who cared to look. And Sybren was seeing.

There wasn't a great deal of traffic and at first the streets were pleasant; well lit, the great houses on either side standing in silent dignity, but as they neared St Bride's the houses became small and cramped, and so did the streets, with discarded Coca Cola tins and greasy newspapers from chip suppers blowing to and fro.

''Another world, isn't it?'' observed Mr Werdmer ter Sane.

Rose said that yes it was, and in more ways than one, she added silently. She had enjoyed every minute of her evening, but it had been like peering through an open door at delights which could never be hers. As he drew up in the courtyard she put her hand on the door, suddenly anxious to be gone, but he leaned across her and covered her hand in his. ''No, wait, Rose, what's the matter?''

She was surprised so that she could only mutter, ''Matter?'' in a stupid fashion.

''That's what I said. You are unhappy, hiding it nicely but underneath that serene face you are on the boil, why?''

She answered him in a hurry. ''Oh, there is nothing. I'm tired; Shirley's been a full-time job. You wanted to know about her; she is doing marvellously; her mother and father...''

He interrupted her. ''Yes, I know. I've had a talk with them. She'll do very well, I think although we can't know for certain just yet.''

She turned to look at him then. ''But you wanted to know about her—you know already—there was no need...''

''None at all,'' he told her coolly, ''but you would have dug in your toes about coming back with me, wouldn't you?''

''Yes.'' It sounded bald, but she couldn't think of anything further to say. He took his hand away abruptly. She heard him sigh as he got out and went round the bonnet to open her door. Anxious to make amends she said timidly, ''It was nice meeting you again...''

''Nice, nice? There was nothing nice about it.'' He sounded mocking and his laugh held no amusement. ''It's a great pity...'' He didn't go on and when she looked up at him he said quietly, ''Good night, Rose.''

An unhappy ending to a happy evening and the quicker she took herself in hand the better. A fruitless task which cost her almost all of a night's sleep.

She would have given a great deal not to have gone on duty in the morning; Mr Werdmer ter Sane would most certainly come to inspect Shirley's leg. Which he did, while she was at her dinner. She wasn't sure whether to be glad or sorry about it when she got back to Shirley, but the wish to see him again was stronger than her relief; he would visit again, she felt sure.

While she was busy with the toddler Sister Cummins came into the room. ''Well, everything is fine,'' she said in a satisfied voice. ''Mr Werdmer ter Sane is more than pleased—thinks everything is as near perfect as it can be. Mr Cresswell came with him, of course, he'll be in tomorrow morning again. Mr Werdmer ter Sane is going back to Holland this evening so I don't suppose we'll see him again. A pity. Now he wants the treatment changed—it's written up...'' She glanced at Rose. ''It's a good thing it's your weekend—you look washed out, Rose. Did the office allow you that week you wanted off?''

''Yes, thank you, Sister. That's in two weeks' time; I'm looking forward to it.''

''I won't say you're a lucky girl because you so deserve it, Rose. Now, as to this treatment, let's get it clear.''

There was plenty of work which was a good thing; she was too tired to think or mope when she went off duty, the days went quickly and the thought of her weekend off kept her going.

Aunt Millicent was glad to see her. Not a lady to show her feelings, nevertheless she had welcomed Rose with real warmth, and as for Maggie, that dear soul fussed round her like a hen with a chick; it was soothing to be made much of and under their kindness Rose's good sense began to take over from her black mood. It happens all the time, she told herself, girls falling in love with the wrong man, I just have to forget him and make up my mind to a career. Indeed, she actually told her aunt that she intended to apply for the post of junior night sister. ''Which will give me a chance to get a ward sister's post if one falls vacant,'' she pointed out. ''It's a good jumping-off job.''

''Yes, if you wish to jump,'' pointed out Aunt Millicent drily.

She wasn't a lady to invite or offer confidences but she was well aware that Rose was unhappy and when it came to talking about her visit to Holland extremely cagey. ''It'll be that surgeon with the awkward name,'' she informed Maggie as the pair of them watched Rose picking peas in the garden. ''And Rose being the girl she is, she'll break her heart silently.''

Old Maggie sighed. ''The dear soul, such a darling girl too! A wife in a million she'd be.'' She sniffed. ''I'll make a Dundee cake for her to take back with her.''

They stood watching her, each of them loving her in their own way. Rose didn't tell her aunt about her visit to Holland until a short while before she had to go back to St Bride's. ''I like Christina very much,'' she explained. ''It will be nice to see little Duert again.''

''And I dare say you'll meet some interesting people—friends of the ter Brandts,'' observed Aunt Millicent casually.

''Oh, perhaps, they have a lovely house, I'll be quite happy just sitting around in the garden all day.''

''You'll go and see the girls you met at the hospital while you were there?'' Her aunt's voice sounded uninterested.

"Perhaps. It's been a lovely weekend, Aunt Millicent, thank you."

"Oh, pooh," said her aunt gruffly, "Maggie and I love to have you. Come again soon, my dear."

CHAPTER SIX

THE SUMMER weather had broken as Rose got off the bus and hurried through the rain to the hospital entrance. Slow drops of rain were falling and great clouds were piling up above her head. There would be a storm before morning and if the weather turned bad it would mean an evening in the sitting-room, drinking endless cups of tea and bandying hospital gossip. She took her case to her room and went down to the canteen for her supper and found most of her friends there. They greeted her noisily, all agog to tell her the news that Sadie had given in her notice. Alice, who always got hold of gossip before anyone else, said, "She decided to get married just like that. Giving up nursing too, her Tom's been offered promotion and they've a chance of a house." Alice added importantly, "We're having a whip round to get her a present."

Having delivered herself of this important piece of news she started on Rose. "We never heard much about your job in Holland. Have you heard how the little boy is getting on? Your Shirley's doing awfully well. He's a wizard, isn't he, that Dutch surgeon? What's he like to work for?"

"Just as nice as Mr Cresswell," said Rose, not wanting to talk about him. "What are we going to get Sadie?"

There was plenty to do on the ward; little Shirley was well on the way to recovery and didn't need as much attention but there were several ill children and a battered baby, a poor scrap, undernourished, unloved and covered in bruises. With care he would become a normal baby again but it was going to take time and patience. Rose was glad to have something to keep her busy and her mind off her own affairs. And after a week, when the baby was beginning to look like a baby once more, she turned her mind to her holiday, only a week away now. Another dress, she decided, something she could wear in the evenings. She found a printed lawn with a frilled shawl collar and short full sleeves in a pale cyclamen pink, belted round her slim waist. She bought two or three T-shirts as well, in pastel colours, and a widely pleated deep cream skirt and cardigan to go with it. Trying them all on after duty she felt quite excited; it was unlikely that she would see Sybren Werdmer ter Sane, but if she did she wouldn't look too bad. Even Alice, that dampener of good spirits, observed that the dress did something for her.

She had heard from Christina; would she get herself a ticket on a morning flight to Amsterdam and someone would meet her there. There was a plane getting in at eleven o'clock, she had written, if Rose could get a seat on it, and if she couldn't would she let her know at once? So everything was arranged and Rose went on duty on a morning four days before she was due to start her holiday to find Mr Cresswell with Shirley.

"Just passing through," he told Rose. "I'll be back for a round; there's no need to get Sister Cummins." He wandered to the door. "I hear you're going over to Schiphol on Saturday, Rose, which flight?"

She was surprised but told him readily enough, and then gaped at him open-mouthed when he observed, "My wife and I are travelling on that flight too. We'll see you on the plane if not before."

"Oh—you're going on holiday, sir? I'm just going for a week to stay with Dr and Mevrouw ter Brandt."

"Yes, yes, I know." He wandered off through the door leaving her to wonder how he knew that, certainly she hadn't told him, still news had a way of getting round the hospital and she supposed that even as important a man as Mr Cresswell might stoop to listen to the grapevine occasionally.

Sadie was to take over from her for the week; now that she was going to leave she was spending her last month filling in for holidays and nurses off sick. Rose primed her well, promised to bring her back a box of the elaborate chocolates they had admired together when they had been on holiday, and packed her case. The weather hadn't broken, her week bid fair to be perfection. She washed her hair, bought a new lipstick and spent a long time applying varnish to her nails. She had pretty hands and she took care of them; the pearly pink varnish suited them very well.

She was at Heathrow in good time, unhurriedly getting herself through the routine. She was wearing one of the new T-shirts and the cream skirt and had tied back her hair with a matching ribbon and looked cool and uncluttered.

She hadn't expected to see Mr Cresswell and his wife, at least not until they were all on the plane, but as she went into the lounge, waiting to go on board, Mr Cresswell waved to her. ''Over here, Rose,'' he commanded.

She went rather reluctantly; they got on well on the ward but now he was on holiday and his wife was with him. She had met Mrs Cresswell in the hospital, being taken round the wards to see the Christmas decorations, and she had liked her; a quiet unassuming woman, the antithesis of her husband's rather forceful manner. She smiled at Rose now and beckoned her to a seat beside her. ''So you're going to Holland too,'' she stated comfortably. ''How long are you staying?''

''Only a week, with Dr ter Brandt and his family.''

Mrs Cresswell nodded. ''We're going for a fortnight but we're not staying in one place for more than a day or two. Do you like flying? I don't.''

They chatted in a desultory fashion until Mr Cresswell got to his feet as they were asked to board the plane, and Rose bade them goodbye, guessing that they were travelling first class, which they were.

She didn't see them at Schiphol; she had collected her case from the carousel and was making her way to a quiet corner to await whoever was to meet her when she found the Cresswells at her elbow.

''There you are,'' declared Mr Cresswell, ''thought we'd missed you. And here's Sybren...''

And indeed it was, looking vast and very much at ease, kissing Mrs Cresswell, shaking Mr Cresswell by the hand and then as

Rose took a step backwards, anxious to get away as fast as she could, flinging a casual arm round her shoulders which effectively rooted her to the spot. ''Hullo Rose,'' he barely glanced at her. ''I'm dropping you off at the ter Brandts' place.'' He picked up her case and led the way to where the car was parked, ushered Mrs Cresswell and Rose into the back, settled himself beside Mr Cresswell, and drove off.

Rose hadn't said a word. She had been surprised, filled with delight and now, having recovered her wits, indignant. It was like being a parcel, for indeed she had had no more chance to speak up for herself than a parcel would have. She said with only the faintest tremor of rage in her voice, ''I was expecting to be met...''

Mrs Cresswell patted her hand. ''Well, dear, I expect the ter Brandts thought this would be just as quick—Sybren dropping you off, I mean.''

It didn't seem worthwhile pointing out to her companion that he was going miles out of his way to do that; Schiphol was right on Amsterdam's doorstep. The Hague was well to the south. She smiled at Mrs Cresswell and fell to contemplating the back of Sybren's handsome head.

To her surprise they all got out when they reached the ter Brandts' house and from the lack of surprise on Corvinus's face, she concluded that they had been expected, all four of them.

Christina came into the hall then. ''Rose, isn't this fun?'' She tucked an arm in hers as she greeted the Cresswells and lifted her face for Sybren's light kiss. ''Duert is on his way home, he'll be here in a few minutes. Sybren, take Mr Cresswell into the sitting-room and give him a drink while I take the girls upstairs.''

She led the way to a bedroom at the side of the house. ''Corvinus will bring your case up presently, Rose.'' She beamed at her. ''I like your hair like that. There are combs and things on the dressing-table if you want anything.'' She turned to Mrs Cresswell. ''How long are you staying with Sybren?''

''Just for two days, my dear. John wants to go to Leyden and then we're going to Friesland to join friends who are sailing there.''

They went unhurriedly downstairs and found Duert had joined his guests, and in the consequent flurry of greetings and handing of drinks, Rose found herself beside Mr Werdmer ter Sane. Light conversation was needed; she sought desperately for something to say, took a gulp of her sherry and did her best. ''What a lovely summer we're having,'' she essayed.

''Weatherwise yes, otherwise no.'' And when she looked at him, he gave her a bland smile which didn't help at all. But she persevered, ''Well, you have had one or two difficult cases, I expect.''

''Indeed I have.''

She said with desperate chattiness, ''Are you on holiday too?''

''No.'' He looked at her. ''I like your hair like that.'' He sighed gently. ''I always thought of you as rather a plain girl, but I see that I was wrong.''

It wasn't a conversation at all, thought Rose desperately, and everyone else was at the other end of the room. She took another good sip of sherry.

''No, you're not wrong, I'm plain; if you see something often enough you don't see it any more, if you see what I mean.''

''A muddled remark, but I get the gist. It is a pity that we can't be friends, Rose.''

She was finding the sherry a great help. ''Yes, it is, but it doesn't matter really, does it? We don't—we aren't—that is, we don't share the same background, do we?'' She added quite fiercely, ''I'm applying for a night sister's post when I get back.''

''Ah—a career girl.'' He gave her a mocking smile and she felt a little sick because she would never be able to say the things she wanted to say to him, only pretend to an enthusiasm for something she had no heart for.

She was saved from answering by Christina who came over to join them and talk about the children. ''We're going to Noerdwijk-aan-zee,'' she told them, ''for a picnic. You must come,

Sybren, we are taking the children too, in a couple of days' time, and don't tell me you're operating because I know you're not.''

''My dear Chrissy, it sounds delightful, of course I'll come.'' The others had joined them and presently they went in to lunch. And shortly after that he stowed his guests back into the car and drove away without having anything more to say to Rose.

Lying in her bed in her charming room after a blissful day, Rose allowed her thoughts to stray to Sybren. She hadn't expected him to be there although she admitted now that she had hoped that in some miraculous way they would meet again. But the meeting hadn't been very satisfactory; he had called her plain—well, not in so many words, but that was what he had meant. And she hadn't done anything about it; if she'd had any spirit at all she would have made him eat his words. There were ways...she could have her hair permed and tinted and assemble a collection of lotions and creams and bright lipsticks. And new clothes, tight jeans and those enormous sweaters and layers of gossamer skirts and tops she had never been able to fathom in *Vogue*. He might look at her then and decide that she wasn't so plain after all.

She got out of bed and went over to the dressing-table and by the light of a brilliant moon bunched her long fine hair around her face, looping it up with one hand and turning and twisting to see the effect. Even by moonlight she could see that it wasn't for her.

She got back into bed, thinking now about her pleasant day; little Duert had remembered her and the baby was gorgeous. She and Christina had spent a lazy afternoon on the lawn behind the house with the baby in a Moses basket and the toddler tumbling between them. They had had their tea there too and then Dr ter Brandt had come home and he and Christina had gone indoors to bath the children and to give them supper and feed them under Nanny's eye. It had been nice to see Nanny again, and even nicer to be staying with such a happy family. Half asleep, she wondered if Sybren and that Mies girl would be happy.

The next day slipped by in a gentle round of gossip, playing with the children, and when Dr ter Brandt came home, an hour's run into the surrounding country once the children were in bed. The roads he took were well away from the motorways, narrow and mostly brick-built, running between flat green meadows, passing through small villages, very quiet because as he explained it was the time of the evening meal for most Dutch households. They went back presently for drinks and dinner and afterwards friends came in and spent an hour casually in the rather grand drawing-room, rendered homely by Christina's knitting cast down on a chair, the pile of papers lying by the doctor's big wing chair and the two dogs, wandering from one to the other. A lovely day, thought Rose, lying in her bed already half asleep, and an even lovelier tomorrow because they were going on a picnic and Sybren would be there.

He arrived about ten o'clock in time to have coffee before they set out. They went in Dr ter Brandt's Rolls with the girls in the back with the children and Sybren in front, the impedimenta necessary for a day's picnicking bestowed in the boot. "So small," observed the baby's doting father, "and half the contents of the house seem necessary for her comfort."

He exchanged a smile with Christina and Rose thought wistfully how marvellous it must be to be married to someone who loved you and you loved too. She looked away and found Mr Werdmer ter Sane's eyes fixed so intently upon her that she put a hand up to her hair; she hadn't even bothered to tie it back but left it to hang down her back. He smiled suddenly and she smiled rather shyly back at him; perhaps it was because he was wearing slacks and an open-necked shirt that he seemed friendly.

Noerdwijk-aan-zee was small, tucked among the dunes, with a single main street, a line of hotels along the short boulevard and a wide beach stretching as far as the eye could see in either direction and although there were plenty of people on the sands there was room and to spare; besides, the ter Brandts had a beach hut at the quieter end where the small town ended and the dunes took over. The hut opened, rugs and cushions and a sun umbrella arranged, the picnic basket and the children's needs dealt with,

Christina declared that she was going for a swim before they had lunch. She gave her husband a speaking glance as she said this and he said at once, "A splendid idea, darling, we can leave these two to baby-sit and they can have a turn while we put the food and drink ready."

The baby was asleep and little Duert busy with a bucket and spade. Rose sat with her back against the hut wall, watching him, while Sybren lay full length on his back, his eyes closed.

But he wasn't asleep. Still with his eyes closed he remarked, "There is a great deal to be said for the domestic life, don't you agree, Rose?"

She looked towards the sea where the ter Brandts were swimming side by side. "Oh yes." She spoke in a rather colourless voice, afraid that she might betray her feelings, longing to be in Christina's shoes, only of course Sybren would be in Dr ter Brandt's and little Duert would be another Sybren and the baby...what would they call the baby?

"Stop dreaming, Rose. Tell me, do you suppose I should make a good husband?"

She said carefully, "I imagine that any man would make a good husband if he loved his wife."

"Don't beg the question."

"You see, I've worked for you in hospital and seen you there but I don't know anything about you. You have a lovely home and I dare say lots of friends. I think you work very hard and like your work and you're successful, aren't you? You're handsome too." She spoke matter-of-factly, while her heart cried out at the idea of him being anyone's husband but hers. "That evening at the restaurant in The Hague, there was a lovely girl with you—I don't know her name; Christina called her Mies. Are you going to marry her?"

He opened one eye. "You think that she would make me a suitable wife?"

She said severely, "How could I possibly tell, Mr Werdmer ter Sane?"

''My name is Sybren. Do I seem very middle-aged to you, Rose?''

She shot upright with real surprise. ''Middle-aged, you're joking. Why, you're—you're not even in the prime of your life.''

He rolled over and sat up. ''Well, that's something. It encourages me to make a sandcastle with my godson.''

Which he proceeded to do. The pair of them were still busy with it when the ter Brandts came strolling back from their swim.

''The water is just right,'' Christina flung herself down beside Rose.

''Whip into your swimsuit, Rose. Duert and I will get the lunch.'' She looked across at Sybren. ''Are you going in, Sybren?''

He glanced up from the careful tunnel he was making. ''Yes, what about this young man?''

''He's going swimming with his Papa, aren't you, my dear?'' She cast a motherly eye at the Moses basket. ''Off with you while I lay the cloth.''

Sybren seemed in no hurry; Rose went away to change into her swimsuit, a sensible affair in navy blue, plaited her hair and wound it into a topknot and went off down the beach to where the doctor and his small son were paddling. The water was pleasantly warm and very clear. She waded slowly and then began to swim, something she could do well. After a little while she paused to tread water and rest and saw Sybren beside her.

''You swim well.''

''Thank you. I used to swim with my father; I'm rather out of practice.''

He had turned on to his back and she did the same. It was blissfully warm and quiet and she could have stayed there for ever; somehow everything seemed so simple, just the two of them floating around in a kind of limbo. What would he say if she told him she loved him? A kind of recklessness seized her and she actually had her mouth open to ask him when he turned over and began to swim slowly towards the shore. ''Time for lunch,'' he told her.

She reached the beach at the same time as he, trembling with a kind of delayed shock at what she might have said. He gave her a sharp glance as they waded ashore. ''Cold?'' he wanted to know. ''You are shivering.'' He added kindly, ''You'd better get some clothes on.''

She felt better by the time she had dressed and joined the others, and over their leisurely meal she became her usual composed self again, keeping an eye on little Duert, sampling the wafer-thin sandwiches and little cheese tartlets, the salad, the hard boiled eggs, the ham *broodjes,* and drinking the lager, icy cold from its container. There was hot coffee afterwards, too, and while she and Christina settled the little ones for a nap the men packed everything away and then strolled off along the sands.

''It's nice here, isn't it?'' said Christina. ''It's our favourite picnic place.'' She smiled dreamily. ''We—we got engaged here.''

Rose rolled over to look at her. ''Oh, did you? How romantic, was it a lovely day like today?''

Christina chuckled. ''There was a gale blowing and it rained torrents. But that didn't matter.''

Rose sighed without knowing it. ''No, I don't suppose it would.'' She looked along the beach to where in the distance the two men were strolling along. ''When I get back I'm going to apply for a night sister's post—the junior one.''

''You like night-duty?''

She shook her head. ''No, but it's the quickest way to get promotion, isn't it?''

''You want to stay at St Bride's?'' Christina sounded casual.

''Well, I expect I'd better; perhaps when I've had a senior post for a year or two, I'll try for somewhere else.''

''Do you mind where?''

She shook her head again. ''No—it doesn't matter.''

''Don't you want to get married?''

She sat up, glancing without meaning to at the two men, coming towards them now. ''Yes, oh, yes. But I shan't so I'll have to be a career girl.''

The two men joined them and they sat around, not talking much, until the children woke and they fetched cold drinks from the picnic basket and then packed everything up, climbed into the car and drove back to The Hague.

Nanny was waiting to see to little Duert and the baby and Rose went to her room and showered and put on a fresh dress and went back downstairs to find the others already on the patio and Corvinus arranging the tea tray just so. She would have liked the next hour to last for ever; sitting in the late afternoon sunshine, listening to the gentle talk around her but not having much to say for herself. They had been discussing a play at the Koninklijke Schouwburg and idly wondering if they should go one evening when Sybren observed, ''Which reminds me I must be going—I've a date this evening.'' He looked hard at Rose. ''Dinner with Mies.''

She looked straight back at him. ''All this fresh air will have given you a splendid appetite.'' She said it just a bit too quickly and at his sudden smile, looked away.

''A delightful day,'' he remarked as he got up. ''We must do it again some time. Kiss the babies good night for me, Christina.'' He bent and kissed her cheek, said something in Dutch to Deurt ter Brandt and turned to Rose. ''I'll see you again, Rose,'' and watched the delight flood her face before she could prevent it. He bent suddenly and pulled her to her feet. ''See me to the car, the exercise will do you good.''

The car was at the front of the house; she walked beside him in silence along the patio and round the corner to the sweep before the door where the Rolls stood. When they reached it she said sedately, ''I hope you have a lovely evening.''

He stood looking down at her, half smiling. She supposed it was a silly remark to make and not worth an answer. He said softly, ''I'm working all day tomorrow, the day after that I'm coming to fetch you before lunch—you can tell Christina I'll bring you back safely after dinner in the evening.''

"But you haven't asked me—I haven't said I'll come..." Her voice shook a little with happy excitement and she hoped it sounded as it usually did.

For answer he caught her close and kissed her. She hadn't been kissed very often and never like this. He let her go very gently, got into the car and drove away, leaving her standing with her mouth open and her eyes wide.

She stayed where she was for a few moments while a succession of thoughts wove their way through her head. Almost all of them made nonsense; a number of them were the stuff of which dreams are made; only a very few were sensible. With a great effort she allowed these to take over; Sybren was no boy; he had had years in which to bring kissing to a fine art; doubtless he kissed all the girls with equal finesse. He was probably feeling sentimental at the prospect of seeing Mies and last but not least he might have kissed her in a fit of absent-mindedness. The last was hard to swallow but it was as good a reason as any. She walked slowly back to where the ter Brandts were sitting to be greeted by Christina's cheerful, "Seen him off in that car of his? A pity he couldn't stay to dinner."

Rose stooped to pat the dogs. "Yes, he's asked me to go out with him the day after tomorrow—for lunch, he said he'd bring me back in the evening after dinner, if that is all right with you."

She didn't see Christina's wide grin at her husband. "Oh, lovely for you—we hadn't planned anything, had we, Duert? You'll be able to see some more of Amsterdam. We wondered if you'd like to go to Scheveningen tomorrow? It's a bit crowded but there's the pier and lots to see. Duert's given himself a day off again; at least what he calls a day off—he'll go to the hospital early and be home by ten o'clock or so and then go in again between tea and dinner. The weather forecast's good, we'll take the children and the dogs for a walk before we go and leave them with Nanny."

It sounded fun, thought Rose, besides she would be able to take her mind off Sybren.

It was as much fun as she had hoped even though the wretched man wasn't out of her head for one single second. They had put the baby in her pram, attached little Duert to his leading reins and with the dogs for escort taken a walk through the quiet avenues around the house and by the time they had got back Duert was waiting for them. There was no hurry; they sat for a while playing with the children and gossiping before they got into the car. That was the nice part about living as the ter Brandts did; no one seemed fussed about time or being late or having to get somewhere; she supposed it was because they had a beautifully run home and devoted staff. She had a sudden memory of racing on and off duty at St Bride's always with an eye on the clock, calculating how much one could get done in a given time on the ward, or just how long it would take to get to the station or go shopping. She sank back, relishing the comfort of the car and sternly stopped her thoughts from wandering to Sybren. He would be working himself now, doing a round or perhaps operating. She jumped guiltily as Duert said over his shoulder, "I saw Sybren—he was at my hospital to see a child with brain damage. I'm to remind you that he'll be with us by eleven o'clock tomorrow."

Rose murmured something and wished she didn't blush so easily.

They went first to the harbour so that she could see the fishing boats and the fishermen's wives in their voluminous black skirts and coloured shawls, their heads covered in snowy caps with the gold ornaments on either side. And having had her fill of these, they drove back along the long promenade to the casino where Duert parked the car while they went on to the pier. It was delightful loitering in the sun, sitting down to drink lemonade and watch the crowds on the beach.

"Is it always as crowded as this?" asked Rose.

"No, only in July and August. We hardly ever come; sometimes in the autumn, it's so quiet then; no one about, only the fishermen."

They lunched at Le Bon Ton, a French bistro, small but Rose guessed that it was expensive. Afterwards they got into the car again and went to Madurodam, the miniature model city halfway between Scheveningen and The Hague. Here they spent more than an hour, treading between the miniature houses and shops, watching the trains and trams travelling to and fro and they saw the barges on the canals sailing slowly along, while the windmills turned, ferries fussed back and forth and in the harbour boats came and went and the planes landed and took off from the airfield.

"Pretty marvellous, isn't it?" observed Duert. "It lights up in the evening you know."

"Why is it called Madurodam? Is there a town called that in Holland?"

"No, it's named after a lieutenant, George Maduro, who died in Dachau. There couldn't be a better memorial, could there?"

They went back to the beach then, and walked along the firm sand by the water's edge and returned finally to have tea in the pier restaurant. "A lovely day," said Rose and meant it, finding it even lovelier because in the morning she would see Sybren again.

He was very punctual but all the same she had been ready for half an hour before he arrived. She was wearing the pink dress and had taken extra care with her face and hair. She had put it up at first, and then taken all the pins out and brushed it smooth and tied it back with a pink ribbon. Soon enough she would be wearing it in a severe bun again, she reminded herself. Only one more day left after this day and then back to St Bride's and hard work. She couldn't bear to think of it.

She had felt a little shy at meeting Sybren again but she didn't need to; he greeted her with casual friendliness, observed that he was glad to see that she wasn't going to keep him waiting, spent five minutes talking to Christina and the children, then stowed her in the car, got in beside her and drove off.

She didn't ask where they were going, she was content enough just to sit there beside him. When they reached his house she got out to find Hans waiting by the open door, his face wreathed in smiles. She wished him good day and added, ''Do you remember me, Hans?''

''Certainly, Miss, a pleasure to see you again.''

The hall was cool and dim and this time she was ushered into a room on the other side of it, smaller than the rather grand one she remembered from her first visit. But it was beautiful, nonetheless, with panelled walls hung with paintings, comfortable chairs and little tables scattered around and a deep window at one end with a window seat piled with cushions. Curled up among them was a black and white cat who took no notice of them at all, nor twitched a whisker when the door behind them was thrust wide and a bouvier came prancing in. Rose had glimpsed one once or twice on her previous visits to Holland but she had never been as close as this. He looked a bit fearsome with his small yellow eyes and great head but she put out a clenched fist for his inspection and bade him a polite hello.

He went to his master first, wagging his stumpy tail and beaming all over his ferocious face and then at a word from Sybren gently nosed Rose's hand and offered his head for a pat.

''William,'' said Sybren, ''and don't ask me why. I've had him since he was a very small puppy and he'll not harm a hair of your head.'' He turned to look at her. ''He knows you belong here, you see.''

She had nothing to say to that; he went on, ''He would make mincemeat of anyone I didn't approve of, though. You like him?''

''Oh, yes, very much. What does he do all day while you're at the hospital?''

''We go for a walk each morning before breakfast and again in the evening. I'm not always away from home, you know. When I'm free we go to the woods or to the beach and he loves riding in the car. During the day Hans takes him out.''

He strolled over to a sofa table behind a brocade sofa. ''What will you drink, Rose?''

And when she hesitated: ''Will you try a long drink? Sherry and tonic with ice? Just right for this weather.''

She found that she wasn't shy with him any more; they had slipped into an easy relationship which permitted of companionable silence as well as talk and presently they crossed the hall again to the dining-room, at the back of the house, a panelled room and furnished very beautifully with a mahogany oval table and chairs and a serving table against one wall. There was a magnificent *stoelklok* on one wall and a vast mirror in a carved frame over the wide hearth. They sat at one end of the table and ate without haste, pausing to talk a great deal. There were potted shrimps, lamb cutlets with potato straws and mouth-watering salad and by way of afters orange ice cream with Courvoisier, all these helped along very nicely with a muscadet and rounded off with coffee served in paper-thin china cups and poured from a massive silver coffee-pot.

Rose accepted it all, as she would accept a lovely dream, querying nothing, knowing at the same time that dreams have a way of ending and that she would wake up presently. But she refused to think of that, just for a little while she was truly happy.

After lunch he took her round the house, so much bigger than it appeared from the street with a vast complex of kitchens and pantries and cellars below ground where she met Hans' wife Jultsje, a big woman with bright blue eyes and a wide smile, and a round dumpling of a girl who grinned and blushed. Hanna was from Friesland just as Jultsje was, being that lady's niece. "There is also a gardener, but he's quite old and comes and goes when he likes," explained Sybren leading the way up the narrow staircase which opened into the back of the hall.

Upstairs there were any number of rooms, some large and beautifully furnished with modern bathrooms cunningly hidden away and some small and cosy, tucked away down narrow passages or up short narrow stairs. It took some time to see everything and when they got back to the big room she remembered so well, the afternoon was almost over.

"We'll have a stroll in the garden, shall we?" asked Sybren and took her out to the long narrow lawn behind the house with William at his heels. They strolled round the garden afterwards and half way down its well ordered length he stopped to say, ''I like your dress, Rose. You should always wear pink.'' He bent and kissed her cheek lightly and then walked on again, his hand under her arm. ''After dinner we'll go for a stroll along the *grachten*.'' And after that he talked about commonplace things; Amsterdam and his home and how the city had changed over the last few years and the differences between Dutch and English law, and Rose sitting beside him on a little rustic seat built round the mulberry tree at the very end of the garden listened to every word.

They went back into the house presently, into the vast drawing-room where Hans had set tea on a drum-table by the window. Rose was pouring their tea when Sybren came and took his cup from her and set it on the table.

He said quite angrily, ''Dammit, there's something I want to say to you—something—I must explain before you go back to England. The trouble with you is that I thought that I knew what you were thinking; now I've got to know you better I'm not sure any more. I'm not even sure if you like me.''

She looked at him then and smiled a little and said steadily, ''Oh, yes, I like you, I didn't mean to though.''

''Good. Rose, what would you say if I were to tell you that I want to get married?'' He paused. ''Do you know me well enough, I wonder?''

He was standing in front of her, for once in his self-assured life at a loss for words, staring down at her plain face so very composed. Her composure was like a fence between them although he had no idea that he had only to give it the slightest push to get rid of it. He began, ''Rose…''

She held her breath, not sure what was going to happen next, aware that her insides were turning over and over wondering what he was going to say.

Only he didn't say it; the telephone rang.

CHAPTER SEVEN

MR WERDMER TER SANE said something in his own language. He spoke softly and Rose couldn't understand him, which was just as well because he was swearing quite ferociously. He went to the phone and listened without comment and she watched his face change back to the blandness she didn't much care for. When he spoke it was to utter only a few words before he put the phone down. He looked at her across the room and she wondered how a face could change so swiftly from warmth to an impersonal politeness; just as though she had arrived unexpectedly and he had felt he had to ask her to stay to tea…

"Don't go—have your tea; I shouldn't be long…I'll let you know."

Something at the hospital, she supposed, something serious too, otherwise why should he have changed from the delightful companion who had shared her day to this polite distant man. She said quietly: "Very well, Sybren," and watched him go from the room. He put his head round the door a moment later.

"It's only fair to tell you that that was Mies."

She felt as though she had been turned to stone. What was fair about it? And what was she supposed to make of his remark? And why in heaven's name had he made it? She sat there while the tea cooled in her cup. Hans came in presently, took a look at the untouched sandwiches and cakes and took away the teapot and the teacups and came back with fresh tea.

"Mijnheer wouldn't like it if you do not eat and drink, Miss," he cautioned her. So she drank some tea and ate a couple of sandwiches and watched the beautiful little carriage clock on the mantelpiece. Almost an hour went by before the phone rang again, and this time Hans was in the room to answer it before she could get out of her chair. "For you, Miss," he told her and went softly from the room.

"That is Rose Comely?" asked a voice; a high little tinkling voice, and Rose knew who it was at once. She said, "Yes, you wanted me?"

"I have a message. Sybren will not be back at his house. He sends his regrets and you are to ask Hans to see you back to The Hague."

"Why is he not coming back here?" asked Rose.

Mies laughed. "That is something you will know, but not just this evening. We celebrate—you understand?"

Rose had no chance to ask any more questions; Mies rang off.

She went and sat down for a few minutes, trying to understand. Why couldn't Sybren have spoken to her himself? And was that what he had been on the point of telling her when Mies had phoned him? There was no point in guessing, she thought wearily, and went in search of Hans, who listened politely to her rather muddled request, assured her that he would get out the second car from the garage and drive her back himself. "For that is what Mijnheer would wish," he told her. "You will not stay for dinner, Miss?"

To dine alone in the splendour of Sybren's dining-room would have been farcical. She refused politely and waited until he went to fetch the car. A Rover, beautifully polished. She got in beside Hans and maintained a conversation of sorts for the entire journey although afterwards she had no idea what she had said.

The ter Brandts were sitting together having drinks before dinner when she arrived. Hans, with a tact which she thanked him for from the bottom of her heart, had rung the bell and gone inside, presumably to explain, for a moment later Christina came out to the car, poked her head through the window and said cheerfully. "Called out, was he? It happens all the time, Rose. You're just in time for a drink before dinner."

She was swept into the house, and Hans, suitably thanked, went off to the kitchen for coffee before going back to Amsterdam. "You'll tell Mister Werdmer ter Sane that I quite understood, won't you?" Rose begged him. "You won't forget."

She had her drink and ate her dinner, looking, if she had but known, as though the world had come to an end, as indeed it had for her. But neither Christina or Duert said anything, but embarked on a lengthy discussion as to whether they should spend Christmas in London or at home, which meant that she could sit between them and murmur from time to time without actually taking part in the conversation. Presently Christina said easily: ''You must be dog tired, Rose. Don't stand on ceremony with us, if you'd like an early night.''

So she went to bed, but not to sleep; she thought about Sybren until her head ached. But not as much as her heart.

Mr Werdmer ter Sane wasn't thinking about her; he was bent over the operating table very carefully removing a blood clot from the brain of a small boy who had fallen out of a fifth-floor window from a block of flats in one of the poorer parts of Amsterdam. That the child was alive was partly due to Mies van Toule who had been taking a short cut through the city in her car and had been forced to stop by a distraught woman who demanded that she should go to the nearest telephone and get help. Her inclination had been to drive on but then she remembered that her dearest friend had told her that Sybren had been seen driving that morning with a girl beside him. She had guessed, quite rightly, that it had been Rose, probably she was at his house now; she had noticed the difference in Sybren's manner of late and this was a chance to get even. She had phoned his house, knowing that he would go at once to the hospital and when he had seen her at the hospital and asked her to phone Rose and explain, she had played the perfect helpful friend and promised to do so. It had all worked out very nicely; she had driven a wedge very neatly between Sybren and Rose. And being clever as well as pretty, she drove herself out of Amsterdam to stay with friends without telling anyone where she was going, thus avoiding possible awkward questions from Sybren.

He wasn't free to phone his home until well after midnight and Hans told him then that he had driven Rose back to The Hague and then delivered her message. Mr Werdmer ter Sane had grunted some reply, told Hans to go to bed and then gone back to the intensive care unit; the child was by no means out of danger.

He got home at four o'clock in the morning; the child, despite all his efforts, had died. He drank the coffee in the flask left out for him by the faithful Hans, showered and changed his clothes and went to his study; sleep was out of the question, he found himself wishing that Rose was there, sitting quietly listening while he went over his night. Sitting there too tired to sleep, he knew that she was all that he wanted. Which was strange, he mused, smiling to himself, he had had no inkling that he would grow to love her when they had first met. Later, when he had finished his morning round at the hospital he would go to The Hague and tell her so. He yawned hugely and closed his eyes and Hans found him there a few hours later, sitting in his great chair asleep.

He was delayed at the hospital. Too late to go to his home for lunch, he ate a sandwich and drank his coffee at the hospital and then got into his car. He was tired now but to see Rose was more important than sleep.

Rose had packed that morning and now she was on the lawn beyond the house with the baby asleep in her pram, little Duert curled up on a rug under the trees and Nanny dozing in a chair close by. Christina had gone to the hairdresser and Duert was at the hospital and they would all forgather for tea presently. She had cried her eyes out during the night and now there were no tears left. Tomorrow she would go back to England and Sybren must and would be forgotten. It wouldn't have been so bad, she thought for the hundredth time, if he had told her that he was going to marry Mies; after all she had guessed that for herself, but it had hurt, his bald message without explaining, and Mies… Rose ground her splendid teeth at the thought of the girl. She had heard the triumph in the girl's voice over the phone. Rose rolled over on to her front; well, good luck to them both.

She didn't hear Mr Werdmer ter Sane's silent approach, and since her three companions were by now all fast asleep, they didn't hear him either.

He had stretched himself out beside her while she was still catching her breath. He said quietly, ''I'm sorry our day had to end like that, Rose.''

She said stonily, ''Please don't apologise. Mies explained. Although I can't think why you couldn't have done that for yourself.'' Her voice had risen slightly despite her best efforts to keep it nonchalant.

''I was unable to phone you myself.'' She glanced at him and he at her. ''I didn't get home until morning.''

Rose sat up straight, her imagination running wild. ''I don't suppose you did.'' She gave a snort. ''Celebrating...I cannot for the life of me think why you asked me out yesterday; it was quite unnecessary, you know. I couldn't care less if I never see you again, not that I shall so that won't matter.'' She gave a great heaving breath, got to her feet and raced away into the house and up to her room, where she walked up and down pausing to look out of the window at Sybren, lying where she had left him on the grass. He looked as though he was asleep and in fact he was.

Of course she had to go down again when Christina came home. She had pulled herself together very nicely and she need not have worried about Sybren; his manner towards her was pleasantly casual, just sufficiently interested in her return to England but evincing no curiosity as to what she intended doing when she got there. Only once, when she happened to catch his eyes inadvertently, did she see the anger in it.

I'm the one to be angry, she thought, listening with a serene face to Christina's plans for Christmas. Christmas seemed a long way off; and where would she be? Rose wondered. On night-duty, more than likely.

Mr Werdmer ter Sane got up to leave. He had refused an invitation to stay to dinner, pleading a previous engagement, but without drawing attention to herself, there was no way in which Rose could refuse his request to accompany him to his car.

She walked beside him, giving the strong impression that she was ready to turn tail and run at any moment and he had nothing to say until they reached the car.

"Where did you think I went yesterday evening?" he wanted to know in a casual voice.

Rose had herself nicely in hand. "You told me—at least you told me that Mies had telephoned… You said it was only fair to tell me."

He sounded amused. "And am I to be allowed to explain or are you to stay like a poker?"

"You have no need to explain and it isn't funny… Mies explained, just as you told her to."

He had stopped by the car and now he lent against it, his hands in his pockets, looking so casual she had a strong wish to box his ears if that were physically possible. "And she said?" he prompted blandly.

"That you—both of you—were together—she said I'd understand…"

"And you understood, of course?" His voice was soft.

"I'm not a fool," said Rose fiercely. Before she could say more, he asked. "And of course you believed her?"

"Why not?" she snapped. "I may be plain and uninteresting but I won't be pitied—or patronised. You had no right to invite me to spend the day with you and let me think…" She stopped before she gave herself away. "I suppose you thought you were giving me a treat."

"You thought that of me, Rose?" His voice was harsh.

She didn't know what she thought any more. "I never want to see you or speak to you again," she flung at him, "and I hope you'll both be very happy."

She turned and ran back to the house and after a moment Sybren got into his car and drove away.

The ter Brandts were sitting where she had left them. They looked at her stricken face and Duert said at once, "We were just talking about your journey home. I've given myself a half-day and we'll all drive down to Schiphol and see you off. We'll be over ourselves before Christmas and we must see something of you then.''

Christina chimed in then, full of ideas and plans, talking easily, giving Rose time to become more the self-contained girl that she was. They left her presently while they went to see the children into bed and she sat on in the cool early evening, her miserable thoughts going round in her head like mice on a wheel. Presently she got up and went up to her room to tidy herself for the evening, wondering what she would do and say if Sybren were to phone. He didn't of course and when she went down to join the ter Brandts she astonished herself and them with her bright chattiness for the rest of the evening.

''Can't we do something?'' begged Christina after she had said good night. ''I do wonder what happened...?''

''Well, my love, you will have to be patient,'' said Duert, ''we can't possibly interfere.''

''No? Couldn't you possibly just hint...''

''No, darling. Sybren may be one of my closest friends, but I won't poke my nose into his affairs.''

''I bet that beastly Mies is at the bottom of it,'' observed Christina.

Duert went to the hospital directly after breakfast with the promise that he would be back for an early lunch and Christina and Rose spent the morning in the garden, playing with the children and gossiping idly.

''Are you on duty tomorrow?'' asked Christina.

''Yes—half past seven in the morning too. It feels as though I've been away for several weeks instead of seven days. I've had such a gorgeous time.''

Rose's pale face belied the words but Christina didn't comment. ''We've loved having you and remember we're going to see something of you before the end of the year. Will you be night sister by then?''

''I'm not sure—I might not even get the post, but if I do I believe the job starts next month.'' Thinking about it, she viewed the prospect with something like dismay.

The morning slid away with her ears stretched for a telephone call which never came and after lunch she was driven to Schiphol to be given a send-off she wouldn't forget, with an armful of flowers and chocolates and warm goodbyes which did something to melt the hard cold knot in her chest.

It was hot and thundery when she got on the bus at Heathrow and as she got out at the terminal great drops of rain began to fall so that once in London she gave way to the extravagance of a taxi to St Bride's. The sky was dark overhead by now and the hospital, never a thing of beauty, looked gloomy and uninviting and when she got to her room it was to find none of her friends off-duty, so she unpacked, got her uniform ready for the morning and went down to supper.

All her close friends were there; over egg and chips, bread-and-butter pudding and cups of tea she painted an enviable picture of her holiday.

''Lucky you,'' declared Sadie, ''while we've all been slaving away...there's a new houseman, though!''

There was a ripple of laughter round the table. ''You'll never guess his name, Rose. Percy Pride, he's quite a lad too—this is his first job and he's very pleased with himself.'' Sadie examined her nails. ''I've been out with him—just for supper.'' She heaved a sigh. ''I must say I'll miss the odd date when I'm married.''

She shot a look at Rose. ''Did you have a date while you were in The Hague?''

Rose had already told them about the picnic and one could hardly call her fiasco of a day out with Sybren a date. ''No,'' and she added lamely, ''there wasn't time—we were always doing something.''

They all liked her too much to pursue the matter and presently, since they were off-duty now, they went over to the home and spent their usual hour or so drinking more tea and eating the packet of Dutch biscuits Rose had had the forethought to bring with her.

She went back on duty to Sister Cummins' ward and found it busier than ever. Little Shirley was making progress, but slowly, and nursing her was a painstaking chore that had to be kept to with exact strictness. Mr Cresswell who was still away had restricted the operating list to routine stuff which his registrar dealt with in his absence.

On her first morning back, Rose met the new houseman. He seemed pleasant enough and anxious to be friendly and impress her, and Rose, being Rose, took him at face value and thought he wasn't too bad. He had a lot to say for himself but the young housemen often had; they were pleased that they had jobs and she didn't blame them for that. She had, in her own modest way, been pleased with herself when she had been awarded the gold medal. Not that she ever mentioned it to anyone.

A day or two slipped by, she wrote her thank-you letter to Christina, phoned Aunt Millicent and was warmly invited to spend her next free days with her, and over and above that she took care to spend her off-duty time with one or other of her friends: that way she didn't find it so easy to lapse into thoughts of Sybren. Only at bedtime did she allow herself to do that; he was the last thing she thought of before she slept and each morning when she woke her first thought was that perhaps by some miracle, he would turn up at St Bride's.

She would have to wait until the end of the following week before she could have her weekend but she was due a day off before then. It surprised her very much when Percy Pride followed her into the office one morning and asked her what she was going to do with it.

She was searching through the charts on the desk and answered rather carelessly, "Oh, nothing much. Have a good sleep and do some window-shopping."

Percy was looking at himself in Sister's looking glass. He was a conceited young man but his ego, flattened by Sadie's flippant treatment, needed a boost. And who better to do that than Rose, unremarkable and at a loose end? She would be grateful for his attentions and once he felt sure of himself again, he could pass on to some of the pretty nurses he had noticed around the place. He arranged himself negligently on the side of Sister's desk.

"How about having lunch with me? I'm free until the morning—we might try a picture gallery or a museum afterwards."

Rose had the charts nicely arranged. "Do get off the desk," she begged him, "I've just got things sorted… Thank you, I'd like to come out with you." She sounded pleased and he puffed out his chest, not knowing that she would have accepted an invitation from just about anyone because that was the only way she could try to forget Sybren.

He got off the desk. "Splendid. Twelve o'clock in the front hall?" He added rather grandly, "I'll be back to check that nephritis. Let me know if you are worried."

He walked off, pleased with himself, leaving Rose wondering what on earth had possessed her to accept his invitation. Still, it would get her through another day and each day would be easier, she told herself.

"He's not quite your type," said Sadie when Rose told her.

"What's my type, then?"

"Oh, someone older, love. Someone who could see what you're really like."

"You mean under my plain face there's a heart of gold?"

Sadie giggled. "Something like that, but our Percy will do for you to practise on, only don't let him practise on you." She got off the bed to pour more tea for them both. "I say, I've been thinking, would it be a good idea if the bridesmaids wore pink but in different shades—light to dark if you see what I mean, and how do you feel about a wreath of flowers or do you want a hat?"

Percy Pride was quite forgotten in the serious business of Sadie's wedding.

They went back on duty together and Rose went straight on to the ward so that the part-time staff nurse could go to her dinner, leaving her with a first-year nurse and Mrs MacCauley, a sensible middle-aged nursing auxiliary. She was checking little Shirley's TPR while the other two did the after-dinner tidying round when Mr Werdmer ter Sane walked on to the ward. Rose turned her head to see what the slight commotion was behind her and saw him coming unhurriedly towards her. She charted the board, which gave her a few seconds to steady herself, but nothing would stop the colour flooding to her face, nor could it check her racing heart. All the same her "Good afternoon, Sir," was uttered in a calm voice.

He stood and looked at her for a moment, smiling in that nasty way, she supposed because she was blushing so fiercely. His "Good afternoon, Staff," was uttered with a brisk politeness. "I saw Mr Cresswell a day or so ago and told him that I would cast an eye over Shirley."

"Yes, Sir, I'll get the registrar."

"He knows I'm here." He sat down on the side of the cot and began a conversation with Shirley. After a moment he looked over his shoulder at Rose. "Are you free this evening?"

"No," said Rose much too fast, and the blush which had almost gone, started all over again.

"Tomorrow?"

"I have a day off; I'm spending it with one of the housemen..."

He raised his eyebrows. "Are you? Nice work, Rose. I take it I'm not forgiven?"

"No." She didn't meet his eyes. "Would you like to see the wound? It's healing well but there's just one area that's oozing..."

She looked up with relief as the registrar with Percy Pride at his heels joined them, and Mr Werdmer ter Sane fell to poking and prodding very gently. At length he straightened himself. "Yes, well I think we're in the clear." He looked at Rose. "Is she chesty?"

"Yes—not much, but I noticed it for the first time this morning."

"Nurse quite rightly reported it to me," interrupted Percy Pride, and was interrupted in his turn by Sybren's quite quiet: "Nurse? which nurse? Or do you refer to Staff Nurse Comely?"

"Oh, er—yes. Sorry. I've written her up for a mist: expect:"

Mr Werdmer ter Sane looked at the registrar who looked back

at him with a poker face, and Rose knowing exactly what was going to happen picked up the chart and handed it to him. ''We don't want a nasty chest, do we?'' he enquired mildly. ''Ampycillin, I think—the linctus of course.'' He glanced at Rose. ''Keep an eye open, Staff Nurse, and let me know if you're worried. I'm here for a few days.''

He handed her the chart back. ''Good day to you and thank you.''

The three of them went away and she nodded at the student nurse who hurried down the ward to open the door and came back beaming with pleasure because Sybren had paused to thank her as though he really meant it.

Rose saw him again the next day; she had gone to the entrance hall at noon precisely only to be told by Bagg the head porter that Mr Pride would be delayed for a few minutes. She was mooning round, examining the marble busts of bygone surgeons and physicians which littered the hall, when Mr Werdmer ter Sane came through the entrance door. Since she was facing the door at that moment she couldn't pretend that she hadn't seen him. He walked unhurriedly towards her, his eyebrows lifted.

He said, very suave, ''Staff Nurse Comely—about to enjoy your day off?'' He looked around him in what she considered to be a sickeningly smug manner. ''Percy not turned up? I must say I consider that you could have done better for yourself.''

She was stung into saying most unwisely, ''Beggars can't be choosers.'' And regretted the words immediately because he said cheerfully, ''I did offer to bury the hatchet; we could have done so most amicably over lunch at Wilton's. Champagne of course; I always placate my enemies with champagne—mushrooms in cream sauce, lobster thermidor, and raspberries and cream...''

Rose who had eaten a slice of toast and had a mug of tea with a tea bag for her breakfast, said crossly, ''Oh, be quiet do,'' and then, ''I'm not your enemy, I just don't like you.''

''Yes, you said so and that, you weren't going to speak to me again.''

"Well, I have to on the ward and it—it would be rude if I pretended not to see that you are there when you are."

He said softly, "All the time I hope, dear girl. Ah, here is your… What is he, Rose?"

"Nothing," she snapped and turned a welcoming smile on Percy Pride.

That young man gave her a casual hullo and a rather more polite "Good morning, Sir" to Sybren who enquired innocently, "Busy, Mr Pride?"

"Day off, Sir. Had a lazy morning, forgot I was taking Rose out actually!" He turned to her, missing Mr Werdmer ter Sane's contemptuous look. "You didn't mind waiting, did you, Rose? There's plenty of time, we can have a snack at the British Museum and then spend the afternoon there."

Mr Werdmer ter Sane uttered a choked sound which he turned into a cough.

"That sounds most interesting." He gave Rose a limpid look. "You'll enjoy that." His smile was quite nasty; she had come to dread seeing it, especially just then; she would have liked to retire to some dark isolated spot and have a good cry, but only after hitting Sybren over the head with something really hard and doing the same for the wretched Percy.

Sybren, watching her, read her thoughts very accurately, she had that kind of a face, for him at any rate. She was in for a dull day, by the end of it she would probably not be on speaking terms with Percy. It served her right for being proud and stubborn and jumping to all the wrong conclusions. All the same he made a mental note to be around that evening, he didn't think that Percy was a young man to splash out on dinner unless he was getting something in return, an aspect which Rose, being Rose, had overlooked.

He said pleasantly, "Well, enjoy yourselves, it's a splendid day."

Which it was, only not a day to spend in a museum, thought Rose, going outside with Percy. They took the bus. He had a car, he explained, but it wasn't worth driving the short distance from the hospital and spending a fortune on parking fees. Rose, anxious to make the day a success, agreed and stood uncomplainingly between a very stout woman with a shopping bag smelling of fish and a youth with a strange hair-do and a radio strapped to his belt. At least she heard the midday news.

When Percy had told Mr Werdmer ter Sane that they would have a snack, that was exactly what he had meant. Rose, eating beans on toast and making every mouthful tell, thought waspishly of mushrooms in cream sauce and lobster thermidor, though Sybren hadn't meant a word of it, and over their coffee listened with all the interest she could summon to Percy carrying on about his career. ''Of course I don't intend to be a paediatrician,'' he told her. ''I'm not keen on kids; they're grubby and sick up. I shall specialise in cardiac surgery, there's a wide field and plenty of money there.''

''Is there?'' Rose was a little vague; she never thought of surgery in terms of money although she was aware that surgeons for the most part were comfortably well off. ''So you'll go to one of the cardiac hospitals when you're finished at St Bride's?''

''Naturally, St Bride's is only a stop-gap until there is a vacancy.''

''But St Bride's does very important work—look at little Shirley—that was a marvellous piece of surgery Mr Werdmer ter Sane did—she'd be dead by now...''

He shrugged. ''She'll have one leg shorter than the other if she lives.''

''Of course she'll live,'' said Rose indignantly, ''and there are such things as surgical shoes...''

''Well, don't let's bore on about work. If you're finished, shall we move into the museum?''

It appeared that Percy liked mummies. He knew a lot about them too; he lectured Rose at length about each specimen and she disliked every minute, trying not to look too closely at the remains he was so enthusiastic about, her thoughts turning more and more to lobster thermidor. Mercifully, he stopped at teatime and marched her along to the cafeteria for a cup of tea and a sponge cake which merely sopped up the tea and left her insides empty. It was over tea that Percy told her that he had the key to a friend's flat. ''We'll nip along there,'' he told her, ''and have a drink—there's food in the fridge; no one will know if you don't get back to St Bride's—I suppose you're on in the morning; well, as long as we're back before breakfast...'' He rambled on happily while she sat staring at him. Was this what Sadie had meant when she had said that he wasn't quite Rose's type? She said clearly, ''I think you've got it wrong. I've no intention of going to anyone's flat with you, Percy. Whatever gave you that idea?''

He lolled back in his chair, still very sure of himself. ''My dear girl, aren't you a bit out of date? Nowadays we live just as we like...''

''Yes, we do,'' said Rose coldly, ''and I don't think we like the same sort of life.''

''My God, you're stuffy.'' The sneer on his face quite spoilt his good looks.

Rose, wishing to be fair, considered this. ''Yes, I dare say I am,'' she conceded. ''Thank you for a very pleasant afternoon, Percy.''

She picked up her shoulder bag from beside her chair, got up and walked away, looking quite composed and under the calm seething.

She was also hungry. On the bus going back to the hospital, she tried to decide what she would do with her evening. Sadie was on duty, her other friends were either on duty too, or had dates. Fish and chips, she told herself philosophically, and the new novel a little patient's grateful parent had presented to her a few days ago. Anything would be better than spending the evening, not the night, with Percy. She shuddered strongly at the very idea, descended from the bus and went briskly across the hospital's forecourt, watched by the patient Sybren.

He strolled towards her as she crossed the entrance ahead of him, blocking her path so that she was forced to stop. ''Had a good time?'' he wanted to know blandly.

He really was the last straw. ''You again,'' declared Rose in a regrettably shrill voice. ''I might have known. And if you've come to gloat, you can get on with it, but don't you dare stop me...''

The voice in which he uttered, ''Now, now,'' would have soothed an ill-tempered baby in the throes of teething. ''You don't have to say a word. I just happened to be here,'' he uttered the fib with a magnificent candour. ''If you could forget that you don't like me and have dinner with me? I dislike eating on my own.'' He gave a fleeting thought to his solitary meals in his home and smiled very faintly. ''If you're not hungry we could cut out the lobster.''

She had meant to say no but her insides rumbled in the silence following his words and he added matter-of-factly, ''You're hungry too.''

She gave him one of her clear looks. ''Yes, I am. I'll come and thank you but only—only...''

''As ships that pass in the night? Oh, that's understood.'' He turned her round smartly and made for the door.

''I'm not—I really ought...'' She began and was silenced by his, ''You can do whatever you need to do while I'm seeing about a table.''

After that he had nothing to say; she sat in the comfort of the Rolls, her head empty of thoughts, in a dreamlike state from which she felt sure she would wake presently. But she didn't; Sybren parked the car and ushered her into the restaurant with a kindly, ''Off you go, I'll be here when you're ready.''

She spent ten minutes doing her face and her hair and wishing that she had been wearing something smart enough for her surroundings. The pink was all right, but she had worn it several times, he must think she hadn't anything else. Apparently he didn't for when she joined him he remarked, ''I like that dress better than any of the others you wear. Pink suits you.''

She thanked him shyly and followed the head waiter to a table by a window, nicely secluded.

''Well, now shall we have champagne cocktails while we decide what we'll eat?'' His manner was just right, the old friend taking out another old friend he'd accidently met. For the whole of their delicious meal he made no mention of the hospital, or Percy Pride or Holland for that matter. He seemed to have an inexhaustible fund of small talk which needed little or no reply on her part. As they went from mushrooms to lobster and from lobster to a magnificent concoction of ice cream, chocolate and whipped cream crowned with raspberries, Rose unwound. Sybren, filling her glass with the excellent champagne he had ordered, lifted a finger for coffee and sat back while their plates were taken away and it was brought. Only then did he ask, ''Do you want to tell me about it, Rose? Regard me as a sympathetic aunt if you wish, or one of your friends at St Bride's. It doesn't matter that you don't like me; I promise you I'll forget about it at once. You see if you bottle it up it will grow out of all proportion and you'll rake it up,'' and when she didn't speak, ''what did you have for lunch? Beans on toast?''

She laughed then. ''Yes, and a cup of coffee...''

''I've never liked beans since I ate them out of a tin when I was a scout.''

''You were a scout?'' She looked so surprised that he laughed. ''It keeps little boys out of mischief. What part of the museum did you visit?''

''The mummies. I—I didn't much care for them and it seems so rude to stare at them when they've been dead for such a long time.''

''True. Young Pride is interested in them?''

''Oh yes!'' She found herself smiling. ''He lectured me.'' She sipped her coffee and didn't look at him. ''We had tea then and he—he told me that he had the key of a friend's flat...''

She glanced at him and somehow he wasn't Mr Werdmer ter Sane any more but someone she could talk to without feeling a fool. It was a facet of him she hadn't seen before although, loving him, she thought that she knew him very well. ''I should have thought of that, shouldn't I?'' she ended.

He said gravely: ''I think that perhaps your friend Sadie would have, but you…no, Rose. You haven't had much experience of men, have you?''

The warm friendly feeling faded. She said woodenly, ''No, for obvious reasons.'' She was suddenly cross because he had spoilt the evening. ''And you have no need to remind me—haven't I been told since I was a teenager that I was plain—homely was the word my stepmother used and she was so right—men don't make passes at homely girls, only when there's no one else available I suppose.'' Her voice squeaked with temper. ''You should know that.''

She put down her coffee-cup and said like a small child, ''Thank you for my dinner, I'd like to go back now.''

Mr Werdmer ter Sane hadn't said a word; he paid the bill, accompanied her from the restaurant, saw her into the car and drove her back to St Bride's, still without speaking. Only as he opened the door for her did he say, ''Good night, Rose—good-bye perhaps?'' He touched her cheek with a gentle finger and got back into the car and drove away.

CHAPTER EIGHT

LYING IN BED, trying to get to sleep, Rose admitted that she had been silly as well as rude; no wonder Sybren hadn't spoken to her on their way back from the restaurant. She was going to have to apologise to him; he would probably be on the ward in the morning. She shut her eyes and drifted into an uneasy sleep.

Sister was back on duty in the morning which left Rose free to attend to Shirley who despite the antibiotic was slightly feverish and pretty peevish. The registrar came during the morning, attended by a sulky Percy, who avoided Rose's eye and, most unusual for him, had nothing to say for himself. The registrar examined Shirley without haste, his face expressionless. He was worried, Rose guessed, and to tell the truth she was worried herself; the child wasn't making progress and she had been doing so well.

''We'll keep her on the antibiotic for another twenty-four hours, Rose,'' the registrar told her. ''If her temperature isn't coming down by then, we'll have to think again. Mr Werdmer ter Sane went back this morning but he'll come over again if we're worried; he didn't want Mr Cesswell's holiday interrupted, he's not due back until Sunday.''

He went away and when she had settled Shirley she went into the ward to get started on the treatments and dressings. It was a day when things went wrong; nothing important, just small irritating things; notes mislaid, a child who should have gone home, delayed, not enough sheets back from the laundry, the dispensary querying Percy Pride's prescriptions; and quite rightly too for he wrote very small and with flourishes which could be taken for anything. Rose went off duty that evening feeling that it had been a day of twice its usual length.

The rest of the week was much the same, too; although she was ready to admit to herself that she was partly to blame; try as she would, she found it quite impossible to stop thinking about Sybren, largely because she had no idea if she would ever see him again. Shirley seemed to get better although she wasn't making the progress she should and she knew that the registrar was worried about her although there was nothing he could put his finger on. Her small chest had improved and yet she was listless and very peevish, not bothering when her mother came to sit with her for hours at a stretch. Rose, going off-duty on Friday evening for the weekend, was vaguely worried about the child; the operation had been a success, there was no doubt of that, and yet Shirley wasn't doing as well as she should. Sister Cummins, drinking her coffee with Rose on the Friday, voiced her unease. ''I shall be glad when Mr Cresswell is back on Sunday; I only wish we could have got hold of Mr Werdmer ter Sane but Mr Farrell tells me he had to go to Munich on some urgent case and can't get here before tomorrow. Still I dare say the three of them will put their heads together. You're pale, Rose, it's a good thing you have this weekend off.''

Rose didn't agree with her; she was going to miss seeing Sybren; he would be gone by the time she got back at midday on Monday. Well, it was her own fault; he had asked to be forgiven. She wondered why; it surely couldn't make much difference to him, she had been—what had he said? A ship which passed in the night.

When she got to her aunt's cottage that lady eyed her severely. ''Rose, what have you been doing with yourself? You're washed out, no colour at all, all eyes and much too thin.''

Rose said with a false cheerfulness, ''Well, that's a good thing, I'm too fat, you know.''

''Rubbish, child. Maggie, we'll have a bottle of that port the vicar gave me for Christmas, and you, Rose, sit down and eat your supper. I know it's late and you are tired, but no one ever slept on an empty stomach.''

It was soothing to be taken so firmly in hand with her aunt on one side plying her with port and Maggie urging second helpings and when she was told to go to bed with the hot milk

Maggie had put into her hand, she went willingly enough and presently laid her head on her pillow and went instantly to sleep.

She was up early, feeling marvellous, drinking a cup of tea with Maggie in the kitchen and then taking Shep for a walk before breakfast. And over that meal Aunt Millicent observed that there was really nothing much to do but if she liked to accompany her to the church to do the flowers she was more than welcome.

The church was small and old and cool and the vicar came along while they were arranging their vases and had a long, rather prosy chat, a pleasant hotchpotch of local news, the amount of honey he was getting from his hives, old Mrs James's poor health and the forthcoming Sunday School treat. Rose found it all very soothing.

''And you, Rose?'' he wanted to know. ''How is life treating you? You are able to enjoy your leisure, I hope; your work is hard but worthwhile and nurses deserve their pleasure even more than the rest of us.''

She assured him that yes, life was splendid and there was always something to do when she was off duty and she had so many friends...

Aunt Millicent, arranging a massive bouquet for the font, for there was a christening on Sunday, glanced at her niece. From the look of the girl, she mused, none of that was true. Telling fibs, in church too, and to the vicar but the dear child was unhappy about something. Aunt Millicent thought privately that she would like to meet this Dutch surgeon Rose was so careful never to mention. Maggie, an elderly spinster and with a romantic heart, had declared that little Rose was in love and Aunt Millicent had a shrewd suspicion that she might be right.

She bore Rose back to the cottage presently to eat a substantial lunch and then take Shep for his afternoon walk. ''For I am quite exhausted,'' said Aunt Millicent, who had never been exhausted in her life but held the view that there was nothing like a good walk in the open air to ease one's feelings.

As for Rose, she walked for miles until even Shep slowed his steps and when she got back to the cottage she looked all the better for it with colour in her cheeks and a readier smile. She was given sherry, told to tidy herself for her supper and plied with good wholesome food before sitting down to a game of bezique with her aunt and then being packed off to bed with Maggie trotting up the stairs presently to see that she drank her milk. The two old ladies' sensible kindness did much to restore Rose's equanimity; a Sunday spent as they always were at the cottage: church, lunch, a lazy afternoon in the garden with tea under the trees edging the lawn and one of Maggie's delicious cold suppers to round off the day, more or less completed the cure. At least it had made her see that life had to go on whether she loved Sybren or not and she would have to make the best of it. She slept dreamlessly and went back to London in the morning. It was obvious that things weren't quite right when she went on duty after her early dinner. Sister Cummins pounced on her at once.

''Good, you're back. My goodness, what a weekend and you not here. Mr Werdmer ter Sane has just gone; Mr Cresswell's still in the hospital if we want him. Shirley took a turn for the worse yesterday, thank heaven both men came back together; she's on a life support machine—fat embolism—you were worried about her chest, remember? They did a tracheostomy last night—there's respiratory failure. Let's hope there's no brain damage. She's unconscious, of course. She's being treated by hypothermia. I've been looking after her and they sent a staff nurse to manage the ward; now you're back, take her over, will you?''

Sister Cummins was tired and, unlike her, ruffled. She allowed Rose to sit her down at her desk and fetch her a tray of tea from the kitchen.

''Who's with Shirley?'' she asked, sugaring her tea lavishly and opening a tin of biscuits.

''Staff Nurse White from the medical side—she's quite good, but she's not dealt with a fat embolism before...''

''And in the ward?''

"The two part-timers and the junior student nurse; they can cope."

"Then Sister, would you agree to going off duty for a few hours? If Doris White could go into the Ward, I'll see to Shirley. Mr Farrell's on duty, isn't he? And he can get hold of Mr Cresswell." She couldn't stop herself asking, "Is Mr Werdmer ter Sane coming back?"

"I don't know. He flew over yesterday afternoon; he was here until a short while ago. He and Mr Cresswell think there's just a chance; she's holding her own." Sister Cummins was reviving rapidly under the influence of strong tea. "Everything was going so well too, and it's a bit late in the day for a fat embolism, I mean, no one expected it after the first few days." She poured another cup of tea. "Now I'll give you a report and take your advice and have an hour or two off. You're on until the night staff come, aren't you?" She added belatedly, "Did you have a good weekend?"

"Lovely, thanks, Sister."

"You look better for it. I'll come back to give the report, shall I? That will leave you free to see to Shirley before you go off-duty. Staff Nurse White can see to the ward—relieve each other for supper."

It was a good thing that there were no other very ill children; all the same, there was more than enough to do and Shirley needed constant care. Rose sipped a cup of tea one of the nurses brought her and hardly noticed the time. When she got off-duty at last she was tired and hungry. Mr Cresswell had been in and so had Mr Farrell and Percy Pride had been with them, out of his depth, she suspected, although he looked as though he knew exactly what was going on. Her last thoughts before she slept were a sure hope that she would never be in a tight corner with him.

She was on all day for the next day or two; she had breakfast with the other girls and was on duty by half past seven, the long day stretching ahead of her but not minding that; it was a good thing to have something to think about, something urgent enough to dispel Sybren from her mind.

It was mid-afternoon with only another couple of hours before she could go off-duty when he came into the ward. He nodded briefly at her, said, ''Let someone know I'm here, will you?'' and went to look at Shirley.

Mr Farrell came almost immediately followed by Percy, and Mr Werder ter Sane asked, ''Where is Sister Cummins?''

''Off-duty, Sir,'' said Rose and when he frowned a little went indignantly pink although she asked reasonably enough, ''Would you like Staff Nurse White here, Sir? She's been nursing Shirley.'' She gave him a calm look, hiding her hurt feelings. He didn't want her on the case any more; well, that was all right by her. She met his cold eyes without a blink. How puzzling it was that she could love him so wholeheartedly and find him such a very tiresome man.

"That won't be necessary, Staff Nurse. Shall we have the charts?''

He was there quite some time, discussing what was best to be done, and presently Mr Cresswell arrived and they stood around muttering and murmuring to each other, while Percy hovered on their perimeter and Rose sensibly got on with her observations, checked her tubes and paraphernalia, taking no notice of the learned gentlemen and their deliberations. They gathered round the child presently and Mr Werdmer ter Sane said, ''If you will continue the treatment, Staff Nurse, and notify Mr Farrell of any change.'' He looked at Mr Cresswell who nodded agreement and who then said surprisingly, ''Good work, Rose, keep it up.''

But Sybren said nothing, merely nodded even more briskly than before and walked away with Mr Cresswell, leaving Mr Farrell to give her a friendly pat on the shoulder as he followed them. Percy would have spoken to her but she said rather crossly, ''I'm busy—do you mind?'' and went back to her dials and tubes.

She didn't see Sybren again, although he was in and out for the next day or so, always when she was off-duty or at a meal.

Little Shirley began to show signs of recovery; a slow recovery but steady. Now it was a question of waiting to see if she had suffered any brain damage and Rose, watching the small signs of returning consciousness, prayed that that had been avoided. Shirley was still on her life-support machine and would be for another few days, after that they could be optimistic.

The weather was unusually warm and Rose longed to be at her aunt's cottage out in the fresh air, taking Shep for his stately walk, doing a little undemanding gardening. She did go for a brief walk each evening with whoever was off-duty with her, but there was only the nearby park and besides the streets round the hospital were crowded by various processions of people chanting for or against something. Usually they didn't come on to the streets until the early evening, but as she went about her work in the early afternoon she could hear a good deal of shouting in the distance. Sister Cummins, coming in to take a look at Shirley before she went off duty, remarked upon it. "I'll be glad to get away from the din for the evening," she observed, "I'm off to Maidenhead. See you in the morning. There is nothing new since I went over the report with you."

Staff Nurse White was in the ward with two student nurses and since half the children were convalescent she would be able to cope easily. Rose began to bed-bath Shirley, still unconscious but restless. She was just finishing when one of the student nurses came into the room to tell her that Percy Pride was in the ward. "Staff thought you'd like to know," she explained. "He's just pottering around."

Rose nodded. "He would, leave the door open, will you? Have the children had their teas? Will you ask Rene if she'll make a pot of tea for Staff and me? You two go to tea at four o'clock, will you?"

She was alone again, bending over Shirley when the world seemed to explode around her, a thunder of sound which rumbled and grumbled to a never-ending crashing of brickwork and masonry and tinkling glass.

Rose wanted to scream, as it was she was terribly afraid and trembling so much that she had to put down the thermometer she was holding, but the discipline of years of training took over; the ventilator, not surprisingly, had come to a halt; she started the manual emergency and switched on the oxygen from the cylinder, aware that Doris, her face as white as her own and shaking just as badly, was at her elbow. ''The windows are blown out, thank God the glass went outside, the floor's sagging...''

''Three of you—four with Percy, if the stairs are safe get the children down to the next floor—stay in the ward, get a nurse on the landing and another at the bottom of the stairs—make a chain; get Percy to help.''

''But you? I'll send Percy here as soon as the children are safe.''

''I'm all right for the moment, and there's the door over there.'' She nodded towards a small door at the back of the room which led to a narrow passage, relic of the earlier days of St Bride's and seldom used. ''Hurry, Doris.''

There was noise all around, but not very close, people shouting, ambulances wailing, running feet. Rose, feeling that she was in the middle of a particularly nasty dream, worked away at her machine and hoped for the best. Someone would come soon and if she gave way to panic both she and Shirley would come to grief.

She could hear frenzied activity in the ward and then silence before Doris called, ''We're empty Rose, and Percy's coming.''

But before he came there was a slow shudder as the outside wall of the ward swayed slowly outward and disappeared. There was still the width of the ward between Shirley's room, and a good stout wall besides, although the door was hanging on its hinges. Rose made a small sound which might have been a sob and then pulled herself together again. They would have to risk making a run for it once Percy came back. They would go through the ward and down the stairs; he could carry the child while she pumped; it would be touch and go but better than staying where they were.

He came in slowly, almost reluctantly, his face pale, ''The stairs,'' he said hoarsely, ''they've just fallen to bits, we'll never get out that way.''

''Then we'll go along the passage: it's narrow and it'll take twice as long but we're sure to find help. You warned someone we're here?''

He looked at her and she saw that he wasn't listening. She said it all again, fear making her shrill, and this time he said, ''Help, no I didn't. We'll never get away,'' he repeated.

She had a blanket ready. ''We'll have to manage without the oxygen—pick her up carefully and don't go too fast or I'll never be able to keep up,'' she said bracingly, more to reassure herself than him. ''There's sure to be someone...''

In the distance someone yelled ''Fire!'' and she froze. ''Get a move on, Percy,'' she managed from a shaking mouth and opened out the blanket.

''I'll get help.'' He had turned and rushed out through the door before she could speak. Her first frantic attempt to shout after him came out as a very small squeak, the second was an ear-splitting yell, unfortunately drowned by the urgent sirens of approaching fire engines. She couldn't believe that he had gone away and left them; he knew, even better than she, that Shirley needed two people to get her to safety. She shouted again still hopeful that he had gone for help and would come back at any moment, but there was no reply, only ominous creaks and groans from the building and the faintest whiff of smoke.

Something would have to be done; anything was better than staying there waiting for the roof to fall in or to be enveloped in flames. She remembered Doris, then, she would have told someone; Rose took fresh heart, snatched up some towels in her free hand, planning to wet them in the wash basin. She would disconnect Shirley, go through the door into the passage and go as fast as she could until she reached the small stairs at its end. They opened into, for some reason which she had never bothered about, one of the underground passages which honey-combed the hospital's foundations. There were several doors leading into the courtyard around the building, once there they could get Shirley on to a portable ventilator. Even as she planned she knew that the chances of the child surviving were small. She filled her lungs and gave a great shout.

This time she was answered. ''All right, I'm not deaf,'' said Mr Werdmer ter Sane, bending his large person so that he could get through the door.

Sybren had been driving towards St Bride's when the bomb exploded, too far off to suffer any injury but near enough to the hospital to have a good idea that it would have been caught in the blast. He parked his car and shouldered his way through the still running crowds. The entrance was damaged but still standing, one wing more or less undamaged excepting blownout windows, but the surgical wing had received a good share of the bomb's force, and Sister Cummins' ward was exposed to the outside world although there was no sign of life there. He had crossed the entrance hall already crowded with patients and nurses and house doctors organising them into a semblance of order when he saw Staff Nurse White. He put out an arm and stopped her. ''Rose, where is she?'' he wanted to know.

''Still with Shirley; at least I asked Percy Pride to go back and help her, they ought to be here.'' She looked round helplessly. ''He said he'd see to everything so I haven't told anyone—I had the ward to see to.''

He said soothingly because she was on the verge of tears, ''Of course—don't worry—I'll see if I can find them.''

There was a good deal of rubble blocking his way and before he reached the stairs outside the ward he could see that it was a hopeless task to get up them. He went back the way he had come, the smell of smoke strong in his nostrils. There would be another way up to the ward; he would have to lose precious minutes looking for it.

There was no need, a door along the passage in front of him burst open and Percy came hurtling towards him. ''We must get out,'' he pushed Sybren's arm away, ''the place is on fire.''

"Where is Rose?" Sybren's voice expected an answer, fire or no fire.

"With Shirley..."

"And you left them to roast alive?" Mr Werdmer ter Sane uttered strong language in his own tongue. "You will get doctors or porters or police—anyone, a trolley, oxygen and a portable ventilator and you will bring them to this door at once and wait here." He added grimly, "If you do not, I personally shall break every bone in your body."

He didn't wait to see how Percy reacted but tore through the door, closing it behind him. The stairs faced him; he went up them at a surprising speed considering how heavily built he was. The narrow passage at the top seemed endless and the smell of smoke was stronger. He saw the door at its end and opened it with a grunt of relief.

Rose stared at him from a pale frightened face, still working away at the ventilator. She opened her mouth to speak but no sound came which was a good thing. From the look on his face he was in no mood to stand any female nonsense. He was disconnecting Shirley from the useless machine and wrapping her in the blanket. "Work the ventilator and keep close," he bade Rose and without more ado he made for the door. It was a tight squeeze going along the passage and even worse on the stairs. Rose performed miracles of balance, her heart in her mouth, her arms aching beyond belief, her eyes stinging from the smoke eddying lazily around them. If she had had any breath left she would have whooped with joy when they reached the door. Mr Werdmer ter Sane gave it a vicious kick and it flew open and they burst through it untidily into instant activity. Percy Pride, doubtless anxious about his bones, had assembled all that Sybren had told him to get. Shirley, connected to oxygen and the ventilator and warmly wrapped, was laid on a trolley and borne away with Mr Werdmer ter Sane in charge and Percy, anxious to make amends, hovering. There were quite a few people in the procession and no one had noticed that Rose wasn't with them.

She watched them go, leaning against the broken door. She felt a little light-headed but sensible enough to reason that it was natural enough for them all to concentrate on Shirley, and probably the burly policeman who was giving a hand had thought she was just being curious when he had moved her gently aside from the trolley and told her to get out of the way. She would have to make her own way to the entrance hall and find Doris and the rest of the children.

Shirley was being taken to the undamaged wing, being hastily organised to take as many children as possible. Mr Cresswell was already there and he and Sybren bent over Shirley, assessing the damage. She was still alive. ''And probably none the worse for it,'' said Mr Cresswell with satisfaction. ''How long has she been off the life-support machine?''

''Rose?'' Sybren looked around when she didn't answer. ''Where's Rose?'' He looked again. ''Did anyone see her? She came through the door with me.''

He didn't wait for an answer but turned and went back the way they had come and found her still leaning against the door. ''What on earth are you hanging round here for?'' He sounded so angry that she blinked at him. He couldn't even rescue her without getting cross about it, she thought wearily. ''I'm going to find Staff Nurse White,'' she said in a voice quite devoid of expression. She added idiotically, ''I'm sorry we were such a nuisance, Sir.''

She had whipped past him and sped around the corner towards the entrance hall before he could stop her.

It took a little while to find Doris; the hall was full of firemen, ambulance men, doctors and nurses all intent on getting the children back into some sort of shelter as quickly as possible. Some were being taken by ambulance to neighbouring hospitals, the really ill ones were being bedded down in the far wing, which was happily undamaged.

''There you are, Rose—I've been so worried about you—Percy got you out? How is Shirley?'' She eyed Rose's face. ''Are you all right? You're a kind of pea green...''

"I'm fine. Are all the children still here?"

"Yes—I'm on my way there just now. I came back to report to Casualty Sister, she's doing all the checking. Come with me—we've got the little ward at the end—you know the one? It's too small but we'll have to manage. I say, you were a brick to stay, Rose..." Staff Nurse White, who wasn't a talkative girl, said shyly, "I wouldn't have dared—I was scared stiff..."

"So was I, if there'd been anyone there to hear I'd have screamed."

"But Percy?"

"Not Percy—Mr Werdmer ter Sane."

Doris White paused in her headlong rush through the crowds. "Him? He rescued you? Where was Percy?" She gulped, "Rose, he told me he was going back for you."

"He changed his mind. At least he did get to us, but he went away again. But don't let on..."

The ward they entered was crowded with cots, beds, nurses and doctors with a porter or two thrown in. The babies were all at one end, bawling with rage at being disturbed, to everyone's relief. The toddlers were two to a bed at the moment, apparently unaware that anything untoward was afoot; Shirley had a bed to herself with one nurse working the ventilator and another one controlling the flow of oxygen. Mr Cresswell was there, so was Sybren; they looked at her as she and Doris went across the ward, Mr Cresswell with a warm welcoming smile tinged with faint alarm at Rose's unfortunate colour; Sybren with a cold eye which apparently hadn't noticed.

All the same he was the one to catch her as she crumpled up in an untidy heap. With a muttered word to Mr Cresswell he strode out of the ward, across the back of the still crowded entrance and kicked open the door of the nurses' home.

There were a lot of people there too, going to and fro in a purposeful manner. He stopped a distracted woman with a fierce hair-do and a blue overall. "Which room is Staff Nurse Comely's?" he barked at her.

She put an agitated hand on her substantial bosom. "You can't come in here..."

"I can and I will, which room?"

"I'm the warden..."

Mr Werdmer ter Sane, not naturally a patient man, was losing his temper now. "I don't give a damn what you are. The number?"

She told him, gobbling with annoyance.

"And why don't you get into the hospital and give a hand instead of wringing your hands here?" he demanded and took the stairs two at a time. .

It was a good thing he was a large strong man; Rose wasn't heavy but she had a room on the second floor. By the time he reached her door he was breathing rather faster than usual.

He laid Rose gently upon her bed, took off her cap, covered her with a blanket and felt her pulse. It was quite satisfactory; he fetched a glass of water from the wash basin and sat down on the side of the bed and studied her. There was nothing faintly glamorous about her; her hair was in a deplorable state, hanging in wisps around her pale face. Her apron had been dragged askew and she had laddered her tights and there was a cut on one arm where she had caught it on some wreckage on their way to safety. He bent and kissed her very gently and waited patiently until she opened her eyes a few minutes later.

"Where..." she began and stopped. Heroines in novels always asked where they were when they had fainted. Instead she said, "I'm sorry I fainted. So silly."

"So sensible. Nature's way of putting you out of action so that you can recoup your strength." He sounded as dry as one of her text books.

She sat up, the pea green had given way, thankfully, to pallor, and she drank the water he was offering. "I'm quite all right, thank you," she told him in a voice which belied her wan appearance. "I'm sure you want to get back."

"How long were you there alone?" he asked.

"Oh, not long. I'm not sure..." She forced her voice to it's usual matter-of-fact calm. ''One doesn't notice time when one is busy.''

''Or when one is scared out of one's wits,'' he commented blandly. ''You're a very brave girl, Rose. You could have killed Shirley if you'd panicked and you could both have been killed there.''

''You came...''

''Yes.'' He got up. ''I'm going to find someone to bring you a hot drink and you are to lie there warm and quiet for at least half an hour, after that you may return to duty. Those are doctor's orders.''

He went very quietly and she put her head back on the pillow, glad to rest it. Ten minutes later one of the home sisters came in with a tea tray. ''I had no idea,'' she began comfortably, ''Mr Werdmer ter Sane came looking for me and told me. You poor child, what a frightful experience, left alone like that. You were doing your duty, of course, but I can think of any number who wouldn't have stuck their necks out when there was a chance of getting killed or burnt to a crisp.''

She put the tray down and poured the tea out and then poured something into it.

''What's that?'' asked Rose.

''Whisky, my dear. Mr Werdmer ter Sane ordered it for you. Drink it up, there's a good girl.''

Rose had swung her legs over the bed. ''I must get back—there'll be such a lot to do,'' she began.

''Bound to be.'' Home Sister was unflappable. ''I popped over a little while ago to give a hand.'' She chuckled. ''He didn't think much of our warden, I might have known she'd go to pieces—still that's neither here nor there. They've got everyone out, no one killed in the hospital, thank heaven, but several poor souls who were out in the street; quite a few children hurt, but not badly—your wing got the full blast, most of the centre and the other wing are more or less intact—and the nurses' home, of course. They have transferred the children who've been hurt and two of the student nurses, one of the porters and a domestic worker. I hear almost all the equipment has been damaged though.''

She re-filled Rose's cup, stood over her while she drank it and picked up the tray.

''I'm going back on duty, Sister.''

''Yes, dear. Put on another apron first and do your hair, you look more like yourself again now.''

Ten minutes later Rose went back into the hospital. There still seemed to be a great deal of confusion but the entrance hall was emptying fast although there were several men there with cameras. She hardly noticed them but slipped back into the ward, had a word with Doris and went to look at Shirley. The child actually looked better; she was checking things with the nurse looking after her when Mr Cresswell joined her.

''Feeling better?'' He gave her a kind smile. ''A nasty experience, Rose, but I—we are all proud of you, it takes pluck to be brave when there's no one there to see. Mr Werdmer ter Sane is in theatre, checking the damage; we decided that you ought to go off-duty until tomorrow but we knew that you wouldn't take any notice of anything that we said.'' He went on briskly, ''Now let's see who we've got left here—I've sent two of the babies over to Margaret's, they've got respiratory failure and they'll do better over there; they can come back when we are straight.''

After that things fell slowly into place. The hospital was full of firemen and police and television cameras but work went on in the wards wherever possible. Rose gathered her team around her and gave the children their suppers and their medicine, re-arranged the cots and beds, sent nurses to their supper in turn, conducted the senior nursing officer round her small patients, did another round with the registrar who had been off duty and had just arrived back, and then found some paper and wrote the report. The Kardex was gone in the ruins; a new one would have to be made out tomorrow, in the meanwhile she made a quick resume of the day's happenings ready for the night staff, most of whom were already on duty anyway.

It was a boon and a blessing when the electricians managed to get the electricity going again and the reserve ventilator could be brought in and fixed up. Rose sent the student nurse who had been looking after Shirley off-duty, conferred with Doris White and did a final round of the sleeping children. "You go to supper," she told Doris, "and take everyone with you, and ask someone to save me some food, will you? I'll be along as soon as the night people have settled in."

Which took rather more time than she had thought; it was long after the usual hour when she left the ward and she was now so tired she loitered along the passage, stumbling a little over the hoses still lying around, not looking where she was going. She stumbled over Mr Werdmer ter Sane's large feet too, which brought her to a sudden halt.

"Oh, sorry, Sir." She looked at him with tired eyes, and her gentle mouth drooped at his curt, "You should be in bed. What are you doing traipsing around?"

"I'm going to my supper," she told him with dignity. "Good night, Sir."

He put his hands on her shoulders, pinning her gently to the spot.

"Oh, Rose, what has happened to us? I thought we had become friends—more than friends. But you don't trust me, do you?"

"Does it matter? And I did trust you until Mies told me." She wriggled under his hands. "Oh, does it matter?" she asked again. "I'm so tired."

He let her go then. "Of course. How thoughtless I am. Good night, Rose and sleep well."

He had gone. She went to the canteen and ate what was on her plate and went to bed. She wanted to cry but she was too tired.

CHAPTER NINE

THE NEXT FEW DAYS went by in a well ordered chaos; it was surprising how swiftly the great piles of debris round the hospital and in the streets around it were cleared away. An army of workmen moved in, mending doors and windows, hanging huge tarpaulins over gaping walls as in the meantime the hospital fell into its routine, or something approximating to it. At least the little patients suffered no discomforts although there was a certain amount of improvisation with equipment and there was, for a day or two, a shortage of crockery and everything which everyone had tended to take for granted as being to hand when needed. But on the whole, they managed very well; all the small tiffs which occurred between the various wards and departments were forgotten, at least for the time being. The laundry supplied the linen to the wards without complaint, even allowed extra; the dispensary forbore from wasting the ward sister's time by querying entries in the dispensary book and there was an unending supply of egg and chips and soup in the canteen.

Rose went about her work, outwardly her usual matter-of-fact self, while inwardly she was as miserable as she had ever been in her whole life. If this is being in love, she told herself fiercely, then the quicker I forget about it the better. Mr Werdmer ter Sane had come twice during the week and on both occasions she had been off-duty. Anyone would think, she mused bitterly, that he had looked in the off-duty book so that he wouldn't have to meet me.

Which was exactly what he had done.

Percy had avoided her but she had hardly noticed that, in fact she didn't think about him at all. She wanted to forget those awful moments when she had been alone with Shirley and he was all part and parcel of them. She would never forget how she had felt when she had heard Sybren's voice, calm and unhurried, and she supposed that she never would.

The ward settled down; Sister Cummins, still brooding over the fact that she hadn't been there when she would have been most useful, had the ward organised by now even though it wasn't entirely to her liking, and Shirley, to everyone's delight and surprise, regained consciousness and began to pick up once more.

Towards the end of the week Rose encountered Percy Pride as she was on the way to the path. lab. He had been avoiding her and she hadn't minded; he had behaved shamefully and he must be feeling awkward about it, besides Sadie had told her that he had been on the carpet and advised to transfer to the convalescent home in Surrey run by St Bride's.

But if she had expected an apology from him she was to be mistaken. He stopped in front of her and said sourly: ''So—how is our little heroine getting on? Did you a good turn, didn't I, leaving you to hog the limelight?''

Rose gave him the kind of look she would have given something nasty under a stone; she wished that she could be like Sadie with a quick, telling retort on her tongue, but she couldn't think of anything to say.

Percy eyed her narrowly and when she didn't speak, "Oh, well, it didn't do you much good with Mr Werdmer ter Sane, did it? He's off home and I dare say he'll forget about brave little Rose once he gets there. You are not quite his cup of tea, are you?''

Rose, holding the path lab specimen in its dish carefully in one hand, reached up and smacked his cheek. It made a very satisfactory sound and was just as good as the kind of caustic remark she was sure Sadie would have made to him. She didn't wait to see the results of her slap but walked on down the stairs into the lab. If she was a little nervous about coming out again in case he was lurking, she had no intention of admitting it, even to herself.

Back on the ward she gave herself no time to think about

Sybren; he was going home, Percy had said, and there was no point in him lying about that, and probably once there, he would forget her. Instead she kept her mind on her work, longing at the same time for five o'clock to come so that she might go off-duty. She had her two days off but she wasn't going to Aunt Millicent's; she would potter around until lunch time and then take herself up to Regent Street and do some window-shopping and there was bound to be someone off-duty on her second day; they could go to Kew Gardens or take rolls and cheese into Regent's Park. She tackled Shirley's small wants with zest and not long after five o'clock she went off-duty.

She was almost at the bottom of the big staircase leading to the entrance hall when she saw Sybren standing talking to Mr Cresswell. She couldn't go back; he was facing her and would have seen her.

As indeed he had; he said something to Mr Cresswell and crossed to the stairs so that they came face to face on the bottom step.

She searched his face and could find nothing comforting in it. "You're leaving—Percy told me." She put out a hand. "So I'll say goodbye..."

He ignored the hand and she dropped it to her side. "You want it to be goodbye, Rose?"

She said in a rush, "Yes, oh yes, and I do thank you for rescuing me and Shirley and I hope that you will be very happy..."

He lifted his eyebrows at that. "Happy, should I be?"

"Well, yes." She wished that she could say all the right things, Sadie would have known; made some witty observations about being married and turned everything into a joke, something which she was quite unable to do.

"I'm glad about Shirley and you must be delighted. When she is grown up she'll think of you with gratitude."

"And you, Rose; you're already grown up, how do you think of me?"

The warm colour washed over her face but she didn't look away.

"I shall think of you as a very eminent surgeon, Sir."

"You flatter me. Goodbye, Rose." He stood on one side and after a moment's hesitation she went past him, across the hall and through the door at the back which would take her to the nurses' home.

She went very fast, trying to run away from her unhappiness. Before she reached her room she had already made up her mind to go to Aunt Millicent. If she hurried she could get a train; the local bus would have left, but just for once she would be extravagant and get a taxi. She hurled things into an overnight bag, tore out of her uniform, showered and dressed, tied her hair back with very little thought as to her appearance, left a message for Sadie and nipped smartly to the hospital entrance, remembering to peer cautiously out into the forecourt first in case Sybren's car was still there. It wasn't. She gulped back the ridiculous hope and went to catch a taxi to the station.

She caught the train with seconds to spare and at the other end was lucky enough to find the vicar's sister, only too glad to share a taxi with her. Aunt Millicent's cottage looked cosy and welcoming under the summer evening sky; Rose flew down the path and opened the door, calling "It's me, Rose," and when Aunt Millicent poked her austere head round the sitting-room door, she dropped her bag and hugged that lady quite ruthlessly, fighting a great desire to burst into tears.

Aunt Millicent took a lightning glance at her niece's face and said heartily, "Well, what a lovely surprise. I was only saying to Maggie this very evening how nice it would be if you were here for a day or two."

She frowned fiercely at Maggie, who had come hurrying from the kitchen, and that lady on the point of saying something quite different agreed instantly and loudly. "And there's a lovely little raised pie just waiting to be eaten," she pointed out. "Just you put that bag in your room and I'll get a tray."

"And a glass of wine, I think," declared her aunt, "and if

you're not too tired we long to hear about that awful bomb. I had such a splendid letter from your principal nursing officer and a charming one from Mr Werdmer ter Sane."

Rose, on her way upstairs, whizzed round. "He wrote? To you? what about?"

"Telling us what had happened and saying that your courage had saved a child's life. He wrote that you were a splendid nurse with a great sense of duty."

Rose said, "Oh, did he?" in a hollow voice. That was the sort of thing one could say about anyone; someone one didn't like overmuch or someone to whom one was quite indifferent. She went upstairs to her pretty room and sat down on the bed and pulled herself together. Presently she went down again and ate the raised pie and drank the wine and with the two elderly ladies on either side of her gave them a tidied-up version of the bombing. After that she was urged to go to her bed with the promise of a nice day on the morrow, doing nothing. She kissed the two kind faces, drank the milk with Maggie standing over her, and went upstairs. She was sure that she wouldn't sleep and she had a lot to think about but the country silence was soothing and the gentle murmur of voices from downstairs acted far more efficiently than a sleeping pill. She slept.

Mr Werdmer ter Sane had left the outskirts of London behind him and was well on the way to the ferry which would take him back to Holland when he slowed the car at an exit, followed it down and round and started driving back to London again on the other side of the motorway. For a man accustomed to having his own way either by arrogance or charm, he found himself singularly helpless. Rose, unassuming, not even pretty, certainly tiresomely obtuse about some things, had wished him goodbye in a matter-of-fact manner which should have left him in no doubt as to her feelings, but her eyes, her lovely gentle eyes, mused Mr Werdmer ter Sane besottedly, had betrayed her. He was at a loss to know why she had taken such a dislike to him—

after all they had gone through too. He put an elegant foot down hard, anxious to get back to St Bride's and find out.

The head porter was unable to help him. ''Saw Staff Nurse Comely go out this evening with me own eyes, Sir—'ad a bag with 'er too.''

Mr Werdmer ter Sane thought for a moment. ''Can you get hold of her friend? Sadie the name is—but that is all I know.''

Old Wilson said stolidly: ''Staff Nurse Gordon, Sir.'' He had worked all his life at St Bride's but he couldn't remember a consultant ever wanting to speak to a staff nurse off-duty. ''She'll be over in the 'ome, being just off-duty as you might say.''

He applied himself to the phone. ''She'll be right over, Sir.''

Sadie came dancing through the door; no one looking at her would have guessed that not five minutes earlier she had been in her dressing-gown, drinking tea and about to wash her hair. Now the dressing-gown had been replaced by uniform and her hair was charmingly arranged under a snowy cap.

She said breathlessly, ''Hullo. It seems silly to call you Sir, but I suppose I must. I thought you'd forgotten me.''

''Impossible—although I must do my best— I hear you are to be married very shortly.'' He smiled, at his most charming. ''Sadie, where's Rose?''

''Rose?'' They had walked into the centre of the entrance hall where no one could overhear them. ''Is that why she went?''

''Where?''

''To her aunt's house at Ashby St Ledgers, that's in...''

''I know, I wrote to her aunt—Miss Curtis—it's somewhere near Daventry.''

''Four miles—go up the M1 and turn left. Too late to go now—they'll all be in bed. It's about seventy miles; that's nothing to you and your Rolls. I say, why do you want to see her, has something awful happened on the ward?''

He shook his head. ''No, nothing like that...''

''You're not going to tell me, are you?''

''No, Sadie, not now.''

"I shall ask Rose when she gets back on Sunday evening."

"By all means. Thank you for your help. I hope you'll invite me to your wedding?"

"I say, will you come if I do? Rose is to be one of the bridesmaids, she is going to wear pink, she looks pretty in pink."

"I have thought for some time that she looks pretty in anything."

Old Wilson peering at them from his little box was shocked when she leaned up and kissed Mr Werdmer ter Sane's cheek. Really, what was the world coming to?

"Good luck," said Sadie, "Rose is a darling girl but very pig-headed."

She whirled away blowing a kiss to Wilson as she passed.

Sybren left London after seven o'clock in the morning, breakfasted on the way and was tooling down Ashby St Ledgers brief main street before ten. He stopped once here to ask the way and presently stopped in the lane outside Aunt Millicent's cottage. He got out and stood a moment looking at it; the windows were all open as was the front door and at the side of the house, given over to the soft fruit, he could see Rose picking raspberries.

She turned round as he shut the gate behind him and started slowly up the path and then came across the grass towards her. His good morning was affable and gave her no clue at all as to why he was there, standing in front of her, an uncanny answer to her daydreams. She put the basket of fruit down carefully and said good morning in her turn and since the silence between them got rather too long for comfort she essayed a little light conversation.

"I thought you were going to Holland."

"So did I, indeed I started my journey and changed my mind. I wanted to make quite sure that you had meant what you had said; that you had wanted it to be goodbye, Rose."

She said very steadily, "Yes, I did mean it. I'm sorry you came all this way..." She paused and being a truthful girl, added, "No, I'm not sorry."

He stared down at her. "I believe that we are at cross purposes; and I think to get to the heart of the tangle I must go back to Holland.'' He studied her face carefully. ''You really mean it, don't you, Rose?''

''Oh, yes. And if you don't mind I'd rather not talk about it.''

He nodded. ''Very well. We'll say goodbye for a second time. Do you not have a saying in English 'Third time lucky'?''

She wasn't going to answer that. It would be so easy to tell him that she loved him; she had only to open her mouth, but there was Mies—such a suitable wife for a wealthy eminent surgeon—waiting for him to go back to her.

She asked politely, ''Have you had breakfast! I'm sure Aunt Millicent will be glad to give you something.''

''I had a meal on the way here. I'll be on my way.''

Not just yet, cried her heart, five minutes more—ten minutes more... Someone, somewhere heard her. Aunt Millicent poked her head out of the kitchen window and called in her no-nonsense voice, ''Rose, whoever that is bring him in for a cup of coffee.''

Aunt Millicent was well aware who it was; it was Maggie who had seen him coming up the garden path and had rushed into the sitting-room to whisper the news, just as though anyone was near enough to overhear her.

''It's him,'' she whispered excitedly, ''I'm sure of it, Miss Curtis—that Dutch surgeon Rose never talks about. Fine as fivepence and a splendid body of a man.''

So Miss Curtis had gone to peer from the kitchen window while Maggie got out the coffee-pot, and since Sybren accepted the offer at once there was nothing for it but to bring him into the house.

Aunt Millicent received him graciously, liking what she saw, and immediately embarked on a series of topics of an impersonal nature until he put his coffee-cup down, observing that he would have to leave if he were to catch the hovercraft from Dover; he didn't specify at what time it went and she didn't ask him, merely observed that she had been delighted to meet him and telling Rose to see him to his car. Rose, who had had almost nothing to say, obediently got to her feet, waited while first her aunt and then Maggie bade him goodbye, and then led the way down the hall and out of the front door. She could see the Rolls parked in the lane and wished it miles away so that Sybren couldn't get into it and drive out of her life. They reached the gate but when she put out a hand to open it he covered it with one of his own.

''I had my life planned,'' he spoke quite quietly, ''unexciting but satisfactory enough and somehow it didn't concern me overmuch. And then we met.'' He paused to stare down at her upturned face, and she said quickly, ''A flash in the pan, that's all it was—you don't need to explain; I don't want you to. It was kind of you to come but I've made up my mind.'' She drew a deep breath and lied convincingly. ''I really don't want to see you again. Please go now.''

She steeled herself against another goodbye and was very surprised when he smiled as though he were genuinely amused about something. ''Sadie said that you were pig-headed.'' He lifted the hand he had been covering with his and kissed it gently. ''*Tot Ziens,* Rose.''

He got into his car, raised a casual hand in salute and drove away without a backward glance.

''He didn't kiss her,'' worried Maggie from the sitting-room window. ''He's gone.''

''He'll be back,'' said Miss Curtis, ''Oh, he'll be back, Maggie. He's not a man to come whining excuses, he's gone to find out what's got between them. I suspect that our little Rose has got the wrong end of the stick and is too pig-headed to let go.'' She nodded in a pleased manner. ''He will make her a splendid husband.''

''I could do with another cup of coffee,'' she went on in her usual forthright tone as Rose came wandering in through the door. ''We'll all have one and then I'll come and help with those raspberries, Rose, it's best to pick them before the heat of the day.

She led the way into the sitting-room and sat down by the

coffee tray while Maggie went off to the kitchen to fetch some more coffee. "A very pleasant man," she commented casually, "and one to be trusted I think. A good trait in a surgeon, not given to talking about himself either."

Rose agreed, it was something she had only just realised herself.

Rose was kept pleasantly occupied for the rest of the day; to sit idle with nothing but one's sad thoughts was what Aunt Millicent described to herself as unsuitable, so Rose picked fruit, bathed Shep, took him for a walk with her aunt for company and then after tea was taken to the village for a whist drive in aid of one of Miss Curtis's worthy causes. She did everything suggested to her in a docile manner, her mind far away, going every inch of Sybren's journey to his home. And on the way back home for supper, she imagined him arriving at his lovely home on the *gracht*. Mies would be there to welcome him, of course, wearing something glamorous, and at the sight of her he would forget all about a girl named Rose... She fetched such a deep sigh that her aunt hurried her indoors with the observation that she had tired herself out. "Supper," decreed Miss Curtis firmly, "and then bed."

Rose was indeed exhausted by her feelings, she slept soundlessly almost immediately her head touched the pillow, still thinking of Sybren.

Aunt Millicent kept her busy all the next day too, doing all the undemanding small tasks which went with village life, and the following morning she went back to St Bride's, fortified by Aunt Millicent's bracing therapy and an enormous cake baked by Maggie, to be eaten with the bedtime cups of tea.

The ward was busy and Shirley, well on the way to recovery now, was demanding: Rose was kept busy which was a good thing; on duty at least she had little time for her own thoughts, although that meant that she saved them up for bedtime, lying awake thinking of Sybren when she should have been asleep. At the end of the week she had lost weight, and her brown eyes looked enormous in a rather pale face. The houseman who had replaced Percy Pride was forced to agree with Percy's rather spiteful opinion that Rose was a splendid nurse but nothing much to look at, although he liked her. She would, in his opinion, make a chap a splendid sister.

Rose had days off at the end of the week, but she had decided against going to Aunt Millicent's, much as she would have liked to. She was aware that she wasn't the best of company, just as she was aware that her aunt and Maggie had bent over backwards to help her when Sybren went away. She spent her days off assiduously touring picture galleries and museums, seeing nothing of them, but they filled the days.

She had a letter from Christina during the next week, full of news and not a word about Sybren. And why should there be? He didn't belong to her world.

Another week dragged to its close and there was no sign of the warm summer weather abating. The idea of another two days spent inspecting museums was too much for Rose to face. She phoned Aunt Millicent to see if she might spend her free days with her and was left in no doubt as to her welcome. She had a free evening before her days off; she had already packed her overnight bag; she hurried off-duty, showered, changed into the pink dress because it gave her pale face some colour, and raced down to the entrance hall. She had cut things rather fine, she would have to get a taxi if she were to catch her train. She tore through the door, straight into Mr Werdmer ter Sane's substantial person.

It was more like walking into a tree trunk, surprise took her by the throat so that she was unable to utter a word, but Sybren, not surprised at all, steadied her with a hand on each shoulder and remarked,

''Ah, there you are,'' taking her bag from a nerveless hand at the same time and steering her towards the Rolls parked within feet of them.

Rose found her voice, albeit a rather squeaky one. ''I've a train to catch—I'm going away, you can't...''

''Oh, but I can, my dearest love, in you get.''

He opened the car door and stuffed her ever so gently on to the seat and then went round the car's bonnet and got in beside her.

"This is so absurd," Rose's voice was a shrill whisper. "You simply cannot...! I don't understand..."

"We will have a little talk later." His voice was soothing as though he were coaxing one of his small patients. He started the engine and tooled the car across the forecourt and out into the evening traffic. And he didn't say anything else at all until they were clear of the densest traffic and in the comparative peace and quiet of Hampstead, on the way to joining the M1.

"You thought that I was going to marry Mies," observed Sybren in a conversational tone. "If you could have asked me I would have told you that nothing was further from my mind. I am going to marry you, my dearest, I didn't realise it at first, but gradually you have taken over my life, my very heart—you and I are hopelessly entwined. I can't imagine living without you."

"But Mies said..." began Rose. Her heart was thudding away to break her ribs but she tried to ignore it. "She said that you were celebrating..."

"And you were a darling little fool to believe her. You are a very silly girl, Rose. You are also brave, honest, a delightful companion and my dream girl." He sighed. "And how I love you!"

Rose didn't speak: she sat savouring the words he had uttered, she had more or less digested them by the time they had reached the M1 and he allowed the Rolls to leap ahead.

She said shyly, "I've been in love with you for a long time, Sybren, only I tried not to be because of Mies."

He laid a hand over her clasped ones in her lap. "It took me a little while to find Mies and discover exactly what she had told you."

"How did you know that I was going to Aunt Millicent's this evening?"

"Sadie."

She asked urgently, "Sybren, do you really want to marry me?"

"Oh yes, my darling Rose, I really do, and if we were not on a motorway I would stop and underline that statement."

With that she had to be content, for he didn't speak again until at last he turned the car off the motorway and made for Ashby St Ledgers. And then all he said was, "What a very beautiful evening it is." And Rose, who had hoped that he would call her his darling again, agreed rather coldly.

But she need not have worried. He stopped the car in the lane outside Aunt Millicent's gate and got out and came to help her out too, and at the gate he stopped. "Darling girl." He smiled and wrapped his arms around her and kissed her in a manner which left her with no doubts at all.

"I don't know anything about you," said Rose weakly.

"Oh, yes you do. Haven't we worked together for weeks on end?"

"But your family? I mean, are you an orphan?"

"Lord no, sweetheart. Four sisters, all younger than I am, and a mother and father, all looking forward to meeting you."

He bent to kiss her again and she kissed him back.

At the sitting-room window her aunt watched them with deep satisfaction. "I said he'd be back," she told Maggie, peering out beside her.

"Lawks, Miss Curtis—he's kissing her." She turned a beaming face to her companion. "I'd best make up the spare-room bed; this time he'll be staying."

0702/73/MB45

Betty Neels Ultimate Collection Official Prize Draw Rules

NO PURCHASE NECESSARY

Each book in the Betty Neels Ultimate Collection will contain details for entry into the following prize draw: 4 prizes of a signed Betty Neels book and a weekend break to Amsterdam and 10 prizes of a signed Betty Neels book. No purchase necessary.

To enter the draw, hand print the words "Betty Neels Ultimate Collection Prize Draw", plus your name and address on a postcard. For UK residents please send your postcard entries to: Betty Neels Ultimate Collection Prize Draw, PO Box 236, Croydon, CR9 3RU. For ROI residents please send your postcard to Betty Neels Ultimate Collection Prize Draw, PO Box 4546, Kilcock, County Kildare.

To be eligible all entries must be received by **July 31st 2003**. No responsibility can be accepted for entries that are lost, delayed or damaged in the post. Proof of postage cannot be accepted as proof of delivery. No correspondence can be entered into and no entry returned. Winners will be determined in a random draw from all eligible entries received. Judges decision is final. One mailed entry per person, per household.

Amsterdam break includes return flights for two, 2 nights accommodation at a 4 star hotel, airport/hotel transfers, insurance and £150 spending money. Holiday must be taken between 1/8/03 and 1/08/04 excluding Bank holidays, Easter and Christmas periods. (Winner has the option of accepting £500 cash in lieu of holiday option.)

All travellers must sign and return a Release of Liability prior to travel and must have a valid 10 year passport. Accommodation and flights are subject to schedule and availability. The Prize Draw is open to residents of the UK and ROI, 18 years of age or older. Employees and immediate family members of Harlequin Mills & Boon Ltd., its affiliates, subsidiaries and all other agencies, entities and persons connected with the use, marketing or conduct of this Prize Draw are not eligible.

Prize winner notification will be made by letter no later than 14 days after the deadline for entry. Limit: one prize per an individual, family or organisation. All applicable laws and regulations apply. If any prize or prize notification is returned as undeliverable, an alternative winner will be drawn from eligible entries. By acceptance of a prize, winner consents to use of his/her name, photograph or other likeness for purpose of advertising, trade and promotion on behalf of Harlequin Mills & Boon Ltd., without further compensation, unless prohibited by law.

For the names of prize winners (available after 31/08/03), send a self-addressed stamped envelope to: For UK residents, Betty Neels Ultimate Collection Prize Draw Winners List, PO Box 236, Croydon, CR9 3RU. For ROI residents, Betty Neels Ultimate Collection Prize Draw Winners List, PO Box 4546, Kilcock, County Kildare.